THE AGE ATOMIC

"If you're not careful, Adam Christopher will melt your face off with *The Age Atomic*: the heat of the prose pairs with searing action. This is fireball storytelling and a rare follow-up that's better than its predecessor."
Chuck Wendig, author of Blackbirds

"Adam Christopher's debut novel is a noir, Philip K Dick-ish science fiction superhero story... a novel of surreal resonances, things that are like other things, plot turns that hearken to other plot turns. It's often fascinating, as captivating as a kaleidoscope... just feel it in all its weird glory."
Cory Doctorow, New York Times-bestselling author of Makers *and* Little Brother

"Christopher's tightly plotted novel is a truly original debut that, while subtly referencing Orwell, Kafka, Marvel comics and Philip K Dick, manages to maintain its own distinctive tone – a genuine pathos and longing for something elusively other. Recommended."
The Guardian

"Adam Christopher maintains a punchy, bestseller prose style that keeps the action rocketing along, and protagonists that seem right both in their own setting, and appropriate to what we already recognise as super heroes. *Empire State* is an excellent, involving read, and it fully deserves to be the start of a new universe."
Paul Cornell, author of London Falling

"A daring, dreamlike, almost hallucinatory thriller, one that plays with the conventions of pulp fiction and superheroes like a cat with a ball of yarn."
Kurt Busiek, Eisner Award-winning writer of Astro City *and* Marvels

ALSO BY ADAM CHRISTOPHER

Empire State
Seven Wonders

ADAM CHRISTOPHER

THE AGE
ATOMIC

ANGRY
ROBOT

ANGRY ROBOT
A member of the Osprey Group

Lace Market House,	4301 21st St., Ste 220B,
54-56 High Pavement,	Long Island City,
Nottingham,	NY 11101
NG1 1HW, UK	USA

www.angryrobotbooks.com
Rad's Universal Robots

An Angry Robot paperback original 2013

ISBN: 978 0 85766 314 6
Ebook ISBN: 978 0 85766 315 3

Printed in the United States of America

9 8 7 6 5 4 3 2 1

For Sandra, always.

To Mur, for getting me into this,
and to Stacia, for getting me out.

AUTHOR'S NOTE

In our universe, the Cloud Club, that Art Deco extravagance occupying the 66th, 67th and 68th floors of the Chrysler Building in Manhattan, was not a nightclub for the bright young things of the city, but instead a lunchtime club for businessmen. They didn't accept female members, they weren't open in the evenings, and despite the opulent surrounds, it sounds... well, it sounds kinda boring.

Much better, then, to turn it into the hottest nightspot of the 1930s and 1940s. Music, dancing, and my goodness, the view! A club where a young woman called Evelyn once danced the night away, before everything went wrong.

I hope readers will allow some artistic licence in creating this fictitious version of New York City.

PART ONE
THE GIRL WHO FELL

"I don't want anyone in or out of my family to see any part of me. Could you destroy my body by cremation? I beg of you and my family – don't have any service for me or remembrance for me. My fiancé asked me to marry him in June. I don't think I would make a good wife for anybody. He is much better off without me. Tell my father, I have too many of my mother's tendencies."

– The suicide note, May 1st, 1947

ONE

At 10.30 am, there is hardly a line at all. The day is bright but cold, and aside from hardy tourists from warmer climes, ten gallon and fur in place and all, today most decide the view can wait for another time.

I'm no good for him.

The man inside the ticket booth is old and nice, he smells of roses and the lick of hair around the edge of his cap is a frozen map of parallel lines drawn by his comb just a few hours before. Behind him the golden wall behind towers, over her, over everyone in the lobby. Her eyes linger over Art Deco rays of sun, as straight as the Ticketmaster's hair. The rays stretch out across the wall, touching all corners of a map rendered in shining gold and bronze.

Welcome to the Empire State.

I'm no good for anyone.

Eighty-six floors in two elevators: one large, one small. There are more people here, having penetrated the first line of defense, now ready for the final assault on the summit. With the fingers of one gloved hand she traces the band of maroon marble that bisects the passageways at near shoulder height. With the other hand she clutches at her throat, at the pearls he gave her.

Please tell him...

The elevator rises and her heart soars. She feels drunk, as though the air is becoming impossibly thin with every foot in altitude gained. She watches the back of the elevator operator's head. She can't see his face but he might be the Ticketmaster's twin. His hat is also straight and the hair on the nape of his neck likewise damp and regulated into perfect lines.

It's windy at the top, and cold, but the morning is glorious. Her grip tightens on her pearls and she looks into the sun directly. Her retinas burn but she doesn't flinch. She wants, needs, to feel it, to feel alive, if just for a short while.

She takes off her coat. It is grey and heavy, but somehow she feels no colder without it. She folds it as though to stow it in an airing cupboard for a winter to come, a winter she knows she will never see. She places it on the ledge, her bag on top. The fingers of her left hand tug at the necklace, counting the pearls like a rosary.

Ten gallon and fur collar walk by, their faces alive. The view, my God, the view. You can see all the way to New England on a day like today. Say, do you think you can see all the way to Texas?

She turns away and walks around, counting, counting in her head, like suddenly she's working to the master plan, the secret mission, the divine destiny. The numbers loom large in her mind.

It's cold. She takes a breath and feels it, now. Cold, like the cold if you were dead.

The breath just taken is held, and she turns on her heel, and...

Eighty-six floors and you can see all the way to Texas.

I... maybe...

Seventy.

Maybe I can fly. I can fly, I can fly.

She holds the pearls and her silk scarf cuts her neck as first it is pulled tight and then it is pulled off.

Forty.

Maybe the Skyguard will catch me. The Skyguard will save me.

Manhattan spins, pirouettes, dances around her as she stays perfectly still.

There is no Skyguard, not anymore.

He can't save me.

Tell him I lo–

Then her body hits the car and Evelyn McHale leaves the world.

He sees it first, a white something caught in the wind, drifting left and right and left again as it rides the cold morning air. It twists like a snake, like something alive. The cop frowns and squints against the bright sky.

That someone's scarf?

If you divide by five the number of seconds between the flash of lightning and the roll of thunder, you can work out how many miles away danger is.

One Mississippi. Two Mississippi.

The thunderclap is heavy and wet. The cop jumps at the sound, hearing the glass shatter and salt the sidewalk, hearing the metal twist and bend, hearing the cries of onlookers and passersby and regular folk who never wanted to be near anything like this, not today, not any day.

He rounds the corner and sees commotion, furor. Some people are running away, but some are running toward. Some have stopped to stare; some have stopped to look away.

She lies in the broken V that used to be the roof of a limousine. The cop sees the tiny flag waving on the hood. An official car.

She lies on her back, eyes closed, one hand clutching her pearls, her feet bare, her stockings torn. The cop thinks that somehow she's asleep. For a second he thinks to go and wake her, before the shock hits and he realizes what has happened. He looks up, in case there are any more people raining down, but all he sees is the Empire State Building, silent, impossibly tall, immobile. The cop's world spins a little as vertigo strikes, so he looks back to the body.

There are more people now. The cop scans the crowd, looking for more of his kind, but sees none.

To his left, a young man raises a camera and presses the button.

PART TWO
WINTER'S TALE

"I feel impelled to speak today in a language that in a sense is new... That new language is the language of atomic warfare.

"To the making of these fateful decisions, the United States pledges before you – and therefore before the world – its determination to help solve the fearful atomic dilemma – to devote its entire heart and mind to find the way by which the miraculous inventiveness of man shall not be dedicated to his death, but consecrated to his life.

"But the dread secret and the fearful engines of atomic might are not ours alone."

– "Atoms for Peace"
US President Dwight D. Eisenhower to
the UN General Assembly, December 8th, 1953

TWO

She was pretty and her name was Jennifer and she was going nowhere, not tied to the chair like she was. She had long brown hair with a wave in it and was wearing a blouse with ruffles down the front that Rad thought looked nice but which meant she must have been freezing.

The man standing next to the chair was less pretty. His name was Cliff and he had a face to match, and he was holding a gun that was pointed at Rad in a way that made the detective nervous. The thug was wearing a trench coat, and beneath the coat were muscles, hard, solid; muscles that spoke of bar room brawls and violence in the small hours. Rad Bradley was a detective now and had been a boxer before, but Cliff's frame made him decide that, when it came down to it, he didn't want to go one-on-one with Cliff, even if he could get that damn gun out of the way. But, then again, a job like his on a night like this, punching someone you didn't want to was likely to be in the cards.

The gun in Cliff's giant fist was a revolver, and the hammer was back.

The back of Rad's throat tickled. He needed a drink, and soon, assuming his stomach wasn't going to be perforated in the next few minutes.

The lopsided slit that was Cliff's mouth twitched into a smile.

Jennifer's wide eyes flicked between Rad and her captor.

Her lips quivered along with the ruffles on the front of her blouse. Rad thought she might burst into tears but then he decided she was more likely composing a particularly choice string of abuse. She was shaking not because of fear but because of the cold.

Cliff jutted his chin out to cut the air between them like an Ironclad steaming out of the harbor.

"Don't tell me," said Cliff in a voice made for radio, which was lucky given his face. "You're too old for this kind of thing?"

"No," said Rad, with more than a little hurt pride. What, crooks thought he looked old now? He squared his shoulders, which helped suck his gut in a little. Cliff's smile opened with a wet click at the corner.

"What I was gonna say," Rad continued, "was that it's too cold for this. The city starts to freeze and now and again it gives a shake or two, and everyone's in a panic. This makes my job a little more difficult than I would normally like, you see."

Cliff nodded, his eyes flicking back and forth between Rad and Jennifer. He adjusted the grip on his revolver.

"The cold is good for business," he said. "Good guys stay indoors, leaving the city to us. And sure, it's cold out, but a job's a job. I thought you'd understand that, detective. The way things is."

Rad nodded. "The way things is," he repeated. Then he laughed.

"Something funny?" Cliff snapped the gun up. With practiced ease the thug slipped his free hand inside his coat and pulled out a silver hip flask.

"Oh, I was just thinking," said Rad, his eyes on the flask. "Reminds me of something everyone used to say, not that long ago. 'Wartime'. Remember Wartime?"

Now Cliff laughed, and the laugh turned into a cough. It

came from deep in his chest, and sounded like rocks banging together underwater. Rad wondered how many you'd have to burn through in a day to get a sound like that in the six months since Prohibition had been lifted.

"I do remember Wartime," said Cliff, uncapping the flask with his teeth and taking a swig. "I fought in it. Even got me a medal."

"That a fact?" asked Rad, knowing full well that it wasn't. Cliff couldn't have fought in the War, because only robots had fought in the War and only one had come back from beyond the fog and it wasn't Cliff. The cold was messing with the goon's head.

Cliff smiled and took another swig. "Sure. But you're right about the cold. They say it's going to get worse too, that it's never going to end."

"That a fact?" asked Rad, this time with a tang of anxiety. He didn't like to dwell much on the problem of the Empire State's never-ending winter, but Cliff was clearly reading the newspaper too.

Cliff shrugged. "The hell do I know? Maybe you're all going to turn to ice like the water. Maybe they'll figure out a way of stopping it. But what I do know is that in the meantime, I've got work to do."

"Uh-huh," said Rad. "Funny way of putting it."

"What is?"

Rad scratched a cheek and pointed at Cliff. "We're going to turn to ice, or you're going to turn to ice?"

Another swig, another smile.

Rad ran his tongue along his bottom teeth. His mouth was dry and the flask sure did look good. But his night wasn't going to plan and it occurred to him that this was now often the case. "Crooks like you got thick skin, then?"

"Yeah. Pretty thick," said Cliff, recapping the flask and slipping it back into his coat.

"Gentlemen!"

Rad blinked. Jennifer's teeth were clenched against the cold, but she was looking at him with narrow eyes. Even Cliff lowered the gun just a bit.

Jennifer looked up at her captor.

"Look," she said. "Tell me what you know. Help me, and I'll help you."

Cliff chuckled quietly. "Lady, you got the wrong guy."

"Of course I haven't," she said. At this Cliff raised an eyebrow. "We're both looking for something. I think we both know that time is running out, so let's cut out the macho and get down to it. Right?"

"Hey," said Rad. "You never said you were looking for something."

Jennifer looked at Rad with something close to disdain. "You don't know the half of it," she said.

"You called me," he said, gesticulating in the cold air. "Said to come down to an address, which turns out to be an old warehouse in a quiet part of town. Said you needed my help taking down one of the new gangsters who've moved in downtown – which is handy, since I've been on the trail of Cliff too. Said that maybe you were onto something else, something big. Only when I get here I find you need my help more than I'd guessed. So maybe you should be grateful I'm here, considering you're the one tied up with the gun pointed at you."

Cliff twitched his wrist. "The gun is pointing at you too, pal."

"Cliff, look," said Rad, "give it up. You and your cronies have attracted the attention of not just people like me but people like Jennifer, and she works for the city. It's only a matter of time before you're out of business."

Cliff's thin lips formed something like a smile. "That so, friend?"

Jennifer shifted in the chair. "Tell you what, Cliff, let's cut a deal." She jerked her head in Rad's direction. "Ignore him. Let's talk. Let's work it out. Because you and I both know the whole city is in danger, right, and when times are tough you can't pick your friends, right?"

Cliff seemed to consider this while Jennifer shivered in the chair. Rad saw her coat lying on the floor in the shadows nearby, a big overcoat in dark green that matched her pencil skirt. Cliff must have dragged it off her so she couldn't slide out from the bonds holding her to the chair. Rad was cold himself – freezing, in fact – but Cliff didn't seem too bothered, even though his trench coat and hat, and suit underneath, were more or less the same as Rad's. Rad thought again about the hip flask. He promised himself to get sorted in that department in the morning, assuming he and Jennifer made it out of the warehouse.

Cliff had picked a good spot too. Since the citywide curfew had been canceled six months ago and the once-regular police blimp patrols halted, crooks had been able to spread out across the city, finding a goldmine of disused, empty buildings that nobody else came near and that the police would never find. The city had become a crime-ridden rabbit warren and there was no shortage of work for Rad, although at times it felt like he was one man against a multitude. The gangs were organized, running under the tight leadership of thugs like Cliff, one of the city's most wanted men, someone Rad had been trying to get a tail on for weeks now. Rad was out of his depth, he knew that; chasing organized crime was liable to earn him a pair of concrete boots instead of a paycheck. Which was why the unexpected call from Jennifer Jones had been something of a relief.

Jennifer Jones. Rad reminded himself once they were home and dry to ask her about what exactly she did, and how exactly she'd gotten his number to ask for his help by name.

The warehouse was the size of a blimp hangar, lined with individual lock-ups, each with a roller door like a one-car garage. The floor space itself was filled with crates that Rad had no clue about at all other than whatever was inside them was packed around with straw. Lots of straw. The stuff was everywhere, all around them on the floor... which meant, Rad thought, that the warehouse was still in use. Perhaps Jennifer had found Cliff's own little hidey-hole, the place used by his gang to hide illicit goods. Rad was just thankful it was only Cliff who appeared to be home at the moment.

Cliff sniffed and waved the gun, his deliberation over.

"Yeah, I don't think so," he said. "If it's all the same to you, I think we need to bring events to their climax. And you two are something of an obstacle."

Jennifer gave Rad a look that asked very clearly for the detective to hurry up and do something already.

"I understand," said Rad, looking at Jennifer.

"Understand what?" asked the thug. For the first time, Cliff moved his head, turning it to look down at his prisoner. It was enough.

Rad kicked out, catching a sheaf of straw on his shoe and tossing it toward the thug.

Cliff ducked instinctively and pulled the trigger, but Rad was already out of the line of fire, Jennifer throwing her chair sideways. Cliff turned at her movement and brought the gun to bear, his attention off Rad for a moment.

Rad's fist connected with Cliff's jaw and brilliant white pain exploded in the detective's knuckles. Rad, surprised at the force of his own punch, swore and staggered backward, but Cliff had gone over sideways. Rad blinked, but Cliff didn't move.

Rad shook his fist, and tried flexing his fingers. They hurt like all hell. Cliff had lived up to his name: it had been like punching a brick wall. Gritting his teeth, Rad slid down to his knees beside Jennifer's chair and with his good hand began to work on the rope holding her in place.

As soon as she was loose Jennifer scrambled for her discarded coat. Rad helped her into it and pulled her close to get her warm, the both of them still on their knees.

"Thank you," she said into his ear with hot breath. She pulled back and looked down at her former captor, then glanced at Rad's hand. "You OK?"

Rad kept his fingers moving, teeth clenched against the pain. "Nothing a little ice won't fix. And we've got a lot of that in the city right about now."

Jennifer laughed, but just as she went to stand the warehouse shook, the vibration rattling the roller doors that surrounded them. The pair waited a moment, crouched together on the floor. Then the tremor passed and Jennifer stood and pulled her coat tight.

"My imagination, or are those getting more frequent?"

Rad stood himself, and moved over to where Cliff lay.

"Yeah," he said. "Stronger too." He peered down at Cliff. The thug was out cold, his mouth slightly open. It didn't look like he was breathing, and there was something shiny on his chin where Rad's fist had landed.

Jennifer joined the detective. "Terrific," she said, nodding at the body on the warehouse floor. "Out with a single punch? Not bad, Mr Bradley."

"I used to box, or so I've been told. I've got a medal and everything." He reached forward with his good hand and felt Cliff's neck, his heart racing a little. There was no pulse and more than that the skin was cold, apparently the same temperature as the frozen air of the warehouse.

"He's dead," said Rad, not quite believing it himself. He looked at Jennifer.

"Depends on your definition of dead, I suppose," she said.

Rad's jaw moved up and down but he couldn't find the right words to answer. He carefully lifted one lapel of Cliff's trench coat with his injured hand and reached inside with the other. Maybe there was some ID, or something else that would be useful. Instead, his fingers closed on the smooth metal of the hip flask. He pulled it out and looked at it.

Well, he needed a damn drink, and it didn't look like Cliff was going to mind much. He glanced back to the body and uncapped the flask to take a sip.

"Wait!"

Rad ignored Jennifer as his nostrils caught fire, reacting to the poisonous fumes from the flask. His throat closed in a reflex action and he choked – then coughed, hard. Through watering eyes he saw Jennifer move in front of him and he gasped as she knocked the flask out of his hand. The detective retched and bent over, and saw the flask on the warehouse floor, a thick liquid spilled from the open top.

"Sweet Jesus," Rad said, his voice a rattling croak. He coughed again and stood. Jennifer scooped the flask up and held it away from her, looking at it like it was about to explode.

Rad's throat was raw. Jennifer tipped the flask upside down, letting the rest of the liquid escape. It was bright green and pooled on the cement floor like oil. The smell was sharp, like gasoline and coal smoke and lemon juice.

Rad managed to find his voice.

"What is that?" He peered closer, fascinated by the evil liquid on the ground. Jennifer crouched near to the floor to take a closer look.

She looked back up at the detective. "It's anti-freeze," she said.

"He was drinking chemicals?"

Rad stroked his chin with his good hand, and looked

down at the dead body in front of them. Dead? His punch hadn't been that heavy, unless maybe the guy had had a fractured skull to start with.

He looked at the wet mark shining on Cliff's chin. Then he swore and knelt down again. He poked at the thug's face.

"Son of a bitch," said Rad as he pushed hard at the shiny patch, enough for the skin to slide back over the bottom of the jawbone.

Except it wasn't bone, not at all. The shining patch was metal, silver. The whole goddamn jaw was made of it.

Rad jerked his hand away, only for Jennifer to take over. She pulled at the torn skin, then gripped at the edge with both hands and yanked. She rocked backwards on her heels as a rubbery beige something that had been Cliff's face came cleanly away.

"They've started already," she said, and she stood, tossing Cliff's face to one side and putting her hands on her hips. She pursed her lips in thought.

"He's a robot," said Rad. "And you're not surprised. Who's started already? More robots? And where do robots like this guy come from anyway? The only robots I know of are the ones that the Navy used to make. He doesn't look like one of those."

Jennifer looked at him and nodded. "It's been modified. Upgraded."

"Oh," said Rad. He had that sinking feeling again; here he was, helping someone who knew more about what was going on than he did.

Jennifer pushed Cliff's head to one side, revealing the rear half of the skin-mask. She pulled the robot's hat off; Cliff's hair was still in place, slick and proper just like any self-respecting crook would like it. But beneath, in the dim warehouse light, his real face shone, all silver and wet and angular, a whole lot of triangles and rectangles that explained Cliff's special kind of handsome. Inside the metal mouth were teeth which looked pearly white and human enough, as did the eyes set into the steel brow.

Rad felt a little ill and rubbed his finger against his pants. He wasn't sure what the flesh-like material was that covered the robot but he had a feeling he didn't want to be touching any more of it. He looked down at Cliff again. For a robot, it sure had gone down easy. Maybe he'd punched out a fuse. Not a great design for a mechanical gangster.

Rad coughed and sniffed and turned away, directing his attention to the closest stack of wooden crates behind him as he wrapped his arms around his chest, trying to beat some warmth into his body. His feet shuffled through the straw on the floor, his toe nudging a small silver metal rod, like half a pencil, the blunt ends wrapped in copper.

Rad picked up the rod and turned, holding it out, but Jennifer was hunched over Cliff. Rad closed his mouth and slipped the rod into his pocket and turned back to the crates.

He pulled on the lid of the one nearest him. The nails slid out with surprising ease; the crate had been opened before, recently.

Rad pushed his hat back on his head and pulled a few handfuls of straw out of the crate, his punching hand functional but sore.

"I don't know what these guys were moving," he said over his shoulder, "but it's not booze or guns."

Rad pulled a gunmetal grey something out of the crate. It was a cylinder about six inches long and three wide, capped at one end by black glass and finished at the opposite with some kind of electrical terminal. Rad shoved more packing out of the crate and found a length of curly cable secured with a wire twist, long plugs on each end, clearly designed to mate with the end of the cylinder. He looked for a third time in the crate, and saw at the bottom a sort of trapezoidal box like a radio with dials and buttons on the front, and a handle in black plastic on the top. He gave the handle a tug but the object didn't move much. It felt heavy.

Rad turned back to Jennifer and the robot, cylinder in one hand and cable in the other.

"You wanna start telling me a little about all this? Because if you want my help then you're going to have to fill me in on this one. And we're going to need to discuss my retainer."

Jennifer stood and looked Rad in the eye. "He said you could be difficult."

"Who did?"

"Captain Carson. Who else?"

Rad blinked. "You know Carson?"

"Sure I do. I work for him – worked, anyway. Nobody's seen him since–"

"Since he walked over the ice and disappeared into the fog," said Rad. "Yeah, I know. So you wanna tell me why I'm rescuing one of Carson's agents from a robot gangster? I would have thought the Commissioners would send the big guns in, one of their own in a mess like this."

Jennifer laughed. "Big guns? There aren't any. Or haven't you noticed? Not since… well, not since before, anyway. Carson had some grand plans, but now with the Fissure and the cold, the whole place is a mess and…"

Rad waved his hand. He didn't like to be reminded of the status quo, because the status quo was bad. Carson, the new City Commissioner was gone, abandoning his post when the transdimensional tear that connected the Empire State to New York City – the so-called Fissure – vanished. And with the Fissure gone the city was slowly turning into a solid block of ice, one apt to shake itself to pieces too, if the tremors were going to keep up like they were.

Rad had heard things were bad at the Empire State Building. There was no one in charge, no one to give orders, no one with any kind of solution, because the one man who knew how any of it all worked had apparently committed suicide.

"Yeah," said Rad. "I got it."

Jennifer nodded. "Carson spoke highly of you. Said you were the best. Said to call you when things got difficult."

"So things are difficult?"

"Something like that."

"You said they'd started already." Rad gestured around the warehouse, his eyes scanning the lock-ups. "I take it you're on the trail of something?"

"Yes," she said. She straightened and moved to the nearest of the roller doors, giving the padlock at the bottom an experimental kick with her boot. She pushed at the door, rattling it, but it held firm. "We need to see what they've got in here."

Rad gently pushed Jennifer to one side and knelt next to the lock. He took a pair of lock picks from inside his coat pocket, holding them up for Jennifer to see. She smiled and folded her arms.

"Useful."

"Hey," said Rad. "Detective's best friend." He turned back to the padlock and got to work. The padlock was large but nothing special, and within moments Rad had it sprung. He stood, one hand on the roller door release, but then paused and looked over his shoulder at Jennifer. He had a bad feeling about this.

"Ready?"

She nodded. Rad sighed, and pulled the door up. As the roller snapped into its housing, he yelled in surprise and jumped back nearly a foot.

"What in the hell?"

Jennifer darted forward before Rad could say anything more.

"God damn," she said, her breath clouding in front of her.

The lock-up was filled with robots, tall and silver and inactive. They filled the space wall to wall, five in a row. Rad stood on his toes and counted ten rows to the back of the space.

"Fifty," he said, his eyes wide. "There's fifty robots in there."

Jennifer stepped closer. Each robot had glassy eyes that were dark. She stared up at the closest one, then reached up and tapped the front of its head.

"Careful!" said Rad, tugging on Jennifer's arm. She didn't resist as he pulled her back, but when he turned her around he was surprised to see her smiling.

"We need to get out of here," said Rad. "I don't like this one little bit."

"Open another."

Rad huffed in the cold air. "What?"

"They're not active," said Jennifer. "Open another lock-up."

Rad was frozen to the spot. Behind Jennifer the ranks of inactive robots stood like life-size children's toys.

"OK," he said, finally, not quite believing what he was doing. He moved to the next roller door on the left and picked the padlock. The door shot up with a bang that made him jump.

Inside were more robots. Another fifty. Rad looked down the length of the warehouse, then turned and peered into the gloom over the other side of the vast space. The building was lined with the lock-ups, at least sixteen on each wall. Sixteen times fifty was...

"He's been busy," said Jennifer. "They have warehouses all over the city. If they're all filled with robots..."

Rad shook his head. "Someone is hiding a robot army in the city?" He swept the hat off his head, the scale of the mystery he'd stumbled into almost too big to comprehend. He licked his lips and decided to focus down on something a little smaller. He moved to the nearby stack of crates.

"What about this stuff?" He lifted out the metal cylinder again. "Any idea what this is?"

"It's a Geiger counter," said Jennifer, "part of one, anyway."

"That so?" Rad raised the cylinder to his eye and tried to look into the end that was black glass, but it was totally opaque.

"It detects radiation."

Rad looked at her over the metal cylinder.

Jennifer blew out a breath and it steamed in the air between them. "Welcome to the age atomic, detective."

THREE

Rad sat in his chair behind his desk. He was turned around, not facing the office door and the grandfather clock in the corner, but the large square window immediately behind his desk. The blinds were up, and it was night, the light in the office turning the window into a big mirror.

Funny how things had come full circle. It hadn't worked out with Claudia, although they'd tried their darnedest, but the truth was their marriage was an echo of something which had never happened, not in this dimension. That was the worst part, knowing what the Empire State was and what it had done to them. It had worried at Rad and it had worried at Claudia, and eventually it had pushed them apart. But maybe that was for the best. Rad didn't like change, although he knew that might have been the Empire State pushing him again. He liked his job and his liked his office. He had looked around for better, of course, but none had that window and the view, so Rad had stayed put and the little room next to the office was still his home.

Rad watched his reflection, and he watched the corners of the room behind him. Then he sighed and took a sip of his coffee and sighed again. The coffee was good. Real coffee, from the other side, from New York. He had Mr Jones to thank for that. Except now the Fissure was gone and the city had begun to freeze, and while the coffee was warming Rad knew he needed to keep an eye on his supply because suddenly it was a limited resource again.

Huh. Jones. Rad wondered if Nimrod's agent from New York and Carson's agent from the Empire State were connected, or even the same person, in a way.

Rad had secured the lock-ups and they'd hidden Cliff's body in an empty crate in the warehouse. He'd be found eventually. Rad wasn't sure if that meant the clock was ticking or not, but he had the feeling that time was most certainly running out. Hundreds – thousands – of robots hidden in warehouses all over the city meant something big was on the cards, something well beyond even the organized gang crime that Rad had been investigating. Something calamitous. Jennifer knew much more than she had let on, but had left without so much as a goodbye. As Rad slinked back to his office he hoped she knew what she was doing.

The chair creaked as Rad shifted his weight. The Fissure was gone and the city was freezing, getting colder every day, but that didn't stop Rad watching the reflections in his office. Reflections – mirrors – were one way the Empire State and New York were connected, at least if you knew the trick. And Rad knew that even with Carson gone on his side, there would be people working on it on the other. The problem of the Fissure would be affecting New York, Rad knew that – New York was the Origin, the template, and it led to a whole wide world, a universe beyond. The Empire State was the Pocket, an imperfect duplicate of New York, reflected through a hole in space-time thanks to the fight between the Science Pirate and the Skyguard, the two former protectors of New York.

But the Fissure did more than connect the cities; it tied them together. One could not exist without the other anymore. Which meant if the Fissure was gone and the Empire State was freezing up, then Rad knew New York would be in trouble too. He only hoped that Captain Nimrod, Carson's "original", hadn't taken a little walk as well. Nimrod had a whole damn government department dedicated to the Fissure. Nimrod was working on it, Rad knew that. He had to be.

Which is why Rad sat in front of the window in his office most nights. Watching and waiting. The mirror-like quality of the window at night would let Nimrod see into the Empire State. And with Carson gone, Rad was one of the few people left in the Pocket dimension who had any clue how the world worked, so it would make sense for Nimrod to get in touch with him first.

So the theory went.

Rad sat in front of the window and the grandfather clock ticked time away in the corner, and he sipped his coffee and flexed the fingers of his sore hand. After a while Rad turned around on his chair to look at the item on the desk.

It was the small rod, the one he'd pocketed. It looked a little like a fuse, and Rad thought that maybe it had fallen out of Cliff's head, loosened by Rad's punch, the reason the robot had gone over so easily. He'd meant to ask Jennifer about it but he'd clean forgotten. He could show it to her next time they met, if there was going to be a next time.

He rolled the little cylinder on the desk, picked it up and looked at it closely, like he would suddenly recognize it for what it was. He put it back on the desk.

"Huh," said Rad to himself. "The age atomic."

Rad jerked his head up at the sound. It was still night outside, and Rad could see himself reflected in the window. The office behind him was still and empty.

The phone was ringing. Rad blinked, then spun around on his chair and grabbed at the stem, pushing the earpiece against the side of his head.

At last, the call.

"Nimrod?" he said. He squinted into the emptiness of his office, like that would improve his hearing.

"I think you have something of mine," said the voice on the other end of the line.

The line was crystal clear and the voice was loud, and more important it didn't belong to Nimrod, didn't have that strange clipped accent he shared with Carson and which Rad had learned was "British." The voice on the phone was a local call.

"Who is this?"

The man on the end of the phone clicked his tongue. It echoed strangely, although Rad wasn't sure if that was the phone or... something else. Maybe a gas mask worn by someone from New York acclimatizing to the Empire State's different environment. There was something else too, in the background. Music. Jazz music; the phone line stripped the bass out but Rad could hear a bright piano and drum beat.

"Where are you from?" Rad asked, before the man on the phone had a chance to say anything else.

"Oh, patience, detective, patience. You have something of mine. You picked it up at the warehouse. I'd like it back."

"Uh-huh," said Rad. He glanced at the clock in the corner. It was three in the morning. He'd dozed off, which explained the crick in his neck. "Must be pretty important for you to call at this hour."

There was a dull scraping on the other end of the phone. "Oh, it's late. I'm sorry. You tend to lose track of time, job like mine."

Another hint, another clue. Rad smiled. "Lot of fancy stuff in that warehouse. Specialized equipment. Not to mention the toys you've got in cold storage. Quite an operation you have running."

Too much information? Rad winced and sucked in his

cheeks. He needed some sleep and possibly not any more coffee.

The man on the phone laughed. It was just a quiet chuckle, slow, steady. Rad listened, but there was nothing else on the line except the man laughing and the faint music.

"Something funny, pal?" Rad sniffed. "Nothing funny about tying ladies to chairs and waving guns around."

"Oh yeah, I heard about that," said the man on the phone, while in the background the jazz reached a crescendo and then stopped. "That's a shame. Tell you what, friend, come up and see me. Bring my property. We can have a drink, and we can have a little chitchat."

"I'll look forward to that." Rad reached for a pen and had it ready, poised over the jotter on his desk. He felt like he'd just made a breakthrough in a case he knew nothing about. "What's the address?"

The man on the phone just laughed again. Rad thought he'd pushed it a little far with a criminal mastermind – well, he assumed the guy was a criminal mastermind, who else rang in the small hours just to laugh at a detective?

The scraping sound came again, like the man on the phone was distracted and turning away from the mouthpiece. Rad pressed the phone into his ear and closed his eyes. The office vanished, and he was lost in the faint buzz of the phone line. The jazz started up again, another number, slower this time.

There. There was something else. The buzz was moving; not interference, but something in the background. Somebody talking, too far away for Rad to know if it was a man or a woman.

The scraping sound came back loud, and Rad opened his eyes.

"There's someone here who wants to see you."

Rad sucked in a breath and leaned forward on his desk.

Eyes wide, just one thought entered his mind.

"Carson's there? Can you put him on?"

The laugh again. "Last I heard the Chairman went out over the ice and into the fog," said the man. Rad could almost hear the smile in the man's voice and he didn't like it one bit.

"Quit playin' around. Look, I–"

"Come north. 125th Street. You can't miss it. Look for the green light."

"What?" Rad squeezed the pen. "What's the address?"

"You'll find me. 125th Street. Tomorrow. Come at night – it's not safe during the day. Drive to 110th, then walk."

"Look, pal, whoever is there–"

"He says his name is Kane Fortuna. I think he wants to talk to you pretty bad."

The phone went dead, and Rad sat very still in his chair with the earpiece still in place for a long, long time.

FOUR

Cold, cold like the grave.

Evelyn smiled, like she could remember what cold was. She knew it was cold because that's all everyone was talking about on the radio and on the television. Evelyn could read the waves of electromagnetic radiation as they bounced between the skyscrapers of Manhattan; she could see, feel, any and all energy. Eventually she'd worked out how to read the information encoded within some of it. Sometimes she regretted her ability, when the barrage of energy packets become a cacophony, a noise so loud she thought she would go insane. She could block it all out, if she really concentrated, but if there was one sensation that remained to her it was fatigue. Blocking out the noise cost energy, and she had precious little to spare to stop herself falling out of the world. So most of the time she swam through the noise as she ran to keep up with the world as it moved away from her.

People had asked her about it all, back at the beginning. She was fascinating and she was pitiful, but although they'd all felt sorry for her for a while, time passed and they got bored. And then she'd had to make them take notice, and take notice they did. She hadn't realized she had that ability, not at first, but it made sense. Any and all energy was available to her. She was energy herself, the quantum signature of a person burnt into the fabric of the universe.

She could, she discovered, do almost anything, and finally people noticed. The United States soon had their own secret weapon, a sentient, intelligent, "living" nuclear deterrent: Evelyn McHale.

The people who knew what she was called her the Girl Who Fell. To others, including the inhabitants of New York who had accidentally seen her as she went about her business on behalf of the government of the United States – or when she wandered through the city on her own, trying to reconnect to the world – she had another name: the Ghost of Gotham.

Wandering, watching. As she was now.

Evelyn McHale floated six inches from the ground on the banks of the East River in the cold night, running with all her might to keep up with the world, trying to remember what winter felt like.

She listened to the lapping of the water and to the creak of boats moored on the docks nearby. She listened to the rats in the subway and the fish in the river and an argument five miles away, somewhere in Brooklyn. Evelyn couldn't remember the last time she'd been in Brooklyn, the last time she'd left Manhattan, the last time she'd done a lot of things. When she tried to remember her old life it just came back to that day, and she remembered that day well enough, although she wished she didn't.

Maybe it didn't matter. Time wasn't particularly relevant to her anymore. She existed outside of time, one step to the left of the world. But she could look back in, at the past, the present, the future. She remembered how time mattered a lot to the world around her and the people in it, which is why she kept count. She watched the world age, sensed the fatigue growing in the concrete and steel and glass and rock of the city.

She counted the decay of atoms in space, and she smiled.

She could do a lot of things since that day.

Evelyn moved forward, floating a little higher into the air and gliding towards the water's edge. As she moved, the soft blue glow that constantly surrounded her grew in intensity as she forced the universe to do her bidding.

She remembered living in the city, one of millions who did just that. She remembered enjoying the crowds, the feeling that she was part of something. And she remembered it all being too much, and the decision that had to be made.

And now she was alone. Alone and falling, again, although this time not from a tall building but from time and space.

Evelyn floated forward, out into the middle of the river, hovering one hundred feet in the air. Her aura flared brilliant blue as she pushed at the world, and she turned, looking out across the city on both sides of the water.

So many people, going about their lives, some long, some short.

People were watching. She could feel them, feel their fear as they caught a glimpse of the Ghost of Gotham. Of course, her occasional excursions drove important people wild in Washington, but that didn't matter. She loved the city, and sometimes she had to go out and see it again.

People were watching in Brooklyn, and they were watching in Manhattan. Phones were ringing, and there was chatter on police radios. Someone had called the coastguard. A dozen people were scrambling for cameras, and four newspaper reporters were right now pulling coats over their pajamas as they raced to get the scoop.

She had to admit, she sometimes enjoyed the effect her presence had on others, on the living, the way her appearances in the city got attention. She listened as word spread, as heartbeats all over town kicked up a notch, as people told their neighbors to shut the hell up and as others began to pray.

Evelyn McHale, the Ghost of Gotham. If only they knew what she really was.

Fear. She wanted to visit everyone in the city, nod and smile and say yes, yes you should be afraid. Fear was powerful, primal. Although the universe was getting further and further away from her, her connection getting fainter and fainter, fear was her ally, its own special kind of energy that she could use, that helped her keep up with the world.

A boat approached, and someone with a camera had arrived at the nearby dock, aiming his lens at the glowing blue woman floating over the river.

Evelyn sighed. She didn't need to breathe but she remembered how to sigh. She remembered sighing on that day. She remembered the effect that gravity had on her mass. She remembered the fall, the spin, watching the curve of the Earth, the vertigo, the fear, the hope, the blue of the sky and the grey of the ground and then the light, the light, the light. She remembered her hope that the Skyguard would save her evaporating as she remembered that there wasn't a Skyguard, that there hadn't been for years, that New York was unprotected. New York was protected now, of course. The whole country was. She'd taken up the job herself.

Evelyn sighed again, and then she was gone.

FIVE

It was blue and beautiful and dangerous, and Captain Nimrod never tired of looking at it. Perhaps it was his imagination, but standing in the light of the Fissure, he felt... invigorated? Not quite the right word. Young. That was it. In the light of the Fissure he felt young, and while he knew that was just his imagination, an impossibility according to the scientists employed by the Department to study the crack in space/time, that didn't stop Nimrod closing his eyes and enjoying the warm bath of energy that swirled in the air around him.

And it made sense, really it did. The Fissure emitted energies that he and his fellow scientists could barely comprehend, although he understood more than the others. Perhaps the energy from the Fissure was making him feel young as it bathed every cell in his body with deadly light, and one day he would simply drop dead, or perhaps do something unexpected like explode over his morning coffee.

Perhaps, perhaps. Nimrod opened his eyes and watched the Fissure in both fear and fascination.

Around the edge of the concrete disc in Battery Park, the usual complement of MPs stood. Nimrod wondered if they felt it too. Usually they guarded the Fissure while it was inside its armored egg-like shell. Opening the shell, exposing the moving, living space-time event was a special, rare event.

Nimrod stroked his mustache. Of course, there was someone else who knew as much about the Fissure as he did: one Captain Carson, native of the Empire State. And right now Nimrod wished his counterpart from the Pocket would make contact. But the Fissure roared and roiled and...

And there was nothing on the other side. It was a glitch, a temporary disturbance on the time-space conduit that linked New York City to the Empire State. That was all, had to be. An entire universe – even a small, city-sized one such as the Empire State – couldn't just vanish.

Could it?

Nimrod brushed his mustache again. He couldn't send any more agents through. It was futile; none had yet returned, not even one of his most trusted men, Mr Jones. Were they dead? Nimrod felt a tightness in his chest, knowing that he would be to blame if that were the case, having sent his own agents to their deaths across a portal between universes with nothing on the other side.

But the other methods of transdimensional travel weren't working either. The hall of mirrors back at the Department was just that, a hall lined with mirrors. Nimrod's team had even tried reversing the electrical charge that danced so delicately across the polished metal surfaces, enough potential energy there to fill your mouth with the taste of vinegar, but to no avail. Nimrod and the others had stood and watched their own reflections for weeks before Nimrod had taken to staring at the Fissure itself. It was prettier than his reflection, for a start.

But it was no different in Battery Park, staring into the void between this world and the next. The Fissure was active and stable and unchanged, but there was nothing on the other side. The connection with the Empire State had been lost.

"Sir," said the MP. Nimrod turned away from the Fissure and instantly missed it.

The Fissure was addictive. Nimrod knew that, and the scowl vanished from his face. The MP looked nervous behind the black goggles they all wore. Nimrod made a note to get himself a pair for the next visit.

"Sir," the MP said again, his voice low and discreet.

"Yes?" Nimrod wondered how long, exactly, he'd been standing in Battery Park. The Fissure played tricks with your mind, with time.

"She is asking for you."

Nimrod blinked, then nodded. "Very well."

"There's this too, sir." The MP handed Nimrod a newspaper. It was fresh, the paper crisp and warm between his fingers. Nimrod cast an eye over the headline on the front page above a blurred black and white photo that showed nothing much except something white floating in the air against the background of what looked like Brooklyn at night.

The MP stood back and saluted, then turned and marched away. Nimrod frowned, folded the newspaper into quarters, and followed.

It was best not the keep the Ghost of Gotham waiting.

SIX

The air was still and as cold as a slap in the face as Rad pulled the collar of his trench coat up and the brim of his hat down. The streets were slick with a thin layer of dangerous black ice, the gutters and the corners of buildings piled with a dry, sand-like scattering of snow, the kind you only got when it had been cold a real long time.

And it had been cold a real long time.

Rad sniffed the air and immediately regretted it, the sudden sting of ice like a firecracker exploding in his nostrils. He exhaled into the collar of his coat and dragged his scarf up over his mouth and nose.

The Empire State was freezing up and here he was, venturing into unknown territory in the dead of night on the back of nothing but a weird phone call. Just like old times.

He'd parked his car a few blocks south, where there were at least some people and light, but as he'd walked it had got darker and darker, as if the city was fading away, dying as he went north. Come at night, the mystery caller had said, as it wasn't safe during the day. It sounded backward, but Rad had kept to the letter of the instructions. He hiked north on foot, through streets a little wider than he was used to, among buildings a little lower than he felt comfortable with.

Rad crossed the deserted street and paused.

He was being followed, but the person doing the following

was hardly a professional. The attempt to match his own footsteps to Rad's was poor.

No problem. Rad thrust his hands into the pockets of his coat. In his left, his fingers curled around the short metal rod taken from the deceased – deactivated? – robot gangster, Cliff. In his right, his fingers curled around the handle of his gun.

Rad kept walking, slowly at first and then speeding up. He broke his step and heard the person behind him pause, so he stopped and turned on his heel, but the street was dark with plenty of shadows for people to hide in. Rad saw nothing, and the night was silent.

Rad mentally counted off the bullets in his gun as he recalled loading it that afternoon. He wondered how accurate it was and over what distance; it really was a small gun designed for point-blank defense, and he hadn't had much of a chance to test it.

If this was Harlem at night – the safe time to visit – then during the day it must be a virtual no-mans-land.

Rad pulled his collar higher and kept walking. He had somewhere to go, and someone to meet.

Kane Fortuna.

Rad shook his head and kept his eyes on the sidewalk. Kane had returned? Was the caller telling the truth? Rad dared to hope he would see his friend again: Kane Fortuna, the Sentinel's former star reporter, with a misguided career as the Skyguard cut short by a little trip through the Fissure. That was eighteen months ago, and despite searches on both sides of the dimensional divide in New York and the Empire State, his body had never been found.

Rad had assumed Kane was dead, that if you went into the Fissure on one side and didn't come out the other, then the universe had chewed you up and that was that. Maybe he'd been too quick to jump to that conclusion, but he really wasn't sure what else he was supposed to think.

Rad picked up the pace as he thought about his old friend. If Kane was alive and well, Rad was prepared to forgive him the naivety that had led him to be influenced by the wrong side. Rad knew Kane; they would talk, and Kane would listen, and they'd work everything out.

Maybe. Rad tightened his grip on the gun in his pocket, and turned a corner. Ahead, on the opposite side of the street, the neon sign of a tavern glowed, a rainbow halo thrown around it as the ice crystals hanging in the air reflected the light.

Rad needed a drink, and some time to think, and a chance to lose his tail.

Smiling beneath his scarf, he skipped up to the door, and went inside.

The tavern was the same as any that Rad had ever been in. Though, if he thought about it, the only establishment he'd ever been in was Jerry's, near his office, despite the fact that there was no Prohibition anymore and the sale and consumption of alcohol no longer attracted the death penalty. But Rad liked Jerry's and wasn't interested in trying anywhere else. Jerry was also rather accommodating when it came to the matter of his tab.

The place was empty, save a barman in a blue shirt, his back to the room. Rad checked his watch, which showed it was eleven in the evening. Maybe the night was young in Harlem. If the daytime was dangerous, then maybe it was at night when it all came to life, like Harlem was operating on an opposing timetable to the rest of the Empire State. Maybe, thought Rad, he'd been a little early, which would explain the person following him and the lack of patrons in the tavern.

Rad slunk to the bar, took off his hat, and unwrapped his

scarf as he perched on a stool. Rad waited a moment while the barman did a fine job of ignoring the only customer in the joint, then he tapped his fingers on the bar.

The barman turned to face him, wiping a glass with a towel. He was a young man, his features sharp, his eyes narrow and his hair so greasy it made Rad's own shaved scalp crawl. He looked like he was chewing something, but whether it was gum or a bad attitude, Rad wasn't sure.

"You open?" Rad said. It wasn't the best icebreaker, but he was nervous, more nervous than he realized. He'd been followed through what had felt like a completely empty, alien world. He didn't like it, and now he had a surly barman to contend with.

"Yeah, we're open," said the barman. Rad tried a smile and the barman returned the expression, although it didn't look that friendly. He was still chewing something, and when he smiled the wet sound was loud and clear. The man's teeth were filthy, and as the saliva squeaked around them Rad saw that it was dark, nearly black. "What can I get for ya?"

Rad frowned, wondering how hygienic this establishment was. He decided to go for something safe.

"Coffee. Lots of sugar."

The barman's smile widened and his nod this time was different, the nod of a man appreciating a fine choice. He even said the same as he straightened up and vanished through a door behind the bar.

Rad reached into his pocket to retrieve his wallet and his hand found the metal rod. He pulled it out and peered at it in the low light.

"Hey, where did you get that?"

The barman had returned, steaming cup of coffee in one hand. He was frozen in the doorway, his eyes wide, locked on the object in Rad's hand.

Rad held the thing up by one end but before he could say anything, the barman dumped the coffee on the bar, spilling nearly half of it, and reached across to push Rad's hand away. Rad snatched the rod close to his chest.

"Hey!"

"Put that damn thing away, Jesus," said the barman. He kept his hands out, his eyes scanning the empty bar behind his single customer. He was breathing heavily and quickly.

"You know what it is?" asked Rad.

The barman leaned across the bar, his face an inch away from Rad's. Rad grimaced; the barman's breath was hot and smelled of acetone. As he leaned back, Rad saw the barman's eyes were bloodshot. The man was either sick or high on something.

"It doesn't matter what it is," said the barman. "It belongs to him, to one of his machines."

"Who?"

The barman was very still, his eyes on Rad's. Rad raised an eyebrow and the barman nodded.

"You don't want nothing to do with him," he said.

Rad shook his head and slid off the stool. Enough was enough. As he moved, the barman jerked forward again and grabbed Rad's forearm tightly. Rad shook it off.

"Bud," said the barman, "you wanna watch yourself. It's not safe."

"So I've been told," said Rad.

The barman flicked his head at the object in Rad's hand. "You're not from round here, are you?"

"Downtown," said Rad.

The barman pursed his lips like he was going to whistle appreciatively. He leaned in to Rad, like a conspirator. Rad found himself getting closer to the man, his nose assaulted by the acidic smell of his breath.

"I heard things were rough, downtown." The barman

said it like it was another place altogether. As far as Rad had seen, that seemed to be exactly the case.

"That so?"

The barman nodded, his eyes glazing over, almost like Rad wasn't there. He chewed and swallowed and spoke.

"Yeah, man, I heard there were riots, and that they'd tried to storm the Empire State Building." The barman tried to whistle but his lips did nothing but pass a narrow current of air through them. The tang of acetone was strong and Rad couldn't stop his nose crinkling.

"I heard there was a hijack," the barman said. "I heard the police tried to come down on a crowd in an aerostat, but the people, they stormed the ship and took it over and were flying it around the place." He moved his hands in the air, clearly impressed.

Rad said nothing. The barman was right; since the cold had set in and Carson had abandoned his post, the city was full of disturbances.

There was a light in the barman's eyes. "I heard there were others, in the city. Y'know? From the other side. Infiltrators, all secret-like, on the down-low. Coming in and stirring things up, right? Trying to overthrow the Commissioner, get their own kind in."

"The other side?" asked Rad.

"Yeah." That fire again, fighting its way out of the barman's bloodshot eyes. "I heard they were called 'Communists'. From New York."

Rad frowned. "Com-you-what-now?"

"The Reds..." The barman almost whispered it, and let it hang in the air along with the stench of his breath.

The man was deranged, whatever the hell it was he was chewing pickling his brain. So he'd heard the news from downtown, about the riots and protests, but infiltrators from New York? The Fissure had closed.

Time to change to subject. Rad pulled the metal rod out again but kept it close to his chest. As soon as it came into view, the barman's eyes widened again and they darted around the empty bar.

"Jesus, mister, you gonna give me palpitations, I'm telling ya."

Rad's eyebrow went up again. "You know someone called Geiger?"

The barman shook his head, quickly. "Never heard of no Geiger, but then I don't know his real name."

The mystery man. Rad's caller, he had no doubt about it. "Who?"

The chewing paused, and this time the barman ran his hand through his greasy hair.

"Either you're playin' me, or you're about to walk into the spider's parlor with a clue, mister."

"I came here because I was asked to," said Rad, raising the tube to his eye line. "Someone wants this back. Sounds like you know who."

"Oh, mister, mister," said the barman, backing away and holding his hands up like Rad was asking him to open the register and start counting bills. "You gotta turn around now. Go back downtown."

"What's so bad about uptown? Who lives up there?"

"Mister, everyone knows. Maybe not downtown, but around here, nothing goes on that doesn't have something to do with the King."

Rad sniffed and placed the rod on the bar. The barman's eyes were glued to it. Rad watched the barman as he slowly spun the rod on the damp wood top.

"Who's the King?"

"Come on, mister!"

Rad stopped moving the rod and waited until the barman dragged his eyes from it to Rad's.

"Who is the King?" said Rad with more force.

The barman shook his head and dragged the towel off his shoulder only to slap it back across the other. He folded his arms and nodded again. "You must know who he is, if you said he wants that back."

"Can't say I caught his name."

The barman shook his head again. "King isn't his name. King is what he is. The King of 125th Street."

Rad smiled. "Seems a funny place to be king of."

The barman didn't seem to like this. His eyes hardened and the thin smile vanished. "But that's where he told you to go, right?"

Rad held his breath for a moment, then let it out slowly. The creepy barman was right. The instructions had been simple: come to 125th Street, come at night. That was all Rad had got. He'd looked it up on a map back in his office but the map hadn't shown anything except a street like any other, running across the upper part of the city, west to east, at a bit of an angle.

"The King of 125th Street..." said Rad, mostly to himself, but his words elicited more vigorous nodding from the barman.

"Lives in a castle."

Rad glanced up from the bar to the barman. "Lives in a... castle?"

"There's a light on the top sometimes, green one."

"Huh," said Rad. He was getting closer. Whoever this King was, he was involved with something fishy involving robot gangsters and a warehouse full of strange equipment and an army of tin soldiers. He could pay the King a little visit, find out more, and take the information to Jennifer Jones.

"But, mister, come on," said the barman, pleading. "You gotta go home. Toss that thing in the river and forget you ever came to Harlem."

Rad smiled and pocketed the rod. He lifted his hat from the bar and placed it on his head. The hat was still cold from being outdoors, and Rad could felt the moisture on the rim against his scalp. Rad patted the pocket of his trench coat, feeling the dead weight of the pistol in it. "Don't worry about me. I can take care of myself."

The barman sniffed. "You don't know what's out there," he said. Then he stood back and folded his arms. Rad watched as he chewed, and he saw that the man's saliva wasn't black, it was green. He thought back to the antifreeze in Cliff's hip flask. Suddenly a reason why the barman was interested in the metal rod came to mind. Rad gasped.

"You a robot?" he asked.

The barman's thin lips split into a lizard grin and he slurped a mouthful of green saliva before leaning back in across the bar. "What, are you crazy? I'm as real as you are."

Rad retreated from the bar, transfixed by the man's chewing. The man wasn't as big as Cliff, and while he wasn't exactly a perfect human specimen there was a certain handsomeness hidden behind the grime and grease.

"What are you eating?" Rad asked, peering at the barman's ever-moving mouth. "You chewing a battery or something?"

The barman stopped chewing and sniggered. "Trust me, you don't want any of the green."

Rad's eyebrow went up. Green? "I guess not", he said. Then he lifted his hat. It was time to go. "Sir, it's been a pleasure. I'll be sure to pass my regards on to the, ah, King."

He turned and made his way to the door, the barman not saying anything but chewing, chewing, chewing.

When the door closed behind Rad, he thought he heard the barman say "good luck" or "go home", but he wasn't sure which.

SEVEN

Harlem was quiet and sharp, the sound of Rad's shoes on the ice-clad pavement the only noise as he walked onward. The street was lit in a dull orange from the clouds above, and ahead Rad could see the black conglomeration of buildings merge into something much larger, a squat skyscraper of the sort more common to downtown, the shouldered setbacks outlined against the dull sky behind. There was no light, green or otherwise, but the building had to be it. He was on 123rd already. Maybe the King of 125th Street was watching his progress, and would put the light on when he was nearer.

Rad stopped. He hadn't seen anyone since leaving the tavern, and the trailing footsteps hadn't reappeared.

Except... there they were. But they sounded different now: not just one set of footsteps but several. They shuffled rather than stepped, a group moving slowly and far away, at least at the moment. Rad thought again that the King might have invited him into an ambush.

Rad ducked into an alleyway that was just a tiny gap between two buildings. The brickwork was rough and layered with ice perfectly clear and perfectly smooth. Rad slid his back along it until he was in the shadows, then ducked down and moved forward to peer around the corner, his hand already reaching for the gun in his pocket.

"They're following us."

Rad jumped at the whisper in his ear, turning his head

sharply to find a face-full of fur. He spluttered and tried to brush it away, before realizing it was Jennifer Jones's hat. Rad hissed, and Jennifer shushed him.

"What in the hell are you doing here?"

Jennifer raised an eyebrow. In his fright, Rad had pulled the gun from his pocket and was pointing it right at her. Jennifer moved the barrel to one side with a finger, then raised her other hand. In it she held a gun, something large and silver that shone in the night, looking more like a hair dryer than a weapon.

Jennifer smiled. "Your little pea-shooter isn't going to be much good around here, detective."

Rad sighed and hunched his shoulders, allowing the upturned collar of his trench coat to touch the rim of his hat. His breath plumed in front of him as he spoke. "You been following me too?"

"All the way from your office," said Jennifer. Then she laughed. "Don't look so surprised, Mr Bradley. You're not the only detective in the city."

Rad looked Jennifer up and down. She was wearing the heavy overcoat, this time topped with the fur-trimmed hat.

"You're not made of metal too, are you?" asked Rad, not sure if he was serious or not.

Jennifer smiled again. "I'm as real as you are."

Rad opened his mouth in surprise, but Jennifer looked up sharply, her free hand waving Rad to keep quiet.

She leaned across Rad to see out into the street. Rad raised himself up to see over her hat.

The black buildings around them looked like theater flats, the streetlight casting a circular pool of dull yellow light.

Something appeared in that light. Rad held his breath and shrank back, but Jennifer edged forward.

It was a man, a big man, walking with a limp so bad he was dragging his left leg behind him. In fact his whole body was stiff, the arms locked straight, the man's back so rigid it was like he was made of…

Rad ground his molars together. The man's torso was flat and shone in the streetlight, a seamless, rounded thing of metal. His arms were metal too, but the boxy forearms ended in human hands. The bad leg was human, except for the foot, which was nothing more than a rectangular shape from which rigid pipes sprang, traveling up the entire limb in parallel before turning at a right angle and connecting to the man's pelvis. The other leg was entirely mechanical, as artificial as the arms and torso.

The man didn't have a head. There was a short metal stem, a neck, with thinner pipes waving about six inches out from the end of it as the creature moved.

Rad recognized enough of the creature to feel the adrenaline pump through his body, making him dizzy and nauseous.

It was a robot sailor, one of the human-machine hybrids manufactured from the citizens of the Empire State to crew the Ironclads that sailed off to war. The thing was incomplete, the human and mechanical parts badly mixed, the whole thing fragile and broken and twisted.

Rad felt his mouth fill with a sour taste. He glanced down at Jennifer, but before he could speak she pulled back into the alley and raised her hand for silence. Rad gulped and risked another look out to the street.

The broken machine was just the first. As it limped forward, others followed, each a twisted mix of human and robot, none complete, all moving with difficultly and perhaps, Rad thought with a growing sense of unease, pain. They were silent, the only sound the shambling, shuffling of their problematic movement.

Rad counted an even dozen, exactly the crew complement of one of the great Ironclad warships. The last Fleet Day had been two years ago, six months before everything changed. Rad knew the naval shipyards down near the Battery were still in existence, but he also knew that they were empty, abandoned by the navy once Wartime ended. They didn't make Ironclads anymore, nor did they make any more crews.

The group on the street was not an ordered rank of robots. They looked like a collection of spare parts, both mechanical and human. Rad suddenly wondered what had happened to all of the crews that must have been prepared for the last great sailing, the one that had been close to happening before Wartime ended.

He had a feeling he was looking at it, and his stomach churned.

"What are they?" he asked. He knew the answer but he wanted to hear it from someone else. The robot gang had stopped under the streetlight, and a couple of them – one with a big square metal box for a head, attached to a very human neck and chest, and another that was the exact opposite, the human head looking ridiculously small on top of the wide rectangular body – seemed to scan their surroundings.

Looking for them.

"I'm hoping your friend will be able to tell us," said Jennifer. She pulled back into the shadow of the alleyway and pointed with her gun towards the north, towards the vast black building that loomed over the whole area.

Rad followed her gaze. "You think the King has something to do with this?"

Jennifer glanced sideways at Rad, then her eyes were back on the street. "That what he calls himself?"

"So I've been told. King of 125th Street."

"Which matches the directions you were given." Jennifer nodded. "It's all connected – our friend Cliff and the army of robots; these poor creatures in Harlem. Something big is about to go down."

"So what's your plan? Follow me to this King character?"

"You bet. You got an invite."

Rad pursed his lips. "Guess you tapped my phone?"

"You guessed right."

Rad sighed. "I'm not sure the invite came with a plus one. And I was planning on bringing you any information I found."

Jennifer shrugged. "Thought I'd save you the effort."

Rad frowned and glanced back around the lip of the alley. "Damn," he said.

Jennifer peered around his shoulder.

The robots – those with heads – were looking right at them. The sound of twelve semi-mechanical bodies jerking into motion was loud in the otherwise silent night.

Rad realized Jennifer's appraisal of his handgun was accurate. He'd bought the thing to shoot people, not machines, and only if he was really in a squeeze. He glanced at Jennifer's gun, the giant silver thing she still had raised up, balancing its weight like she couldn't really lift it.

"You gonna point that thing at them or what?" Rad asked, not bothering to lower his voice.

Jennifer hissed through her teeth. "Last resort only." She glanced towards the north, to the big building. It was hard to tell, but to Rad it looked at least three blocks away.

"We're gonna have to run," said Jennifer. "On three."

The robots were slow but closing. They didn't appear to be armed, so Rad imagined the general idea was to tear them limb from limb.

Rad and Jennifer locked eyes. Then she nodded.

"Three!"

Rad pushed at the ice-covered brick of the alley wall as he sprinted forward, away from the robots. He instinctively reached one hand behind him to grab onto Jennifer, but his hand met empty air. He half-turned and saw the robots stagger as they caught proper sight of their targets and adjusted their own course. He turned around and saw Jennifer had a good ten yards on him, the shiny leather of her knee-high black boots flashing in the low streetlight from beneath the flapping edge of her coat.

"Hey!"

Rad clenched his jaw and stepped up the pace. Jennifer Jones wasn't going to slow for him, not at all.

He checked over his shoulder. The robots were gaining, their ramshackle, almost random movements making Rad feel ill. He turned again, focusing on outpacing the robots without slipping and breaking his neck on the icy street.

A new street appeared, ahead on the left. Rad saw a shadow move in that direction: Jennifer. He huffed and sprinted towards the corner, then almost collided with the agent's back, only just sliding out of her way and grabbing onto her shoulder to stop himself from tripping.

Jennifer's shoulders rose and fell as she caught her breath. Rad looked ahead, following the aim of her big gun – pointed at a large group of robots blocking the street. There were thirty, fifty, maybe more, the sound of their engines and motors and boilers and clockwork hearts and electric insides buzzing and fizzing and ticking and hissing in the night.

The robots didn't move. Rad turned at a sound behind them. The other robots had caught up. They were boxed in, trapped on either side by a long block of brownstones, with robots between them and the intersections in front and behind.

The group of robots in front parted to let one of their own kind walk forward. It was intact, perfect, two arms and two legs and a head, the whole thing standing near to seven feet tall. It was entirely silver, like Cliff and the robots in the warehouse, its polished surfaces catching the weak streetlight well. Another upgraded model, although this one without the human disguise on top.

Jennifer trained the gun on the silver machine. The robot had a face, complete with nose and metal eyebrows. The thing's jaw was a separate piece, square with a sharp edge. Rad's knuckles ached in sympathy as he remembered punching a jaw not entirely dissimilar just a night ago. Only this time there was a cigarette hanging from the corner of the robot's mouth.

"Oh, you're in the wrong place, lady," said the robot, slowing walking towards them, cigarette flapping as it spoke. Its voice was male and perfectly nuanced, although it echoed like it was coming out of an old radio set.

Jennifer was still, unmoving, the gun pointed at the robot. Standing at her shoulder, Rad watched a gentle ripple in the fur of her hat as it caught the air.

"Don't come any further," she said, and the robot stopped. It held up its arms like anyone would when someone was pointing a gun at them. Rad could have sworn the expressionless jaw was smiling.

Jennifer nodded at the robot. "You the King of 125th Street?"

The robot laughed. Rad found it unnerving.

"My name is Elektro," it said, and it spread its arms wider. "And nobody gets out of here alive."

EIGHT

Rad raised his gun, his finger tightening on the trigger. This was it. They'd had it.

"I hope you got a plan," he said from the corner of his mouth.

"Plan stays the same, detective," said Jennifer. She spoke in a loud, clear voice. At her words, Elektro lowered its arms and tilted its head. Then it took the cigarette from its mouth and flicked ash to the ground.

"Ms Jones," said Rad, "I have no doubt of your abilities, but we seem to be surrounded by robots." Rad waved his gun, like he was showing Jennifer around a yard of used cars. "It's been nice working with you, if you want to call it that, but I pretty much believe our tickets are punched."

Jennifer lowered an eye to the top of her gun. "Get ready," she said. "I'll clear a path. On three…"

Rad frowned, but he found himself tensing his leg muscles, ready for action. Maybe the big silver gun really was going to get them out of this.

"Funny," said Elektro, replacing the cigarette before taking a step back and to the side. He turned his silver head to the robots crowding the street. "Time to teach these two a lesson, friends."

The robots surged forward, so quickly a few fell and were trampled by the more able-bodied behind them. Those that still had human heads or faces leered horribly, while the metallic faceplates of those more complete machines made Rad think of the robotic sailor that had made its way from the ground to the top of the Empire State building just eighteen months ago, leaving nothing but destruction in its wake.

That's when Jennifer pulled the trigger.

Her arm jerked up with the recoil that followed the whump the gun made, like a rocket being launched. Rad felt his ears pop and his mouth filled with the taste of lemon, and there was a pressure behind his eyeballs, the kind of buzzing he'd felt when he'd visited New York. He blinked, and saw Elektro twist as the air buckled in front of it. There was no flash or explosion, but it hurt to watch, like staring into the midday sun.

Elektro screamed, the sound an echoing, electronic screech as the robot vanished, leaving nothing but a single silver arm to fall to the ground, smoking cigarette in situ between two metal fingers. The other robots came to a halt, some sliding on the ice, the circle around Rad and Jennifer now small and tight, unmoving.

Blue smoke curled from the end of Jennifer's gun as she held it aloft, barrel skywards. She was breathing hard. Rad glanced around, his own weapon seeming terribly small.

Jennifer didn't move. Rad looked at her, and saw her eyes glance left and right, her throat moving as she swallowed. Rad had a sinking feeling.

"You going to shoot some more robots?"

Jennifer didn't look at Rad. She adjusted her grip on the gun. "It needs time to recharge."

Rad pursed his lips. "I guess that's a no then." One of the robots had moved forward and was examining the single remaining limb of their leader. The machine pivoted awkwardly at the waist and picked up the arm, then rotated its square head in their direction. "I think you pissed them off."

Jennifer lowered the gun and looked over her shoulder, like she was searching for a way out that wasn't there.

"I was aiming for the big group," she said, and then: "Shit."

The robots took a step forward. Maybe their timing was coincidental, or maybe they all spoke to one another by radio. Maybe there was a whole conversation, a debate, raging in the air around them.

Rad's free hand found his coat pocket and he gripped the little metal rod. He wondered if it was valuable to the robots like it was valuable to the King.

Rad held his breath. The robots stepped forward again. Then there was a roar.

Rad felt his body brace itself. The robots in front of him were lit with a bright green light, and Rad's and Jennifer's shadows stretched out long before them. The roaring grew with the sound of screeching, the sound of fast wheels skidding on the slick road.

Rad leapt to one side, dragging Jennifer down with him. The air was filled with the hot smell of gasoline and rubber, and as Rad hit the deck and he slid on the ice, he got another face full of Jennifer's fur hat.

Rad blinked, his ears ringing, and looked up.

The car was long and low, the chassis rounded like a teardrop. It was entirely black, polished to a grand piano's mirror-like finish. Two tiny windows peered out from above the expansive hood, which curved gracefully down to two headlights, blazing green, mounted deep within the bodywork. The car shook as its engine revved, flames licking from the rear exhaust.

The suicide door opened wide, exposing both the front and rear seats. The driver sat, impassively, hands on the wheel. He turned to look at Rad with circular glass eyes set into a flat metal face. He was covered in a mass of black fur.

The driver pumped the accelerator and flicked the edge of his thick fur coat off the passenger seat next to him.

Jennifer pushed herself off Rad and Rad started to yell at her, tried to grab her arm, but she was too quick. She made for the car, the driver waving her in.

The man had driven the car straight through the crowd of robots, spilling them like skittles. They rolled on the street, unable to gain a foothold on the black ice. But the robots that had backed away from the thundering car and remained upright were now slowly creeping forward.

The man pumped the accelerator again. Jennifer had slid into the front and was pulling the door closed already. The robots started to move more quickly.

Rad dived headfirst into the car's backseat, and rolled against the leather as the driver pushed the pedal to the floor.

The vehicle's roar was even louder inside. Rad closed his eyes and pulled his feet in as the door swung back against its hinges.

The door slammed shut, and Rad opened his eyes. Jennifer was twisted around in the front seat, watching him. He gave a nod and she laughed and turned to their savior. From Rad's position lying on the backseat, all he could see was a ridiculous amount of fur and the back of the man's... mask? Helmet? Or was the driver yet another robot?

Rad righted himself in the back of the car.

The driver pointed ahead. They were driving fast but in a straight line, towards the giant black building. Rad heard Jennifer gasp and pulled himself forward to see out the tiny windows.

Almost on cue, a green light came on at the top of the building.

The driver changed gear, the car lurching as it sped

up, throwing Rad against the leather. In the front he saw Jennifer lean forward to peer out of the narrow windshield, looking up at the building ahead of them.

"Welcome to 125th Street," she said.

NINE

Nimrod stepped into the elevator, surrounded by expensive walnut panels and men in suits. He glanced up, as he always did when he entered the main elevator of the Chrysler Building, and admired the silver mirrored Art Deco sunburst design on the ceiling. He looked at his own reflection, twisted by the design of the mirror, and took a deep breath, trying to remove the fear, uncertainty, and doubt from his face.

It had been only a short walk from the Empire State Building, where his own Department was hidden on the middle levels behind a company nameplate that said TISIPHONE REALTY – apparently nothing more than a upmarket, private real estate firm that handled the kinds of accounts that came from countries rich in oil, with clients who liked to vacuum up little parcels of the United States without much fanfare. That the other department should be secreted in another famous New York landmark seemed appropriate, although their particular choice of office was unusual.

Atoms for Peace, founded by President Dwight D. Eisenhower. An olive branch offering of scientific cooperation and endeavor that stretched out across even the Iron Curtain. But in reality, a secret government department, an initiative to research technologies "acquired" from the Empire State, with the aim of building a defense against...

well, Nimrod wasn't entirely clear on that point and neither, it seemed, was Eisenhower. Granting Atoms for Peace carte blanche had only turned the new organization into the blackest of secret government agencies.

That they were tasked with handling research related to the Fissure and beyond was what bothered Nimrod. The Fissure was, well, it was his. He knew more about it than anyone else, in this dimension anyway.

He didn't like Atoms for Peace, and he knew the feeling was mutual.

From the offices of Tisiphone Realty, Nimrod could see the Chrysler Building. He stood at the window often, watching. He wondered if the Director of Atoms for Peace, the remarkable Ms Evelyn McHale, did the same from the Cloud Club, the former cocktail lounge at the top of the Chrysler Building that Atoms for Peace had co-opted into their headquarters. He didn't really think she did; from what he'd heard, Ms McHale had something of a phobia when it came to the Empire State Building. Perhaps that was part of the problem she had with him, and the Department.

Nimrod glanced at the men around him. There were five agents – two standing behind, one posted on his left and one on his right, and one in front. They each wore a black suit; each had a narrow black tie against a starched white shirt. Each wore a hat, black, of course. They were not Secret Service, but they did a fairly good impression. They were certainly better dressed than his own agents, but then his own agents had to melt into the general populace. Atoms for Peace were different. Their agents rarely made public appearances.

Nimrod wondered what his escort was for, exactly. The agents certainly weren't for his protection (not inside their own headquarters) and they certainly weren't for hers. The agents who stood around him in the elevator – and

Nimrod, too – were nothing but insects to her, as was every other human who inhabited the city, inhabited the whole country.

Nimrod stroked his mustache in thought and the elevator glided to a halt, a bell announcing their arrival.

The doors slid apart, revealing an elegant lobby swathed in maroon carpet, the walls heavy with more of the walnut paneling. The lead agent stepped forward, Nimrod following and finding himself ankle-deep in the carpet pile. He heard the other agents' feet swoosh as they walked behind him.

Opposite the elevator, across the lobby, was a large set of double doors, the bottom third of which were more of the beautiful walnut. The upper two thirds were frosted glass panels, acid-etched with sunburst rays and other geometric shapes. To a casual eye, they looked like just more of the Art Deco theme that filled the entire building. To Nimrod, the designs were a little off, a modern copy somehow altered.

Captain Nimrod glanced to the agent on his right, and saw the man was sweating inside his elegant suit. Nimrod smiled to himself. They were afraid. Nimrod was too – how could you not be, when you were about to have an audience with the ghost of a woman who had appeared as a glowing blue terror after the Fissure had almost been destroyed eighteen months ago, her phantom somehow expelled from the shadowlands between dimensions, granted with the appalling power to see and to interfere with the universe on a subatomic level.

Nimrod tapped his foot in the absurdly deep carpet as they waited. Finally, one of the double doors opened, and another man in a black suit nodded to the lead agent. He glanced at the party, and then looked Nimrod in the eye.

"The Director will see you now."

The Cloud Club had been among the city's finest, most

exclusive establishments. In the early days, Nimrod himself had received numerous invitations to attend functions there, but he was never comfortable in social engagements, and besides, he preferred to drink his scotch at ground level. Over the years, as he worked at the Empire State Building just a few blocks away, probing the mystery of the Fissure and what lay beyond, the fortunes of the Cloud Club declined as the Great Depression and then the Second World War took their toll. The top of the Chrysler Building had been closed for several years by the time Atoms for Peace were brought into existence.

The main clubroom had been left untouched: a cavernous space interrupted at intervals by dark square marble pillars, with ceilings two floors high. One wall was nearly entirely glass. The wall opposite was covered with a continuous mural depicting the cityscape in minute detail. Nimrod had no doubt that club patrons had spent many an hour studying the illustrated city while behind them, through the glass, the real thing winked in the night.

The room, once filled with tables, was occupied now by a single desk, standard government issue, at one end. Two Cloud Club armchairs sat in front of it.

Nimrod walked towards the desk, studying the mural behind it. This section was an enlargement, a stylized rendering of the Empire State Building that took up nearly the whole wall. Nimrod smiled and took a seat.

The room was empty, the agent who had opened the door having decided to wait with his colleagues in the lobby. Nimrod crossed his legs and let his eyes wander over the mural. He felt his back teeth begin to ache, and he held his breath.

"Captain Nimrod, so good of you to come."

Nimrod's smile was tight, his teeth clenched against the pain spreading along his jawline. He knew the pain would subside shortly. It was always like this.

She stepped out of the corner of the room on Nimrod's left. There was no door there, just the two murals meeting in a slight shadow cast by the nearest marble column. One moment Nimrod was alone, the next he was not. No matter how many times he had an audience with the Director of Atoms for Peace, her sudden appearances unnerved him.

She glided forward an inch from the floor, glowing only slightly. Nimrod wondered if she was making an effort to fit in, though if so it was a token attempt. Her tweed suit was out of date, monochrome, like something from a film, as was the matching hat and lace veil. Nobody had dressed like that in years.

Nimrod's fear melted, replaced by sadness. He felt sorry for her. She wasn't alive, and yet here she was, doomed to an eternity of slavery to the Federal Government. It was no wonder she looked miserable behind her veil.

"Director, a pleasure as always," said Nimrod, and it was a lie but he didn't think she noticed. He didn't think she ever did.

Evelyn glided closer to Nimrod, keeping her back to the Empire State Building mural. He found himself sitting up a little straighter, his heart beating a little faster. He couldn't imagine what it must be like to work with her. It was bad enough just being in the same building. Although he really didn't know where she spent most of her time.

Which reminded him…

"There have been reports of another sighting," he said. Then he steepled his fingers and brought them to his lips. "The Ghost of Gotham, as I believe they call you. It is on the front page of both the New York Courier and The Record."

Her mouth curled into a smile. Nimrod wasn't sure he liked it when she smiled.

"I didn't plan it to be quite so public," she said. She turned in the air and floated over to the long wall. She reached out, her fingers trailing the line of the East River.

Nimrod frowned and stood, moving to join her at the wall. He drew breath to speak but she tapped the wall with her finger, making the mural go slightly out of focus around the contact point. Nimrod felt the hairs on the back of his neck stand up.

Evelyn jerked away from the wall and looked at the Captain. Nimrod blinked and shrank back; her eyes were bright and clear with an impossible and terrifying depth and lit with something fierce and blue. A light with which he was intimately familiar. The light of the Fissure.

"Our department operates with the upmost secrecy," she said, her lips in a sly grin and her blue eyes unblinking, "but sometimes I need to... go out. See things for myself. Reconnect."

Nimrod pursed his lips. Conversations with Ms McHale were frustratingly vague.

"You called me here, Director," he said. "And while I am happy to oblige, I do have a department of my own to run. If we could perhaps progress to the matter in hand, whatever that may be?"

Evelyn floated away from the mural, towards the windows opposite.

"Change is coming, Nimrod. Neither you nor I can stop this. A moment is approaching, one in which we will both have roles to play."

Nimrod brushed his mustache with a thick index finger as he considered.

"I'm not sure I understand."

Evelyn turned in the air so they were facing each other. The smile was back.

"War is coming, Nimrod. You must be prepared. We all must."

Nimrod felt the color drain from his face. "War? With whom?"

Evelyn laughed, the light of the Fissure sparking in her eyes and making Nimrod's jaw hurt. Her blue aura grew, and Nimrod stumbled backwards, each blink of his eyes casting a fiery negative image of McHale inside his lids.

"The Empire State, Captain. Soon we will be at war with the Empire State."

Nimrod felt dizzy. He rubbed at his forehead and tried to blink away the afterimage of McHale's glow, but it was no use. He felt ill. Suddenly the world made no sense.

He stumbled forward and grabbed the top of the nearest armchair.

But at least it seemed the Empire State still existed on the other side of the Fissure. The disconnection was temporary.

"What–"

There was a knock at the door, and one of the black-suited agents entered. Nimrod tried to focus on him, on the faint red line on his forehead from where his hat had so recently sat, but his vision was obscured by the echo of Evelyn's aura.

"Director," said the agent, "it is time for your briefing with the doctor."

McHale floated towards her agent, and Nimrod saw the man shift slightly on his feet.

McHale nodded. "Please show Captain Nimrod back to the world."

The agent held out his hand, gesturing towards the main doors. Nimrod turned back towards Evelyn, but she was gone. The pair were alone in the Cloud Club.

Nimrod frowned, and turned to the agent.

"Do you ever get used to that?"

The agent smiled but shook his head. He gestured to the door again. "This way, sir."

TEN

Rad turned away from the window. He was standing in the lobby of a disused theater, and all he could see outside was the outline of a street and buildings, empty of cars and people – and robots, thank goodness – all bathed in a deep emerald light. He rubbed his eyes, and green spots danced in his vision.

"What's with the green light?" he asked.

Their rescuer, the driver of the remarkable car, was silent, standing between Rad and Jennifer. The giant fur coat was gone, revealing a chauffeur's uniform, complete with knee-high boots and jodhpurs. The only thing missing was a hat, but considering the driver's rounded metal face and two goggle eyes, even Rad thought that might look a little silly.

The driver was another robot – built to drive the car, it seemed, not for conversation.

"Talkative, isn't he?" said Jennifer. She looked the driver up and down, but the robot ignored her. Rad wondered if it had been switched off.

The car had brought them up to the theater, which sat in front of the tall building Rad and Jennifer had assumed was the King's Harlem fortress. The awning was in still in place over the entrance, but the signage above was old and mostly missing, only three letters – an "A", and then after a gap two "L"s together – visible above the empty marquee.

The driver had led them inside to the theater's lobby,

where they now stood. Ahead of them was the remains of a concession stand or ticket counter, and on the left and right shallow, elegant stairs wound their way up and around, vanishing into the darkness of the upper level.

"Anyone home?" Rad's voice echoed.

"Rad!"

Rad turned and saw Jennifer facing the stairs on the right. She pointed as a figure broke away from the shadows.

"Detective, detective," said the man trotting to meet them. He grabbed Rad's hand with both of his own and pumped the detective's arm up and down with some vigor. "Why, you made it! Safe and sound, safe and sound. I'm so pleased to see you!"

Rad sniffed, and put on a smile, at least until he figured out what the hell was going on. The newcomer was perhaps in his early sixties, his grey hair cut so short that it stood on end, with a neat beard trimmed into a triangle so precise it looked lethal. He was wearing a suit of dark blue velvet, double-breasted, with a brown shirt underneath and an orange handkerchief in the pocket that matched the color of his tie.

The man was smiling from ear to ear. Rad scratched his chin.

"Ah, yeah, hi there," he said. He nodded at Jennifer. "I don't think you've met my friend."

The man's eyes lit up and his smile grew wider, stretching into an almost open-mouthed expression of delight. He placed one arm behind his back, executed a theatrical bow, and took one of Jennifer's hands in his own, gently drawing it to his lips.

"M'lady," he said, breathlessly. "Charmed, I'm sure, Miss...?"

Jennifer pulled her hand carefully away from the man's grip.

"Special Agent Jennifer Jones," she said. The man's eyes widened.

"Oh, splendid, splendid," he said. Rad didn't like the way he wouldn't take his eyes off Jennifer. He cleared his throat.

"Would you be the, ah, King of 125th Street?"

The man turned and clicked his heels together. "I have the pleasure of holding such high office, Detective Bradley." He clasped his hands behind his back and looked between Rad and Jennifer, his face split with a grin. "I'm so glad you could make it. Really, I am."

Jennifer shook her head. "We're here on official business, sir."

The man's smile didn't falter. He looked Jennifer up and down and then winked at Rad without trying to hide it. Rad raised an eyebrow.

"I was only expecting one, of course," said the King. He clicked his tongue and glanced back at Jennifer. "But I'm not one to complain about such pleasant company."

"Ah, yeah," said Rad. "Pardon me for saying, sir, but you don't look like much of a king."

The King laughed. "Well, it takes all sorts, my man..." He looked down and seemed to study the carpet. Rad sighed and exchanged a look with Jennifer, but she seemed as bewildered as he was.

Rad said, "Hey, buddy?" In the pocket of his coat he could feel the rod from the warehouse. "Your majesty?"

At this, the King clapped his hands and threw his head back in a booming laugh. When he looked at Rad again his eyes were streaming tears, which glinted green in the light from outside.

"Look," said Rad, "you wanted me to come here because you wanted something back, something that I picked up downtown. But more important, you said Kane Fortuna was here. So where is he?"

The King slapped his knee. "My, you do like to get right to business, don't you detective?"

Rad ignored him. "Let's cut to the chase. You take me to Kane and I might give you the component back. But I think Special Agent Jones here might have something to say about that. See, I don't think she likes whatever racket it is you're running, and I'm not sure I do either. But hey, there's a lot in this city I'm not sure I like, and this little ice age we got going on is one of them. So let's get moving before the ice outside gets any thicker and we all need to start sipping antifreeze like your friend at the bar down the street."

The King had started laughing as Rad spoke, a mild case of the giggles turning into a full belly laugh. The detective shook his head in frustration. It figured. The man was a lunatic. What other kind of person would call himself the King of 125th Street and lock himself into a disused theater?

Jennifer stepped up to the King, who was leaning over, recovering from his fit of mirth.

"Look, sir," she said. The King looked up at her and waved her to continue as he took deep breaths, coughing as his laughter threatened to return.

Jennifer glanced at Rad, then looked back at the King.

"There's something going on in the city. I have a lot of questions I need to ask you. I'd appreciate your cooperation and I'd prefer it if we could do this in a civil manner, but we can do this in a more formal capacity downtown if required."

The King of 125th Street finally stood. He sniffed and stuffed his hands into his pockets, then looked Jennifer up and down again before turning back to Rad.

"Come," said the King, patting Rad on the forearm. "Let me give you the grand tour, so you can see how we run this joint." He glanced over his shoulder at Jennifer. "Feel free to tag along, sweetheart. You sure do brighten the room."

He laughed and headed towards the right-hand set of doors that led into the theater.

Jennifer sidled up to Rad. "He's psychotic."

"The man thinks he's a king," said Rad. He removed his hat and rubbed his scalp, then glanced at the driver. The machine was still standing, immobile, silent. "The king of what?"

"King of the robots?"

Rad drew breath to answer, but the King reappeared through the doors.

"Hey, friends, Romans, countrymen, lend me your feet and walk this way!" He vanished back into the theater.

Jennifer looked at Rad and Rad gestured for her to lead the way. She sighed, gripped her silver gun, and headed for the doors.

Rad watched her back, and then as she went out of sight, turned to the driver. "Why do I get the feeling this is going to be a long night?"

The driver said nothing. Rad huffed, and followed Jennifer.

Alone in the lobby, the driver turned its head towards the double doors that were still swinging from Rad's exit. Something flashed behind the driver's round glass eyes, and there was a sound from behind the grating that formed the robot's mouth. It was quiet, and low: the sound of chuckling.

The driver watched the doors for a second or two, then jerked into life, heading towards the nearest staircase and jogging up them two at a time.

There were things to be done.

ELEVEN

It was cold, and getting colder.

The man on the bridge frowned, his breath steaming in a huge cloud before him as he peered ahead. Behind him, the wall of fog was as dense and impenetrable as ever, but ahead the view was clear.

But... he wasn't sure.

The night was quiet, like it wasn't just the bridge and the water beneath it that was frozen solid. It was like the air itself was too cold even to allow sound to pass.

A moment later the ice beneath the bridge cracked, the sound like a muffled gunshot echoing around and around. The man shuffled, the knob of his wooden leg scraping the roadway, as the bridge shook, the tremor strong enough to knock him over. The man grabbed the rail next to him and clung on, pressing his chest against it, ignoring the way the cold of the metal cut through his thick jacket. The tremor stopped, but the man held on a moment longer, just to be sure. He glanced over the edge. The ice had cracked, a great zigzag fissure opening directly below the bridge.

The tremors worried him. They were getting stronger and more frequent, far more so than when he had left the city.

He straightened up. And how long ago had that been? How many years had he been traveling, lost in the fog? Too many, and somehow far more than had apparently passed here.

If this was the same place, the right place.

He had to admit, he wasn't sure. The buildings on the other side of the bridge were dark and apparently empty. The sky was clear but completely black. The fog bank behind the man cast a dirty orange glow over the bridge.

The bridge was the problem. The city was alone, isolated, surrounded by a wall of fog. Beyond the fog was nothing but the lands of the Enemy.

Or so he had thought. He knew, now, that his knowledge of the universe was incomplete. There was plenty beyond the fog. The Pocket was larger than he had ever dreamed, stretching far beyond the reach of his instruments.

But the bridge, that was different. He hadn't known about it before. But as the cold had gotten worse the fog had receded, exposing the structure at the very northern tip of the island. It provided the perfect watch point, the airship anchored to it quite securely, hidden just behind the fog bank. It wouldn't pay to take any chances and leave themselves exposed, if the city was the wrong place.

And the bridge was the one thing that made him pause to consider whether this really was the right place.

He dared not go any further across it. Not yet. There were still tests to do and measurements to make. He stared ahead, trying to judge distance, to recognize any part of the cityscape before him.

There, perhaps, due south, where the air was a little misty, where the glow was captured, the lights of something big, the lights of civilizations, of something more substantial than the collection of empty shells that crowded the end of the island, on the other side of the bridge.

Perhaps it was the right place. Perhaps he had found home.

Perhaps.

The man on the bridge slapped his cheeks to get the

feeling back into them, rubbed his thick mustache to get the ice out of it, and turned carefully on the frozen bridge. Looking down, he stepped forward slowly so as not to slide on the ice, and vanished into the fog.

The interior of the airship was silent until the man returned, his wooden leg tapping loudly on the floor as he made his way to the pilot's seat on the flight deck. He fell into it, and began pulling his gloves off. In front of him, the windows of the craft were opaque with frost.

"Have you come to a decision?"

The man paused and looked up at the ceiling, then shook his head as he dropped his gloves onto the control board.

"No. I can't be sure. We need something else."

A shadow flickered in the room. "We could fly in and investigate."

The man chuckled. "And look what happened last time," he said, banging the end of his wooden leg against the floor. "No, we need to wait. We need to be sure."

"We cannot wait here forever."

That was true. The man sniffed and tugged at his beard. "If only there was a signal of some kind, something we could home in on."

"You only found me because I activated the ship's beacon. It is unlikely we will find such a signal out there."

The man hrmmed, and scanned the controls. It was worth a try.

"A distress beacon, no," he said, flicking a series of switches. On the control board a row of orange lights came on. "But maybe there will be something else. See if you can boost the output of the number two power cell. Perhaps we'll be able to pick something up from the city – radio, perhaps, anything that might give us the information we need."

The shadow moved again. "Very good, sir" said the voice, this time nearer the door.

The man sat back in the pilot's seat, and looked at the frosted windows.

Perhaps it was the right place. Perhaps it was home.

But he had to be sure.

TWELVE

"We can do great things together, you and me."

Doctor X ignored the voice, and focused instead on the clipboard an inch from his face. He ticked some more boxes and scrawled a note in a hand he knew he would not be able to decipher an hour from now. His handwriting was poor at the best of times, but today she was coming to the laboratory to visit. And she expected much, even though she didn't perceive time the same way as everyone else. He glanced out of the corner of his eye and adjusted his round-framed glasses. She could appear from anywhere, which, if he were honest, scared the living crap out of him. And at such a delicate phase of the operation, he needed his wits about him.

"I know you're listening, pal."

The doctor held his breath and flicked a switch on the panel in front of him. The voice wasn't doing much for his nerves either. It filled the space, echoing against the hard surfaces of the laboratory. It was a male voice, eerily calm and muffled slightly, like someone on the end of a long-distance telephone call.

Not that Doctor X knew much about that kind of thing. He'd only been introduced to the concept of "long-distance" in the last year. Imprisoned in the laboratory as he was, he still didn't quite understand what it meant that there was more than just the city outside.

The doctor ticked another box.

"You know I'm speaking the truth," said the voice.

The doctor shook his head, and put the clipboard down.

"I think we're almost ready, Dr Richardson." No response. Doctor X turned on his heel, but he was alone in the laboratory. Well, the Project was there, trying hard to get his attention.

"Laura?"

The thin plastic safety door at the back of the laboratory flapped open as the doctor's assistant came in, wheeling a trolley covered with electronic equipment. She leaned forward on the trolley, picking up the pace.

"Sorry, doctor," she said, bringing the new equipment to a halt by the laboratory's main workbench. "The guys on the door were being jerks again."

Doctor X nodded. "Well, the Director will be here shortly. No wonder they're jumpy. The whole facility seems to be on alert."

Laura began unpacking small trays of components, arranging them on the workspace. "You'd think she wouldn't need to come in and see us. I mean, can't she see the whole city at once?"

"I think she likes to visit in person. It makes her feel like she's still one of us."

"Creepy," said Laura. She set down the last tray and pushed the trolley out of the way. Then she turned to the mesh cage. The door was open in preparation for the next phase of the operation, allowing access to the Project within.

The Project stood in the center of the cage, leaning back against an angled metal slab, around which was an elaborate framework of hinged struts, cables dangling.

The Project itself was huge, seven feet tall and made of polished silver. It's head was a rectangular box, with a man's face crudely constructed out of moving metal cutouts: a nose, even eyebrows. Its jaw was a separate piece and it had two red lights for eyes, which lazily moved from the doctor to his assistant.

The robot had only one arm; the metal of its right-hand side was tarnished, the innards exposed along the flank, sheered clean off, the damage reaching as far down as the hip and upper thigh. From the open side, a dozen cables fed out to the instrument banks in the laboratory proper, with several more connected to the framework suspended over the slab.

"You and me, kid. What a team we could be," said the robot, its amplified voice echoing around the laboratory like it was coming out of a PA. Laura flinched and turned quickly away. Doctor X just shook his head.

"The Project has been in fine form this morning." He returned his attention to his clipboard. "Are we ready for today's test?"

Laura nodded and moved to the largest instrument bank nearest the cage. "The new cell is calibrated. All we have to do is install it and turn it on when the Director gets here. She should be impressed."

Doctor X frowned but, secretly, he agreed. The Director couldn't fail to be impressed with their progress after seeing the latest prototype in action. He put the clipboard down and moved to the table, pulling a large dust cloth off a squat metal cylinder a foot in length and half that in width. Each end angled inward, and around the top rim were a series of slots. Doctor X peered into the top of the cylinder; just below the rim the object was capped with a black glass circle.

"Be a gem, pal," said the voice. "Let me out and we can show the world what we got."

The doctor ignored the voice.

Initially, the Project hadn't spoken. In the first weeks in

the underground laboratory, the doctor's prime objective had been to get it to talk, because he thought if the robot could talk, it would make the work easier. Of course, he'd assumed the robot would be cooperative, just like all the other robots he'd seen as special advisor to the City Commissioner, back in the Empire State. True enough, the Project didn't look anything like the machine hybrids constructed for the Ironclad fleets, but the doctor did recognize the design from early upgraded prototypes the Navy had been toying with.

But then one morning he woke up in another place. His head hurt like all hell, but she'd made it better, made the pain go away. He recalled that morning, lying in an unfamiliar bed in what seemed to be a prison cell, a glowing blue woman floating a foot off the floor beside him.

Doctor X removed his glasses and rubbed his eyes. She would be here soon. He had to get on with his work.

The robot – the Project, as the Director had called it – had started talking, eventually. But clearly it had been damaged in the transfer between here and there. It spoke nonsense most of the time, trying to get the doctor to free it, despite the fact that it was badly damaged and missing an arm.

Doctor X soon realized the machine would not be of any help. Over the next months he'd learned to tune out the incessant, deranged ramblings of the robot.

"Sweetheart, just think of it. Think of the possibilities."

The Project has turned its attention to the doctor's assistant, Dr Richardson. A bright young thing from Columbia University, at just twenty-four she had advanced the field of electronics more than Doctor X ever had. The Director had brought her in before his arrival to prepare the laboratory. How exactly the Director had known he was coming was one of the mysteries that surrounded her; one that had led Doctor X to believe she could see the future.

As Laura would say, creepy.

Suppressing a shiver, Doctor X walked into the cage and opened the front of the Project's casing. The robot lay motionless against the slab, but its red eyes fixed on the top of the doctor's head.

Inside the chest cavity was a circular port, six inches across and stretching clean through to the other side of the torso. The walls of the port were slotted at the compass points, and there were a series of small, glass-capped ports spiraling around the inside wall.

"You gonna give me back my heart, pal?"

The doctor looked up, despite himself. When he looked into the robot's eyes he thought he saw something else, something moving, like the eyes were the windows to some kind of machine soul.

Doctor X cleared his throat. Ridiculous. He stepped back out of the cage.

"Prepare the fusor," he said. He didn't take his eyes off the Project's, but behind him he heard Laura walk to the other bench to start the warm-up procedure. The doctor licked his lips. "The cell can sit hot for a while. Then we just need to wait for the Director."

"I am here, doctor."

The doctor turned quickly, and blinked, the spell of the Project's red gaze broken. From the other end of the laboratory, Evelyn McHale glided three feet from the floor, her monochromatic form outlined in electric blue. As she got closer Doctor X felt the weird sensation behind his eyes again, the pressure, the buzzing in his head, the nauseating feeling of being pulled away, back to the other place.

"Director," the doctor began, swiping the glasses from his face and polishing them on his lab coat before replacing them with shaking hands. "Thank you for coming. I felt it was important for–"

"Are you ready for the next phase, Doctor X?"

The doctor glanced sideways at Laura, then stood to one side as the Director floated towards the cage to examine the Project.

The Project's head rocked back and forth, the red eyes scanning but seemingly unable to get a fix on the Director. It didn't speak, but the doctor could hear a faint sound, a whine, coming from it, like the machine's voice box was jammed. Or like the machine was... in pain.

Ridiculous.

"Doctor X?"

He jumped and found the Director looking at him. He nodded, then moved to join Laura at the instrument panel, where she was gently coaxing the controls. A series of dials sprang to life, along with a row of lights the same shade of red as the Project's eyes.

The doctor watched the dials for a moment and then nodded. He turned back to the Director and almost reached out to touch her shoulder, but thought better of it. He coughed.

"Sorry, yes, we're ready. If you would please step... ah, move... away from the cage, we can begin."

The Director turned in the air, and the doctor suddenly found himself very near indeed to her veiled face. He held his breath, his skin tingling from the sensation of standing so close to her event horizon. She was beautiful and his heart raced, but not out of attraction. She looked grey and sad, but her eyes were electric blue and terrifying.

What things could she see, he thought, and then he gulped. The Director smiled and drifted backwards.

"How is the isolation cage performing?"

Doctor X paused, the question a distraction. The cage in which the Project was placed was a remarkable device in itself, and, if the doctor was honest, perhaps even more of an achievement than the fusor reactor. Anything within was isolated from the universe around it; in theory, a simple application of the properties of the tether that connected New York to the other place which allowed the interior of the cage to exist elsewhere, while still being an accessible part of the workshop. In practice, Doctor X hadn't quite been able to get his head around it. It was the Director herself who had done much of the work.

But it worked. And if anything went wrong with the experiments – anything nuclear – the cage would contain it. That was some comfort, at least.

"Doctor X?"

He blinked, and shook his head. "I'm sorry. The cage is performing admirably. The isolation field removes all interference from the instruments well."

The Director nodded, apparently happy. "Please," she said, "continue."

The doctor turned back to the instruments and clutched at the edge of the console, pressing his fingernails white. He had to get a grip, had to control himself. It would not be long now and the work would be complete. Of course, what fate the Director had in store for him afterwards he could only guess. He hoped – prayed – that she would simply forget him as his usefulness diminished.

"Dr Richardson, are we ready?"

"Ready."

Laura moved to push a small wheeled console close to the door of the cage. The Project's red eyes rolled lazily in her direction.

"Sweetheart, you're killing me here."

The doctor coughed, and lifted the cylinder from the trolley.

"Does it often talk?"

The doctor froze. He glanced back at the Director, but she

was watching the Project. He hefted the cylinder against his chest and adjusted his glasses with one hand.

"No," he said quickly. From the corner of his eye he saw Laura glance sideways at him.

Doctor X moved into the cage and lifted the cylinder, mating it with the port in the Project's chest. He twisted it slightly and carefully pushed it in until the black rim of the cylinder was almost level with the top of the port. Reaching up, he pulled a three-pronged clamp connected to a sprung arm down, and adjusting the spread of the fingers, attached them to the slots on the cylinder's rim. Clamp connected, he gripped the sprung arm and twisted, using the leverage to rotate the cylinder further. At half a turn, there was a click as the cylinder was aligned with the slots on the inside of the port, and the unit slid another inch into the Project's chest. At once, the glass cap on the end of the cylinder brightened to a reddish glow. The doctor peered into the cap, and then turned to his assistant.

"Go ahead, Dr Richardson."

She nodded, her hands moving over the controls.

"Reaction engaged," she said. "Magnetic field stable. Ionization rate constant. Injection to commence in five, four..."

The doctor detached the clamp from the cylinder as Laura began the countdown, and then quickly moved out of the cage. As the countdown reached one, he swung the door closed and engaged the catch, then stepped back. He risked a glance at the Director watching him, a smile playing over her face.

"One."

The reddish glow from the cylinder flared to a bright orange-red, the light moving in a clockwise spiral. The Project's eyes rolled, but it remained silent, save for the quiet whining.

The doctor peered over Laura's shoulder, reading the dials on the console. He nodded to himself.

"You have made much progress, doctor," said the Director.

The doctor looked up and nodded again, removing his glasses.

"Yes, Director. The fusion reaction is stable, and the power output exceeds our estimates by a considerable margin. More than adequate for our needs, but–"

There was a whining sound, a low thrum like the engine of an aircraft slowing down. The lights in the laboratory flickered. In the cage, the Project twitched against the slab, banging its back into it loudly. The light in the chest cylinder flared again, then faded. Two seconds later it was out.

The Director glided closer to the cage.

"But there is still work to be done. Progress remains slow, doctor. The fusor must be fully functional if we are to go into production on schedule."

"The test was successful," he said, puffing out his chest a little. "I said the reaction was stable. I didn't say it was sustainable." He glanced down at the console. "How long this time, Dr Richardson?"

"Eighteen seconds."

The doctor looked up at the Director, a wide smile on his face. Eighteen seconds was a vast improvement, twice as long as the previous test. He was pleased with his work; producing nuclear fusion in a portable, virtually hand-held reactor was quite a feat. Eighteen seconds of stability was incredible.

The Director was smiling too. The doctor's expression faltered. He didn't like it when she smiled.

By the time Doctor X drew breath, the Director had vanished into thin air.

He watched the space where Evelyn McHale had been just a moment ago, and then slowly removed his glasses and rubbed his forehead with shaking hands. His skin was hot, slick with a thin layer of sweat. He closed his eyes, squeezed the bridge of his nose, and finally sneezed. It was a nervous reaction. He sniffed loudly and dropped his glasses onto the console.

"Laura, detach the fusor and prepare for reset."

"Yes, doctor."

The doctor turned to the cage. The Project's eyes were on him.

"Philo, my friend, we could do great things together, you and me."

Doctor X blinked as the Project used his first name, and wondered if it had been speaking the truth all along.

THIRTEEN

"Quite a set up you've got here."

Rad was lying. He exchanged a look with Jennifer, but their tour guide didn't seem to notice the sarcasm in his voice.

The King's 125th street "castle" was a theater, it was as simple as that. Leading them first through the main double doors, the King had turned quickly through a side passage, taking his guests through a series of narrow, twisting corridors filled with random doors and random intersections, and even random spiral staircases rising up in dark levels above. Most of the walls were brick, and most were painted thickly in a dirty white or equally dirty black.

The King laughed and kept marching forward. Rad stopped and wondered several things: what the hell he was doing here, what the hell this wacko with a beard and a blue velvet suit had to do with not just robots but anything at all, and where the hell was Kane Fortuna?

"You planning on standing there all day?"

Rad turned. Jennifer was right behind him, wry grin on her face, but he noticed that her finger was resting on the trigger of her gun.

"You expecting trouble?" he asked.

She adjusted her grip on the weapon. "Always."

Rad huffed and nodded down the now-empty corridor. "He sure doesn't look like a criminal mastermind."

"Looks can be deceiving," said Jennifer.

"You mean it's an act?"

Jennifer waved her hand around. "Well, we are in a theater."

The King appeared again at the end of the corridor. Even from this distance, his broad smile was easy to pick out.

"You're dawdling! There's still plenty to see, plenty! This way!"

Jennifer squeezed past Rad in the narrow corridor.

Rad sighed and stuffed his hands into his pockets. At least it was warm inside. In fact, it was getting warmer. Frowning, he pulled out a hand and placed it on the painted brickwork on his left. His fingertips prickled at the contact. The wall was not quite hot.

The King waved like a showman from the doorway at the end of the hall. As Jennifer approached, he bowed and gestured for her to step through. Halfway across the threshold, she shot Rad a look over her shoulder.

Rad raised an eyebrow. "What?"

"I think you're going to want to see this."

Jennifer turned back and stepped through the door.

The King had led them to the main stage. Rad paused in the doorway, and swept the hat off his head. He looked around, rubbing his scalp absently.

"You've been busy, your majesty."

They'd entered from stage left. The performance space in front of them was a vast platform of polished wood, sweeping out towards the orchestra pit and a row of footlights, all but one blazing in the dark space. Beyond, lost in the gloom, the theater stalls stretched back and up before disappearing into the darkness. Above, the theater circle – Rad could see it still had seats, all red velvet and gold painted wood. Unlike the stalls.

The stalls had been emptied, torn out, replaced with what looked like a junkyard, metal scrap collecting against the edge of the orchestra pit like frozen waves. At first Rad thought the theater's roof had collapsed, bringing with it rubble and tons of roofing lead. But as his eyes adjusted, Rad could see there was some kind of order, pieces stacked according to size or shape. Several clear paths – the theater's original aisles – led straight out from the stage to the back of the room.

"I think we're in the right place," said Jennifer. Rad frowned and shook his head, rolling his hat in his hands.

The scrap was robot parts. Rad saw arms and legs first, then torsos and breastplates, some intact, some in halves like clamshells. Large elliptical waist joints were racked over poles like hula-hoops. There were limb components, individual feet and hands and elbows, and smaller parts that looked like shoulder collars or articulated elbow joints.

And heads. Stacked like coal scuttles, one inside the other in teetering, curved towers. Robot heads, or the external shells of them anyway.

It was a robot graveyard.

The huge stage was filled with materials too, but here the order was more regimented, the space a workshop. Trolleys, racks, shelves, and workbenches were arranged around three large tables, which looked to Rad like the slabs from a hospital mortuary. Every surface but the slabs was covered in more of the robotic parts, most in considerably better shape than the junkyard collection in the stalls. Metallic body parts that were not stacked and arranged neatly were held in various bench clamps and cradles, some opened like fruit, tools ranging from giant wrenches to fine surgical clamps protruding, wires thick and thin trailing out to the banks of equipment ranging from small tabletop boxes to floor standing cabinets. The equipment buzzed and the smell of ozone was rich in the air, and lights flashed red and yellow and blue.

"Rad, look."

He felt Jennifer's hand on his arm as she spoke breathlessly. He turned, and whistled.

The back of the stage was occupied by a tree, growing out of the floor on the left side, the trunk curving up towards the center. The tree was enormous, the branches starting just below the remains of the stage lighting rig hanging high above them. The branches spread out evenly and thickly, obscuring the ceiling in a mass of leaves that glistened wetly in the dark. It looked to Rad like the tree was growing into the structure of the building, the curve of the trunk almost penetrating the wall, some of the back branches growing flat against it.

"What the hell?" Rad whispered. He replaced his hat as he looked up at the tree. Jennifer turned to him, her eyes wide, a smile flickering across her mouth.

"Welcome to my workshop!" said the King, strolling towards them. He ignored the pair of them staring at the tree, and instead moved to one of the nearby benches, on which sat a phonograph, complete with large horn. The King flicked the machine on, and the workshop was filled with jazz. "As you can see," he continued, "I have rather a lot of equipment, but the space here is more than adequate."

Rad and Jennifer exchanged a look.

"Some hobby you got," said Rad, while Jennifer walked over to the tree.

"Not a hobby, Mr Bradley, a vocation, a calling! My work here is very important, very important indeed. Believe me when I say that the future of the Empire State itself depends upon it."

"The tree," said Jennifer, looking up at it. "It's... it's beautiful."

The King walked over to her, his hands clasped tightly behind his back. "The tree brings me luck. It was here before me, of course. The theater belongs to it, I think." He pointed to a patch on the trunk that was worn smooth and shiny. "There. Rub it for luck. Go on!"

Jennifer looked at Rad but Rad just shrugged. Jennifer rubbed the patch on the trunk as the King watched.

"How does it grow inside, with no light, or rain?"

The King shrugged. "It was here before me. It's part of the theater."

"I think we got more important things to worry about," said Rad. "Like the fact we've found the source of our robot problem."

"Ah yes, the robots," said the King, rolling the "R" like a circus magician. "I'm sorry you got tangled up in that, but I did warn you not to come until very late. I can only keep the lantern lit for a few hours a night, and then it takes the rest of the day to recharge the power battery. You were lucky – my instruments reported movement a few blocks south, so I dispatched the Corsair to investigate. It seems like he reached you just in time."

Jennifer scratched at the slab in front of her with a gloved finger. "The Corsair?"

"Ah, the Corsair!" said the King. "My... ah, assistant, shall we say? He's not very talkative, but he is possessed of certain skills that come in useful."

Rad raised an eyebrow. "He'd make a good getaway driver."

The King clapped his hands. "Oh, isn't that car something else? I built that as well. My own design, of course."

Jennifer said, "What does the green light do, exactly?"

"It keeps the robots away," said the King. "It's not green; that's just how we see it. But to them, the light is something else – it interferes with their sensors. More than that, in fact. I have discovered they will actively avoid it, as if it causes them pain, in some way."

Jennifer nodded like she understood. Rad just shook his head.

"You're gonna have to explain why there are robots roaming the streets in the first place. You seem to know a bit about that."

"Oh yes," the King said as he walked around the stage, bending down to inspect various readouts on the workshop equipment as he passed them by. He tapped his fingers along the bench tops in time with the music. "When Wartime ended the Naval dockyards were in full production for another Fleet Day. A day which, of course, will now never come. They claimed most of the robots were deactivated, but I think you and I both know that the crews of the Ironclads are not entirely mechanical. They are men – were men – and unable to be deactivated, short of killing them. So they were released."

"Just like that?"

The King clicked his fingers. "Just like that."

Rad and Jennifer exchanged a look, and she asked, "So why are they all up here? The Naval robot yards are a long way from Harlem."

"Ah, that is my doing," said the King. "I am from downtown, actually. One night, among the chaos, I had my own little encounter. I discovered the robots – all lost, afraid, hiding in the shadows." He held his hands out. "I decided to help them."

Jennifer stepped around the slab with a speed that surprised Rad. "Help them? How could you help them?" She leaned over him as she pressed her questions, her face pale.

"Ms Jones, please! I am both an engineer and a doctor. I thought there might be a way to reverse the process of robotization. If the mechanical and electronic parts of these poor creatures could be removed, maybe the men trapped inside their steel prisons could be freed, and return to normal life."

Rad hrmmed. This sounded like the kind of endeavor Captain Carson would have had a hand in, being the guy who had helped invent the damn robot technology in the first place. The fact that Carson had instead vanished and this guy had set up what was starting to look like a crazy person's backstreet robot surgery crossed Rad's mind as not particularly good signs. He raised a hand, but stopped when he saw the look on Jennifer's face.

She was standing even closer to the King now, her eyes wide, her lips parted. Rad could see the rise and fall of her chest.

"Is it true?" she asked the King, her voice a breathy whisper. "Can you save these people?"

The King still had the smile on his face, and he nodded.

Rad jerked his thumb over one shoulder. "What about those robots outside? They don't look much fixed to me." He stepped up to Jennifer and pulled her away from their host. When she looked at Rad there was a spark in her eyes: she was hot on the trail of whatever it was she was looking for. "And what about our erstwhile friend, the amazing Cliff? There's warehouses full of robots just like him downtown, all packed up like toy soldiers, waiting for something. That anything to do with you?"

Rad pulled the metal rod from his pocket. The King's eyes lit up and he smiled before holding out his hand. Rad pulled his own away and shook his head. "I met a guy earlier who didn't like the look of this little thing one bit. Was scared of it even. You care to explain why?"

The King raised an eyebrow and slipped his hands into the pockets of his velvet jacket. "Oh, probably thought it was some bad hoodoo. My work here makes some people nervous, although I can't think why."

Rad sighed and held the object out. "OK, fine, knock yourself out," he said.

The King took it slowly, his fingers wrapping around the cylinder. Then it quickly disappeared into a pocket.

"Kane Fortuna," said Rad. "Now."

The King nodded. "Come."

The King walked toward the backstage door. Rad followed, but when Jennifer moved after him the King stopped, turning on his heel and holding up a hand.

"Ah, Ms Jones. Please make yourself comfortable here. Mr Bradley and I won't be long."

Jennifer met Rad's eye. Rad frowned.

"Where are we going?" he asked. "Why can't she come?"

"Trust me," said the King. Then he smiled the infuriating smile and turned away, vanishing through the door.

Jennifer sighed. "I don't like this."

Rad adjusted his hat. Neither did he. He glanced around the theater, his fingers playing over the pistol in his coat pocket. He was armed... but so was Jennifer. The big silver gun still hung from her hand.

"We'll be fine," he said, drawing in close, his voice low. "If I can keep his majesty busy, you can take a look around, see what you can find."

"OK. But be careful."

Rad flashed a smile and knocked the brim of his hat with a knuckle. "You too," he said. Then he followed the King through the door, wondering what he was going to say to Kane Fortuna.

FOURTEEN

They came to a large door, unlike any Rad had yet seen in the building, studded with rivets and reinforced with bolted metal plates. As they paused, Rad could hear a sound close by, what sounded like bellows, or machinery. Heat wafted off the door. There must have been a boiler or a furnace beyond it, providing the King with his own prodigious power source.

The King placed a hand on the door's handle and turned to Rad.

"We are here."

The room beyond was large and low: another workshop, almost identical to the one on the theater stage upstairs, although crowded, messy. The walls were lined with electrical equipment in more of the tall cabinets, and there were workbenches, toolboxes, and stacks of robot parts. The difference here was that these parts looked new, freshly fabricated, their metal surfaces unblemished and shining.

The King gestured for Rad to enter first. The detective raised an eyebrow and stepped across the threshold.

There were three slab-like tables here, as on the stage upstairs, but they were occupied by long metal boxes that fitted their tops nearly perfectly, leaving just an edge two inches deep on all side. The boxes hummed and ticked: machines rather than just containers. Rad stood still, listening, as the unmistakable sound of someone breathing heavily, as though in sleep, filled the air. Rad threaded his way between the workshop benches until he was at the head of the slabs.

Two of the three machines were empty. He gave them only a cursory glance. The middle slab had his attention.

The man was young, brown hair greased and damp with sweat, big eyes closed, their lids and surrounds dull red. His chin was covered with a green encrustation that, along with the faint tang in the air, reminded Rad of the barkeep he'd met in Harlem what felt like a million years ago.

Rad swore under his breath, and took off his hat to rub his head. His scalp was crawling with beaded sweat, the adrenaline-fuelled fight-or-flight response that had kicked in somewhere in the theater upstairs now threatening to make his heart leap out of his ribcage.

The man in the machine rolled his head, and his eyes flickered open. Rad's own were wide, his jaw was loose, and he couldn't find anything to say.

"Rad? Is that you?"

Rad remembered how his tongue worked. "Kane Fortuna. All my days."

Kane smiled and closed his eyes. "Nice to see you too, partner."

FIFTEEN

Jennifer traced her fingers along the painted brickwork as she explored the corridors of the King's bizarre theater complex. She'd retraced her steps back to the former lobby and had then taken one of several plain doors that clearly led into what would have been the hidden workings of the theater, the areas not meant for public view. Behind the tattered but still decorative facade of the theater, the corridors were plain and the rooms she had found so far functional and mostly empty.

She was surprised to find herself alone, left to her own devices, the King apparently confident that she would be a good little woman and sit in the main workshop like she'd been told. Like the fact that she was a Special Agent operating on behalf of the City Commissioners somehow didn't matter.

Jennifer stopped in the corridor, and smiled to herself. Of course, that had been a little lie. But sometimes little lies got you places a lot quicker than otherwise. And besides, it wasn't entirely incorrect; it was just... well, just a little out of date. But the King was a crook and a crazy person who was going to help her, had to help her, so what did it matter.

And Rad was right – with the King otherwise occupied, it was the perfect opportunity to search the place.

Rad Bradley, private detective extraordinaire. He was a

nice guy. He was going to be disappointed when he found out who she really was, but that didn't matter. Because when that time came, Jennifer hoped to have solved the little mystery at the heart of Harlem and to have found her brother, James, and that was all that mattered. And the answer lay somewhere inside the King's theater, she was sure of it.

Jennifer took a breath and ventured onwards.

She'd been working on her own for a long time, too long. She still remembered the day of chaos, the day the Empire State Building had been torn apart from the inside-out. In the aftermath there had been no one to stop her borrowing one or two things, like the experimental silver gun that swung heavily from her right hand. That, and as much of the surveillance data on the robot gangs as she could stuff into an old briefcase without anyone noticing what was missing. And the logs from the naval robot yards, the ones indicating that James had gone in but that his section hadn't begun processing before a halt was called to the operation.

The risk was worth it, as had been calling Rad. That had paid off in spades, because he had led her to the King, which would lead her to her brother, she was sure of it. And once she'd found him and got him to safety, she and the detective would be able to clear up the little problem of the robots and the wacko calling himself the King of 125th Street. And then she could go back to the Empire State Building and maybe take charge herself. After all, she would be the city's savior, and she had a very big gun.

Jennifer rounded a corner. Ahead was a large, low space, with a set of wide sliding doors forming most of the far wall. In the center of the room was the car, vast and black and silent. She'd managed to get herself back to the garage. She'd lost track of time, and she was now far enough away from the main workshop that she wouldn't be able to hear the others return. She also knew that she shouldn't be here, not really, and it occurred to her that she'd entered the domain of the King's robot driver.

Jennifer waited in the doorway a moment, but the garage was quiet except for the slow ticking of the car's engine as it cooled.

"Hello?" She raised the gun and stepped forward, eyes wide, alert. There was no other exit aside from the big sliding doors, and no real place for the robot to hide. Jennifer jogged forward and ducked down to peer into the car's interior, but it was empty. She tried the door, which opened with a click and swung backwards smoothly.

She leaned in to take a better look at the remarkable vehicle. She'd never seen anything like it, although the controls seemed just like any other car. The car was powerful, she knew that, and fast too. It would make the perfect getaway vehicle if she and Rad had to make a speedy escape. Even better, the car had a large button in the center of the dash that said START. Jennifer just hoped it was that easy.

She stood and moved to the garage doors. There were four windows set high; on tip-toes Jennifer could just make out an empty, narrow street, more like an alleyway. She tried to remember the route they'd taken to get to the theater just a short while before. She could remember the way, she was sure of it–

An arm enveloped her chest, a gloved hand pressed hard against her mouth. Jennifer cried out but she couldn't breathe, and the sound died in her throat. She struggled, half-turned, and got a face full of thick black fur.

She pushed against the robot as it dragged her backwards towards the car. Jennifer's arms were held against her body but she could bend the gun arm at the elbow. She raised the weapon, trying to angle it in her hand to point it at her attacker, but the gun was knocked away with a clack almost as soon as she moved. It flew through the open door of the car and was lost somewhere in the vehicle's cavernous interior.

The robot stopped moving. Jennifer tried to pull away, and found some slack in the robot's iron grip. She twisted, thinking this was it, she'd found her moment, only for the robot to yank her back hard against his body. Her mouth and nose had been released as the pair wrestled, but she drew breath for a scream before the robot's leather-covered hand clamped over her face again.

Eyes wide, nostrils flaring in panic, Jennifer tried to pull back as the robot brought its black metal face close to hers. Jennifer could see her own terrified face looming large in the two black glass eyes.

"Jennifer Jones," said the Corsair, and then it laughed. Jennifer's heart hammered, fear and panic joined by shock and surprise. She felt ill, and behind the robot's hand the taste of bile was hot and bitter in her mouth. She jerked again, trying to get free, but the robot's grip only got stronger.

"Hey, don't make this difficult, Jen. It's for your own good."

Jen. He called me Jen. My brother called me Jen and he called me Jen and I've found him I've found him I've found him oh god I've found him and it's too late too late too late

Jennifer slumped a little, her eyes flickering, and the hands holding her relaxed their grip.

Her deception successful, Jennifer drew a deep breath and screamed Rad's name.

SIXTEEN

After showing Rad into the workshop, the King had excused himself and, in his shock, Rad hadn't stopped him. Instead, Rad sat next to Kane's machine for a while, having dragged a tall stool out from one of the workbenches. But after their greeting, Kane had drifted into unconsciousness. Rad hadn't wanted to disturb him – the machine looked too much like an iron lung for his liking – but his mind was made up, at least. Rad's priority was now getting Kane out of the place and to the medical attention he clearly needed. But first he had to talk to the King, find out what the machine was actually for. He desperately hoped it wasn't keeping Kane alive. He also wanted to see what Jennifer had found, if anything.

Rad stood, and quickly made his way back upstairs.

Rad found the Corsair first, standing stock still in the lobby of the former theater. Rad let the door close quietly behind him, unwilling to disturb the mausoleum-like silence.

He checked his watch. It was now four in the morning. Maybe the King had gone to bed.

Rad looked the Corsair up and down and then cleared his throat. "Ah, you know where the King is?"

The machine didn't move.

"OK," said Rad, regarding the twin doors on either side of the lobby that led into the theater itself. "Guess I'll have to find out for myself."

He started to turn, but then jerked back in surprise. The robot had turned its head and seemed to be looking at Rad with its round glass eyes.

"Huh," said the detective, looking over the faceplate of the robot. There was something about the shape of the eyes he thought he'd seen somewhere before. "You know, you remind me of someone."

The robot said nothing.

"Oh, yeah, the strong silent type, I remember. Well, so long." Rad waved over his shoulder as he left, but as he walked towards the doors he was suddenly afraid to turn around or even look behind him. One thing was for sure: the Corsair was as creepy as hell.

The King was busy on the stage-workshop, sitting on a stool so tall his feet didn't touch the ground. There was a jeweler's eyepiece lodged firmly between his cheekbone and eyebrow, and a thin trail of smoke drifted towards the branches of the magical tree above as he soldered something minuscule on the bench in front of him. Jazz, something soft and melodic, filled the room.

Rad paused, then strode down the center aisle between the stacks of parts, making his footfalls heavy enough that anyone should have been able to hear his approach over the music. He hated surprising people.

"Mr Bradley, welcome back." The King didn't look up; his mouth was a grimace of concentration. Rad took off his hat and waved it, then felt stupid and replaced it on his head. Apparently finished with his work, the King replaced the soldering iron in its cradle and looked up at the detective, jeweler's eyepiece in situ.

"Ah, hi there," said Rad. He stuffed his hands in his pockets, and felt the hard shape of his gun. His fingers curled around it. "Where's Agent Jones? I think we all have a little talking to do, don't you?"

The King shuffled on his stool. "I'm sorry?"

"Talking," said Rad. "You, me, Agent Jones, just a little pow-wow about what the hell is going on here. You've got a building full of weird and my old friend is lying in some kind of machine downstairs. I think we need to clear some stuff up."

The King slid off the stool and walked to the edge of the stage. He looked down at Rad, his mouth still in the same expression of concentration as when he'd been soldering.

"Mr Bradley," he said, "to whom are you referring?"

Rad paused. "What? Kane?"

The King shook his head. "No, the other... Jones, was it?"

Rad's jaw went up and down, and then he let out a breath, slowly. "Where is Jennifer Jones, your majesty?" He pointed at the King with his hat.

The King shook his head and smiled. "I'm afraid you have me at a disadvantage, Mr Bradley. I don't know who this Jennifer Jones is."

Rad blinked. He was feeling more ill at ease with every passing moment. He raised his hat again, stabbing it forward as he spoke.

"You tell me where Special Agent Jennifer Jones is right now, or I swear I'll turn over every piece of junk in this place to find her." He thought then that maybe he should have been pointing with the gun, and not his hat. The man in the blue suit in front of him seemed not even a little bit disturbed. He looked down at the detective with something like wry amusement.

Rad huffed and dropped his hand. He needed to get help, get the police up here. He still had some pull down at the Empire State Building, and once they'd discovered one of their own had vanished into the far north of the city, he'd be able to come back with a whole posse, more than enough to deal with the robots outside and the King and the Corsair, and they could get Kane out and search the whole building.

Or... maybe the King had killed Jennifer? No, that didn't make any sense – why kill her and not him? And there had been plenty of opportunities to bump them both off since they'd arrived. Maybe Jennifer hadn't found anything and had gotten tired of waiting and had left. Maybe that was the sensible option. She seemed to like doing her own thing.

"OK, fine, whatever, your majesty," said Rad, throwing his hands up. "I'm gonna go get some help and we're going to turn your little operation upside down."

Rad turned on his heel, thinking his plan over, wondering whether he was making the right decision to leave Kane behind, helpless in the downstairs workshop. Lost in thought, his eyes fixed to the floor, he almost walked straight into the Corsair. Rad sucked a breath through clenched teeth and swept his hat off in surprise.

"What the hell?" he said. "Excuse me, I'm going to the police."

Rad went to move forward, but the Corsair grabbed his arm holding the hat with lightning speed. Rad swore and pulled against the grip, but it was held firm.

"Hey!"

"It is not safe outside, Mr Bradley," said the King. Rad looked up at him, the small man with the pointed beard now very tall and imposing on the stage. "The robots will have returned, and I'm afraid you would not make it very far."

"Then turn your fancy green light on, your majesty."

The King shook his head and tutted, almost with regret. "The lantern is still recharging. It will be nearly a full twenty-four hours before it can be lit again."

Rad pulled again at the Corsair. The robot didn't even rock on its feet, and Rad's arm remained locked in place. A cold fear began to creep into Rad's bones.

"I ain't joking, your majesty," he said, gritting his teeth and pulling, pulling, pulling at the robot. "Where are you keeping Jennifer? She locked up downstairs too?" Rad had an uneasy feeling. "You gave her the same story too, huh? Too dangerous to leave?"

The King shook his head. "It is for your own good, Mr Bradley. The robots will kill you for sure. You must remain here."

The Corsair pulled Rad closer and shoved a handful of cotton wool in his face. Rad gasped as the unmistakable sickly sweet stench of chloroform assaulted his senses. He held his breath, but he knew that was no defense.

"Lock him up with Kane," said the King, his voice a hundred thousand million miles away. Rad's lungs were on fire. He released his breath, inhaled deeply, and the last thing he saw was the Corsair's oddly familiar black metal face spinning in his vision.

SEVENTEEN

Nimrod watched the floor indicator lights as the elevator carried him up the spine of the Empire State Building. There was no polished walnut here, no mirrors or brushed Art Deco steel. The elevator was a service one, spare and functional. It did the same job.

He had walked the few blocks from the Chrysler Building to his own, enjoying a clear, if cold, day. The agents from Atoms for Peace who trailed him from the Chrysler Building didn't make much of an effort at disguising their movements as they followed him from one block to the next.

Nimrod frowned. Atoms for Peace putting agents on his trail did not surprise him, but it did worry him. It wasn't personal. No, it was the position, the job they were watching. He was a threat. He was protector of New York City in many ways and custodian of the Fissure. His position meant, in theory, he was the custodian of her, because she was part of it, an unliving, unbreathing embodiment of the Fissure itself.

Nimrod chuckled. That was a fudge, of course, something similar to what the President had been told. She was a quantum copy of a woman who had died long ago, who had somehow been caught in the gap between the universes by physics so far beyond the comprehension of mortal men.

Atoms for Peace. Nimrod felt uneasy. Evelyn McHale had appeared only a few short months ago, and the whole

110

operation was so new but wielded such power with a certain branch of the establishment in Washington, the kind of people who worried Nimrod, those who thought that America was under attack not from the Soviets or Castro or China, but from within, by intellectuals and artists and people who liked to ask questions.

Nimrod certainly included himself in that last group. The country was still reeling from the televised hearings led by that Senator McCarthy, and while Nimrod suspected the Senator's influence was on the decline, there was no doubt that people were still afraid of the Red Menace.

The elevator indicator continued its slow curve to the right.

The Red Menace. Maybe he'd be labeled as a Communist. That would make it easy for Atoms for Peace to move in and disestablish his department. He wondered what their Director thought, if she was even still capable of comprehending the politics of the situation. To her it would be like understanding the politics of a termite colony.

Maybe it wouldn't be so bad. Maybe he could resign, pass the torch and they'd leave him alone.

Alone.

That was the real fear, wasn't it? To be surplus to requirements, cast aside, to be alone.

Nimrod rolled his most recent conversation around in his mind. She had said they were preparing for war. War against the Empire State.

It was impossible, of course. Inconceivable.

And yet... the other side of the Fissure was closed. Something was happening in the Pocket universe. Clearly something bad. And, despite her vague suggestion that he would be involved, only Evelyn knew the truth. The future.

Nimrod had to know. He didn't trust Evelyn – how could anyone? She wasn't even human, not any more. And, as far as he was concerned, his own position was still pre-eminent: he was custodian of the Fissure, his department the overseers of the tether between the Origin and the Pocket. And, therefore, the first line of defense for both.

The elevator pinged and the doors rolled open. Nimrod exited, and quietly strolled through the lobby of his floor, past the little lounge and the agent stationed on duty who sat flipping through magazines, disguised as someone patiently waiting for an appointment. Nimrod knocked on the door of Tisiphone Realty, spoke the password, and was allowed entrance.

Nimrod paused, surveying the office before him. Agents and staffers were going about their usual business.

"Mr Grieves?"

At Nimrod's call, the lead agent appeared from behind a pillar, drained his coffee, and marched towards his superior.

"Sir."

Nimrod paused. Was this the right course of action? What was the threat, and where did it come from?

Was it from the Empire State? Or was it from the Chrysler Building?

Mr Grieves shifted his weight. "Sir?"

Nimrod brushed his mustache. The decision was made. "Call in all agents, Mr Grieves. This department is now on high alert. We must secure the Fissure at once."

Mr Grieves nodded. He turned, then paused and turned back to Nimrod. "Have Atoms for Peace issued a warning, sir? What's the threat?"

Nimrod sighed, and shook his head. "There was a warning, agent, yes. But I fear the threat comes from the Cloud Club itself."

Grieves's eyes went wide. Then he nodded and walked away, beginning to issue orders.

Nimrod watched his office spring to life, wondering again

whether he was concerned about a threat to this world or the other, or for his own survival.

EIGHTEEN

Doctor X had not been let out of the laboratory complex in as long as he could remember. He had free run of the main lab and his cell-like quarters, and everything in between, which included storage rooms, a kitchen, bathroom, communal toilet, and a large common room, the latter two of which were really only used by him and Laura. But the corridor that led from the main lab to his quarters ended at a large green door with an arched top. It was locked, of course. He'd never seen it open, but he was aware of its presence, its potential. It was there in the morning, closed, solid, unmoving. It was there in the evening, in the same state. He'd begun to find it reassuring, strangely – maybe it was the fact it was green, as green as the grass that he hadn't seen for months. It was a doorway to another world.

He'd asked Laura about other places; she came from somewhere called California. But the distance, the scale she had described, made his mind spin, made the buzz saw vibration behind his eyes return. He had acclimated to the Origin universe, but occasionally the world around him liked to remind the good doctor that he was a visitor here.

In fact, he was a prisoner – and a dangerous man, according to the President. Doctor X had even met him once, when he came to open the facility. The ceremony had been secret; only the President and a dozen uniformed men even knew that there was more to Atoms for Peace than just a speech given to the United Nations General Assembly. The President, introduced to Doctor X as Dwight D. Eisenhower, had been one of those uniformed men too, once. That explained it, in a way; it explained Atoms for Peace, the way the President had looked at the equipment, the way he held himself when the Director glided around, explaining their set-up, the reason why he had employed the extraordinary for his secret purpose. He'd kept a distance like Doctor X was electric, like he was dangerous.

But it wasn't him that was dangerous. It was the machine, the Project, the thing in the cage that they needed to be worried about. He hoped they knew that, all of them. The Project was a wonderful and deadly thing.

"Well now, look who's back!" said the voice from the cage. "So, you live to fight another day, eh, bud?"

Doctor X ignored the Project as he walked into the laboratory. It was late, and Laura had already left. Just today she'd made a minor alteration that allowed the latest test fusor reactor to run for nearly three minutes before the overload shut it down. A dramatic improvement, even if three minutes was of as much use as eighteen seconds. If he was honest with himself, it was Laura doing the heavy lifting now.

Then she was in the laboratory, her blue glow mingling with the light from the bench lamps in a way that made Doctor X feel ill.

"Are you going to kill me?" he asked, not quite meaning to but wanting to fill the silence with something. His usefulness was up, he knew. He was a prisoner and he was expendable, and the bulk of the work had been done. But he regretted asking it, and when the Director didn't reply he finally did look up into her face. She was smiling sadly behind the veil.

"You have much work to do, doctor," she said. "The fusor reactor must be stable according to the original calculations. Atoms for Peace must have a never-ending power source. We cannot proceed without the power. When the prototype reactor is complete, we can go into full production."

Doctor X closed his eyes and took off his glasses. "I've told you–"

The Director was suddenly standing – hovering – beside him. He tried not to flinch, but he did anyway. She didn't seem to notice.

"Do not delay, Dr Farnsworth. We must prepare ourselves for war."

Doctor X blanched. She never used his name; she refused to acknowledge that he existed in this universe. For her to use it now filled him with a cold fear, as cold as the waters of the East River. Then she disappeared from the workshop; Doctor X barely noticed.

"She's going to kill you," said the Project. "Maybe not today, maybe not tomorrow, but some day. Some day."

It was right. The Director was going to have him killed, and Atoms for Peace would install the young Dr Laura Richardson as their Chief Scientist. It was just a matter of time.

"You and me, buddy, we'd make such a team."

If he fixed the fusor, got it working as required, providing power for the terrible machine army Evelyn was building, then he was unnecessary. Perhaps more important, with the fusor operational, war would come: the Director would have her army; the results would be terrible to behold.

But if he could delay fixing the fusor…

Doctor X removed his glasses with a shaking hand.

If he delayed the work, deliberately, then his life would be prolonged and war would be postponed, if not averted altogether. Doctor X could save himself and the lives of countless others.

"The things we could do. Oh, the things we could do."

But she would find out, and he would be killed, and the work would continue.

But maybe there another option, an alternative, one that would not only keep him alive... maybe it would set him free? If the fusor was operational – if the Project was operational...

Doctor X shook his head and slipped his glasses back on. He pulled the stool out from under the bench and sat heavily on it.

"Just you and me against the world, pal."

Doctor X glanced at the cage. The Project was locked into the frame, but the bright red eyes were on him, unmoving.

The Project wasn't just running through a set of recorded phrases. It was... alive, in a way. The Project was aware of its surroundings, was aware of the situation. Its offers of assistance... perhaps they were genuine.

And with a fully operational fusor installed, the Project would be unstoppable, the first – if the Director had her way – of a whole army, a wonderful, terrible robot army.

Doctor X cleared his throat. He was alone in the laboratory – it was nearly three in the morning now. How long had he been sitting at the bench? The artificial lights blazed high above, removing any sense of time.

Alone, except for the Project.

He looked at the workbench. Then he asked, "How much do you know about the fusor reactor?"

The Project laughed. "Oh, Philo, my friend. I thought you'd never ask. That thing, I can feel it working when you put it inside me. It's a real buzz."

Doctor X took his glasses off. "You can... feel it?"

"Sure. I can also feel what's wrong. But don't feel too bad. It's an easy mistake – anyone could have made it. But don't sweat it. You and me, we can make it work. No problem."

Doctor X said nothing. Was it that easy? Was the solution sitting inside the isolation cage, just a few feet away? He replaced his glasses. "Can you help me?"

As soon as he said the words they felt inadequate, incomplete. He needed to explain himself, explain the situation, explain what he thought was going to happen.

Then he laughed. He was tired, exhausted. The Project was a machine, like the many others that filled the laboratory. The silence grew in his ears like the roaring of the ocean. He closed his eyes.

"Yes," said the Project.

Doctor X gulped a breath and held it. When he stood, he felt dizzy, his heart racing, and when he opened his eyes the world was fuzzy at the edges. He moved to the cage, lightheaded, like he wasn't in control of his own body. His eyes were dry and he blinked and blinked and rubbed them, and when he opened them again he saw the clamps holding the Project to its frame were unlocked, open.

The Project was free. Doctor X took a step back, looking at his own hands; he didn't remember releasing the locks on the frame. Now this was it, really it. Because now the Project was going to kill him. But it was better this way. He'd be dead and the fusor reactor would be unfinished and there would be no war.

"I'm not going to kill you," said the Project. It turned its head left and right and left again, and the glassy red eyes rolled back and forth in their sockets.

"Can you read my mind?" It was a ridiculous question but he asked it anyway.

The robot's head stopped moving, and it looked at the scientist.

"I don't need to read your mind, Prof. I can read your face like an open book. Remind me to play poker with you sometime."

Doctor X stared at the robot, not quite following the conversation. The robot turned its head again but was otherwise motionless.

"Little help here, buddy," said the Project.

Doctor X's jaw went up and down, and he looked around him like he didn't know where he was.

"Hey, Prof, there." The Project didn't move, but its eyes indicated to Doctor X's left. On a table was a replacement arm. "Gonna need that back. And I need me some juice, real quick."

"Juice?"

"The fusor, dummy. You need to install it."

The doctor turned around and shook his head.

"But it isn't ready. Even with the modifications it can only run up to three minutes now. That's not enough."

"I know," said the Project. "But I'll tell you what to do. So let's get it up and running and then we can get moving along, nicely nicely."

"How do you know my name?"

The Project's face was fixed, a metal sculpted approximation of an artificial man, but the laugh that came from behind the faceplate sounded surprisingly warm and real.

"Philo Farnsworth, the hottest ticket in the Empire State. I've got a friend who speaks highly of you, pal."

Doctor X nodded. His knees wobbled and for a moment he thought he would hit the floor with them, but he stayed upright.

The Project's eyes rolled as it watched Doctor X. "You don't look so good. Looks like you could do with some juicing yourself."

Doctor X took his glasses off again. He closed his eyes and rubbed them until he saw blue spots dance.

"Hey, don't worry about it. We'll fix you up," said the robot. "And you can call me Elektro.

"And you and me, we're going to set the world on fire."

NINETEEN

The laboratory was empty when Laura arrived for work. That wasn't unusual, although she did worry for Doctor X's health. He didn't get enough – any – natural sunlight living underground, which would play havoc with anyone's circadian rhythms. She only hoped he was given vitamin D tablets with his food. He'd taken to working at night too, when she wasn't there, appearing late in the afternoon. It was almost like he didn't want to work with her, which was a shame. She knew she was the only person Doctor X ever really saw, apart from a few auxiliary staff and the silent, black-hatted agents that accompanied them. And the Director of course, but she didn't count as a person, not really.

Laura shrugged off her jacket and slipped on her white lab coat, glancing around as she did so. He'd been busy during the night. Very busy. Laura allowed herself a little smile; at least his scientific curiosity hadn't left him.

"Good morning, Laura."

Laura jumped, her hand clutching her chest. She spun around, recognizing the voice.

"What–" Her hand found her mouth.

The Project stood next to the cage, its left arm replaced with the new limb she'd built just a few days ago. Its eyes glowed brightly, as did the circular window in its chest. Laura found her gaze drawn to the red light pulsing and spinning like a radar screen.

The fusor... the Project had a fusor installed: an operational, functioning portable fusion reactor. She blinked, her surprise fading as her professional interest took over. She took a step forward, wanting to see the work, and then she screamed.

The Project was standing next to the cage, but the frame within was not empty. Wired to the cradle around it, cables and wires dangling, connected to banks of dead equipment, was Doctor X. His eyes and mouth were open. His head lolled to one side.

His lab coat was a brilliant pinkish red. It took Laura a moment to realize that the heavy fabric had acted as a sponge, absorbing the blood from the cavernous chest wound. There was a smell too, the smell of meat at a butcher's counter. Laura felt the bile rise in her throat – hot, sticky, making her choke.

The doctor's chest had been opened down the middle, the two front halves of the ribcage removed entirely. Laura glanced down, and saw on a small trolley near the cage a mound of black and red material, oily and wet. Doctor X's eviscerated insides.

The hollowed-out torso was filled with wires, all connected to the apparatus inside the cage like they had been when it had been the Project occupying the frame.

Laura doubled over and closed her eyes. She spat her breakfast onto the floor, and sucked in a breath, determined to stay conscious as the world spun around her.

It was fine, it was fine. She just needed to call for help and the workshop would be filled with agents. And the Director... she could see what was going on, right? All Laura had to do was to call out, get her attention, and everything would be fine. Maybe the Director could even put Doctor X back together again.

"Anyone ever tell you you're a pretty girl?"

Laura jumped. The Project was nearer now, moving with remarkable silence. The circular swirl of red light from its chest was almost hypnotic.

"Things didn't go so well with me and the Prof, see," said the machine. "But I think I got it fixed. Know where I went wrong. I'm good now."

Laura backed away, feeling around the bench behind her. The workshop was large and there was plenty of room to run. She just had to judge her moment. There were agents near, there always were. She just needed to get to the door and–

"He was a great guy, you know."

Laura froze. She didn't want to die, not today. Not like Doctor X.

The Project stepped forward.

"Your boss, I mean. The Prof. What a guy. Fixed me up too, real swell." It raised its new arm and flexed it like a circus weightlifter before tapping the index finger against the glass window in its chest. The sound was loud but dull. "All systems go. Course, I told him what to do, but nobody's perfect."

Laura spun on her heel, but came face to face with a computer cabinet, not the exit she had expected. She cried out in surprise and turned back around. The Project was closer, within touching distance. She looked around, looking for an escape, for a clear route out.

"It's a shame about the Prof. But, y'know, sometimes you just make an honest mistake. I mean, c'mon, what can you do, huh?"

"What can you do?" Laura repeated. It sounded like someone else speaking, like her ears were stuffed with cotton wool.

The robot continued to creep forward. "But never mind.

Let's talk about you and me, Laura. We're gonna do great things, you and I. Oh boy, you'd better believe it."

Laura nodded. Out of the corner of her eye, she could see it: one of the claw-like clamps that were used to install the fusor reactor in the robot. Install... and remove. If she could get to the clamp, all she would need to do was jam it into the robot's chest and turn, just once, to unlock the fusor. The power would be disconnected instantly, and without the external power supply provided by the cage, the Project would drop where it stood.

It sounded easy. The Project was up and moving and unrestrained, but it seemed slow, like a drunk person concentrating very hard on not being drunk. Even so, the machine would pull her to pieces like tissue paper if she tried to get the clamp in place... unless she was quick, quicker than it was. And all it would take was a twist. A single twist.

Laura sidled to the right. The robot didn't move, just followed her with its eyes. The clamp was on the bench, just there, almost in touching distance, next to the back-up prototype fusor. The reactor looked different somehow.

Eyes fixed on the Project, Laura moved again, one step, then another, then another. The robot didn't move. She glanced to her right, to make sure the clamp was really there, then looked back at the robot.

She reached out, not looking. Her fingers found the clamp. The metal was cold.

"Not so fast, honey pie." The Project jerked to life. Laura jumped back to her left, clamp in her grasp. She pulled it off the bench and it fell downward, yanking her shoulder painfully. The clamp was much heavier than she remembered.

She backed away, knowing that she was out of room and out of time. She raised the clamp in front of her. It had a handle like a gun, complete with a trigger to lock and unlock the three articulated fingers.

The robot ignored her, turning its attention to the other fusor reactor on the bench. It lifted it with one hand like it weighed nothing at all, and turned to the doctor.

"Ta-da," it said. "Neat, right? We got them fixed. Portable nuclear fusion. Virtually unlimited power." The robot shook its head; Laura almost imagined it was in quiet appreciation of the technology. The Project was right. Each reactor could power a city. Laura had hoped they would be used for good, of course. They would change the world. Unlimited power, so cheap as to be virtually free, inexhaustible, safe. First every city would have a fusor, one single cylinder replacing a dozen conventional power stations. And who knew what was possible with such power? That was the whole point, the whole thing about science. It wasn't what you could imagine now; it was what you could imagine five, ten, twenty years from now. What possibilities would the power offered by the fusor reactor unlock in the future? Every city would have one – how about every home? What if every single human being in the United States of America had one each? Their own personal spark of creation, a flame captured from the embers of the Big Bang itself. Contained, nurtured, tamed.

It made the mind reel.

But it was too much. She knew that. Atoms for Peace were going to put one into each of a thousand machine soldiers. That was too much power, a recipe for disaster. If anything went wrong...

Laura watched the fusor reactor swing in the robot's hand. A portable power source. A portable Little Boy or Fat Man, or worse. A whole army equipped with fusors would have enough power to knock the Earth off its axis.

"Now," said the Project. "I'm gonna try a different approach."

Laura squeezed the clamp's trigger, making the three fingers flex, making a clicking noise that was as loud as an atom bomb. The robot took a step forward, and she took a step back and hit something tall and hard. She was up against the computer cabinet with nowhere to go.

"Me and the doctor," said the robot as it walked slowly forward, "we had this thing going on. Quite a plan, see. But, you know, things the way they is, it's down to you and me now. I mean, I wouldn't say no, right? Right. So here I am thinking, hell, we got a whole bundle of these babies, so why not, right?"

The robot raised the fusor in front of it, pointing the flat end of the cylinder directly at Laura. It took another step forward.

"Sure, why not," said Laura, her voice barely a mumble.

Didn't the Director see everything that was happening in the city? Was she watching now, from the Cloud Club, as her precious Project ran amok in the laboratory?

Of course she was. Laura felt her heart kick. This was part of it. A test of the fusor reactor. An experiment to be observed.

Laura shook her head. The robot took another step towards her.

"Screw you, bitch," said Laura under her breath, and she powered forward, using the cabinet behind her as a springboard. Squeezing the trigger, she pushed the clamp forward as she moved, hoping that after dozens of installations she could estimate automatically the mating point of the clamp and the reactor in the robot's chest. All it would take is one turn, just one turn to the left, not even a five-degree rotation, and the reactor would disconnect and she would save herself and maybe she would save the whole damn world.

The Project threw its arms up and leaned back – as

though surprised – as she flew at it, and Laura wondered what the noise was, the sound that reverberated around the workshop. She looked up into the eyes of the robot, their red lights rocking back and forth in the sockets like a child's broken toy, and she realized the sound was her, screaming in anger. She was up against the robot, its metal casing cold and hard, her fingernails trailing silently across the chest. She screamed and screamed again, raising her arm up, her yanked shoulder protesting at the weight of the clamp. Why was it so damn heavy?

The clamp slipped, and Laura tried again, this time tearing her eyes away from the robot's pretend face to look and align the clamp. There wasn't much time; any second now she'd be tossed like a sack of wheat clean across the laboratory.

A twist of the wrist, and the clamp still wouldn't lock. The metal fingers slid across the glass port of the reactor, failing to find any slots at all. She twisted the other way, yelling in frustration.

Her cry died in her throat and she almost coughed. The fusor reactor, it was different. There were no slots in the rim for the clamp, nothing to grip on around the edge, no way of removing it, not by her. The clamp was redundant.

"Lady, please," said the robot. "Have a little patience."

Laura pushed away and let the clamp drop to the floor. She turned, desperate to make a getaway. There was no other option.

"It's OK, I understand." The robot grabbed Laura by the collar of her lab coat, lifting her until her feet left the floor. "Don't worry about a thing. I got this honey. Power, I get it, I understand. And trust me, you wouldn't believe what this thing can do."

"What are you doing?" Laura struggled, but the robot's grip was firm, her lab coat cutting into her armpits.

"You need an upgrade, that's for sure. I tried it on old Philo but it didn't take. But it's OK – I know what I did wrong now."

Laura shook her head, her eyes wide. Couldn't the robot distinguish between living creatures and machines like itself?

"I can't use the fusor," she said, "I don't need it!"

The robot almost tutted. Then it lowered her to the floor and pushed her hard against the computer cabinet with the end of the fusor reactor, squeezing the air out of her lungs. With the other hand it tore open the front of her coat, then her blouse underneath, then snapped the front of her bra off, exposing the pale skin over Laura's sternum. The robot tilted its head, and moved the reactor, lining up the flat end between her breasts. Laura gulped in air, each breath pushing her skin against the end of the cylinder. The metal was cold.

Laura cried out again – not a scream of fear, but of anger, screaming at the goddamn robot that was going to kill everyone, including her, as the robot pushed, breaking bone, breaking flesh, as it tried to upgrade her.

TWENTY

Rad woke in a hot sweat, his mouth filled with a foul, chemical taste. He coughed and rolled over, banging into the side of something hard. Looking up, he saw through watering eyes that it was one of the slab tables in the downstairs workshop.

He sat up, yanking the scarf from his neck and awkwardly pulling himself out of his trench coat. It was hot in the workshop, the chloroform-induced headache giving Rad a sudden rush of claustrophobia down on the floor. He grabbed the lip of the table and stood, leaning against it as his coat fell to the ground, where it hit with a dull thud. Rad bent down and picked it up, slipping the gun out of the coat pocket and into the back of his waistband. It was careless of his captors not to have searched him, but he was grateful.

He stood, leaned against the left-side slab and took long, deep breaths as he oriented himself. A breath caught in his throat and he coughed as he saw the machine on the slab, empty earlier, was now occupied. There was a robot lying it in, a flat, unfinished metal head sticking out of the dark green box. Rad watched it as the thumping in his head subsided. The face was crude, nearly featureless save for two short slots for the eyes and a longer one for the mouth. The robot didn't move.

Rad turned and, leaning his back against the machine, began rolling his shirtsleeves up. He laughed, remembering what it was like up top, in the city, with its ice and darkness.

Then his laugh turned into another cough and he was suddenly desperate for a drink. He glanced around, but there didn't seem to be a faucet in the workshop.

"Rad?"

Kane. His voice was weak. Rad moved over to the head of the machine and looked down at his old friend. Kane was sick, there was no doubt about it.

"I'm here, buddy," said Rad, pulling the stool closer and perching himself on it.

Kane smiled, and closed his eyes.

Rad sighed. He'd known Kane for... well, for as long as he could remember. He was older than Kane by a fair margin, but he remembered those first jobs, hiring the teenage Kane first as a runner and messenger around town, but then, as his charisma and prowess became apparent – the uncanny way in which he seemed to be in the right place at the right time, his knack for talking to people in just the right way – Kane had become more than a messenger boy. They became friends, and Kane helped more and more, particularly after he got a job at The Sentinel, the Empire State's first, foremost – and only – newspaper. Kane used that charisma to build up a network of contacts that stretched right across the city, and his work with Rad not only got Rad's cases solved a lot quicker but provided the material – sometimes sensationalized, of course – for Kane's newspaper.

Rad scratched his chin and coughed again. He was feeling a little better, more awake, despite his thirst and the oppressive heat of the workshop.

Kane Fortuna. Rad knew that wasn't his real name, but he had never known any other. Sometimes it didn't pay to think too much about the past in a place like the Empire State.

Rad's last memory of Kane was burned into his mind's eye, so much so that it was the last thing he saw when he closed his eyes and went to sleep, and the first memory he had when he woke up each morning. Kane Fortuna, wearing the powered armor that used to belong to the Skyguard, one of the two protectors of New York City – whose very actions had led to the creation of the Empire State itself. Kane, in the armor, pulling against the energy of the Fissure as he stood across the threshold between one universe and the next, caught like a fly in honey.

Rad rubbed his face, and watched his friend sleep. He'd tried to help him, done his best, his very desperate best, but Kane had been confused, mistaking Rad for... well, for someone else.

But the image was there, in Rad's mind, as bright and fiery as the rippling blue corona of the Fissure itself. Kane had realized, all too late. Realized who Rad was, but more, realized what he'd done, how he'd been tricked and manipulated by others. And it had been too late. Kane had fallen into the Fissure in the Empire State and had not come out the other side in New York.

Then a year of rebuilding the city, with Captain Carson taking charge, walking into the role of the City Commissioner like it was his destiny, a year that now felt like some ridiculous golden age. Things were getting better. There was cooperation between both sides of the Fissure, Carson and his equivalent in New York, Nimrod, working together. It was secret still, of course. The existence of the two universes was known only to a select few on each side.

And then the Fissure had vanished. Rad had been busy with his detective agency. It was a distraction, and a welcome one, especially after he and Claudia had finally given up on their marriage that never was.

Rad had also been busy with Carson. The old man seemed like he needed the company, despite his high office. And, looking back, Rad knew that there had been something lurking, a black cloud over Carson that had culminated in his apparent suicide shortly after the Fissure vanished and the city entered a winter that got colder every day.

Rad watched Kane. He looked older, but then he imagined he did as well. He had no idea what Kane's injuries were or what the machine was, but it occurred to him that Kane might be stuck in it forever, unable to survive without the King's treatment.

Kane had nearly destroyed not only the Empire State, not only New York, but the whole of both universes. The Fissure was more than a doorway, it was a tether, a connection that both universes needed, lest they unravel.

The irony was the Fissure had closed anyway. The tether was severed, the Pocket cut off from the Origin and slowly dying. It would have been better, Rad thought, if they'd just popped out of existence, zip! And then nothing would have mattered anyway. But a slow death by a long cold worried him. How long could they survive? How bad would it get before the end?

"Rad?"

Rad jerked his head up. Kane was awake, smacking his lips and trying to look up at his friend.

"You're the last person I expected to see again, buddy." Rad gave him a broad smile. Kane managed one in return, and Rad saw his teeth were stained yellowy green. Rad frowned, and thought back to the barman out in Harlem.

"Rad Bradley saves the day again," said Kane. His voice was quiet and raspy but seemed strong. "So, you here to get me out of this joint?"

Rad laughed and held up his hands. "Let me work on that. What the hell happened to you anyway? Where did you go?"

Kane narrowed his eyes, like he was thinking very hard or hadn't understood the question. Maybe a little of both.

Kane licked his lips. "I remember falling," he said. "I was going backwards, falling down, like I was being pulled."

Kane managed a small smile. "I don't know, maybe I was going upwards. Up, down, didn't really feel like anything."

Rad leaned in. "Then what?"

"Then..." Kane frowned and winced again.

"You OK, buddy?"

Kane nodded. "Yeah. My head's a bit sore. Happens, it's OK. The guy in the suit will be here with the medicine soon."

Rad chewed the inside of his cheek. He put that nugget of information to one side, and pressed on with his questions. "Where did you end up, after you fell through the Fissure?"

Kane rolled his lips, and shook his head. "I hit the floor. Hit it bad, felt like every bone in my body had broken. I remember... I remember lying on the ground, and there were all these people around me. Then there was this noise and this light, I don't know, and then all the people were gone, and there was this guy standing there. Everything looked green. Maybe that's just the way I imagine it. But I could see this guy standing there, standing over me. I was saying something, but... I don't remember what. Then I was here, in this place."

"You were here?" Rad clicked his tongue.

"Yeah. I knew you'd find me, Mr Super-detective."

Rad shook his head. "Kane, you fell through the Fissure eighteen months ago. It swallowed you up, and you didn't end up in New York."

"Huh," said Kane. "Guess it's the Fissure's thing with time, right? Guess the Fissure threw me forward."

The room shook, rattling the equipment. Rad looked at the ceiling and grabbed the edge of the machine to keep his balance on the stool. The tremor stopped after a long ten seconds, and Rad let out his breath.

"What was that?" Kane's eyes were wide open. "An earthquake?"

Rad frowned, but Kane had already closed his eyes, his

head resting back against the pillow. "Something like that," said Rad. "You picked a crummy time to make your glorious return, buddy."

But Kane was asleep already.

Kane slept for hours. Rad had been around the workshop several times. There was plenty he didn't understand, lots of equipment and gadgets and junk that obviously were to do with the construction – or deconstruction – of robots. Rad wasn't entirely sure what went on underneath the hood of a car let alone the inside of a robot, but the way the parts in the room were all shiny and new made Rad think the King hadn't quite given him the full picture. Finding lost robots, bringing them back to the workshop, turning them back into men. It was a fine idea, a great one even, a real service, if it was possible. But with no more robots being made down at the dockyards, the King's workshop should be filled with old parts, not new ones. Either the King was reclaiming new parts from the old robot factories at the bottom of the island, near the Battery, or he was making his own. Whichever it was, Rad didn't much like it. But stuck in the workshop with the heat turned up to eleven, he didn't see that there was much he could do.

The workshop had two doors. One was hot to the touch and presumably led further down into the bowels of the building, to a furnace or boiler room – unlikely to be the most useful route of escape.

Which left the other door. It was wood painted green, the wood itself ancient and as solid as iron, reinforced with black iron bands. It was locked with a bolt on the outside, and when Rad banged his fists on it it was like pounding on the brick wall that surrounded it, the door carrying no vibration, no movement at all.

No, Rad couldn't open this door. He'd have to wait until

the door was opened for him. Which, according to Kane, would be soon, because the "man in the suit" was going to deliver the medicine.

Rad turned and scratched his chin, surveying the workshop as he ran that particular piece of data around his brain.

Rad eyed the stack of apparently new robot head shells on a nearby bench, and shuddered. He might have been a little less in shape that he would have liked, but he was attached to his body and he didn't feel like switching any part of it for something made of metal.

"They're coming… marching. Them… the red… red lights. They're coming…"

Rad darted back to Kane's side. His friend's face was slick with sweat, his hair damp across his forehead, as he twisted his head from side to side, his eyes screwed up in pain. Rad placed a hand on Kane's forehead. He was burning up.

"Hey, Kane old buddy, hang in there," said Rad.

"Machines… it's her… it's her… blue… her eyes are blue… her eyes are blue… cold and fire and cold and cold… machines… blue…"

Rad raised an eyebrow. Some kind of flashback to falling through the Fissure? Wouldn't be a surprise. He'd been between universes twice himself, and that was shock enough.

But whatever Kane was dreaming about, Rad didn't like the way he mentioned machines.

"Easy, buddy, easy," said Rad, his voice a whisper, his eyes flicking up to the workshop door. *Come on, you spooky son of a bitch*, he thought. *Come on with the damn green potion.*

"Soon, soon, soon, soon…"

"Soon what?"

"Soon, soon…" Kane said, and said again, faster and faster.

Rad shook his head and looked up. Maybe Kane needed the green stuff after all. "Hey! Your majesty!" he yelled. "Get your ass in here with the medicine!"

"They're marching... the machines are marching... she's coming... no! No!" Kane shook his head violently. Rad grabbed Kane's head between both hands and tried to keep it still, but Kane's strength was surprising. Rad gritted his teeth, hoping this wasn't some kind of seizure.

"No!" Kane cried out, so loud Rad flinched. "She's coming, her machines are coming here... she's going to end it all... they'll destroy everything... everything!" Kane's eyes snapped open, and he looked at Rad. Rad swore that he saw a light in the eyes of his friend, a distant blue and white spark dancing in his pupils, spinning like the stars, flaring like the Fissure that had once stood in the middle of the Battery.

"Soon," said Kane, "they're coming soon."

"What? Who are? Kane, speak to me, buddy. What's going to happen?"

Kane shuddered in Rad's grip and then he blinked, licked his lips, and slumped. Rad realized that his whole body had been thrashing inside the machine.

"OK," said the detective, sliding off the stool and pushing his fist into his open palm as he surveyed the laboratory again. Time was running out, fast. He had to get them out and find Jennifer. "Hang in there, buddy. I gotta do some thinking here."

Kane muttered something, but when Rad looked at his friend he was asleep.

TWENTY-ONE

Twelve agents from Atoms for Peace had the machine at gunpoint, a dozen automatic pistols spaced evenly in a semicircle in Doctor X's robotics laboratory. The doctor sagged inside the cage, nearly six pints of blood pooled on the cement around him. On the other side of the lab, the tall computer cabinet was covered with something red and black that was getting sticky as it dried.

Elektro stood in the middle of the circle of agents, his red eyes rolling around them, but the machine appeared to be patient. It was humming something fast and happy. The dozen agents knew they would need more than nine-millimeter ammunition to stop it.

Evelyn McHale floated into the circle of agents, one moment not there and the next there. Elektro's eyes fixed on her blue form as the Ghost of Gotham drifted closer, and the robot stopped humming.

The Director regarded Elektro, tilting her head, her lips parted, like she was trying to read something in the machine. Elektro said nothing and remained still.

"You killed Farnsworth and Richardson," said Evelyn, finally.

"Hi, boss," said Elektro.

Evelyn floated to the door of the cage, but stopped just short of the threshold. She ignored the remains of Doctor X on the slab and instead seemed to be examining the edges of the cage door.

"I didn't see this. It hadn't happened."

"Sorry about the mess," said Elektro, its head spinning around to watch the Director. "But it's OK, I'm good. I figured out where I went wrong. Third time's the charm, right?"

"The cage. Isolation." Evelyn floated backwards, her eyes fixed on the structure. "I understand."

"Say, how about you and me cut a deal? Just imagine what we could do, huh? It's enough to make the mind reel, boss. Ah, boss?"

The Director was now in front of Elektro. The robot's head swiveled back to her as she reached out to touch the spinning red disc in the machine's chest. Her fingers stopped an inch from the glass.

"You understand the principles of the fusor reactor?"

"More than that, lady," said Elektro. "I got the damn thing working. Our old friend there was close but no cigar, as the saying goes. Hey, you got any cigarettes around here?"

The Director smiled and drifted backwards. "Agent Carter will give you his. Agent?"

Behind her, one of the agents twitched into life. He glanced sideways at his colleagues, then slowly lowered his weapon. He pulled a packet of Lucky Strikes from his jacket and handed them over.

"Much obliged," said Elektro, flipping the pack open and extracting a cigarette. "Smoking'll kill ya, but who wants to live forever, right?" His eyes flicked to Evelyn's.

"With Doctor Farnsworth and his assistant dead, I need someone to complete work on the fusor reactors and prepare the army for war," she said.

"Huh," said Elektro, cigarette dangling from his metal jaw. "I can fix 'em up but you're gonna need a central reactor to time them all, give them a kick-start."

"The structure is prepared. It just needs your adjustment."

The Director smiled, and the end of Elektro's cigarette flared blue. The robot took a drag and exhaled a cloud of smoke that went right through Evelyn's body like it wasn't there.

"Lady, you got yourself a deal. When do I start?"

TWENTY-TWO

The green door of the workshop shuddered once as it was unlocked, and swung open. In one hand the Corsair carried a tray supporting a pitcher of water and two other, smaller vessels, each containing a dark green liquid.

Rad frowned, realizing the "man in the suit" wasn't the King. He'd hoped for an old fashioned escape – wait until the jailer arrived, then jump him. Simple, but effective. Only the jailer wasn't the little man in the blue velvet suit, it was his robot, which Rad didn't want to tackle. Time for plan B.

Rad stood. "About time."

The Corsair swung the door closed and walked forward in silence. It placed the tray down on the bench nearest to the three slabs.

"You keeping us here forever?"

The robot released the tray and faced the detective, but made no sound.

"Tell the King I want to see him," said Rad. The robot didn't move but Rad ignored it, taking the pitcher of water from the tray and pouring himself a glass. The liquid was cool and refreshing, and just reminded Rad how hot it was in the underground workshop.

The Corsair jerked into life, taking one of the small vessels of green liquid and a long pipette from the tray. Filling the pipette, it moved to Kane. Rad backed away, clutching his own drink tightly.

"What is that stuff anyway?" Rad asked. The robot ignored him.

Kane opened his mouth and closed his eyes as the Corsair gently lowered the end of the pipette onto Kane's tongue and squeezed the rubber bulb between two fingers. Kane seemed to stiffen as the medicine was dispensed, and Rad could smell the tang of battery acid.

"How's it taste?" he asked Kane. Kane grimaced like he'd just taken a shot of something strong from under the counter of the cheapest dive in town.

"Pretty smooth," he gasped. "Could do with a little more tonic." He laughed, and quickly his laugh turned into a dry cough. He turned his head, and thick green saliva ran down his face from the corner of his mouth.

"You're in a bad way, buddy," said Rad. He looked at the tray, eyeing the second tiny bottle of green liquid. "Hey, Jeeves, you think I'm taking that and you've got another thing coming to you real quick."

"Detective, you are indeed fighting fit, fighting it!"

Rad turned to find the King of 125th Street standing in the doorway of the workshop, hands deep in the pockets of his jacket.

"Your majesty," said Rad, watching the King enter. "I got a feeling you're starting to believe your own legend."

The King smiled at Rad, but it was an expression devoid of any warmth or emotion; it was just his face making a shape. The Corsair stood to attention and the King nodded.

"That will be all. You may leave the tray." The robot did not acknowledge the order, but left.

The King walked around the detective until he was at the head of Kane's machine. He stood between Kane and the other machine, and looked between them. Rad glanced at the robot head that was sticking out of the other box, and starting thinking certain things about why the Corsair had brought two bottles of the green medicine.

Now was his chance, but Rad paused. Get out of here? How could they? Kane was injured or ill or both, and clearly in no shape to move either way. He needed to find Jennifer, and fast. Knocking the King over the head wasn't going to help much.

"Mr Fortuna cannot leave here, Rad," said the King, as though reading his mind. At this Kane craned his head to look at his captor. Then he looked at Rad, his big eyes wide and wet, his expression fearful. Rad wondered what the machine was hiding.

Rad sighed. "How bad is he? Can we get him out of this... this machine?" Rad waved his hand at it.

"Kane cannot sustain his own vital functions," said the King. "When I picked him up out there, in a dark alley in Harlem, he was dying. I got him here just in time. I had these machines built in case I ever encountered refugees who needed a more complete life support than most as I operated on them, turning them from machine back to man. I hadn't used them yet. Kane was my test case."

Rad stepped forward, eying the long, green box. It looked like nothing more than a large coffin, the curved upper surface a series of plates, riveted together like the hull of an airship. Looking closely, he could see one horizontal seam was not sealed. The box had a lid.

"So Kane is stuck in this forever? Like someone with polio?"

The King nodded, then moved to the other machine. He took the robotic head and held it between his hands. "Close enough. In order for Kane to be released, I will have to reverse the procedure. My plan was to help the robots of the city become men again. For Kane, it will be the opposite – to survive, he needs replacement parts."

Rad and Kane exchanged a look.

"Seems like you've been doing that already," said Rad. The King smiled sweetly but his attention was on the robot in the other machine.

"Look, your majesty, we've got a problem here. You gotta see it from our point of view. You've locked us up, and one of us has gone missing. It all worries me just a little. You got robots outside, you got quite the setup in here, and all the while the Empire State – the whole damn city – is dying. Turning the Ironclad crews back into people is a fine endeavor, don't get me wrong, and maybe if we can work this out then the Empire State can help you out with that. But all this isn't going to mean a damn when we're solid blocks of ice."

The King looked up. Rad ran a finger around the collar of his shirt. The King must have been cooking inside his blue velvet suit, but the skin of his face was pale and dry.

"Unless," said Rad, lowering himself back onto the stool, "you turn everyone into a robot. Then the cold won't matter. I really hope I've got you wrong on that, your majesty."

The King pursed his lips. He let go of the robot's head and turned towards the other door, that one that was hot, the one that led deeper into the theater.

"It's time to show you something, Mr Bradley. Come."

Rad had braced himself for more heat, but the corridor beyond the green door was cooler than the workshop. Rad began to roll the sleeves of his shirt back down.

"I'm afraid to say that the winter of the Empire State is my doing," said the King, without pausing in his march down the corridor. Rad stopped, one shirtsleeve rolled, the other halfway done. He stood, frozen in the corridor, thinking about the heat and about Kane and about the fact that he hadn't been to the bathroom in a while and kinda needed to go, and whether or not the King had really said what he thought.

"Excuse me?"

The King stopped ahead, at another door – one in heavy blackish metal, reinforced with bars – and turned on his heel.

"Mr Fortuna is important, detective."

"Ah, well, yeah, he is. I'm sorry, I–"

"No, detective. Kane is important to everything. To you, to me, to the city, to the Empire State, and to New York. He is integral."

Rad sniffed. "That a fact?"

"It is a fact, yes," said the King. "And to save him, I had to make a choice – the city, or the man. And it had to be the man, of course."

"Of course." Rad vaguely remembered the old saying that a madman should be humored, and he wondered whether this was actually wise advice. He was alone with the King, who was both older and smaller than him. The King's robotic servant hadn't followed them and, Rad thought, maybe there was a chance the workshop door was still open. So really, all he had to do was stick his fist in the King's face and hightail it back down the corridor, flip the lid on Kane's machine, and they'd be gone.

Assuming the King was lying about Kane, of course. Assuming Jennifer was still alive, somewhere. What Rad really hoped was that Special Agent Jones had gotten out and was heading back now, even as he and King walked down the underground passage, bringing with her that army of agents he knew the Empire State Building had at its disposal.

If only Carson were here.

Rad coughed. If only a lot of things.

"So to save Kane Fortuna, I created my masterpiece, my pièce de résistance."

The King extracted a set of keys on a large black ring from the pocket of his jacket and unlocked the door. Beyond was a light, white and blue, that waxed and waned and seemed to lick at the air like smoke and flame. A light that made Rad's head hurt, that started up a buzzing, a vibration behind his eyeballs.

Rad very much wanted a drink now. Something strong, like the kind of drink he and Kane used to share in Jerry's speakeasy, back when the Empire State was a very small place and they didn't think too hard about the world in case the Empire State pushed back.

"The Fissure has not gone, detective. In fact, you've been talking to it for hours."

Rad frowned. The King was talking in riddles.

"Kane Fortuna fell through the Fissure while it was unstable. He fell, and it became attached to him, tethered, like the Empire State was tethered to New York. He fell, and like elastic, the Fissure pulled him back. When he returned, the tether – the elastic – snapped. Kane is like a magnet, drawing the energy of the Fissure into him. He is the Fissure now. He and it are inseparable – the tether no long connects the Pocket to the Origin, it connects Kane to himself.

"I saw him fall into the city like a shooting star, hot and blue. Had I not found him, detective, not contained the power, the Fissure – the power within him – would have destroyed the Pocket entirely. But I got to him quickly, the fallen star burning in an alleyway, the energy consuming him, on the brink of implosion. That is why he cannot leave the machine, detective."

Rad shook his head. "The machine – the box – is containing the power?"

The King nodded, and gestured to the white and blue light that filled the doorway.

"Not only that," he said. "After you, Rad Bradley."

TWENTY-THREE

Black and white and blue and white and her eyes burning blue they are blue her eyes are blue cold blue the light at the end of the

Marching. The machines are marching. Silver stiff as toys silver and tall like men. Marching marching marching the red light spins and spins. Counting down down the machines count down and then

She is there. She stands in the darkness, she is the darkness. She spreads her arms and her army marches through the fog through the blue light the blue light her eyes are blue they are cold and blue and she left the world and was dragged back from

She is looking. She is looking at me. She is looking at me but she can't see me and she is falling falling falling falling falling falling

Run.

They are coming. They are marching. The atomic army marches.

Run.

Her.

She will destroy all to destroy herself.

It is written.

Run.

She is coming for me and

Kane woke with a start, his throat tight. He'd screamed; after who knew how many days and nights of this, he recognized the signs now – he couldn't touch his face but his skin felt cold and wet, and his neck was sore, as were the muscles that bunched at the back of his jaw. When he licked his lips he tasted the residue of the medicine and something else, something metallic. Blood. He ran his tongue around the inside of his mouth and instantly found the wound in his cheek. He'd bitten it as he slept. He often did.

But his throat was dry. He tried to clear it, but it felt like two pieces of sandpaper rubbing together, and his larynx rattled and rasped. If he'd screamed, like he thought he had, it wouldn't have been too loud.

He craned his neck, but the machine he was in was so large he couldn't see much. There was no mirror, not like on an iron lung, so all he could do was look at the ceiling, or at a stretch of wall behind him, upside down. When he tried that he could feel himself moving inside the machine.

Kane flexed his fingers, and they seemed to work, although he wasn't sure whether it was his imagination, a muscle memory echo of where he thought his hands should be. Maybe there was nothing left. Maybe he was just a head on a box. Maybe it would have been better if he'd fallen into the gap between universes and not returned.

Kane sniffed, and took a deep breath, then let it out. No, he was all there, he was sure of it. He could breathe, and breathe normally, under his own control. Whatever the machine was doing, it wasn't controlling this basic function. Just to prove the point, he held his breath, held it until it became uncomfortable, then a little more. Then he released it, gulping air as his throat burned. But that was good. And if he could breathe and feel his lungs and feel the walls of his ribcage move, then maybe when he flexed his fingers, his toes, then maybe the rest of him was OK too.

Kane closed his eyes, and maybe he slept. The next thing he was aware of was a click. He opened his eyes and rolled his head to his right, where he saw the King's robot manservant standing over the other machine. It was holding the head of the robot in the other machine – no, it was stroking the metal cheek of the other robot with one hand.

Kane licked his lips. He wasn't sure whether he was awake or asleep. He wiggled his toes again, and tried to remember if he'd been able to do that before, and whether that meant anything at all.

"Rest easy." The Corsair's voice was quiet, a whisper. It was male, and very human, muffled slightly beneath the metal face.

Kane gulped, painfully. He'd never heard the Corsair speak before; he had assumed it didn't.

The robot lying in the other machine twitched, and the head moved slightly as the leather-covered hands of the Corsair continued to stroke its face. And there was a sound, a sigh, an exhalation from the robot in the machine, from the horizontal slot that formed the mouth.

"Shhhhh," said the Corsair. The robot's head twitched again and there was something else, a voice, a whisper behind the metal that Kane couldn't hear. The Corsair leaned over his charge, like it was listening carefully to the faint words. Then it stood straight, and hushed the robot again, and turned around.

Kane closed his eyes, hoping he was quick enough that the Corsair hadn't seen him watching what he felt, strangely, was a private moment. He tried to remember how long the other machine had been occupied, and realized the robot lying within it had appeared soon after Rad arrived.

Kane felt the sweat trickle over his eyelids, and he felt his forehead twitch. There was a gentle sound of glass on glass, and Kane risked a peek. Between narrow lids he saw the Corsair preparing the second bottle of medicine, dipping the long pipette into the bottle, drawing it up, then turning back to the other robot. As Kane watched, it carefully inserted the narrow glass tube into the slot mouth, and squeezed, emptying the dropper.

The robot in the machine jerked once, twice, as it coughed and gasped. Its head turned, suddenly facing Kane.

Through the mouth slot, Kane saw human lips, delicate and dry, maybe female. They moved, and the tip of a tongue stained pale green poked out as it tried to moisten the lips.

Kane coughed in surprise. He rolled his head back to stare at the ceiling as the Corsair, apparently startled, moved to loom over him, bending down low so the flat metal face was right over his.

Kane fought against unconsciousness, but it was no use. And maybe he was asleep already, and this was all a dream, like the flexing of his fingers and the visit from his old friend Rad and the dead woman with the blue eyes. The green medicine.

Green, like the pair of human eyes staring into his own from behind the flipped-up goggles of the Corsair's mask.

Kane cried out in surprise, and then the darkness claimed him once more.

TWENTY-FOUR

The room was a basement or cellar, much like any Rad had ever seen. He'd stood in quite a few, he reflected, as they were places associated with bad deeds, where last stands were stood, where bodies were hidden, where victims and suspects and the innocent alike hid when above them was danger and chaos and violence.

Rad blinked as his eyes adjusted to the brightness. The glow, blue and white and alive, was coming from what looked like a furnace or boiler. Set against the far wall, it was large and square, taller than Rad, with a fat black chimney that vanished into the ceiling. There were gauges and dials and controls, a couple of large wheels and several smaller ones. It was industrial, but nothing out of the ordinary.

Except for the light. The furnace had a door, convex and square, with a large sprung handle, horizontal across the front, that was almost the size of Rad's forearm. The door had a window, and through the window shone the light.

Rad felt ill, partly because of the effects of the unusual light – an effect he hadn't experienced in more than a year, a sensation long forgotten but suddenly, instantly familiar the second he was exposed to the source – and partly due to the realization that the King was telling the truth about the Fissure. And if that was the case, then chances were he was telling the truth about the rest of it. Where this left the mysterious disappearance of Special Agent Jennifer Jones

– a woman the King now claimed never to have met – Rad wasn't sure, but he was sure the conversation was about to come around to that topic.

"What the hell have you done?" asked Rad, raising his arm in front of his face as he approached the furnace. The heat from the window was intense but just bearable – like sitting too close to an open fire – even though the door was closed. Rad didn't remember any heat from the Fissure when it had been in situ down in the Battery, but things were clearly different here. "I thought you said the Fissure was inside Kane."

The King nodded. "He is the Fissure now, at least part of him. With Mr Fortuna in the machine out there," he said, pointing in the direction of the workshop, "I can channel the power of the Fissure in here, allowing me all the energy I need for my work."

Rad shook his head. "What about the city?" he said. He waved at the walls of the basement, indicating everything, the totality of the pocket dimension. "Without the Fissure we're all dead – the city needs the energy. The whole place is breaking up. You must know that."

As if to emphasize Rad's point, the floor shook and the pipes on the furnace rattled. The tremors were certainly stronger here, in the north.

The King stuffed his hands into his pockets and smiled.

"We will survive," he said.

"Robots, isn't it?" Rad took a step closer. "You're going to turn everyone into robots. Then it won't matter how cold it gets."

"You misunderstand, Mr Bradley. There is a greater danger approaching the city. One that will destroy us, if we do not act."

"Greater danger than freezing up or shaking to pieces?"

"Kane has a unique perspective. His connection to the

Fissure allows him to… see things. The future, perhaps."

Rad thought back to Kane's feverish dream. He also thought back to the green liquid he was being fed. "You sure your drugs aren't making him hallucinate?"

The King laughed, the sound explosive. "Kane has seen them coming. Don't you get it, detective? He can see the future, and the future is nothing but an army marching towards us. An army of machines, of atomic soldiers."

Rad scratched his head. The King sounded delusional, paranoid – if it wasn't for the fact he'd heard Kane talking in his sleep. "A machine army? You mean robots, right?"

The King tapped Rad on the lapel. "Got it in one." He was still smiling, like Kane's apocalyptic vision was nothing at all. Rad frowned.

"Robots from where?"

The King stepped up to the furnace, and almost pressed his face up to the glass of the door. It must have been terribly hot, but he didn't seem to notice. "Where do you think, detective?"

"New York?" Rad's eyes widened. The robots hidden in the warehouse, and the King's little enterprise suddenly made sense. "You mean to tell me a robot army is on the way here, and you're building your own to defend the city? Based on something Kane saw in a dream?"

The King was staring into the window of the furnace. He didn't answer.

Rad took a step forward. "Ah… hello?" The King didn't move. Rad sighed and weighed his options. He paced the small room, processing this new information. Finally he came to a decision. He walked up to the King and addressed his back. "You going to let us go?"

The King said nothing.

"You going to tell me where Jennifer Jones is?"

Nothing. The King was stationary, staring at the door of

the furnace. Rad leaned over, looking at the King's face, and saw it was frozen, the man staring blankly into the blue light.

"Hey, anyone home?" Rad reached out to nudge the King's shoulder, but somehow he didn't want to risk it. The man wasn't even blinking.

A cry echoed from elsewhere, back down the corridor.

Kane.

Rad swore under his breath.

"Play your games, your majesty, whatever the hell you like. We're out of here."

He turned to leave and felt a hand on his shoulder. He pulled against it, then cried out in pain as the King's fingers bit into his collarbone through the thin fabric of his shirt. Rad instinctively dropped, trying to ease the pressure and slide out from under the King's hand, but the King was faster. His other hand grabbed Rad's upper arm and pulled him around.

Rad's feet were yanked out from under him as the King – a man half his size and twice his age – threw Rad halfway across the basement. Rad hit a stack of packing crates, splitting the wood and spilling the straw from within, but he recovered quickly and rolled to one side, ignoring the pain in his back from where he'd landed on the gun tucked into his waistband. Pulling himself to his feet, he swung around, fists raised, years of experience automatically preparing him for a brawl.

"What in the hell?" Rad shook his head. The King walked towards him, slowly, calmly, his hands in the pockets of his blue velvet suit, like he'd never laid a finger on Rad.

"You cannot leave, Rad Bradley. Kane Fortuna is important. Kane Fortuna is the key."

Rad flexed his fingers, his mind racing. He had the gun but shooting an old man – even one as remarkably strong as the King – seemed a little over the top. He realized he'd have to lead with his left, considering his right was still sore from its little meeting with Cliff's metal face.

Rad lunged, teeth gritted, eyes fixed on his target. In that second before his fist was thrown forward, he actually enjoyed the sensation. This took him back. It occurred to him that he didn't do as much punching as he used to, and rightly or wrongly, when he was younger that was the part of the job he enjoyed.

Rad's left fist connected with the King's cheek, and there was a crack. Rad felt two of his knuckles slide out of position with a nauseating tug before snapping back. The King rocked slightly on his feet, but was otherwise unaffected by Rad's attack. Rad cried out in pain, praying that his hand wasn't broken, and reeled back towards the door.

The King smiled, and Rad saw his punch had done something. At the corner of the King's mouth, the pale flesh of his face split, revealing something silver and bright beneath.

Rad backed away, shaking his fist. He moved the fingers, and they all still worked; he'd been lucky. He'd just put his fist into a metal face for the second time in a few days.

The robot King of 125th Street smiled, and stepped towards the detective.

"You have got to be kidding me," said Rad. He reached behind his back and pulled out the gun, and when he pointed at the King the man stopped and looked at it. Then he laughed.

"You wouldn't shoot a defenseless old man, would you now?"

"No, I wouldn't," said Rad. "But then you're not a man, are you? You're another machine, like Cliff. One of the 'upgraded' models." He raised the gun.

"Mr Bradley, please. Violence is not the answer."

"Not always, but sometimes," said Rad. He took a step backwards and his right heel touched the stairwell behind him. He was running out of room.

"Besides, robots are bulletproof. Or hadn't you heard?"

Rad gritted his teeth. He thought back to Cliff and the little metal tube. Was it a weakness? He'd felled that machine with a single punch, but, Rad knew, either his blow had been very lucky or the robot had been faulty or damaged in some way...

"You cannot leave, Mr Bradley," said the King. "I need Kane's power. I have a city to protect, and I need you and Jennifer Jones for my army. I need you alive to begin the process, but I do not necessarily need you to be... intact."

The King stepped forward and reached towards Rad, his fingers curled into claws and the serene smile still on his fake face.

Rad was out of options. He raised the gun, aimed along the barrel at the King's head, and fired once, twice, three times.

The first shot tugged another chunk of artificial flesh off the King's face, but the second hit his left eye. The orb shattered in a shower of glassy splinters and the King staggered backwards, his head dipping so that Rad's third shot cut a strip off the robot's fake scalp.

It wasn't the result Rad had been hoping for, but it wasn't bad. As the King raised his head, thick black liquid oozing from the damaged eye, he snarled and lunged forward. Rad stepped back and nearly tripped on the stairs, but forced himself to take rough aim at the King's head. As he fell against the staircase, he fired five more times, hoping that at least one round would hit the mark.

The King pulled up as he was hit, the artificial flesh of his face shredded by the shots. There was a louder bang and his head was thrown back, then flopped forward.

Rad had hit the other eye. The robot was now blind.

The machine screeched, the sound inhuman and terrifying, enough to snap Rad back to reality. The robot lunged forward again but Rad pulled himself up the stairs and out of the way with ease. As the King fumbled on the bottom stairs, Rad braced himself against the railing and kicked out, sending the robot cartwheeling backwards. It hit the furnace door and shrieked again, like it had been burnt, and as it tried to pull itself back upright Rad saw its head was at a slight angle, like the neck was damaged. It moved forward, arms outstretched, but it was slow and awkward.

Rad saw the opportunity. He ducked back down the stairs and, pushing the King's shoulder, spun the robot around, easily avoiding the outstretched hands. With the King's back to him, Rad reached around and plucked the keys out of the robot's jacket pocket. Then he gave the King a shove. The robot screeched and overbalanced, falling to the floor.

Keys in one hand, gun in the other, Rad took the stairs two at a time. He slammed the reinforced door of the furnace room shut and locked it. Then he took off back down the corridor.

TWENTY-FIVE

The lobby outside the doors of Tisiphone Realty was empty except for a man sitting in one of the two couches, silent but for the rustle of the newspaper he was holding. There was a coffee table, on which was scattered a few copies of Life and Time, and by the window a water cooler – the kind that came with those ridiculous paper cone cups that you couldn't put down anywhere. The window itself looked out over West 34th Street. Today the sun was shining. It was a beautiful morning in New York City.

The man on the sofa recrossed his legs and flicked the center of the New York Times he wasn't reading. His shift was due to end in fifteen minutes, when he'd be replaced by another man in another suit. The first man would fold the newspaper nosily and deposit it on the table and check his watch, complain about being late for an appointment he'd forgotten downtown, and dart off towards the elevators while his replacement grabbed a cone of water and took in the view.

This scene would be repeated every four hours.

The agent scanned the article on page five of the newspaper for the tenth time. His name was Jan Holzer, and he was looking forward to getting back to his apartment in Queens and getting some coffee and some sleep. Jan drank coffee for the taste – ten years with the Secret Service had made him immune to the effects of caffeine – and a cup of joe (milky, a habit he'd picked up from his German-English parents, to the horror of his friends) was the perfect nightcap after a shift at the Empire State Building.

Jan flicked the paper again and collapsed it in half, then half again. He uncrossed his legs, crossed them again in the opposite direction, and checked his watch.

His replacement was late. This wasn't unusual in itself, nor any particular reason for concern. The security details had some leeway programmed into them, so agents could come a little early or a little late; a few minutes here and there didn't make much difference, and it added to the cover, if anyone happened to be watching.

Although this time Jan's replacement, Eddie Ellroy, was ten minutes late. This was, strictly speaking, against the rules, but Eddie was Eddie.

Jan sighed. He didn't like Eddie. Eddie always cracked a joke about Jan's German heritage and found it hilarious to call Jan "Einstein" because, as a security agent for a government scientific department, Jan was clearly working beneath his station and really should have been behind the door they guarded, working on the affairs of state with the other brainiacs.

Eddie Ellroy was a real jerk. And right now, he was a real late jerk.

The door of the Department opened. Jan tensed, ready for action, years of Secret Service training kicking in, preparing him for anything. Expect the unexpected. In Nimrod's world, the unexpected was very often the case.

A young man in a grey suit emerged from the Department, his hair slick, his shoes shined. He let the door swing closed behind him and, without a glance at Jan, took off down the corridor.

Jan clicked his tongue. Things were in a real state in there, he imagined, since the whole Department had suddenly gone on alert. But as a security agent it paid to keep out of such things, keep his mind clear, focus on the job at hand. Departmental alert or not, his job didn't change.

The elevator pinged, out of sight, and the lobby was silent again. Jan got back to reading the front page of the newspaper for the one-hundredth time.

A moment later the elevator sounded again. Finally. Jan braced himself for the one-way delivery of jokes at his expense, and stood to get another cup of water. All part of the act.

"The traffic today is the pits!"

Jan turned at the voice, cone of water halfway to his mouth. Eddie Ellroy was still absent. Standing in the lobby was a woman, dressed in expensive furs and high heels, a hat that was really a little too large for her balanced on top of a haircut Jan hadn't seen outside the pages of Life magazine. The woman smiled, the movement of her chin making the veil in front of her face move.

Jan drained his cup and crushed the paper cone in his fist. "Excuse me?" he said, outwardly polite, inwardly wondering who the hell she was and where the hell Ellroy had got to. Jerk.

The woman sat on the edge of the sofa and began shuffling through the magazines on the coffee table. Selecting an issue of Time, she sat back and studied the cover intently.

Jan reached for the inside pocket of his jacket, sliding the fingers of his right hand between the buttons of his suit. In a hair under two seconds he could have his gun out and trained on the intruder. There was no reason for anyone who wasn't involved with Nimrod's Department to be on this floor, and his replacement security detail had failed to show, all of which was totally wrong. There was a telephone on the wall; all Jan had to do was keep the gun on the woman and call for more security.

"You're a little premature there, Mr Holzer," said the woman. She lowered the magazine just a little and peered over it at the agent. Holzer gulped, his hand moving further into his jacket, his fingertips caressing his concealed automatic. Time to drop the act.

"This is a restricted area, ma'am. I'm going to have to call security. They'll want to ask you a few questions."

The woman slapped the magazine down on the table and sighed, rolling her eyes as she reached for the handbag on the floor. Jan watched her and took a step forward, the gun that was once inside his jacket now out. He took another step and pointed the weapon at her.

The woman glanced up as she rifled through her bag, and shook her head with a smile. "Relax, agent. I'm standing in for Ellroy today."

Jan raised the gun.

"Here we go," said the woman. She pulled a folded card from her bag and offered it to Jan. Jan took it, keeping the gun aimed at her forehead, and flipped it open. He read the ID aloud. "Special Agent Irena Dubrovna?"

"Got it in one, agent." It took Jan a second to realize she was holding her hand out, waiting for him to return the card. He did so, and he lowered his gun, but he didn't replace it inside his jacket.

"I don't know you," said Jan.

Irena shrugged. "I don't know Ellroy either, but I've heard he's a real jerk. Anyway, get. I'm here."

Jan frowned. Irena looked right, he had to admit, dressed well enough to pass as a potential client for the real estate company Nimrod's Department pretended to be. Her manner was casual, but their very public exchange had blown any kind of cover. Not that anyone was watching. Jan rolled his shoulders and glanced around. The door to the Department was closed, and the corridors were silent.

Jan sniffed and nodded, slipping his gun out of sight. Irena ignored him, her attention back on the magazine.

Feeling uncomfortable, but looking forward to coffee and sleep, Agent Jan Holzer left.

Irena waited a moment, and then rested the magazine on her lap. After watching the Department door for a minute more, she stood and walked to the windows. She looked out across the city, towards the Chrysler Building, on the beautiful morning.

She reached up, sliding a gloved hand beneath her veil, and touched the earpiece buried deep in her right ear. It was new technology, advanced, but one of the advantages of her cover was that her hat was big enough to carry both the radio's battery and transmitter.

"Alpha One, in position."

She listened, nodded, and then helped herself to a cup of water.

TWENTY-SIX

Security agent Jan Holzter had been on the money. Behind the closed doors of Tisiphone Realty it was organized chaos.

Every desk on the floor was occupied, half by men, mostly in rolled-up shirt sleeves, cigarettes burning bright, filling the air with a thick fog of tobacco smoke. Some shuffled paper, a lot held telephones between shoulder and ear as they jotted down notes. The other half of the staff were women, most looking considerably less flustered than their male counterparts as they focused on typing and filing, filling the air with a machine gun clatter of keys striking paper. The cacophony that filled the office wasn't loud, but it was constant and unending.

Nimrod watched the hubbub through the open door of his office. Behind him, the ticker tape machine sprang into life, slowly feeding paper onto the floor. Mr Grieves quickly picked up the tape and began to read.

Nimrod folded his arms and turned around. "Well?"

The agent pulled the tape through his fingers. "All departments acknowledge the alert and are awaiting further information. The Vice President has been taken to a secure location and the President is currently at the State Department in DC."

"Very good."

"Also the Secretary of Defense wants to speak with you, urgently."

Nimrod sighed. He should have expected this, but it was exactly the kind of distraction with which he didn't want to deal. Nimrod was keenly aware that it was Atoms for Peace, not his Department, in favor with the Secretary. "He can wait."

Mr Grieves smirked as the phone on Nimrod's desk rang. Nimrod nodded and Grieves picked it up. He listened a moment, and as Nimrod watched his smirk quickly faded.

Grieves held out the phone to his superior. "It's the Secretary."

Nimrod gritted his teeth and closed the door of his private office. Then he took the receiver.

"Mr Secretary, we were just talking about you."

The Captain smiled at Mr Grieves and walked around his desk, phone pressed tight against his ear.

"Yes, Mr Secretary. I believe so."

Nimrod sat heavily at his desk and listened a moment longer, then barked a laugh.

"Bad? My dear chap, 'bad' does not begin to describe it. What I am talking about is nothing less than the end of the world."

The door to the Department opened, and Captain Nimrod stormed out. Irena lowered her newspaper, trying to keep the surprise from her face. But it wasn't an issue, as the target wasn't watching. Nimrod muttered under his breath and waved one hand in the air like he was arguing with someone who wasn't there as he strode the short distance across the lobby and vanished into the corridor leading to the main elevators.

Irena listened until she heard the elevator ping and the doors open. A moment later the doors rattled shut and silence returned.

Irena leapt from the sofa and crossed to the window to

get the best reception. She looked down, trying to get an angle on the street below, but the stepped shape of the Empire State Building hid the main entrance.

The radio clicked in her ear.

"Cloud Club, this is Alpha One," she said. "We have a problem."

TWENTY-SEVEN

The lobby of the Chrysler Building was deserted. Nimrod noted the fact, but didn't pause as he strode across the marble floor and into the walnut and silver interior of the elevator.

She would know he was coming, of course. She saw everything in the city, some said, though Nimrod knew that if this was so, she ignored most things. Maybe she had heard the conversation between him and the Secretary of Defense, the conversation Nimrod cursed himself for not expecting. But that would have been like trying to pick a single conversation out of a stadium full of people; even the Ghost of Gotham had her limits. Besides which, he doubted she found it very interesting. For someone – something – with such power, she was remarkably single-minded. Perhaps that was not surprising. Nimrod had often tried to imagine what it was like, to die and be brought back, granted with all the power of the universe. If your mind didn't break, then, with the universe at your fingertips, surely your perspective changed somewhat.

The Secretary's decision was a disaster waiting to happen, Nimrod knew that now. The order to hand over all responsibility and duties to the Director of Atoms for Peace and allow her department to proceed with their operation was not just ridiculous, it was foolhardy, perhaps even suicidal.

There was no alternative. He had to see her, talk to her, convince her to change her mind, make her understand that they should be working together, not fighting. Nimrod just hoped there was enough left of a human being inside the Ghost of Gotham that he could make her see reason.

The elevator pinged, and the doors opened. Nimrod felt his mustache bristle as he stepped out into the lobby of the Cloud Club and found himself alone. Ahead of him, the giant doors of the Director's personal domain, with their silver sunray decoration and frosted glass, were closed.

Beyond, the former nightclub was quiet. The room was truly cavernous, and Nimrod had the odd sensation of walking through a cemetery, or into a mausoleum. The Cloud Club was a relic of another era, when New York City had been an entirely different world. Nimrod pondered this as he walked to the single desk, the one the director of Atoms for Peace had no need for. He noticed, for the first time, that the desk was dusty. His eyes moved over the murals on the wall. For some reason they looked dull, faded.

Maybe there was something left of Evelyn McHale. In a way, she was like the room, a relic of another era. She had been plucked from time and then dumped in an alien world. She may as well have been taken to Mars.

Nimrod walked to the great glass wall and looked out over the city. The Empire State Building sparkled in the sun, and below the streets were filled with people and cars. Nimrod smiled. None of them knew they lived in just one universe out of... well, who knew. None of them knew about Atoms for Peace or the Director, although there would be plenty in the city who remembered Evelyn McHale. Many had even seen her ghost, glowing in the night.

Nimrod turned back to the empty room.

"Director?" His voice didn't echo as much as he thought it would. "Evelyn, I need to talk to you," he said to the ceiling.

There was nothing, not even an unusual breeze or a drop in temperature or a knock on the wall, one rap for yes, two for no.

Nothing. No one came, not the dead woman, not agent or guards. No staff at all; the Cloud Club was empty.

Nimrod frowned, and then wondered how far he could go before the orders from the Secretary of Defense circulated around the building.

Nimrod straightened his tie and brushed down the front of his safari jacket, and marched towards the door.

It was time to find out what Atoms for Peace were really doing.

In the elevator Nimrod punched the button for level B6, the last-but-one sub-level listed on the panel, and to his surprise the key lit around his thumb. If Atoms for Peace were hiding anything, it was going to be down there, under the city.

Level B6 was a series of plain corridors, lined with polished grey concrete and lit by functional utility lights. Nimrod's footsteps echoed as he walked down one corridor after another, each intersection he came to presenting him with a choice of three equally featureless alternatives. He counted each as he passed through: First right, second straight, third straight, fourth left. There was no signage, no doors, no cameras, no mirrors. He had passed no security stations, no gateways or doors or screens. He was alone.

Was it normally like this? Or were Atoms for Peace otherwise engaged elsewhere, their Director included? Nimrod stroked his mustache as he walked, aware that his unimpeded progress was likely deliberate. They were letting him in, giving him free reign. Setting a trap.

After five minutes, Nimrod arrived at the first obstacle, a tall green door. Underground and despite counting the intersections, Nimrod had lost his sense of direction, though he knew he must be several blocks out from the Chrysler Building already. His own Department was just a floor of the Empire State building and some of its sub-levels. It was staffed and run more or less like any government field office, albeit one more covert.

This... this was something else. Atoms for Peace were building a web under the biggest city in the United States. How far the web crept, Nimrod was now determined to find out.

The green door opened at a touch, and led to a short corridor that ended in an identical door. Halfway along the corridor were two smaller doors, black iron with shuttered windows like the doors of a cell. One was locked, the other opened into a small, sparsely furnished office. Nimrod didn't much like the idea of working underground, where you would never be able to keep track of the time. Standing in the doorway, Nimrod glanced around the office. There was no clock.

The other green door was also unlocked, and led into a laboratory-cum-workshop.

"Hello?"

Nothing. Nimrod's voice echoed up to a high vaulted ceiling, much higher than the ceiling in the corridors outside. The concrete here was older, damp stains trailing down from the ceiling. The room was old, part of something else – the city's water or sewage system, reclaimed by Atoms for Peace.

Against the opposite wall was a square metal cage. Its doors were open, and within was a frame with horizontal armrests, though it looked far too big for a man. The frame was connected to pieces of electrical equipment inside the cage and out. The main slab was shiny at the center and dark around the edges, like it had been recently cleaned. On the cement floor in front of it was a large, irregular dark patch that reminded Nimrod of spilled blood.

Nimrod stuffed his hands into his pockets and turned slowly on his heel, taking in the contents of the workshop. There was a regular oscilloscope, a rotometric signal dampener, and, against the wall, next to a small coat rack with six hooks to hold laboratory coats, a sequential field inverter, the device as big as a car, with modifications and upgrades Nimrod didn't recognize.

He stopped, and found his heart rate was a little high. He had been hired by the US Government for a number of different skills, one of which was his expertise with electronics, cybernetics, and robotics. Although he was not as knowledgeable (or as pompous) as his Empire State counterpart, Captain Carson, he was expert enough to understand the purpose of the facility.

It was a robotics workshop, similar to the ones set up in the aftermath of the Empire State incident. As had happened at the end of World War II, when Nazi rocket technology had been stripped out of Germany and taken to the United States along with Germany's scientists, so the Empire State had surrendered some of its robotics technology. There was a rumor that a scientist had been brought across as well, a Pocket universe version of someone who already existed in the Origin universe; Nimrod had dismissed the story, but now he wasn't so sure. That would have explained the office, and the cell-like quarters. If a scientist had been brought across, to allow him the freedom of the city would have been far too dangerous.

Nimrod turned back to the stain on the floor. He was getting a very bad feeling about what Atoms for Peace were doing in their secret laboratory.

It was time to go lower.

The button lit, and the elevator descended. Nimrod knew now that his journey was being controlled from elsewhere, that he was being observed.

Level B7 – the last button on the elevator panel – appeared to be the same as the floor above: concrete corridors, utility lights, and not a soul. Nimrod decided to head in a straight line, and thought that he had, but soon found himself back at the elevator lobby. He shook his head, and rubbed his mustache, and checked his watch – he'd been stalking the underground portion of the Atoms for Peace base for nearly two hours, and he was tired and footsore.

The elevator was still open, and Nimrod walked into it, his eyes on the floor, his hands in his pockets as he considered his next move. He reached for the elevator controls and stopped, his hand in midair. The panels in the elevator were different – there were just two floor buttons: "1", which was currently lit, and "2", beneath.

Nimrod frowned. He was in a different elevator.

Nimrod punched "2" and the doors slid shut.

The descent to level 2 was longer than Nimrod expected, the elevator taking him deep underground. When the doors finally opened, the scene was very different from the floor above. The architecture was still bare concrete, but the elevator opened directly into a single corridor, lit in a deep, flickering orange from the opposite end. Raising his hand to shield his eyes against the light, Nimrod saw the corridor end in a black door with a square window, through which the fire-like light shone.

Reaching the door, Nimrod could see nothing through the window except a bright point of orange light and a lot of black space. The room beyond was clearly enormous.

The door opened onto a viewing platform, constructed out of metal grilling. Looking down, Nimrod could see through to the floor beneath, thirty feet below. To his left and right metal staircases headed down, weaving back and forth twice before they reached the bottom.

Nimrod stepped forward, and gripped the platform's handrail as he looked out into the space. The metal was cold against his palms, and as he looked out he gripped them tight enough to feel the cold against his bones.

The space was truly cavernous, as big as the largest Air Force hangar he'd seen above ground, hidden in the desert. It was lit from above by large white floodlights, but they did little to dispel the orange glow coming from the center of the room, where a huge torus was held in mid-air by a framework of silver struts. Above the torus was another black metal platform, perhaps octagonal, around the edge of which looked to be control panels and instrument banks. Two twisting black staircases led from the platform to the floor.

The torus was the source of the light. The entire object was glowing orange, like iron in a fire: darker around the edge and almost white in the center. A brighter light moved around the ring, anti-clockwise, throwing the orange light around the hangar, and across the robots assembled on the floor – robots surrounding the central structure from one side to the other, filling the room wall-to-wall, end-to-end.

Nimrod gasped. Robots. Hundreds of them, maybe thousands. Each identical, tall and silver, row upon row upon row. Nimrod counted fifty units from one side of the room to the other, then lost count as he tried to count the rows going back.

The robots were vaguely man-shaped, but huge; from his elevated position, Nimrod estimated each was at least seven feet in height, with rectangular torsos that were wider at the shoulders than at the waist by a considerable girth. The worst thing was the heads – each had a face, each identical, a toy-like parody of human features: triangular eyes, and a mouth that stretched across the square face. The mouth was a black plate, angled and vicious, a separate piece that could clearly open and close like the robots could… eat something.

Each robot had a black circle in the center of its silver chest; as his eyes adjusted to the orangey gloom, Nimrod could see the discs shine, like dark glass portholes.

Nimrod squeezed the handrail and shook his head, trying to understand what he was looking at, remembering the Director's talk of war.

And here was her response. Atoms for Peace were indeed preparing for war. They were building an army. An army of robots.

The robotics laboratory was one thing; this was entirely another. The Secretary of Defense be damned – this was going straight to President Eisenhower.

There was a sound as Nimrod turned, like a button of his jacket clicking against the platform railing, an innocuous sound he barely registered before a black bag was yanked over his head and his arms were pulled back sharply.

He cried out and got a mouthful of dry cotton. He spat the fabric out and struggled, pulling his shoulders around, trying to break free, but the needle that entered his neck was thin and sharp, and the last thing Nimrod felt was pain and then numbness and the last thing he heard was the roar of the ocean, far away.

TWENTY-EIGHT

The night in Harlem was cold, the world frosted with ice, the air heavy with freezing mist.

The streets were empty, the buildings too: empty shells staring with empty black eyes out onto deserted streets. It seemed the very fabric of the place was rotting away, brick crumbling, concrete fracturing like wet chalk. If the Empire State was an imperfect copy of Manhattan island, then the Pocket universe's Harlem was where the data degradation was worst. The cold wasn't helping, nor the tremors. The whole world shook as it fell apart; here in Harlem, the quakes loosened mortar and pushed stones, making cracks, weakening everything.

The people stayed inside, huddled in small communities that gathered around fires to keep the dark away, to keep the creeping cold out. Some areas were better than others; here people could move around, try to continue some semblance of normal life, with shops and bars and businesses struggling onwards as the endless night drew on and the temperature dropped, and dropped again.

The area around 125th Street was not one of the good places. Here the night was stained a violent green when the lamp atop the tower at the back of the King's theater was lit. Other times the shadows were deep, the darkness a perfect place to hide. Nobody walked these streets, not anymore, because the King had gathered his faithful from all over the city to this one spot, and here he kept them in darkness until they were needed.

So they waited, in small groups and sometimes ones larger. Their numbers fluctuated as the King took them inside his operating theater, where they were saved.

He was a great man, they said. A great man, blessed with miraculous skills. He would save them all, return them to their old lives, the ones they had before they marched willingly into the robot yards downtown, before answering their conscription papers, or, for some, before they were snatched in the dead of night and woke to find themselves in the middle of a slaughterhouse, waiting their turn for their limbs to be separated from their bodies and their hearts removed and replaced with rubber pumps to push machine oil around their internal mechanisms.

Tonight, the green lantern flicked on, bathing 125th Street and the surrounds of the theater in a deep, sickly haze.

It was necessary. The King said so himself. The green light kept enemies away, kept them safe. And it would not be long now; the King had said so, many times. When the green light came on, when the pain started and the robots scurried to the shadows to escape its hellish glare, the King and his servant would appear, on the veranda that jutted out from the front of the theater, out over the main entrance. They would stand on this platform, this stage, and the King would tell them that everything would be fine, that everything was going to plan, that soon they would be saved, all of them, from their torment. Just a little while longer, just a little more time, and then they would be ready.

Because, he said each and every time, the city owed them. The Empire State had taken their lives away, stolen them. It had treated them like machines, like just more tiny cogs in great wheels, sending them off into the fog, never to return. Feeding them to the Enemy, to keep it complacent, satiated.

And when the time was right, when the work was complete, the King would lead them back downtown, where they would liberate the Empire State from itself, and take back what the Empire State had stolen from them.

Then, after he had spoken, the green light would turn red, and the relief would be a blessing. The robots could come out and bathe in the light, the light that healed, energized, the light that gave pleasure, not pain. And then the King would be on the street, within reach of the pawing hands and claws and clamp and servo units. And with the help of his servant, he would administer the nourishment, the magical green elixir that kept them alive while they waited to be called into the theater.

But tonight was different. The green light had come on, but there was no appearance, no speech. Robbie and the others hid in the shadow of a stairwell close to the entrance; it was a good spot, and his group had fought hard to claim it, and every night defended it as best they could. It was difficult, dangerous, and soon Robbie's gang had been reduced to the strongest – Robbie, with his telescopic arms and domed head filled with stained glass; Ratings 112363 and 112463, two soldiers nearly intact; and a small man who refused to give his name, who appeared to be more human than robot but when he moved – and move he did, so very quickly – there were flashes of silver beneath the ragged blankets he wrapped himself in.

The green light had come on, and they'd waited, but there was nothing. Robbie sat with his back against the stairs, facing away from the theater. He waited, ignoring the rambling conversation of the two Ratings, each repeating the words of the other, not quite in time, over and over until it became too much for Robbie's ambient microphone to bear and he turned the input volume down. With his telescopic arms wrapped around his legs, he sat and rocked his curved carapace against the cement of the stair block.

He needed it. Oh boy, did he need it. He could feel it, that aching deep within his alternator, a sensation, a tension, creeping out across his hydraulic system, a chill that cooled his valves until he thought their glass would crack. He licked the roof of his mouth – he still had a tongue, although his upper palate was a plate of copper, unfinished and corroding, like most of his torso. He rocked against the stairwell, leaving verdigris stain on the bricks.

The green light suddenly went off, and there it was – the red. He could feel the relief coursing through his circuits, even from here, hidden in the shadow. He looked ahead to the street, the icy ground bleached pink-red.

Oh man, all he had to do was stand up and walk out into the light, and he'd get the first part of the hit. He almost couldn't stand it, it was like the control gyros where his stomach used to be were shorting out, going haywire, creating a pins and needles sensation that swept across his framework, like being tickled with a feather back when he had skin. Perhaps that's all it was; maybe his motivation dampener was too cold and was accessing the memories of the man he used to be, memories that were supposed to be locked away, suppressed forever.

Robbie didn't like it. The King hadn't spoken, and while the green light had gone off and the red one had come on, something was up. If he stepped out into the red, and the King wasn't there to dispense the green, the hit, then the pain that followed would be too much to bear. It was better to stay here, unmoving, corroding into the brick and concrete than to suffer that pain. The relief of the red was intense, but temporary – to get the hit, you had to have the green too, not the light but the elixir, and that was dispensed by the King and the King alone.

"My brothers!"

Robbie's head rotated almost automatically at the sound, as the directional microphones mounted next to the primary optical unit behind the angled stained glass filters in his head kicked in. There was movement near the theater, near the main doors, not on the balcony. Something wasn't right, but the voice was crosschecked and identified: it was the Corsair, the King's servant.

"My brothers," came the voice again, "the King has sent me to bring the green. Come and receive the green from your King, and rejoice in his majesty."

Ratings 112363 and 112464 chattered excitedly, their shared words piling over each other and vanishing into a rush of static. Robbie could understand the feeling, the want, the need to get the hit, to get the green.

Robbie retracted his arms and stood, his body rotating towards the theater. His optics adjusted to the red light and he saw the Corsair standing in the doorway of the castle, holding out one hand. Robbie zoomed in, and saw the small rectangle of something dark on the Corsair's upturned palm. Nearly a whole ounce of green. On the ground next to the King's servant was an open metal box, and within, stacked in neat piles, more wrapped hits, one for each robot, except the larger ones that needed two.

The absence of the King himself was unusual, but it didn't matter – his servant had brought the green instead. Already there was movement across the street as robots pulled themselves out of shadows and out of alleyways, from behind stairwells, up from basement entrances. The street was soon filled with moving machines, although perhaps fewer than the night before. More had succumbed to the cold, the low temperature sucking the life from their batteries. The green fixed that, or at least it made it feel like it did.

The nameless robot in the blanket behind Robbie didn't move. Another one gone.

The robots moved across the street, but Robbie was closest – that was why his group defended the stairwell with such desperation, because it was closest to the theater, which meant Robbie was first in line for the hit.

The Corsair turned towards him as Robbie approached. Robbie's rubber skirt slid on the ice, making it look like he was gliding if it wasn't for the slight bobbing up and down of his short steps. The Corsair held out his hand; Robbie paused, the red light flooding his sensors, the knowledge that the hit was just seconds away almost too much for his logic gates to handle. He heard them clicking inside his carapace, and gears moved inside his head as the optics zoomed in on the Corsair's gloved hand and the prize it held.

The other robots, knowing the hierarchy, fearing the might of Robbie and his Rating companions, fell into line behind him in silence. While most were happy to fight out territory elsewhere, there would be no skirmish here, not in the red light, in the presence of, if not their King, then his royal servant.

Robbie bowed his head, and gears whirred inside his head as his voice box came to life.

"GREEEEEEEEEEEEEEEEEEEENN."

The Corsair nodded in return; his black metal face was expressionless, but switching spectra to penetrate the opaque glass of the Corsair's goggles, Robbie could see the eyes behind the mask. He wondered what kind of a man he had been, to be so strong to have resisted and overcome conversion in the Naval robot yards and to have sworn to help those less fortunate than he on their journey back to humanity.

"WHENWILLITBETIIIIIIIIIIIME?"

The Corsair chuckled behind his mask, and when he spoke it was a sibilant whisper.

"Soon, my brother, soon. Soon we will be ready to go downtown, and claim that which is rightfully ours."

The Corsair's black fur coat moved in the wind as he began dispensing the green to the King's loyal subjects.

TWENTY-NINE

Rad retraced his steps at a run. He remembered a short journey from the underground workshop to the furnace room, but now it was confusing, with more doors and turns that he'd noticed coming the other way. All he could do was try not to think too much and hope his subconscious knew the way. He was too busy worrying about how long the locked door behind him would hold out against the King, however damaged the robot was.

Rad burst through the green door, into the workshop. He turned, but the corridor behind him was silent, with no indication the King had managed even to climb the stairs of the furnace room yet. Rad threw the door closed behind him.

"Kane, buddy, time to go." Rad raced to Kane's side. The former reporter blinked and squinted at Rad, and began to shake his head. Rad waved his hand and turned to scan the workshop.

"Oh no," said Rad. "No, no, we're going. That guy who calls himself a king? Turns out he's just the same as the Corsair, one of our metal friends. Aha–" He spied a long crowbar-like metal rod among the robot parts and grabbed it. Then he returned to Kane's machine and began trying to force the two seams of the machine apart.

"Rad, listen to me," said Kane, his voice a dry, cracking croak. "We can't leave, not without–" His voice dissolved into a dry cough.

The metal rod slid against the smooth surface of the machine, Rad almost connecting his chin with it as he fell forward. He swore, readjusted his grip, and tried again. This time he got purchase and forced the end of the rod into the seam. There was a click, and a small gap formed, from which shone a bright light. Rad frowned, gripped his hands together, and tried to leverage his weight. He puffed his cheeks out as he worked.

"We ain't got much time," said Rad, teeth clenched. "I did some damage to our robot friend and locked him in the other room, but he'll get out eventually." He heaved again. "Although a robot with a robot servant, now, there's something. Seems like they're building some kind of society of their own."

"Rad!" Kane said. "There's someone in the other machine!"

Rad paused, his eyes scanning the other machine. The robot's head was turned away from him, and at the base of the neck he could see brown hair bunched under the edge of the metal.

Rad yanked the rod from Kane's machine and it snapped shut again, cutting the light out. Rad felt the room spin a little but got to the other machine. The one holding Special Agent Jennifer Jones.

He carefully rolled her head so she was looking at the ceiling. What he'd thought was a robot head was actually a mask or helmet, hinged at the top, held together with simple pins. This close, he could see Jennifer's eyes through the holes in the mask. She sighed, and Rad could see her teeth through the slot mouth.

"OK, OK…" said Rad, his hands moving over the mask, locating the pins holding the mask in place. There were four, and they came out easily. After dropping them to the floor, he lifted Jennifer's head carefully and pulled at the front of the mask. It swung up, and the back panel loosened; within moments it was free. Rad tossed it to the floor, and then swore.

There was another mask, smaller, covering Jennifer's face from hairline to chin. Rad ran his fingers around the edge, which stopped just short of her ears, trying to find a strap, but there was nothing. The mask was brilliant gold, shining, the front an elegant Art Deco sculpt of a woman's face, with delicate eyebrows and full lips.

Rad pulled at the edge, but the mask didn't shift. He pulled again, harder this time, but the mask was firmly attached. Rad merely lifted her entire head, making her to moan in discomfort. Jennifer was alive, at least. He could worry about the golden mask later.

Kane coughed. "The Corsair isn't a robot... it's a man. I saw his eyes."

Rad nodded, processing the new information. "OK, OK... so the King is a robot and his robot is a man. Great. Let's work out the why and the how and the who later. We've gotta get out of here, but it looks like I'm the only one up and moving."

Rad swore and shook his head. It was time to think of something big and great that was going to work. There was something he was forgetting, he was sure of it.

"The King said I can't leave the machine," said Kane.

"The King said a lot of things."

"Some of which were true."

"Yeah," said Rad, still holding Jennifer's head. "But some of which was a little less so. Like the fact he was a robot, for a start. So who knows what else he's been saying?"

"What reason would he have to lie about me? Why would he want to keep me here?"

"Ah, yeah, about that."

Kane raised up his head. "About what?"

"Well," said Rad, "seems the King wants to keep you around as his own personal power generator."

Kane shook his head. "What?"

Rad shrugged. "Long story. You've got the Fissure inside you. Neat, right?"

"I... what?"

"Look," said Rad, "we're on the clock here. So let's save it and work on this marvelous escape plan."

"I'm glad you have one," said Kane, resting his head back on the pillow.

"Ah, yeah, and it's marvelous, believe me."

There was a bang from somewhere beyond the green door. The blind King had climbed the stairs, then.

Rad looked around the workshop. They had to leave, and it wasn't like he could wheel the two machines out. But the Corsair was absent, and the outer door was, as Rad had hoped, still open.

Jennifer coughed. Rad felt her pulse, under the edge of the mask. It felt fine, strong, and she was breathing normally and her eyes looked clear and were blinking as usual through the eyeholes.

"Rad?"

"We meet again, Special Agent. How do you feel? Can you move around inside this thing?"

Jennifer grunted with effort, and her head slid on her pillow as she struggled with something.

"I'm strapped down. I don't think I'm hurt. At least I can't feel any pain, and I can move my arms and legs."

"OK," said Rad, retrieving the metal rod from the floor. "Let's just hope they didn't have a chance to get started on you properly." He felt along the seam of the machine, and began to work the rod into the gap.

Kane watched them from his table.

"What do you mean, get started?"

Rad huffed as he worked at the lid of Jennifer's machine.

"It's what we thought. The King isn't turning robots back into people. He's turning people into robots. This place is full of robot parts – new parts, not ones he's taken from the refugees. He's creating his own little machine army, and he's using power from the Fissure to do it."

"The power that's inside me."

Rad paused. His back was to Kane, and he was glad that Kane couldn't see the expression on his face. "Seems so. But first things first."

The rod slid home, and Jennifer jerked as Rad opened a two-inch crack between the machine's lid and the base. No light flooded out, so Rad adjusted his grip and heaved. There was a loud crack, like he'd broken a catch, and then another, and then the rod moved easily, Rad levering the lid up.

Jennifer was held down to her slab with thick leather straps across her chest, her legs, each arm and ankle. Rad made short work of the buckles, and Jennifer only needed a little help to sit up. She stood, and Rad helped her step over the high lip of the machine and onto the floor. She looked down at herself and straightened her coat.

She seemed fine, just dandy, but Rad flinched when she looked up at him through the metal mask. She noticed, and laughed, her voice echoing behind the metal.

"It's strange, it doesn't feel like there's anything there." Her fingers ran over the mask, tracing the seams, feeling the contours. "It has no weight. It's like it's a part of me."

Rad nodded. "Then it won't slow you down. But Kane is the problem right now. We can't get him out of the machine, but we can't carry him out in it either."

Rad clicked his fingers. Of course… he turned to Kane.

"When you landed, what happened to the suit?"

Kane coughed. "Landed?"

"Landed, crashed, fell on your ass, whatever," said Rad. "When the great reporter fell from the sky, were you still dressed as the Skyguard?"

"Ah, yeah, I guess."

"So what happened to the suit?"

Kane frowned. Then he looked around the workshop from his horizontal position.

"It must be here somewhere. I don't remember."

"Maybe the suit is part of this all?" said Jennifer. "Maybe they reverse-engineered it for the technology, used it to help build the robots?"

Rad nodded. "Maybe," he said, picking up his coat, hat, and scarf off the third, empty machine. He began putting them on and then paused, one arm in his coat. "You're one of Carson's Special Agents, right?"

Jennifer nodded, but Rad noticed a pause before she did so.

"OK," he said, "I'm going to ask about your significant pauses and whatever it is you're not telling me later, but listen, if you worked for Carson, that means you know at least a little about the Fissure."

"Yes, of course."

Rad shrugged his coat on properly. He began pacing the workshop, casting his eyes over the shelves, tables, cabinets and stacks of equipment. There were enough robot parts in the room to build a dozen walking machines, but he couldn't see what he was looking for.

"The Skyguard's suit is really a machine, like a robot," he said. "Last time I saw it, it was doing a pretty good job of channeling or absorbing the energy of the Fissure itself." Rad turned to Kane. "That was the whole point of the plan, right?"

Kane nodded. "The Science Pirate made some changes

to the suit so it could absorb ambient energy. The plan was to drain energy from the Fissure, and then feed it back by overloading the suit's batteries."

Rad held a hand up. "Stop right there," he said. "Drain energy from the Fissure, right?"

"Right."

Jennifer nodded. "I get it."

"Exactly," said Rad. "This machine Kane is in is containing the power, channeling it into a contraption in the other room."

As if to emphasize the point, a distant bang sounded again as the King pounded on the furnace room door.

"So, find the suit," said Rad, "and maybe we can get Kane out of the machine and into it before he blows the place sky-high."

"If the suit is still in one piece," said Kane. "Might've been wrecked when I came back."

"Or maybe the King pulled it to pieces," said Rad. "But have you got a better idea?"

He glanced around the workshop. "We have to find that suit before the Corsair comes back, even if we have to turn this place upside down."

They'd been searching for what felt like hours. At first, fearful the Corsair would make a surprise return, Rad and Jennifer had stuck together – first turning over the downstairs workshop, and then cautiously moving out to examine the rest of the King's domain. But when there was still no sign of it – of him – Rad suggested they split up to widen the search.

Jennifer headed up, telling Rad she was going to start at the top and work her way down. The former theater was huge, and the green light was mounted at the top of the building. The King was bound to be using rooms above the theater as well.

Jennifer paused in a dark corridor three levels up. The floorboards creaked and the place smelled musty and old, and aside from the rustling of her long coat and the odd echo of her breath inside the mask, the place was silent. The corridor in which she had stopped was short, no more than a stairwell landing before continuing up to the next level.

She moved forward, the floor creaking again. It was lighter here, thanks to a long, low window with an arched top. It was frosted with ice on the outside, which diffused the streetlight, bathing the landing in an eerie glow.

Jennifer moved to the window; it was set low, more like a decorative alcove on the landing than a window. It had a wide sill, and she sat and pressed her face against the glass to try to see out. She recoiled at the sharp tap her new metal face made as it came into contact with the glass, but then carefully rested it against the window. She could feel the cold through the glass, not just through her gloves as she rested her palms against the window but through the metal mask itself, like it was a part of her.

Strangely, that didn't bother her, and she wondered whether that in itself should be a worry. But the thin metal mask was weightless, not so much comfortable as feeling like it wasn't there at all. It didn't impede her vision. She had no trouble breathing, or speaking. She hadn't eaten yet, and she wondered what would happen then given there was no articulated jaw, just a narrow metal slot though which she could only poke the very tip of her tongue.

She pulled back and looked at her reflection in the glass. The mask – the metal face – was beautiful, not just a functional part of… what, a robot? Not like any robot she'd ever seen. Maybe the King was an artist, too, creating not just an army of robots but an army of machines formed to his exact specifications. Perhaps he was not only building soldiers but machine people too.

There was movement outside, breaking her reverie. She leaned forward and again touched her metal forehead to the glass.

The street outside was lit in a pinkish-red glow that seemed to hang in the ice-laden air like sugar syrup. There was plenty of movement too: there were robots, lots of them, huddled together at the far end of the street, the group getting narrower as it approached the building until Jennifer could see a queue of them, single-file. At the head of the line, almost directly beneath the window, stood the Corsair. He was facing the line of robots, and as each machine approached he handed something out like a priest at Sunday mass.

Jennifer squinted, and her breath caught in her throat as her vision zoomed forward. She felt like she was falling, the world spinning around her as vertigo threatened to take hold. She gritted her teeth and hissed as a wave of nausea spread over her, and reached out with her hands instinctively, her subconscious mind instructing her limbs to grab onto something, anything, to stop the fall. But her hands banged the glass of the window almost as soon as she moved them. Then her vision stabilized, the drunken sensation ceasing. She turned her head a little and her vision blurred and then refocused, all while her forehead touched the glass.

Her hands moved over the glass, then down, and found the sill and the sill's edge. Jennifer sighed in relief. She was still sitting, looking through the window – and her vision was still fuzzy as she looked through the patches of frost – but somehow the scene below had been zoomed in like she was looking through a pair of binoculars. She realized, awestruck, that it was the mask, responding to her thoughts.

She concentrated, and her vision blurred, filled with nothing but rough white and black shapes. She let out her breath and relaxed her body, letting her shoulders drop and her hands rest on her lap, and the image resolved into pin-sharp clarity.

She had a perfect, close-up view of the street below. She watched the Corsair as he handed out small silver rectangles; they looked like pieces of metal, the size of a box of matches, until the next robot in the line – one that looked more or less completely human, except for one silver, articulated arm – took the item, bowed his head to the Corsair, and then tore off the silver wrapping with his teeth. He pressed whatever it was into his mouth, and his eyes closed as he rocked on his heels. There was movement behind him; Jennifer zoomed out and saw the two robots immediately behind become agitated, until one nudged the creature at the front. The robot-man jerked, then shuffled out of the way, and Jennifer zoomed in to his face. His chin and mouth were covered with something dark and liquid, though it was hard to tell what it was in the pinkish light.

There was a flash of white, and Jennifer's vision swam before she regained control. She was now looking at the street below in what appeared to be normal light... no, not normal light, it was something else, the scene was so sharp, clearer than she had ever seen anything before, such incredible detail, from the pebbles on the road to the ice crystals drifting in the air outside, to the green mess on the man's chin.

The green. The Corsair was handing out green, little rations of it.

Jennifer looked back at the Corsair, her miraculous new eyesight refocusing as she did. The Corsair was wearing his big black fur. There was a breeze in the street, catching the giant collar of the outfit, swirling the thick hairs. With her enhanced vision Jennifer thought she could count every single one as they swayed in the wind, the patterns of motion mesmerizing.

And then she saw it; she zoomed in further instantly, without conscious thought. Under the high collar, occasionally visible on the back of the Corsair's helmet: a ridge, almost like the fin of a fish. It was triangular, the top edge coming out of the back at ninety degrees, and then angling down to the base of the helmet.

It was familiar, Jennifer knew it was – something from the Empire State Building. The ridge was an attachment point for something, something in particular. Jennifer ran her eyes over the back of the Corsair's head, and finally the pieces came together in her mind. The black helmet was incomplete, missing a front-flanged section that would normally come together at an angle over the face, then curve out and up to form two fluted metal wings that stuck out on either side of the helmet.

The Corsair was wearing the Skyguard's suit – what was left of it, anyway. Whether it was damaged in Kane's return or altered by the King or modified by whoever was inside the suit now, Jennifer had no idea. But she'd found the suit. Now she had to get the Corsair out and Kane in.

Something played at the back of her mind, something important, something she'd discovered... but the thought was gone as she tried to grasp it.

Jennifer decided to find Rad before the Corsair had finished doling out the small parcels of green to the assembled robots. She moved a little, her metal face squeaking against the cold glass of the window.

Suddenly, the zoomed-in view of the Corsair blurred, the furs and black uniform caught in quick movement. Jennifer pulled her head back and her eyes adjusted, zooming out and refocusing.

Jennifer gasped behind her mask, and for a second it felt like she couldn't move, couldn't take her eyes away from... him.

The Corsair was looking up at her – not just at the window, but at her, into her eyes. Had he heard the noise? It seemed so unlikely, but if the Skyguard's mask was operational he would have picked it up.

She watched and saw him blink behind the mask of the Skyguard; she zoomed in until his eyes, his human eyes, were the only thing filling her vision.

They were green, a bright, bright green, shot through with yellow like precious gems, two glittering crystals shining in her artificially enhanced view.

Eyes she recognized.

Jennifer gasped and almost fell off the sill as she scrambled backwards.

She remembered now. Remembered lying on the slab, inside the machine. Remembered the pain, remembered the green, remembered the voice whispering in her ear, the voice that called her Jen.

The Corsair was gone, the robots left to mill around. The queue was already beginning to break up as ones from further back moved forward to find out what was going on.

But of the Corsair – of her brother – there was no sign.

Jennifer pushed herself off the alcove and raced down the stairs.

It was getting colder, and not just because Rad was moving further and further away from the workshop and the furnace room. He'd found himself in an empty square room, devoid of anything at all except a light bulb hanging from a single cord, and a big door in one wall. The door was metal, and bulbous, with a large lever for a handle, looking very much like a walk-in refrigerator. Quite what such a device was doing inside an old theater was a question Rad didn't expect he'd find the answer to, because he knew that maybe the building never had been a theater, despite the stage and the awning outside and the missing letters above the front door, despite the rooms he'd found full of props and costumes slowly moldering away. Because in the Empire State, a lot of things never were; for all he knew, this place had sprung into existence as was, derelict and unused and rotting, until the King and the Corsair had found it and taken it over.

His search had been so far unsuccessful. In one room, Rad thought he'd hit pay dirt, seeing the Skyguard's voluminous cloak rolled up in a corner, only to find it was just extra curtain fabric for the main stage.

And the more Rad searched, the less confident he felt. He'd moved from the workshops and engineering areas with their robotic spare parts and components into the leftovers of the theater itself, and more than once Rad realized that if the King had taken the Skyguard's suit to pieces, he might well have already seen most of it spread out across various workbenches and not know it.

He needed to get back to Kane. He was hoping that Jennifer could look after herself.

He was also looking for her gun. He'd seen it take out the crazy leader of the robot gangs, the one that had called itself Elektro, with a single shot. Even with the recharge time, he thought it would come in handy.

Now he was in an empty room with a freezer installed. The temperature outside was so cold the freezer seemed unnecessary. But... he'd better check it. He wrapped his scarf firmly around his face and reached for the freezer door.

The freezer hummed. Rad checked that there was a working handle on the inside of the door – he wasn't going to fall for that one – and stepped inside.

The freezer was filled with shelves, making the place less a butcher's meat locker and more a laboratory storage area. There were containers and boxes stacked everywhere, and large items wrapped in plastic sheeting. Everything was covered with frost.

Rad stepped forward. He didn't know why the Skyguard's suit might have been kept in a freezer, but he was here now and it would pay to check. Just a quick look in, and then he'd head back to the warmth of the workshop. Maybe Jennifer had had better luck, and...

Rad stopped, and squinted at one of the wrapped items on the nearest shelf. There was a pinkish color showing through the sheet. Rad peered closer, then reached out and tugged at the sheet. It slid easily, shedding frost onto Rad's hands. He pulled hard, and began to unwrap the long, thin object, rolling it on the shelf as the plastic was pulled out from underneath it.

Rad swore, the plastic sheeting dropping to the floor. On the shelf was a human arm, intact, the terminal of the shoulder neatly trimmed, exposing the round joint, perfectly clean and white. The arm was male, and it was a little thin, like the arm of a young man.

Rad stepped back and looked at the rest of the shelf. There were many more wrapped objects, some the same size and some smaller. Rad puffed out a great lungful of steam and carefully peeled back another sheet to reveal a single hand. He rubbed the frost off one of the jars and saw it was filled to the brim with a frozen liquid, red, swirled with yellow.

Rad looked around him. The freezer was full of body parts.

He backed away, rubbing the frost from fingers now numb from the cold. He felt numb elsewhere, somewhere deep inside, where maybe he thought the King was trying to do something and maybe Rad didn't quite understand it but that was OK, that was good, because someone was helping those in the city who couldn't help themselves, who had been tossed out by the government and forgotten, completely and utterly, creatures destitute and desolate and not even considered to be people.

But this... this was something else. This was macabre, a horror show, the freezer of a loony tune doing something untoward in the unknown dark and empty places of the Empire State.

Rad shook his head, muttering under his breath. The sonovabitch. He was keeping the human parts removed during his procedures. Why, Rad didn't know and couldn't guess. That was for later, when he and Jennifer Jones and her friends at the Empire State Building came back to sort out the mess.

Rad's back touched the shelf behind him, and he jumped in fright. He sighed, his breath clouding the air, and turned.

Something caught his eye. There was a large object on the shelf, square, wrapped in plastic sheeting that hadn't yet frosted over. There was something pinkish within, and there were marks on the shelf where the frost had been scraped off. The object was new, placed there only hours ago.

Rad didn't want to see what it was, but he had a feeling it was important.

He grabbed the trailing corner of sheeting, and pulled. It moved easily, the plastic cold but still pliable, silky. Three turns and the object was exposed.

Rad felt the bile rise in his throat. The object was a glass head, like the kind in a fancy hat store. Except this head was bare – but for the front. Spread across the sculpted glass features was a face, a real human face, made of flesh and skin, with eyebrows and lips and nose. The glass face underneath was a standard model, and the real face adhering to it didn't match the structure, not completely, resulting in a strange, distorted visage.

But it was enough for Rad to recognize. He coughed, and felt a hot bitterness against the back of his throat. He turned away from it, and almost tripped out of the freezer. He slammed the door behind him, then crashed his back into it and closed his eyes, taking deep breaths of air that were cold but warmer than in the freezer.

That settled it. They'd walked into a house of horror, the likes of which Rad had never seen before. In the dark places of the city, the King of 125th Street was putting into motion an insane plan, a plan that had to be stopped before his army of robots was activated, unleashing who knew what hell on the city as the Empire State plunged into a war with New York.

Rad pushed off the door, determined to get back to the workshop and find Jennifer and get them all out of there.

He was equally determined not to tell Jennifer he'd found her surgically removed face on a glass head in the freezer.

THIRTY

Rad found Jennifer in the workshop, and felt a surge of relief that she hadn't run into the Corsair.

"The Corsair saw me."

Scratch that. Rad nodded as he caught his breath. As he stood in the doorway, one hand on the frame, he couldn't help but stare at the agent's golden face. It was a beautiful piece of work, like a fine sculpture. He'd have to tell her about what was in the freezer, have to.

Jennifer took a step forward and Rad jerked back in surprise.

"What's wrong?"

"Nothing," said Rad quickly. He darted to the door on the opposite side of the workshop and opened it. He listened a moment, but the corridor was empty and there was no sound from the furnace room. Rad closed the door and turned back to Jennifer. "So the Corsair's coming?"

"He was outside," said Jennifer. "He saw me. Then I think he came back in, but he's not here. But–"

"Did you have any luck?"

Jennifer held up her hand. "That's what I'm trying to tell you. The Corsair is wearing the Skyguard's suit. What's left of it, anyway."

Rad swore and swept the hat off his head. He knew there was something familiar about the face, and now he could picture exactly what it was. Take away the wings and the square grille that should have been in front of the face like the visor of a medieval helmet, and you were left with the austere features of the Corsair, just the vertical slots of the mouth and the round eyes of the Skyguard recognizable. Small details, but enough.

"I think he knew, as well," said Jennifer.

"Knew what?"

Jennifer didn't say anything; she just stood there as Rad waited. He could see her eyes blink behind the mask, but nothing else; her face was beautiful but frozen, immobile.

Rad stepped away from the door. "He knew what?"

"That I should have killed you when I had the chance."

Rad spun around. The Corsair stood in the doorway, fists clenched, wrapped still in the giant black fur coat. Rad and Jennifer backed away and the Corsair pulled off the coat, revealing the chauffeur's uniform. At the neck, Rad saw the bodysuit – the remains of the Skyguard's suit – disappear under the collar of the uniform. Rad just hoped that most of it was still intact beneath.

The Corsair stepped forward, forcing Rad and Jennifer against the edge of Jennifer's slab. Behind his back, Rad felt for the bar he'd used to pry the machine open.

"So you gonna tell us who you are," asked Rad, "or is that a mystery we'll just have to live with when we're far away downtown, until we see your mug shot in the newspaper next week?"

The Corsair stopped, and looked at Jennifer. He hissed, like he'd just realized something, or was surprised.

"What?" Rad asked, glancing at Jennifer.

Jennifer took a step forward.

"Now, wait a minute," said Rad. His fingers pulled the metal bar closer until he could get a proper grip on it.

"She hasn't told you, has she?" said the Corsair. There was amusement in his voice. There seemed to be something about power-mad loons in masks that made them a little too pleased with themselves for Rad's liking.

"Kane, you listening to this?"

"Sure am," came Kane's voice from behind his machine. "Wish I could see the show. Sounds like fun."

"Uh-huh," said Rad. "Might have to do something about that."

The Corsair chuckled. "Mr Fortuna can't leave the machine."

Rad snorted. "That a fact?"

"It is."

"He's right," said Jennifer. "You know that, Rad."

Rad's eyes flicked between her and the Corsair. "Oh, you're on his side now?"

"Of course not. But we can't take Kane with us."

Rad's fingers wrapped around the bar. He adjusted his footing.

"We gotta get past this guy first, anyway," said Rad, nodding at the Corsair. "Nice trick, pretending to be a robot, while the real robot does the meet and greet. Can't imagine you get a lot of guests around these parts, so why so much trouble for the double act? But, hey, each man and robot to his own."

The Corsair clenched his fists. "Anybody ever tell you that you talk too much, Mr Bradley?"

"A talkative detective is gonna be the least of your problems in a minute."

The Corsair shook his head. "You cannot leave," he said, moving forward quickly. Rad braced himself, hoping Kane had gotten the message. The metal rod slid in his sweaty hands. A lot depended on him getting this right.

"Stop!"

Jennifer stepped between the Corsair and Rad. The Corsair backed away. Rad didn't move; he was too busy trying to hold the bar still.

Jennifer turned to Rad. "He'll let us go," she said. She turned to the Corsair. "Won't you?"

Rad saw his chance. He let out his breath, nice and slow, and took another in.

"Hey, Kane," he said.

"Waiting on you," Kane replied.

Rad darted to one side, swinging the metal rod out from behind him. Jennifer ducked out of the way, and Rad saw the Corsair hesitate, uncertain. Rad really hoped the Skyguard's suit was working, because the fact that the Corsair hadn't sucker-punched him already was a little worrying, and what he was about to do might kill them all.

Rad ran to Kane's machine, jamming the bar with both hands into the seam around the lid. The rod slipped, and Rad's heart skipped a beat before the rod caught on something and stopped; Rad pushed, pushed as hard as he could, and the rod slipped through the gap. There was a click as a catch was snapped open. Then, with a yell, Rad pulled down on the rod with all his might. His cry of desperation continued long after the rod slipped free and hit the floor, Rad's chin connecting with the slab as he hit the deck.

Rad looked at the floor, which was suddenly illuminated in a brilliant white and blue light. Rad felt his eyeballs trying to drill themselves out of their sockets as a pressure settled on the back of his skull, a headache from hell.

Rad screwed his eyes tight and wished he was dead, but he knew the feeling would pass and everything would be fine, everything would be OK, so long as Kane could control it. Control the power inside him.

Rad rolled onto his back in time to see Kane pull himself up out of the machine – he was nothing more than a hot white outline, a walking flame, incandescent tendrils of energy streaming off him and whipping around the workshop, around the machine and the table, around Jennifer and around the Corsair.

"Jennifer," Rad shouted, unsure whether his voice could be heard over the roar of the unleashed Fissure. He saw her jerk as he called her name, her metal face searching, unable to see. From his shadowed position by the table, Rad jerked forward and grabbed her arm, pulling her down on top of him. She fell, blocking the light, and Rad felt an instant relief from the buzz-saw vibration in his skull.

"Hey, Corsair," said Kane, a million miles away. "You got something that belongs to me."

THIRTY-ONE

Hoffman Island, Lower New York Bay. Eleven acres of not much at all: an artificial island, created from landfill back in 1800 and who cares.

General Fulton Hall liked Hoffman Island. He liked the regularity of it, the way it looked like a near-perfect trapezoid on the big map one of his staffers had got out back at base. He also liked the fact that it was artificial, a product of engineering and effort, a symbol, in a small way, of man's mastery over nature.

General Hall liked that a lot. It was like his job, overseeing military research into the secrets of the atom in the continuing effort to find the biggest bang of them all, the ultimate weapon, the one the Russians would never see coming before it wiped them off the face of the planet. That, too, was man's mastery of nature. With the power of the atom at their beck and call, Hall knew he was helping keep the United States the most powerful nation of them all.

Hoffman Island, one mile out from South Beach, Staten Island. New York City lay directly behind Hall and his retinue, shivering under the tarpaulin marquee that had been erected in front of the crumbling ruins of the old quarantine station. Hall didn't think it would have been any warmer inside the concrete shell, and besides, there was a small but not insignificant risk of collapse if the test on Swinburne Island went wrong. The Quonset huts on the other side of the island would have been better, but they didn't have such a good view.

Hall adjusted his binoculars, fixing them on the smaller but equally artificial island a hair under a mile south of Hoffman. He could see the test rig clearly: a steel pylon looking something like an oil derrick, with an arm coming out at ninety degrees from the top. At the end of the arm, something small, silver; a teardrop shining in the cold New York air. The test device.

He frowned. Conducting an atomic test so close to populated areas – Staten Island, Manhattan just further north – was a damn strange thing, but he'd been assured it was all under control. The whole harbor was cordoned off by warships, all shipping and transport temporarily halted for a "training exercise." And, well, Swinburne Island wasn't worth jack shit to anyone and had been left to the birds for years. Nobody was going to miss it.

Everyone was nervous, everyone except Hall, although when he licked his lips and tried to swallow he found his mouth was dry, and the hand that scratched at his cheek shook a little. But that was normal. What was that old saying? If you're not nervous, you're doing it wrong? Hall's frowned turned to a smirk as he lowered the binoculars. This was a test, just like any other, a little demonstration by an associated department of the US military. That's what the job was all about: pushing the limits, pushing the might of the United States. It was the only way forward, the only way to keep ahead of the game. And boy, the way the world was these days, the United States was the only damn thing between life and death, freedom and liberty or total extinction.

But today was different. Hall wasn't entirely sure what the demonstration hoped to achieve. Truth was he hadn't really read the briefing properly, he'd just skimmed it over a cigarette and coffee in bed this morning. Not his bed, either.

Hall grinned to himself and glanced to his left. In front of him, Captain Mary Poole stared out at the rig a mile distant, her brown hair shining as a sliver of light caught it. Hall sniffed, remembering the smell of her hair and wondered whether he could make up another excuse to his wife to stay, as they say, late at the office.

"Sir, ten minutes until test commencement."

Hall nodded at the adjunct providing the report, but the staffer just nodded in return and didn't walk away. He kept his eyes on the general, even though Hall was trying to ignore him. The man didn't move but his lips were quivering.

Hall sighed and wished he had a cigarette. "Spit it out, corporal."

"Ah, sir," the man began. "It's... well..."

"Corporal, you'll be on duties as yet unimagined by the time we get back to base if you don't let go of your dick and tell me what the damn problem is."

At this the corporal came to attention. Hall's lip curled at the corner. That was better.

"Sir, our guests have yet to arrive. Base reports they haven't arrived there yet, either. Team needs an A-OK to continue without the VIP."

Well, wasn't that typical. A test order arrives with hardly any notice at all from the Department of Defense, with a whole lot of nonsense about a liaison from Atoms for Peace, and then the VIP in question hadn't even turned up on time.

"Maybe she stopped off at the Statue of Liberty," said the General.

"Sir?"

Hall shook his head. "The VIP doesn't arrive at T-minus

zero-six we're closing this circus down. I've got better things to do than freeze my fanny in the Lower Bay."

"Sir," said the corporal. He slinked away.

Hall glanced around, towards the transport choppers sitting on the other side of the island. He presumed the VIP was coming by helicopter too, but the air was silent. There was no way she was going to arrive in time. He would have a word with the Secretary about this. There was work to be done, important, scare-the-Soviet-shitless work. He didn't have time for this.

And as for the VIP, well, he wasn't impressed by the so-called Director of Atoms for Peace. He'd never met her, but she sounded like a right PITA. In all the communications he'd seen that mentioned her, it was always in a strange, almost abstract way, like someone was hiding something. Probably embarrassed some civilian pencil-pusher had managed to land the top job, and a woman at that. If the work of this Atoms for Peace was so important, it should have had some brass in charge, someone from the Pentagon, a man who knew what he was doing. Even the name didn't gel. Atoms for Peace? Some Commie-appeasing BS from Eisenhower... to think that man had led the US to victory in both Europe and the Pacific less than ten years before, too. Jesus.

Hall went to spit into the grass, but his mouth was dry again. He was going to meet Evelyn McHale and... and he felt nervous. He didn't like it and he tried to ignore the growing anxiety in his chest. But truth was, he'd heard other things about the Director. Rumors, mostly, tall stories he'd dismissed without a second thought.

Until now.

He coughed and checked his watch.

"OK, show's over. Pack it up. We can go bird watching some other time."

"General Fulton Hall?"

The General sucked in a breath and turned. Standing behind him, under the marquee, was a woman in a smart dress suit, hat and veil, like she'd just stepped off Fifth Avenue. Fifth Avenue, 1947, that is.

She was also blue, monochrome behind a glowing aura that made Hall's eyes vibrate like he was drilling concrete. A glowing blue woman floating six inches from the ground.

Hall remembered the whispers, the stories, and at the back of his mind something broke. His ears were filled with the roaring of the ocean and the memory of his mother.

He coughed again. Around him, his staff were staring at the woman who had not been there and was then there.

"Ma'am?" General Hall's voice was a dry croak.

The woman glided around the trestle table at the back of the marquee and looked out across the water, oblivious to the reaction of those around her. There, Swinburne Island was a silhouette, the test rig a dark outline against the pale sky.

"Commence countdown," she said, her voice full of something that made Hall want to cry and leap off a tall building.

Hall didn't move; he just watched her. After a moment, some of his staff appeared to come to their senses.

"Sir?" The corporal again, his eyes fixed on the Director.

The General nodded, and tried to swallow, but his throat was parched.

The corporal spun on his heel and made a circular motion in the air with his index finger. At once, the assembled team sprang to life, sitting at desks, manning binoculars and telescopes, while several sat themselves behind a large bank of high-powered radio equipment and began murmuring into close-fitting headsets.

A PA squawked.

"T-minus six, zero-six, to test commencement."

"What exactly am I looking at here?"

Someone had produced coffee out here in the middle of nowhere; General Hall had drained three paper cups of the stuff already, but his throat felt drier than ever.

And worse than that was the fear – it was cold, something deep at the heart of his very being. It came, he knew, from standing next to her. Her, the impossible, the magical, the powerful, the terrifying. Her, the dead woman, the one who didn't belong here, the one who, Hall had felt deep down – the same place where that heart of ice was threatening to creep up and swallow his whole soul – didn't want to be here. Hall gulped again, and wondered if maybe the test had something to do with that.

War, she'd said.

T-minus two minutes.

Everything was going as planned, every eye on the rig a mile away, protective goggles ready to be pulled down at the very last second.

All except her. She stood – floated – next to the General, unprotected. Hall wondered if she could even wear the goggles, if she could touch anything at all. She hadn't yet, she just... hovered, dressed for a busy afternoon trawling Manhattan's famous stores seven years before.

Hall found himself looking at her again. He couldn't help it; she was magnetic, powerful, even though Hall knew it was somehow dangerous to be next to her. It was the feeling of incompatibility, the feeling that she didn't belong, not to here and not to now, and if you got too close to the shimmering blue event horizon that surrounded her you would be dragged down with her, out into the nothing where she really existed.

She turned and met Hall's eye. He felt ill.

She said, "War is coming," and Hall barked the order for the countdown to be paused.

He hadn't read the briefing properly, disregarding as he always did the bullshit that came out of Atoms for Peace. But now she was here and Hall regretted every thought, every rash decision, every casual dismissal he'd made. She was real, and more important, so were the stories about her.

The United States government had a goddess working for them, and suddenly General Hall felt his own work, his job, were insignificant, unimportant.

"What are we testing?" he said, his voice a whisper so low only she could have heard it.

"It's a... device," she said, turning back to Swinburne Island. Hall watched her face; it was like she was looking at something else, the way her eyes were unfocused, the way her mouth was open, her lips just a hair apart, like she was watching fireworks on the Fourth of July or admiring a priceless work of art.

"It's the Russians, isn't it?" Hall knew it. "The Reds are coming, finally."

And suddenly he felt... better. Those Communist bastards. This was it. War... the curtain was going up on World War Three, and the United States of America, God bless her, had a goddess on her payroll.

Hot dog.

Now he understood. This was a threat, a very real one, the logical culmination of world events since 1945. And... OK, the Director of Atoms for Peace was a goddess with powers to match, but dammit, she was American, and she was here, asking for his help, here to show him the magic tricks her team had been working on.

"Are you feeling all right, General Hall?"

Hall blinked. She was smiling at him. He straightened his

back, and raised his chin.

"Never better, ma'am." He fought the urge to salute; his hand twitched by his side, and his vision went fuzzy at the edges.

God bless America.

"Now, Madam Director, we're all eager to watch this demonstration of the... device. Can you fill us in on the specifics?"

The Director's smile didn't falter, and after a beat she turned and looked back towards the test rig. Hall followed her gaze, squinting into the bright morning. Then he raised his binoculars again. The device glinted in the sunlight, hardly anything more than a shining star in Hall's vision.

"It is called a fusor, General," the Director said. "It's a portable nuclear fusion reactor, which operates by direct injection of ions into the containment field. The power output approaches maximum when the ion velocity–"

"OK," said the General, waving a hand. "I've got it. You're here to test a nuclear reactor."

The Director inclined her head with a smile. "Not exactly, General."

"A portable reactor, you say? Is it intended as a civilian or military power source?"

"Neither," said the Director. "The fusor is powerful energy source. But it has another application, one I am here to show you. Recommence the countdown."

Hall turned to the technicians at the desk behind him, but they were shaking their heads. At the back of the marquee, Hall saw the countdown clock resume even as the technician was giving the directions to his colleagues.

"Sir," said the technician, "the countdown has recommenced of its own accord. Recommend we–"

Hall held up his hand, and the man stopped. He looked at the Director, but her attention was fixed on the test rig. "Sir?"

"Stand-down. We're good to go," said Hall. "I think the Director has this under control."

"Sir. T-Minus fifty – five-oh – seconds and counting. Goggles down."

The General and his staff donned their protective eyewear. Through the dark smoky glass it seemed to Hall that Evelyn shone even brighter, her blue glow electric in his eyes. He could see the pulse on her neck quicken as the countdown neared its end.

Hall glanced down at the folder of briefing papers in front of him. He flipped it open and, leafing through, found a summary of the fusor's blueprints. It was a cylinder, and not a very big one either, about the size of a small artillery shell, no more. The General didn't know the expected yield of the device, but he had to assume they – and the good people of New York – were far enough away from ground zero.

"Ten... nine... eight..."

Then Hall looked at Evelyn, and she turned to look at him. She stared into his eyes, and he felt the cold spread. Through his goggles her eyes were aflame, glowing, smoking coals, tendrils of energy drifting out of the featureless sockets. Her lips parted as she smiled, and Hall saw she was glowing inside, smoke wafting out of her mouth.

Hall's chest felt tight. He couldn't breathe... he couldn't think... she was beautiful and she was dead and she was... she was incompatible, and she was not here, not really. These thoughts crashed through Hall's mind. He didn't know anything about her, but he could feel it, feel her presence like waking up in the middle of the night to find the covers being pulled off and a dead, cold weight sitting on the middle of your chest. The eyes under the bed, the something evil in the closet, the creaking floor downstairs.

Hall wanted to run, to grab a boat and get to Swinburne

Island, where he could go up with the test, end it all, his very existence unendurable misery. And still he looked at her, and still she smiled, and Hall remembered the fear and remembered the dark when he'd got lost in the wood when he was four years old.

"Three...two..."

She turned back to watch. Hall felt the tears pooling inside his goggles.

"One!"

There was nothing for a second, and then the test rig – Swinburne Island itself – vanished into a featureless white light. The staff around Hall flinched, some even looking away as others, despite the goggles, raised their arms in front of their faces to shield themselves from the brilliant intensity. Hall's eyes were wide, as was his jaw, as he watched. He'd seen atomic tests – most people under the marquee had – so he knew what to expect: the flash, the roar, the pressure wave, the heat, and then the spectacle of the expanding spherical cloud that would evaporate in seconds as the famous mushroom cloud of death slowly rolled skywards.

This... this was different. The flash of light was brighter, but the explosion was quieter, the pressure wave not so intense. Standing in the light, the Director was suddenly a person, her skin pale but alive, her clothes no longer monochrome but blue and green, her scarf white. She was wearing make-up: the lipstick a bright red, matching the nail polish on her hands. The blue halo was gone, and for a second it looked like she was standing on the ground, not floating above it.

Hall turned back to the test. The white light faded, replaced by rolling oranges and reds as the explosion cloud collapsed and a column of smoke rose directly upwards. As Hall watched, he saw lightning flicker within the column, arcs shooting both up and down. Of the other artificial island in Lower New York Bay, there was no sign.

Through his goggles he could see the blue glow of the Director beside him; she was as she was before – not a woman, but a ghost and a god.

Then the pressure wave arrived, and Hall didn't see anything else for a while.

THIRTY-TWO

When Rad opened his eyes, all he saw was green.

He sat up with a yell and rubbed his eyes, but the green was still there. He ran his hands over the ground beneath him: it was smooth, like glass, a little wet under his fingertips, and very cold. Ice. It was a dark night. He was outside. The King's magic lantern was back on.

He shook his head and looked around. He was lying in a narrow alley in Harlem, and there was a man standing in front of him, wearing a tight, leathery coverall. A helmeted head tilted as the man regarded Rad on the alley floor.

Rad swore and pushed himself backwards until he hit something soft. He turned, sliding on his backside, and saw the prone form of Jennifer Jones lying next to him on the sidewalk, up against the wall.

Rad spun back around, and tried to replay the last few minutes. He remembered the light, he remembered Kane getting out of the box, and then...

He looked up at the man standing over him wearing the leather base of the Skyguard's suit – without the armor plate, or cloak. The Corsair must have been wearing it underneath the chauffeur's uniform.

"That better be Kane Fortuna in there."

The man waved his hand dismissively. "Oh, that guy?" he said, and then he laughed.

Rad raised an eyebrow, and returned his attention to

Jennifer. In the green light her form was completely grey. "What happened?"

"I got you out of there, didn't I?"

Rad frowned as he reached forward. He dug around Jennifer's collar and found the pulse on her neck, which was going just fine, although her skin felt cold. As he pulled away, his fingers brushed the edge of her metal face, and he hesitated.

"I found some things in the theater that I really think we need to talk about," he said.

"We need to get moving first."

Rad nodded and pushed himself to his feet. He was a little unsteady and the ground was treacherously slick, but he balanced himself against the brick wall with one hand.

"So you gonna tell me what happened? You got the suit off that guy. Where is he?"

Kane turned away and began pacing the alleyway. "Trust me, I dealt with him and I got us out."

"Hey, you didn't..."

Kane stopped pacing and turned around, hands on hips. His face was completely hidden behind the black metal mask, which Rad didn't like. He didn't feel like conducting such an important conversation through a piece of metal.

"Kill him?" asked Kane, and then he waved his hand again, a casual dismissal of a joke over a drink. "We can pick him up later, once we get more agents back here. First up, we need to get downtown."

Rad looked Kane up and down. "You seem to be OK."

Kane nodded, still pacing, restless. "It's the suit. It's even better than the machine. If anything, it was the machine that was making me sick. Draining off the power of the Fissure."

"Not to mention the sweet little something they were feeding you."

At this Kane stopped again, looked at Rad. "Some kind of drug? A sedative?"

Rad nodded. "Dope of some kind, could be. Keep you docile, cooperative. The fever and delirium are probably just side effects. Maybe he thought if you knew the power you had inside you, you would have caused problems. You could just have blown yourself out, without my help." Rad looked around, at the walls of the alley and the buildings around them. They were at the side of the theater; looking up, silhouetted against the sky, he could see the branches of the King's lucky tree as they stretched up through the roof at the back of the theater. The tree was in full leaf, untouched by the winter outside.

"Huh," he said.

"What?"

"The tree. The King said it brought luck. Seems he was right." Rad turned back to Kane. "So... suit working OK?"

Kane laughed, then placed both hands on his chin. Using his thumbs for leverage, he lifted the edge of the mask. Immediately a brilliant white-blue light shone out, forcing Rad to look away, shielding his face with his hands.

"Neat," he said. "We're gonna have to figure out how to get all that back where it should be and get the city plugged in again."

"First things first," said Kane.

Rad nodded and looked down at Jennifer just as she groaned. For a moment it sounded like the mechanical voice of a robot, but then she mumbled something and it was her, albeit muffled behind her golden mask. Rad offered his hand.

"You OK, agent?"

Jennifer pulled herself up, and dusted her coat down. As Rad watched, her hands went to her face, and she trailed her gloved fingertips over the contours of the mask. Then she nodded, and looked at Kane. "Where's the Corsair?"

"He's fine," said Kane. "Secure. The police can collect him."

Jennifer took a step forward. "No! We're going back to get him. Now."

Rad reached out for her arm, but she shook him off and spun around. Rad jerked back from the mask. "She's right," he said. "We should bring him in now, not wait."

"And what about the robots, Rad? This whole place is crawling with them."

Rad shook his head. "We're safe out here so long as the green light is on." He pointed, and immediately the green light went out, leaving the alley in darkness.

Kane sighed. "You were saying?"

There was a sound from the other end of the alley, from 125th Street itself – a shuffling, metallic, meshed with the organic rustling of ordinary people. The robots were moving.

"There," said Jennifer, pointing. Rad turned and saw long shadows dancing on the street, thrown from around the corner of the alley. Lots of shapes, people – robots – moving in their direction.

"Kane, can you fly in the suit?"

Kane shook his head. "No. Jets are all missing. Whole system has been stripped out."

"You got anything that can hold them back?"

"Not sure." Kane examined the watch-like panel on his wrist.

The sounds from the alley increased.

"We gotta get out of here."

"Here we go," said Kane, and his wrist panel began emitting a faint pulsing sound that Rad thought was more than a little ominous. "No," said Kane. "Wait a minute–"

"That thing going to blow up now?" said Rad, not sure if

he was joking.

"No, it's the communicator. Hold on…"

Rad turned back to the street. As he watched, the shadows cast by the robots came to a halt and stood swaying in the streetlight. Then they resumed their march, changing direction. They were heading straight for them.

"Dammit, Kane, those things are homing in on the signal." Rad spun around, scanning the alleyway. "Hey, where's Jennifer?"

The alley was filled with a roaring sound, so loud Rad ducked instinctively. From the other end of the alley, a brilliant green light flooded the road. Rad stumbled in surprise and turned towards it, but could see nothing except a green light speeding closer. He shielded his eyes from the glare and saw two lights, mounted on the front of something.

The King's car.

Rad and Kane jumped to opposite sides of the alley as the huge machine came to a halt between them, the rear end snaking on the icy roadway. The passenger door was flung open, Jennifer leaning over the wheel.

"Get in!"

Rad didn't argue. He practically fell into the passenger seat and scrambled to close the door behind him, while Kane did the same in the rear.

Jennifer released the brake and the car fishtailed again. Then it propelled forward fast enough to push Rad back into his seat.

"What the hell? How did you find the car?" he managed, glancing sideways at Jennifer. She had one hand on the wheel, one hand on the shifter, and her golden mask was staring dead ahead, tinged green by the car's headlamps.

"Found my way back to the garage when I was looking around the theater," she said as the car cleared the alleyway and she pulled a sharp right. "It opens into the alley just back there. Now shut up, and let me drive."

Jennifer pulled around another corner, and swore.

Dead ahead was the robot gang, so large it filled the street as far as Rad could see. The robots in front recoiled from the green light, and Rad was sure they were screaming in pain and in fright, but he couldn't hear anything over the roar of the engine.

"Hold onto something," said Jennifer as she floored the accelerator and aimed the car directly for the center of the group.

THIRTY-THREE

In the ruins of the King's workshop, the Corsair lay unmoving, his body bloody and broken, partially covered by twisted metal still hot from the explosion of energy and movement that was Kane Fortuna.

Something clattered to the floor; the Corsair groaned, but the sound didn't carry past the ruin of his mouth. He coughed, and nearly choked on the blood and broken teeth, and then felt a slicing sensation of pain travel along his jawline, where the bone beneath was fractured in seven places.

He blinked, then realized his eyes had been open all along; they were just filled with viscous dark blood. He blinked again and some of it cleared, leaving his view of the workshop floor fuzzy and dark but unobstructed enough to see the carnage.

The slab on which Kane's machine had lain was split in two, collapsed in the middle of the room. The slab behind had been shifted out of position, but the third, which had so recently housed Jennifer Jones, was intact and untouched, save for half of a new robot's torso shell, the metal bright and unblemished, lying on its top.

More movement, out of the corner of his eye. The Corsair tried to move his head but the sudden pain was too much and when he opened his eyes again he was moving, sliding along the floor, leaving a trail of debris and thick blood.

"Master, I, Master, I..." said a metallic voice from somewhere above him. The Corsair let himself be dragged across the floor. Then he was pulled into a sitting position, his back to the wall.

There was a man above him, a short man in a blue suit that was torn and smoking. The man was standing by the intact machine, but was fumbling, moving his hands over the slab and the box on it like he couldn't see. As the Corsair watched, the hands finally found the lid and lifted.

The Corsair blinked, and when he opened his eyes he was inside the machine. He was in pain now, his whole body alive with it, brilliant and sharp and fiery. He looked up, seeing the blackened walls of the workshop. There was a fire, somewhere, lighting the otherwise dark room in a flickering light that threw long shadows. Then the Corsair realized the light was not orange and yellow but white and blue, and was coming from the door that led to the power room.

The Corsair cried out in pain, screamed as loud as he could.

The man who had saved him – why couldn't he remember who that was? He knew him, he was sure of it – was busy at the controls. The Corsair could just see the dark blue velvet over the lip of the machine. The man was hunched over, like he was in pain, like there was something wrong, like–

He turned around, and the Corsair screamed again. The man was the King of 125th Street, he remembered now, his faithful robot, the first one he'd made from a homeless person who had stumbled from the naval robot yard, not yet converted into an Ironclad sailor but put through the mental processing and then left, abandoned as Wartime ended suddenly.

The man's face was hanging in strips from a silver skull, the artificial flesh quivering as the machine man rocked slightly on its heels, the scalp peeled over to the left. The robot's eyes were two blackened, burnt-out holes, a liquid, thick and black and oozing, streaming out like syrup. The robot's jaw, still clad in fake skin, moved up and down as the blind machine struggled to help its master.

"Master, I, master, I..." said the robot. It shuddered as it spoke, its hands moving over the edge of the machine, fingers flexing, searching.

The Corsair tried to shake his head, but there was a thick leather strap over his forehead. He tried to move his body, but he couldn't even feel it. It was like it wasn't there at all or it didn't belong to him.

"Master, I, master, I... I will get them back. They. Can. Not. Escape." Each forced syllable made the King rock. "Master, I, master, I... I will repair you save you make you well. Army the army the army has been activated. They. Can. Not. Escape."

The Corsair screamed until his mouth filled with blood and his throat felt like it was being flayed with knives, as the blind robot King of 125th Street threw a lever and the lid of the machine slammed shut.

THIRTY-FOUR

The man stirred in his bunk. How long he'd been asleep, he wasn't sure. Time passed strangely where he was, although maybe that was his imagination. Years of solitude, years of travel had taken their toll.

The signal was a constant pulsing tone, not loud enough to have woken him, just loud enough to have entered his dreams, the signal becoming a flashing blue light, the light of the gap between one universe and the next.

The man rubbed his good eye and pulled thick fingers through his white beard, and then he lay on his bunk and stared at the ceiling of the ship as the tone continued.

Maybe this was a dream too. Maybe the signal was his imagination, an auditory hallucination. Maybe it was the outside tricking him. It had a habit of doing that; he'd discovered many places on his travels, some of which were cities, whole countries where life went on. Others were places that seemed to be alive themselves.

And they liked to trick him, make him see things, make him hear things. After years of this the man wasn't sure what was real, not anymore. Maybe he'd died a long time ago, on that day when the ice was thick and the fog was deep, the day he'd stepped into it and left the world.

"Sir?"

The man jolted on the bunk, suddenly wide awake. He sat up too quickly, his hand pressing his forehead as the room spun. He waited a moment, then swallowed and glanced at the door to the flight deck. On the control panel in front of the pilot's seat he could see one of the row of orange lights flashing in time with the tone.

A shadow moved around the flight deck.

"I have located the source," said the voice.

"A signal? From the city?"

"I believe this is what you have been waiting for, sir."

The man heart raced as he listened to the tone. He blinked. The signal was… wait, the signal was…

He looked back to the ceiling. "That's not a regular transmission."

The shadow moved, but the other voice said nothing.

The man swung himself from his bunk, the end of his wooden leg loud against the floor of the ship. He reached for his walking stick, and went to heave himself to a standing position, but then he paused, head cocked, looking at the floor and listening, listening.

"I recognize it. The signal, it's–"

"I quite agree," said the other voice.

The man pulled himself up and stumbled into the cockpit, using the pilot's chair to kill his momentum as he dropped his walking stick and stared through the main window. Outside the fog was thinning; the lights of the city were faintly visible as a multicolored smudge of twinkling stars. The frame of the bridge was barely there, a smudge dissolving into the orangey-grey world.

The man gripped the top of the pilot's seat and licked his lips. He was alone in the cockpit. He was alone in the entire ship.

He allowed himself a small smile.

"It's him, isn't it?"

There was a pause, and then a second voice sounded from somewhere behind him. "I believe so."

"So, he found his way back."

"As you once predicted, sir. The arc of his transit returned him to the Empire State."

The man nodded. "Like a comet in orbit around the sun." Then he laughed, and swung himself around into the pilot's seat. He smoothed down his mustache and beard, and glanced across the controls with his one good eye. He frowned, and lifted the eye patch that covered the other, and squinted. Satisfied, he let the eye patch flip back into place, and he clapped his hands and rubbed them together.

"I do believe we shall be in time for tea. Byron?"

"Yes, Captain Carson?"

"Trace the signal, and get a lock on its position. We shall collect them en route to Grand Central."

"Confirmed. Tether release in five seconds."

Captain Carson clapped his hands again and laughed. After all this time, they were going home.

THIRTY-FIVE

It was no good, and Rad knew it.

They'd charged the main group of robots in the car, and Rad was glad that Jennifer was driving because she was unwavering, fearless, as she accelerated and plowed straight into them. The robots had tried to part, to get out of the way as the car hurtled towards them, but there were a lot of them, and several went flying over the long hood of the car, some rolling up over the windshield before sliding down the side. Rad was amazed the car could stand the punishment, but looking down the length of the hood he saw it hadn't even been scratched.

But the numbers were against them. Jennifer slowed, the car losing momentum and power. The robots still trying to get out of the green headlights that seemed to cause them so much pain were now pushed against the hood, rocking the car.

Jennifer threw the vehicle into reverse, turning to look out the back as she tried to find an exit. Rad turned as well. It didn't look good.

"We need to head south," said Kane, lying in the backseat. "Downtown!"

"Tell me something I don't know," said Jennifer, expertly threading the car backwards through the closing mass of robots behind them, then swinging back around as they returned to 125th Street. She shifted gears, and without hardly a pause at all, they shot off down the empty street. As they sped onwards, Rad noticed the cone of green light in front of them was off-center: one of the headlamps had been smashed. So, the car wasn't indestructible after all.

"Dammit."

Rad looked up. On their left, another group of robots came out of a side alley, another ragtag bunch of shapes and sizes and in varying stages of deconstruction. Jennifer dodged them as they stepped out into the road, but looking back Rad could see more coming out of a street opposite. Perhaps they were attracted to the sound of the car, knowing that it meant the King was out and about, saying hello to his loyal subjects, maybe choosing the lucky ones who would come back to the theater and be saved.

Kane righted himself in the back, and grabbed the top of Rad's seat to pull himself forward. "They're coming out of everywhere. How many are there?"

Jennifer kept her eyes on the road, but she shook her head as she drove. "Who knows how many the King had waiting. My guess is Harlem is full of them."

Rad frowned. "And that's not counting the warehouses downtown. The King has thousands of robots – a whole army – hidden across the city."

Jennifer turned her golden face to him, and Rad raised an eyebrow. He could see her eyes through the slots in the mask.

Rad said, "The Harlem robots, they're the refugees, gathering around the King of 125th Street, waiting for him to get to work, turning them back into people."

"Yes," said Jennifer. "Only he isn't. He's finishing the job, converting them fully into robots."

"Then shipping them downtown, putting them in storage–"

"But keeping a few active, like Cliff, to look after them

until they're ready."

Rad whistled. "And in the meantime, Cliff and the others like him, they're organized, working to a plan. They pull crimes, stealing equipment, materials, that the King needs to keep working. The robot gangs. Now it makes sense."

Kane shook his head. "Robot gangs? Sorry, I've been out of town."

Rad grimaced. "Don't sweat it. We just need to get out of here first." He turned to Jennifer. "What happened to that gun of yours?"

She glanced over her shoulder, into the backseat. "Actually, it might be in here."

Kane ducked down. "Bingo," he said after a moment. Then he bobbed back up and passed the weapon to Rad.

Rad turned it over in his hands. "How do I check the ammo?"

"You don't," said Jennifer. "But it should be charged. It's good for one shot and one shot only, remember?"

"OK," said Rad, adjusting his grip on the gun, getting used to the awkward weight of it. "Last resort only." He turned around to Kane. "You remember anything about your dreams?"

Kane sighed and sat back. "A little. There's a woman, a woman with blue eyes. And movement, lots of movement."

Jennifer glanced at Rad. "Dreams?"

Rad nodded. "As well as powering the King's operation, seems the star reporter here can see the future. The King thinks Kane's dream is about an army invading the Empire State from New York."

"An army of what?"

"Guess," said Rad.

Jennifer sighed. "So that's why the King is building his own force?"

"Got it in one."

Nobody in the car spoke for a while. The road ahead was clear.

"Agent Jones," said Rad eventually, "what did the Corsair mean when he said you hadn't told us?"

Jennifer didn't say anything.

"You were on the trail of the robot gangs before you called me. What else were you looking for?"

Jennifer shook her head, and then said: "I'm looking for my brother."

Rad whistled and drew breath to ask the next question when the car slid on the icy road as Jennifer yanked the wheel, hard.

She swore, leaning against Rad as the car turned. Looking out his window he saw the road slide past sideways as the car spun around. Ahead, the road was blocked by a huge group of robots, much larger than the pack they'd charged near the theater. These robots were silver, uniform, marching in a slow step in perfect time. In the Harlem night dozens of red eyes shone like coals.

Rad clung to the handle above his door as Jennifer pushed the huge vehicle to its limit. They shot down a side street, the side mirror on Rad's side clipping the iced brick of the building on the corner. Then Jennifer pulled left, heading south via a different route. But it was no good; there were more of the warehouse robots blocking the road. Jennifer swore again and took the next left, turning just in time to kiss the first row of machine men with the rear of the car. The vehicle jumped and Rad bumped his head against the ceiling.

"Looks like they've rolled out the cavalry for us," said Rad as the car skidded on the slick road as Jennifer pushed it down the next street. "Ah, this isn't good."

The road ahead narrowed alarmingly, but that wasn't the worst part. A building had collapsed across the street, blocking their way entirely.

Jennifer jammed on the brakes and the car jackknifed, sliding on the ice. Rad grabbed the handle above his door with two hands as the car turned like the hands of a clock. Rad could see Kane lying flat on the floor in the backseat, thrown there by the sudden braking, and Jennifer's hands were on the wheel, moving it, coaxing the car around, trying to regain control.

The rear of the vehicle collided with the rubble on the road, and the car kicked, the wheels spinning. Jennifer gunned the accelerator, her hands moving the gearshift, but Rad could hear the wheels spin on the ice and dirt even above the roar of the engine. The car jerked a little, but a wheel was caught on something. Rad and Jennifer both strained to see out of the back window as Kane pulled himself up. Jennifer played the accelerator, and the car rocked gently from side to side, but they weren't going anywhere, not anymore.

Kane pointed forward.

"Ah, guys?"

Rad and Jennifer spun around to see. The end of the street from which they'd just come was now filled with robots. There was five hundred yards separating the group and the car, but the gap was closing fast. The robots marched forward, their pace slow but sure. They were going to box them in.

"Last resort," muttered Rad. He wound his window down and raised himself up on the seat until he could get his whole upper body out of the car. He pointed the gun, not sure what to aim at, and pulled the trigger.

Nothing happened. Rad glanced at the weapon, but aside from the trigger it was featureless, with no other controls.

"Thought you said this gizmo was recharged?" he yelled.

"It should be," came Jennifer's voice from inside the car.

Rad frowned and tried again. Nothing. The weapon was dead.

"Well, ain't that swell," said Rad.

"Get back in!"

Rad obliged, the silver gun useless in his lap. The car's engine barked and the whole vehicle shook, confirming Rad's fears that there was more damage than a jammed wheel – until he realized the sound was from outside the car. A second later, the roadway was filled with a bright white light. As Rad's eyes adjusted, two wide beams stabbed downwards. They swept back and forth across the road before one focused on the car, the other on the robots. The robots came to a halt and as one their red eyes pointed to the sky as they all looked up.

"What the?" Rad and Jennifer leaned over the dashboard to see, while Kane fumbled to get a window open in the back.

Something large descended onto the street, throwing a downwind that blew frost up from the road in huge, glittering clouds of particles that glinted like stars in the spotlights. The object moved over the car, towards the robots, then turned with surprising speed and touched down. It was an airship of some kind, although not one of the now-retired police aerostats. This was more like...

Rad's eyes went wide. More like the Nimrod, the airship of Captain Carson. Rad raised a hand to cut out the glare and caught a glimpse of silver and metal

This thing was much larger than the Nimrod. And the last time Rad had seen the Captain's explorer craft, it was jammed next to the bulk of an Enemy airship, the pair locked together and piloted out into the fog by the Captain's companion, Byron.

Jennifer floored the accelerator with a yell and the car sprang free of the rubble, skidding to the right as the spinning wheels hit the ice. She turned, hard, but the road was too slick and although the car began to turn, it was still moving forward, towards the ship. Whatever it was, they were going to hit it, and Rad was fairly sure the car really was going to be wrecked this time.

Then the light cut out. For a moment the darkness was disorienting. Then the green of the car's one remaining headlight flooded the view ahead, like there was suddenly a wall right in front of them. Rad flinched, throwing himself to one side instinctively, and the green light faded as the car continued to turn. There was a soft, deep thud as the car hit something and came to a stop.

Rad pulled himself upright.

They were inside the airship – it had opened a cargo door. The white spotlights illuminating the street were now out beyond the bay doors. Ahead, Rad could see the rubble of the collapsed building.

The car had collided with a collection of wooden crates and sacks of something softer, destroying several boxes and spilling the contents of the sacks. The air was filled with a harsh scraping – the sound, Rad realized, of the car's stuck engine. Jennifer killed it, and the floor of the cargo bay tipped. The car slid against the wall, and the view of the road outside vanished as the airship lifted off and the cargo bay doors began to close.

Lights were thrown on outside. Rad looked around, and saw Jennifer and Kane were as surprised as he was that they been suddenly, unexpectedly, rescued from a dead end.

"Mr Bradley, a pleasure, as always," came a voice, metallic and echoing, coming from all around them. The voice over the ship's PA filled the cargo bay.

Rad felt Kane looking at him.

"Is that...?"

Rad nodded. Then he opened his door and swung a foot

out. He leaned forward and looked at the cargo bay's high ceiling. The place vibrated as the ship's propeller engines carried them up and out to safety.

"Captain Carson, you sonovabitch."

The PA squawked as the voice laughed.

"My dear detective, such a way with words," said Carson. "Now, come up to the main deck, all of you. Follow the stairs. I'll open the doors."

Rad cracked a grin and slapped the top of Jennifer's seat. "About time I started to count these blessings we all seem to have. Come on."

He swung himself out of the car, Kane right behind him. Rad pointed to the narrow metal staircase ahead of them, leading to a walkway that ran around the hold halfway between the floor and ceiling. On the walkway at the back of the hold was the bulkhead door.

Kane took a step forward, but Rad turned back to the car. Jennifer hadn't moved from the driver's seat.

Rad peered in to the car's interior. "You coming?"

She nodded, and Rad helped her out. But as she walked forward he kept his hand on the small of her back.

They had a lot of talking to do, all of them.

Especially Special Agent Jennifer Jones.

THIRTY-SIX

Carson led the way from the Nimrod, unbuckling himself as soon as the craft had touched down in the dark tunnel. He had hardly spoken except to bark the order to follow as he hobbled off the flight deck, wooden leg and wooden stick banging on the floor. Rad was right behind, grateful that his old friend was still alive but wondering what the hell had happened to him out beyond the fog. Along with the wooden leg and Santa Claus beard, Captain Carson was older by a decade.

Despite Carson's disability, Rad and the others had to jog to keep up with the old man. They walked out of the tunnel into a huge chamber, a concourse of elegant marble, the blue ceiling immensely high and studded with lights like the night sky.

"What is this place?" asked Rad as they crossed from one side of the chamber to the other.

Finally Carson broke his silence. "It is called Grand Central. It has been here always, although never used. It is a train station."

Carson led them up an inclined passageway and then down a set of wide, shallow stairs. Rad jogged alongside him. "There are no trains in the Empire State."

Rad saw Carson grin under his beard. "Precisely," he said. "The City Commissioners were never interested in this place. A veritable fortress, right in the heart of the city! I

232

always thought it would be useful one day, so I had one of the tunnels converted to an airship dock. Splendid, isn't it?"

"That's one word for it, sure," said Rad.

"Oh, Mr Bradley, you haven't changed, haven't changed a bit." Carson clapped, his face lit in a grin Rad remembered well. "And, Kane, my dear fellow," he said, turning to the younger man, "it is a sheer delight to discover you did not perish as we all thought. The Fissure is a strange and wonderful thing."

"It's good to see you again, Captain," said Kane.

"Aha!" Carson came to a halt. In front of them was another large room, as impressive as Rad's fleeting glimpse of the concourse above, but in a different way. Here the ceiling was lower and curved into great vaulted arcs, illuminated by up-lights that cast triangular shadows against the walls. The vaulted ceiling came together to form the inside of a flattened dome in the center of the room, creating a series of separated spaces like the segments of an orange. There were tables of varying sizes scattered around, and plenty of chairs, like the place was some kind of restaurant.

Carson hobbled forward and pulled out one of the chairs.

"Now, then," he said, gesturing for the others to sit. "It is time we had a good, old-fashioned chat."

Jennifer filled Carson in on recent events.

Rad watched as the Captain studied her golden mask, his one good eye moving over the features constantly. Something bothered Rad, and Jennifer had left out a couple of details from her account – like her search for her brother and her own investigations.

Rad rolled his fingers on the tabletop. Finally, he turned to Jennifer. "We've got a robot army coming for us, but the thing that bothers me is that your old boss here doesn't seem to know who you are. You wanna tell us about that?"

"I–"

"And about what your brother has to do with the King of 125th Street?"

Jennifer sighed behind her mask and looked at the three men seated at the table. She pulled off her gloves, and played her fingers along the edge of the wood. Rad felt a jolt of surprise when he realized that her naked hands were now the only part of her, apart from her hair, that was visible. He knew his turn would come to explain to the others what he'd found in the theater freezer, and he wondered what her reaction would be when he told her about the glass head.

"I wasn't an agent," she said. "And I didn't work for Carson, I worked for the City Commissioner – the other one, during Wartime. I was just an ordinary desk clerk, like a hundred others.

"I was attached to the group liaison between the robot yards and the Empire State. It was fine, we were fighting a war, but… I found things out about the ratings used on the Ironclads."

Rad nodded. "That they're people?"

"Yes. I mean, why did nobody know? People – men – marched down to the Battery and into the factory, and they never came back, never. Then every Fleet Day the robots would march down Fifth Avenue until the ticker tape was a foot deep on the sidewalks, and they filed onto their Ironclads, and off they'd sail with fireworks and brass bands and… that was it. How could nobody figure that they were men? How could people be forgotten? Friends? Family members… everyone who volunteered or was conscripted?"

"The same way nobody remembered that the last Fleet had never returned from beyond the fog," said Kane.

Jennifer turned her golden mask to his black one.

Carson brushed his mustache with the back of his index finger. "The Enemy," he said, "is a living thing, an entity that is also a city. Nobody knew that either, except me, and the City Commissioners. But one thing we didn't understand, didn't even consider, was that if the Enemy was a thing alive, then so was the Empire State. The city fights against those in it. It makes you forget, Ms Jones – it has to. Otherwise our entire world, the whole of the Empire State, the whole of the pocket universe itself, becomes a logical fallacy, an impossibility."

Jennifer shook her head slowly, clearly failing to follow the Captain's explanation. Rad waved his hand. "Doesn't matter, and I don't understand it myself. But that's not everything you found, right?"

"No," said Jennifer. "It was my brother. He'd volunteered to join the navy. I knew that but... but I forgot. When I discovered the robots were men, I looked up the enlistment records, just to make sure I wasn't misunderstanding something. I found his name there, and then I remembered. My brother, I lost my brother."

The others around the table were quiet. Rad glanced at the Captain, and saw his eye narrow, his brow knitted tightly in concentration. He wished that Kane and Jennifer didn't have to wear the masks; it felt like they were robots as well.

He turned back to Jennifer. "That's why you were on the trail of the robot gangs, right? You were looking for your brother."

"He was in the last enlistment, and then the Chairman vanished and Wartime ended. I wasn't in the Empire State Building when the robot, the one from the Ironclad, tore it up. But afterwards everything was in chaos. I got through to some people I knew in the robot yards. They were just shutting down, closing everything up. And they just... they just let them out, all of them."

"The robots?" asked Kane.

Jennifer nodded. "They had several Ironclad complements ready to go, as well as four other batches that were partway through conversion. But I couldn't get any information, things were... well, they were crazy. I tried to match up the records, but nothing tallied. It looked like they also had a whole lot of volunteers and conscripts who they hadn't started processing yet."

Rad nodded. "Your brother among them?"

"I didn't know, but that's what I hoped. There was no way to check who had already been turned into one of those monsters, or who had escaped. But the navy just... stopped. The doors opened, and they were left to fend for themselves. Where could they go? They were built and programmed for war, but now they had no function. They couldn't go back to their old lives, because they didn't remember them, and neither did their own families."

"They're in Harlem," said Kane. "The ones that hadn't been finished, they ended up there."

Rad steepled his fingers and tapped his top lip. "The refugees. The King of 125th Street said he'd worked in the robot yards. So he gathered the leftovers up and began work."

"Except he was a robot himself," said Kane.

Rad nodded. "That was a just a diversion. The real king was a man, working while his mechanical assistant collected more refugees and kept them doped on that green stuff, making them dependent on it so they'd have to stick close."

"Yes," said Jennifer. Then she fell silent. Rad wished he could see her face, what she was feeling, thinking, but her golden mask was frozen. But he had a feeling about what was coming next.

"I found him," she said.

Rad nodded. "The Corsair."

Jennifer shook her head. "James. His name is James. He was a doctor, a surgeon. When he volunteered, they said they could make use of his skills. I thought that if he had survived – if he hadn't entered the processing – I thought maybe he would have done something. He would have tried to help."

Carson stirred. "And help he did. Although perhaps not quite in the way you expected."

"No," said Jennifer. "They... they must have started the processing, the mental conditioning, anyway. He... they changed him."

Rad nodded. "And then after finding Kane and discovering his vision, instead of turning robots back into people, he was continuing the work, turning people into robots."

"To defend the Empire State," said Kane.

"To prepare for war," said Rad.

"He thinks – thought – he was doing the right thing," said Jennifer. She raised both hands and fanned them out on the tabletop. "Maybe he was."

The table fell silent. Then Carson hrmmed loudly.

"I see," he said. "I come back to find the place full of robots, while the city itself crumbles away as entropy increases. It seems I have returned just in time."

"Where did you go?" asked Rad. "And what happened to you? You've only been gone three months."

"Well," said Carson, stroking his beard. "By my reckoning, I have been away ten years, at least, although beyond the bounds of the city measuring time is a difficult task.

"But, yes, I abandoned the Empire State. And for that I am deeply sorry. But in the chaos that followed the... well, the you-know-what... while I was trying to pull the city back together, get everything running, removing Prohibition and the restrictions of Wartime and so on and so forth..." Carson rolled his hand in the air. Then he paused and let it drop to the table. "Well, it was Byron. Byron was gone; he had sacrificed himself to save us all. But I wondered, always, at the back of my mind, what had happened to him. Did he survive, perhaps? Did he fly out into the fog and into another world? Did he manage to detach from the Enemy airship and escape? Or did he land? Did he crash? So many possibilities, so many uncertainties. I just had to know. Every time I looked out into the wretched bank of fog I thought of him, and I remembered the two ships, stuck together, vanishing as they left the borders of the Empire State."

Carson wrung his hands and sighed. "I didn't know what to do. What could I do? The city was a mess and needed my attention, but always, always I thought of him, of Byron. And then..."

There Carson paused. Jennifer and Kane exchanged a look, and Rad leaned forward a little.

"And then..."

Carson looked at Rad and smiled sadly. "And then there was a signal. It was very faint, picked up by the Empire State Building but largely ignored. So I searched for it myself, and there it was. Faint, but unmistakable. It was a mayday call, automated certainly and the signal alone may not have indicated anything at all but... it was my signal, the mayday from the Nimrod. Which meant he was out there, somewhere. And that was... well, that was that. I had to go."

Rad shook his head. Byron had survived? Or at least the Nimrod had, and was out there somewhere. Rad couldn't blame Carson, but still.

"You had to go?" he asked. "You would abandon your post like that?"

Carson sighed again and smiled again, and reached out

and patted Rad's hand on the top of the table.

"Oh, my friend, what would you do? The signal was the final straw, the culmination of everything. Suddenly I had clarity. I had purpose. Byron was alive, and I had to find him."

Kane whistled. "So you walked out over the ice, just like that?"

"Ah!" Carson laughed. "Reports of my departure were largely exaggerated, as they say. Yes, I walked, and yes, I was on my own, but I was not unprepared. You may recall, the both of you, that I – or at least my counterpart in the Origin – was a polar explorer of some fame. I knew what to do, because I had always known what to do, even though the skills and memories of the past were not mine and not complete. So I was prepared. All the equipment I needed for a solo hike across the ice and into the unknown was at the house. I prepared myself and left."

Carson looked around the table with a smile, but Rad could see something in his eye. There was a tightness there, and it wasn't just the miraculous increase in years the man had suffered on his journey.

"And?"

Carson rolled his lips, the action moving his entire beard.

"It was hard, but I succeeded. I came first to the land of the Enemy, a dark, dangerous place. The cold was reaching there too, and they looked to be in even worse shape than our own city. It was a ruin, and I stood on the banks of the... well, the shoreline opposite, and as I watched I saw buildings fall, collapsing like sand into the water. There was other movement too, the people, if you can call them that, all moving at once, back and forth, like ants. I could feel it too. The Enemy was there, and it was fighting with something, or against something – against the dissolution of its world, I suppose. It saw me as well. I knew it, and

I... well, I ran. My very presence there seemed to help the thing coalesce, perhaps even hasten the destruction of the city."

Carson looked across the table, but his eyes were unfocussed. He held one hand out, like he was reaching for something, but he was lost in his memories.

"That was... many years ago. I ran. There was ice and fog, and darkness. Eventually the Enemy turned away, or perhaps I simply got used to it. But one day I felt I was alone, and I could get back to tracing the signal. I had a device, a radio of sorts, but I had run for so long from the darkness that I wasn't sure where I was, or how far I had gone, or whether I would even be able to find it again. Time passed – how long I have no idea – but then I heard it, the signal. It was far away, so off I went.

"I found other places. A great city they call New Amsterdam was my home for months as I recovered from my flight. But I had to follow the signal, so as soon as my strength was back I continued.

"I saw war and horror. I saw cities burning, cities destroyed, cities empty. And then I found him."

Rad blinked. "What? You found Byron?"

Carson smiled and seemed to snap out of his reverie. He turned slowly to Rad, and Rad saw a tear roll down his cheek.

"Yes, I did. He's upstairs, in the ship."

Carson led them back to the ship, via the main concourse. This time, as they approached along the incomplete platform, Rad had the opportunity to view the ship clearly, although much of it was obscured by the curve of the tunnel.

It was the Nimrod, although it was different. Larger, longer – the lines were harsh, the armor plating pierced and pitted. The Captain's original airship had been in a poor state of repair when Byron had piloted it away. This machine was the same, but a nightmare version. It felt wrong somehow.

Rad felt a hand on the small of his back. Carson leaned in to him.

"It's a different ship, yes. Well, it is the Nimrod, but a Nimrod from another world. I had to fight for it," he said, tapping his eye patch. "But I found him inside."

Kane walked back from the ship's door, leaving Jennifer to gaze up at its dented walls.

"How many other worlds are there?"

Carson's eye narrowed again. Rad decided he didn't like it when the Captain got that look.

"I thought there was only us and New York," said Rad. "And the Enemy, of course."

Carson nodded. "So did I, or at least that was as far as Byron and I had been able to penetrate. But I had always surmised there were more realms, further out. Perhaps even an infinite number of other universes and worlds."

Kane folded his arms. "And you were right," he said.

"Indeed," said the Captain, and he smiled the smug smile that made Rad laugh and think of tea and sawdust shortbread in the Captain's palatial residence. Then he realized that those days were a very long time ago for the Captain.

"If Byron was in this ship, how did you know it was really him?"

"Oh, that was easy. He had the taken the signal device from the Nimrod – the other Nimrod – and kept it with him. He knew I would be listening."

"So why didn't we meet him when we came back here? You're saying he's still inside the ship?"

Kane said, "It was empty when you picked us up."

Jennifer ducked into the Nimrod's side door. "Ah, everyone?" she called out from inside. "There's someone here all right."

Rad looked at Carson, and pulled himself into the doorway. Ahead of him, a black shadow seemed to sweep past Jennifer. She stopped and looked around her in surprise.

Rad turned back to the Captain, his eyes wide. Carson laughed loudly.

"Byron can't leave the ship, detective. He's a ghost. He's haunting it!"

THIRTY-SEVEN

Carson led them onto the flight deck, where he directed Jennifer to sit in the co-pilot's chair while he occupied the pilot's.

Kane pulled on Rad's arm, leading him to the side while the Captain examined Jennifer's metal face. Rad kept one eye on them, well aware of what he'd found in the freezer.

"You're telling me you believe this?" Kane's whisper was muffled behind the mask.

"Believe what?" Rad hissed out of the corner of his mouth. "That this really is Captain Carson?"

"That, and that he thinks his airship is haunted by his dead friend."

Rad's eyes darted around the cockpit. There were plenty of places for someone to hide. Plenty of places for shadows to collect.

"The past few days, I'll believe lots of things," he said.

"I can hear you, gentlemen."

Rad and Kane pulled back from each other, each glancing around the room. The voice had been a low whisper too, as though from a third person standing close. The voice was deep, accented like Carson's.

Rad saw the Captain looking in their direction, he face split by an annoying smile.

Rad looked at the ceiling. "Byron?"

"At your service," came the voice, this time from behind

Rad. He spun around, but there was no one there.

"OK," said Rad, nodding as he turned back to Kane. "Byron, fine. Hi, there." He raised his hand, unsure where Byron was.

"A pleasure to see you again, Mr Bradley," said Byron.

Kane laughed. "Well, I'll be damned."

"And Mr Fortuna," said the voice, and Rad could have sworn Byron gave a little bow, even though he was nowhere to be seen, nothing more than a dark moving shape in the corner of his eye.

The Captain turned back to Jennifer.

"It is no use," he said, slapping his hands on the top of his thighs and leaning back into his seat. He glanced up at Rad. "The mask cannot be removed. It, dare I say it, appears to be part of her face now. It's a remarkable design, remarkable. The improvements in technique are quite staggering."

"So," said Rad, his eyes on Jennifer. "You know what happened to her? What the mask is?"

Carson nodded, but before he could speak, Jennifer shook her head.

"It's fine. I know what happened. It was James. He did this to me. He started the process."

Rad shook his head in disbelief, but Jennifer stood up and walked toward him.

"He wanted to save me," she said.

Rad pursed his lips. "Look, there's something I have to tell you," he said.

Jennifer tilted her mask, her hands on her hips.

Rad rubbed his chin, looking at the floor. "I found something in the theater, when we were looking for Skyguard's suit."

"Well?"

"The King has parts in storage."

Carson shuffled in his seat. "Robot parts?"

"Body parts," said Rad, shaking his head. He pointed at Jennifer. "Look, point is, that mask can't come off, Agent Jones. Not unless we can pull the Corsair – your brother – out of there, maybe see if he can reverse the process."

Carson let his hands fall into his lap. "I see."

"It's OK," said Jennifer. "We'll get him back, and he can fix me."

"He thinks he was doing that already." Rad held his hands up in apology. "What I mean is, I'm not sure we can count on that."

"How did you find us?" said Kane. Rad turned to him, leaning against the wall, arms tightly folded. He was grateful for the change of subject.

"Ah," said Carson. He barked a laugh and pointed to Kane. "This time I followed your signal, my friend. Your timing was exquisite, as I had been watching the city for some time, but I was unsure. Until, that is, I received your signal. Then I knew."

Rad glanced at Kane, who was now peering at the panel on his wrist. Rad turned back to Carson. "You've been trying to get back?"

"Oh, yes," said Carson. "Once I found Byron and this ship, it was imperative we return to the Empire State. But after so many years of travel, it was... difficult to plot a return course. On the way out, detours to avoid the Enemy aside, I had Byron's signal to home in on. But coming back, we had nothing to follow. We came to city after city, never sure whether we had seen them before, never sure whether they were real, or illusions, or echoes of the Enemy.

"And then we found a bridge, and we followed it until we reached the shores of another place. A dark city, cold, so very, very cold. But there was something about it, I could feel it. But we couldn't be sure, so we stayed just outside its perimeter while I investigated. But then came the signal, and that was the final piece of data I required. We came home."

Kane pushed himself off the wall and stepped closer to the group.

"So now you're home, what do we do? Go back to the theater and bring them out? Go down to the Empire State Building and come back with agents and police?"

"We have to go back," said Jennifer. "James is still in there."

The Captain puffed out his cheeks. "That would be unwise. If the King has activated his robot army early, it will be to recapture Kane. We have no idea how many machines we may be up against."

Rad pulled at his bottom lip. "There's still the New York connection. If Kane's dream is going to come true, it sounds like the gateway only operates in one direction now. We don't know how long we have before we have another army knocking on the door. But if New York is still there, maybe there's a way of getting in touch with Nimrod."

The Captain looked up at Rad, his small eye wet and bright.

"Actually–"

"Mass detection," said Byron, his voice booming out across the flight deck.

Kane and Rad looked at each other. The Captain looked at the ceiling.

"Byron, report!"

"Units approaching Grand Central from all sides."

Rad looked at the Captain. "Units?"

"Confirmed." Byron's voice rang out in the cabin from everywhere. "Grand Central is surrounded by robots."

They stood outside on a large balcony, in front of one of the great arched windows that allowed light to fall into the main concourse. Rad brushed the frost off the glass and peered inside; the concourse floor looked a very long way down.

There was a railing in front of them; Carson stood at it like a general surveying a battlefield, complete with binoculars. Rad noticed that when the Captain brought them up to his eyes, he flipped up the eye patch.

Rad didn't need to use the binoculars to see the problem.

The streets were filled with machine soldiers – the perfect, silver models that Rad and Jennifer had found hidden in Cliff's warehouse. The King had activated his army, and red eyes shining in the night they marched slowly, in perfect step, towards the building on all sides.

Kane shook his head. "How many of them are there?"

The Captain lowered the binoculars, his eye patch flapping against his cheek. "Hundreds, certainly. Thousands, perhaps. The entire robot army may have awakened."

"To get Kane back," said Rad. "They need his power."

The Captain nodded. "Indeed."

Rad looked down the street, Park Avenue, heading south. Grand Central was a roadblock, the avenue splitting into two around it. In front of them was a square, into which jutted half a bridge, connecting Grand Central with thin air, the unfinished end coming to an abrupt halt one hundred yards out.

The square was filled with robots, as was the street that ran horizontally across the front of the square in both directions. If this was the southern aspect, then Rad imagined it would be worse on the other side of the building. They were totally surrounded.

"Can they get in?" he asked.

"No," said the Captain. "Or at least not for some time. I had this building fortified, but I did not expect to face an army of robots."

"What about the police? Surely they can't have missed this?"

Carson tugged his beard. "As with the general populace, I imagine they are keeping well away. There were not many left. My fault, I'm afraid. So eager was I to change the city that I fear I may have weakened its defenses."

Kane stepped forward and looked back at the building, leaning to see the dark sky directly above. The perpetual cloud was very high, barely visible, the cold almost pushing it away from the city. Kane pointed up. "Can we fly out in the Nimrod?"

"Possibly," said the Captain. "If they haven't blocked the tunnel exit."

Rad pulled at Carson's shoulder to turn the old man around. Rad pointed at robots out in the street, the square. They were eerily quiet, just a low-level ticking and thrumming disturbing the cold night.

"We can't stop them, can we?" said Rad. "Four people and one ghost against that lot. And even if we could get out, and gather up all the police and all the agents we could, we can't deal with this. There is a whole damn army. We can't face this alone."

Carson frowned. "What are you suggesting, Mr Bradley?"

Rad sighed. "I mentioned Nimrod before, and you were going to say something. Do you know how to contact him, with the Fissure gone?"

Kane joined them. "What if Nimrod isn't in charge anymore? What if my vision comes true? We'll have two robot armies going to war."

Rad waved a hand. "Maybe, but we don't know for sure, do we? Not unless we can get through to Nimrod and find out. They've got resources, people. If anyone can help us it's got to be Nimrod and the others in New York."

Carson tugged his beard, and turned to Jennifer. She was

leaning across the railing, scanning the crowd.

"You're very quiet, Ms Jones."

"I'm looking for him."

"James? The real King of 125th Street?"

"Yes," she said. "Maybe he's here, leading his army. Maybe we can talk to him, make him understand."

Kane shifted and folded his arms. He looked at Rad, and Rad had a bad feeling.

"Yeah," he said. "Maybe. But let's keeping work on plan A. Captain?"

Carson nodded, and was about to speak when a voice came up from the street below.

"Your new friends can't help you, Jenny."

Jennifer raced back to the railing, the others on her tail. In the street below, the robots parted in a clatter, forming a corridor between their ranks, allowing another of their kind: tall, silver and shining, new, different. Upgraded. Rad peered down at the machine.

"Is that Elektro?"

Jennifer shook her head. "No, it can't be…"

The silver robot laughed, its voice reverberating around the streets until it came from every direction at once. It held its arms out as it addressed the group on the balcony of Grand Central. "Elektro was the first. He was a test, a metal man, my creation.

"I am James Jones, the King of 125th Street, and I am the second."

THIRTY-EIGHT

They stood in the center of the Grand Central concourse, the four of them, as all around, from every door, every window, came the sound of the robots resuming their slow march on the building. Hundreds of perfect machine men, programmed for warfare, commanded by a man who had become like them.

The concourse was cavernous and Rad felt very small indeed. The sound of the chaos outside was an ocean of noise, echoing, reverberating around the hard marble surfaces of the giant room.

They were stuck. Rad sighed and rolled his shoulders.

"New York. Nimrod," he said. "It's the only way. Can you do it, Carson?"

The Captain hrmmed and glanced at Kane. "Mr Fortuna, how much functionality does the Skyguard's suit have remaining?"

Kane looked down at himself, and raised his arms. The suit was really only the inner lining of the Skyguard's original armor, a tight leathery jumpsuit with slots and catches where the rest of the suit was supposed to fit.

"It's keeping me alive," said Kane from behind the plain black faceplate. "The King – James – must have been using it dead, because it's feeding off my energy now."

Carson nodded. "And if you breached the suit... for example, near the wrist." The Captain lifted one hand and

250

flexed it, showing the heel of his palm to Kane.

Kane nodded. "If I breach the suit, then the energy of the Fissure would leak out..."

Carson smiled. "Indeed. A small gap, just so, and you could direct the energy." The Captain glanced up at the constellations in the ceiling. "And more than that, if you concentrate, feel the power within you, understand how it flows... perhaps you could fly, without the rocket boosters."

Rad watched the two of them with growing alarm.

"Mr Fortuna," Carson said. "You are one with the Fissure now. If you concentrate, focus, you can control it. We need your help. Now."

Kane nodded and took a step back, shaking his arms like he was about to do the clean and jerk. He held his head up and Rad could hear his breathing heavy behind the mask. As he watched, the familiar blue glow of the Fissure began creeping out around Kane's body, forming a faint but clear aura. Rad glanced down, and saw Kane was floating an inch above the floor.

Carson clapped. "Capital, Mr Fortuna. We need you to hold the robots at bay, for just a short time. I have work to do. Do you understand?"

Kane nodded, and lifted a little further from the floor. Before Rad could say anything, Kane looked down, took a breath, and shot a full six feet in the air. He laughed.

"This is going to take some getting used to."

Carson waved. "Off you go!"

Rad whistled. "You gotta teach me that trick someday, pal."

Kane laughed as he bobbed in the air. "Sure thing. Teach you over breakfast tomorrow." He gave a mock salute, and rose in the air in a graceful curve, so high he almost touched the star field on the ceiling. Then he dived down, and shot out through one of the great arched windows. The glass exploded, and the sound of the robots outside was suddenly so loud that Rad ducked instinctively. Light flashed outside the window: blue and white, the kind that made Rad's eyes hurt. The power of the Fissure.

"You've turned Kane into a weapon?"

Carson nodded, his smile tight. "So long as the Fissure remains within him, yes."

"And when it isn't?"

"When it isn't, he'll be dead," said the Captain flatly, before turning to Jennifer. "That silver gun, the one I saw Mr Bradley waving around with such panache but such little effect. If my plan is to succeed, I need to repair it." He held out his hand.

Jennifer stepped closer to him, ignoring the hand. "Kane will kill my brother."

The Captain tutted and rubbed his forehead like a particularly exasperated teacher.

"My dear young lady, your brother's actions have put the city at risk. I fear there is little hope for him now – although believe me, I will do my best."

"But–"

Carson put his hand on her shoulder. "Trust me, like I trust Kane. Now, if you so please?"

Jennifer and the Captain stood face to face, eye to eye, until Jennifer sighed. "It's in the ship."

"Splendid," said the Captain. "Now, the pair of you, listen. I don't know how long it will take, but I will need you close at hand."

Rad sighed. "How long it will take for what?"

"To the ship," the Captain called over his shoulder as he hobbled away. "Back to the Nimrod."

Jennifer had been pacing for minutes, walking from one side of the cabin to the other, reaching out and touching the wall as she completed each length, her golden face inclined to the floor. Rad didn't blame her. He had no idea what was going through her mind, but the situation was tight and her brother – the brother she had been so desperately searching for – was right in the middle of it all.

Rad stood by the door, his arms folded tightly. He breathed out, trying to relax, but his body was reacting to Jennifer's barely contained frustration.

"Any luck?"

Captain Carson mumbled, bent over the control console, Jennifer's weapon spread out in little bits in front of him.

"What was the plan, again?" Rad asked. "Because I sure as hell don't remember you telling us."

Carson said something unintelligible, and with a sigh and a roll of the eyes, Rad pushed himself off the wall.

"Look–"

The Nimrod rocked, and Jennifer came to a halt. The Captain hissed as a screwdriver rolled to the edge of the console.

Rad looked at the ceiling. "Another earth tremor?"

Carson nodded. Jennifer stomped to the main door and hit the control next to it. The door whined, but remained closed. Jennifer spun around.

"James is in danger." She advanced on Carson. "Let me out, dammit. We have to talk to him, make him see reason."

"I'm afraid he is beyond reason," said Carson, turning back to his work. Rad noticed he had the eye patch flipped up. "I am delighted you chose this particular weapon to steal from the Empire State Building, however. Most opportune."

Rad looked at Jennifer. "You really think you can talk to him? Get through to him, somehow?"

"Of course," she said. "He's still James, whatever you and the Captain might think."

Rad rubbed his head. "See, thing is, he was planning to turn us both into robots. He even made a start on you and now he's done it to himself."

"Maybe that's the only way to survive," she said.

"Maybe I'll take my chances."

"You ever thought that it's his fault?" said Jennifer. She jerked her thumb at Carson. "He invented the things in the first place."

Rad shook his head. "Ancient history. Meanwhile, your brother has sent the works to come get us."

"Our friendly detective is quite right," said Carson, face still in his delicate repair work. "James needs the Fissure to continue his work. We all need it to survive, of course. The robots will not stop until they have Kane back." Carson leaned closer to the console, and Rad heard a sharp click. "Aha!" said the Captain, sitting back to admire his handiwork.

"That's it," said Jennifer. She marched to the console, brushing the Captain's tools off as she searched for the locking mechanism. The Captain made to stop her, but she pushed him clean off the pilot's chair. He hit the floor awkwardly, his wooden leg unable to provide enough purchase to regain his footing.

"Hey!" Rad rushed forward to help the Captain, but Jennifer pushed him back. She found the switch releasing the lock, and the cabin's door slid open. She quickly turned and made for the exit, but Rad grabbed her arm, swinging her back around to face him. She struggled, but Rad was stronger.

"You can't go out there," said Rad. "At least not until the Captain fills us in on his plan."

Jennifer screamed, and pulled at her arm. It came free from Rad's grip but she fell to the floor. As she scrambled to her feet, Rad darted forward, but she kicked out. Rad stepped neatly to one side, avoiding her boot, and grabbed her arm again.

"Get the hell off me!"

Rad gritted his teeth and held firm, but Jennifer didn't let up. The two struggled in the middle of the flight deck.

The Captain tutted. "Please, Mr Bradley, Ms Jones."

Rad turned to look at the Captain and felt Jennifer yank herself away. Then all he could see was the barrel of Jennifer's gun, now pointed right at him. He held up a hand.

"Captain, this is becoming a habit."

"My dear friend, I really am sorry."

"No!" Jennifer screamed, and lurched forward. Distracted, Rad tried to dive out of the way, but it was too late. Carson pulled the trigger, and the universe evaporated in a blaze of white and blue light, Jennifer's cry still ringing in Rad's ears.

PART THREE
FEARFUL ENGINES

"I am become Death, the destroyer of worlds."
– Quote misattributed to J. Rober
Oppenheimer, on witnessing the
successful Trinity nuclear test,
July 16th, 1945

"It worked."
– Eyewitness account of what he actually said

THIRTY-NINE

The room was large and hot, that much Nimrod could tell with the black bag still on his head. He was bound hand and foot in a wheelchair. Underneath the cloth the sweat poured off him.

They'd drugged him again, just before the last transport, just enough to keep him quiet and still. It had been a plane this time; they'd put him in a wheelchair and he'd banged the base of his skull against the back as they rolled him up a ramp and into the heart of the beast.

Military, of course. It all was. Standard procedure for moving important and dangerous prisoners. He hadn't expected such rough treatment, but clearly the influence of Atoms for Peace stretched very far indeed. And now they had made their move, taking over the Department, making the inconvenient Captain Nimrod disappear. A new regime was required to control New York, to control the Fissure, and what lay beyond.

There were people in the room; Nimrod could hear their breathing, then a couple of coughs, and some paper shuffling. There were footsteps too, which stopped and started and then stopped again with precision. Military police. Through the bag Nimrod could smell wood and paper and the familiar musty tang of hot venetian blinds and dust. They were in a government building, in a big room. Throw in the plane trip and Nimrod suspected he'd been shipped to Washington, DC. Which meant…

The black bag was pulled off sharply, and Nimrod blinked in the light. He squinted and turned his head, his eyes adjusting enough to see the white helmets of the military police around him, and beyond, shuttered windows leaking in pale daylight. Nimrod's face was damp with sweat but he suspected the men seated in front of him were not at their most comfortable either.

His wheelchair was in the center of the room, in front of a large raised semicircle of dark wood. There were twelve men seated behind the curved expanse; they sat high, their faces in shadow, as they looked down at their prisoner.

The shadows did not hide them completely. Of the round dozen, half were military, their buttons and badges gleaming despite the gloom, a variety of peaked caps arranged on the wood before them. The others were in suits, their faces flaring in the light as they leaned forwards or backwards to whisper to their neighbors. Nimrod recognized some, guessed others. Senators Mackenzie and MacNamara; some officious oaf he'd dealt with at the DoD once or twice too often; Wagner from the FBI; Grimwood from the CIA; two others he thought he knew. The rest were doing a better job of staying in the dark. Nimrod closed his eyes and barked a laugh, and when he opened his eyes again some of the people had shifted and the whispering had stopped.

"Do you find this amusing, Captain Nimrod?"

Nimrod focused on the man directly in front of him. He recognized the voice instantly: his old foe, the Secretary of Defense. Beside him was another military man, a general by the name of Hall, Nimrod thought. The General was rotating a pen between his fingers and the half of his face that was in the light looked nervous and twitchy.

"My dear Secretary," said Nimrod, "there is much I find amusing in this world, but let me assure you that this situation has gone beyond the comedic and into the farcical. Now, if you would be so kind as to release me, I shall go directly to the White House and have a little chat with that President of yours."

The Secretary seemed to tick something off a piece of paper in front of him. "You're a funny man, Nimrod."

Nimrod smiled tightly. "I think you'll find I have the authority to do precisely as I please, which includes dissolving this committee and, I might add, expelling each of you from your posts."

"That authority has been rescinded," said the Secretary, "as has your rank."

Nimrod kept his smile tight. Atoms for Peace had done a good job. They'd even got to the President, it seemed. Nimrod wondered if their Director was watching now.

The Secretary turned a page over in the dark. General Hall twitched again. Then the Secretary spoke.

"You are a Communist spy placed here by Soviet Russia in order to subvert departmental operations and gain control of the Fissure."

Nimrod sniffed. "Is that really the best you can do? Even McCarthy was better than that."

"You will be taken from this committee and held until a military tribunal is convened to pass sentence. That is all."

"I want to speak to the President."

The Secretary made another tick. "You have no such right."

"I want to speak to Evelyn McHale."

At this the chairman paused and the committee began to murmur, the sound like bees trapped in a jar. It was only General Hall and the Secretary who did not join the gossip. As Nimrod watched, Hall raised a hand to rub his forehead. Even in the bad light, from his position below the committee, Nimrod could see Hall's hand shake.

The Secretary's silhouette nodded.

"Take him away."

The military police on either side of Nimrod snapped to attention, and a second later Nimrod's world went black as the bag was replaced.

FORTY

The eyes under the bed, the something evil in the closet, the creaking floor downstairs. The darkness moved, becoming thick, alive, intelligent, something from somewhere else. And then the pressure on the chest, someone holding him down, someone pulling the covers off and

"No!"

The woman lying next to Fulton Hall shrieked as the general sat bolt upright in bed, his skin shining with a cold sweat, his fingers clutching the sheet to his chest. He ignored her, unaware even of her presence, as he breathed and breathed and breathed, his eyes searching the corners of the bedroom, his nostrils flaring like he'd just run the New York marathon.

The woman slid her bottom up against the headboard and reached out to grab her lover's shoulders, but he flinched at the touch and she quickly drew her hands back, using them instead to pull the yanked sheet tight to her neck.

"What's wrong? Did you have a nightmare?"

Hall heard her voice, somewhere in the back of his mind, but his attention was drawn to the closet, to the gap between the bottom of the door and the thick carpet. The gap was a black strip of nothing in the dark room, but when Hall blinked it flashed blue, light, the color of the sky on a hot summer's day. The light at the end of things. The light that burned in her eyes.

Hall flinched again as Mary flicked on her bedside light, and he turned in the bed, face red, vein in his forehead pounding, ready to unleash his rage on his mistress. But as she shrank back the feeling evaporated, replaced by a creeping cold somewhere in Hall's chest. The whole bedroom felt like an icebox.

"Fulton?" Mary's voice was small, timid.

He let out a breath. "I'm fine. It was a bad dream, that's all."

He turned away, drawn once more to the gap under the closet door. Mary said something but he didn't hear it, but her light went out and she turned over, leaving Hall to contemplate the darkness. He listened to her breathing a while, listened to her as she lay perfectly awake, terrified in the middle of the night.

Terrified? Hall sniffed and lay back down. What did she have to fear? She'd been there, at the test. She's seen her. She knew too, she had to.

Hall lay still, as still as he could, as he watched the closet. War, she'd said. War was coming. Well, that was his job. He was a soldier. War was his business.

But… but there was no pleasure to be had in war. Satisfaction, yes. Perhaps even ambition. But war was not a thing to be enjoyed, or savored. And the way she had said it, like she was appreciating a fine vintage wine. She was looking forward to it, the woman who didn't even exist in the same world as the rest of them.

Hall blinked, his eyes dry. The gap under the closet door remained black this time.

She was going to destroy the world. He knew that now. Mankind didn't matter to her. The test, out there in the harbor, it wasn't for him, it was for her. She had to be sure the device would work, not for anyone's benefit except her own.

What did she fear, if not the end of the world? Hall gulped a lungful of air that was too cold and Mary moved beside him, clearly listening, waiting for him to fall asleep.

Nimrod. She feared Nimrod, so much so that she'd had him removed, using her puppet, the Secretary of Defense. Nimrod was the final obstacle, that had to be it.

He knew what he had to do now. She'd said he would have a part to play, and play it he would. Only there was a chance, he knew, to defy her, to control his own destiny. She could be stopped. He couldn't do it, but Nimrod could. He held the key.

She would be angry, of course. The wrath of a goddess. Hall pulled the sheets to his chin, his body folding into a fetal position beneath the covers as he watched the closet. If he could save the world, it wouldn't matter. He could stop her. He could also... escape from her.

Hall swept the covers off and stood. Mary turned in the bed and watched him, but she remained silent.

He felt relief and he felt a calmness, like he was floating in a warm bath. He moved to the closet, and with a final look at the gap beneath the door, opened it and took his uniform from where it hung on the back.

"You're leaving? I thought you said you would stay the night."

Hall paused only a moment, then slipped the jacket off the hanger.

"Sorry," he said, knowing she wouldn't press any further. He heard her move on the bed, but he didn't turn around. He thought he should perhaps say goodbye, say it properly, explain everything, but knew that she could be watching, listening. He had to act now, quickly.

Dressed, he picked his cap off the dresser and turned back to Mary. She looked at him with wide eyes that glistened wetly in the dark, and he thought of the blue light that spun in the eyes of Evelyn McHale. And he thought of how he would be free at last.

He said goodbye, said he loved her, and closed the bedroom door behind him.

As Mary turned over, in the gap between the bottom of the closet door and the thick carpet, a blue light shone.

FORTY-ONE

It was cooler in the holding cell, which was a relief. Gone were the bag and the shackles, allowing Nimrod some small comfort, at least.

He couldn't sleep. He paced the cell, a space hardly more than twelve feet by ten, his eyes on the cement floor, watching the toes of his boots. They were scuffed, and the boots – knee-high riding boots, his particular favorites brought with him from England thirty or more years ago – needed a clean, a wax and polish. He paused in his pacing and examined the toes of the left. The leather was thin, worn. Maybe he needed a new pair. If he ever left the cell.

He began to pace again. How many hours he had been kept locked up, he wasn't sure, but dawn was just a couple hours away.

He knew his arrest and incarceration was most likely illegal, the charges certainly fabricated, the whole charade engineered to remove him cleanly and without fuss. Rather than a straightforward disappearance, the accusations of Communist leanings and his subsequent public confession would be used to shut him and the Department down, allowing Atoms for Peace to step in and take over the whole operation, lock, stock and barrel. Controlling New York, controlling the Fissure. The Director would have what she apparently needed to enact her terrifying plan: access to the Fissure, unimpeded.

Nimrod paused as someone walked past his cell. The door had a small square window, which was shut, but the relatively thin metal of the cover allowed sound to penetrate the cell admirably. Although he hadn't been able to see anything through the black bag when he'd been brought in, he imagined the corridors outside the cell swarming with MPs.

Nimrod chewed on a thumbnail. He had to see the President. While it was clear the Director had got to him, the President was a good man and an old friend. And even if he was dazzled by the wonders that Atoms for Peace – the very organization the President had created – could offer him and the country, he would listen, Nimrod was sure of it. Nimrod's position within the hierarchy of government was unique; his influence spread far and wide. He could not be ignored.

However, time was running out. They would remove him quickly. He doubted there would be a military tribunal – on paper, certainly, records could be created, a transcript composed. But Nimrod knew that the next journey would be to the gas chamber or the electric chair, whichever was available in DC for the federal death penalty.

More footsteps outside. Their volume increased; then they stopped. Nimrod turned. Either it was time to be fed, or this was it. The Department would be no more; he would be executed while federal agents and MPs massed at the Empire State Building, arrested all agents, consigned every file in the office to sealed secure document boxes for burial in the Nevada desert.

Keys in the door, loud, taking forever. Nimrod thought of the old days, the freedom of flying his airship across the polar skies.

The door was opened by an MP, who smartly stepped back to allow an officer in. The door remained open as General

Hall ventured inside the cell and removed his hat. Beyond, Nimrod could see two MPs waiting outside in profile, each staring at the other's nose.

Hall saluted, and Nimrod found himself doing the same.

"Captain Nimrod, I'm here to ask you one question and one question only. I hope you'll answer me truthfully and that you won't take much time about it, because time is the one damned thing that the whole world is running out of. Do you understand me?"

Nimrod could swear the General spoke with a slight slur, but he couldn't smell a thing on the man's breath. He looked Hall up and down, remembering the officer was responsible for the most terrible of weapons the United States had at its disposal. General Hall talking about time running out didn't fill Nimrod with confidence.

Nimrod's mustache rolled above his upper lip. "Is that the question, or is there another one coming?"

General Hall's right eye twitched, the nervous tic so severe it almost closed his eye entirely.

"What?" Hall's voice was high, fast. Something was playing on his mind.

Nimrod looked Hall in the eye. "Are you working with Evelyn McHale?"

The General flinched as though Nimrod had slapped him, and Nimrod could see his eyes fill with tears.

Then the General smiled widely, like a used car salesman who has found his mark, like a lover over a conquest, like a killer with his finger on the trigger. Nimrod had seen that smile before. The smile of the insane.

"I... met her. She..."

The General closed his eyes, pinching the bridge of his nose between forefinger and thumb. Nimrod watched as the general shook his head like he was punch drunk. Then the officer sucked in a wet breath and spoke.

"Can you stop her?" he asked, his eyes still closed.

Nimrod frowned. "Are you feeling quite well, general?"

Hall's eyes snapped opened and with his free hand he grabbed Nimrod's lapel.

"Just answer the damn question, Nimrod!"

Nimrod glanced down at the hand gripping his jacket. Then, slowly, he uncurled the General's fingers himself. Out in the corridor, the two MPs were ignoring a conversation well above their pay grade.

"Perhaps," said Nimrod, keeping his voice calm, quiet, not because of the MPs outside, but because he could see Hall was fighting against her. He had seen it many times; contact with the Director of Atoms for Peace could break a mind. General Hall had been changed, and he would not be the same again. The only question now was what form Hall's madness would take, whether he could hold out just long enough.

The General muttered something, and his eyes closed again as he nodded furiously like a child. And then he blinked and straightened up, the model officer. He snapped a salute and Nimrod could see it in his eyes, the spinning blue of eternity, the light of the Fissure.

The General called to the MPs over his shoulder. Nimrod heard their boots snap on the cement floor and the pair marched in.

General Hall looked Nimrod up and down. "Take the prisoner to helipad five. Transport is waiting."

One of the MPs glanced at his companion, doubt passing over his face. The other's eyes flicked between the General and Nimrod. But for both of them, years of military life had ingrained the chain of command.

"Sir," said the first MP, before taking Nimrod by the arm and pulling him towards the cell door. The reluctant MP paused a moment, almost as though he was waiting for a second order from the General, one that fit their earlier instructions regarding the prisoner.

The General smiled, and Nimrod saw the corners of his mouth flecked with white foam.

"Where are we going, General Hall?"

"New York, of course. Sergeant, secure your prisoner. Let's roll."

They were alone together in the helicopter. General Hall was a fine pilot, and Nimrod sat next to him in the cockpit, headphones on, watching the officer at the controls. The flight from DC to Manhattan took an hour and a half, and during that time the General remained silent except for the required radio communications.

If Nimrod's removal from the holding cells had been unauthorized, nobody appeared to have noticed, at least not while General Hall and the two MPs led him, unchained, unbagged, through the facility. There were several checkpoints and guarded doorways, but at each the personnel on duty merely saluted and let the General through without delay, without a glance at his charge.

At the helicopter, the General dismissed the MPs and invited Nimrod into the cockpit. Nimrod supposed that, by now, the MPs would have reported the General's activity to their superiors and all hell would be breaking loose in the office of someone important, but there was nothing on the radio except air traffic, and as the lights of Manhattan crept into view, they hadn't yet been approached by any aircraft sent to apprehend them.

Nimrod didn't speak, not daring to distract the General, knowing the officer was concentrating not only on the complex task of flying the helicopter but on fighting against her influence, an influence spreading inside him like a cancer.

But as they flew over Manhattan, towards the Empire State Building, Nimrod judged the time was right.

"Why did you release me, General? You were at the committee meeting. I'm a Communist spy according to the US Government, and what you are doing is most certainly treason. We're both for the gas chamber now."

"You still don't see it, do you?" said the General, his voice bursting with static, the microphone on his headset too close to his lips. "She's going to destroy us, destroy everything."

Nimrod sighed. "And you think I can stop her?"

The General pulled the helicopter around into a tight turn, forcing Nimrod against him. Nimrod saw they were now coming in to approach one of the helipads on the Empire State Building.

"Who else is there? You're the only one she fears. There has to be a reason for that."

Nimrod looked at him and frowned. "And what about you? She will be watching. She may fear me, but you, well, you've interfered. You won't be able to escape her."

The General shook his head as he eased the chopper closer, preparing to set down.

"That's all taken care of, don't worry. Your job is to stop her. She's going to destroy not just this world, but all of them. I think you know what I mean."

Nimrod's eyes went wide. "So that's why she wants access to the Fissure–"

The General looked at him for the first time in the flight. "Yes. She's getting ready to send an army through. That army will destroy everything. *Everything*. She's got to be stopped."

As soon as he spoke, the General winced, his shoulders hunched, and the helicopter wobbled as it hovered. Then he shook his head and nodded, and returned his attention to their destination. The helicopter bobbed in the wind, then slid sideways in the air and touched down on the helipad that protruded on the west side of the setback at the Empire State Building's eighty-first floor.

Nimrod wondered how far they were going to get once inside the building. A handful of personnel were at the helipad, the usual staff and three of the department's agents, two attempting to smoke in the stiff wind.

Nimrod released his harness and swung himself out of the helicopter. He turned to talk to the General, but the General was still sitting where he was, hands on the controls.

"General?" Nimrod had to yell over the noise of the rotors.

Hall flicked a switch and they began to wind down. Then he turned to Nimrod and shook his head. "Go, and do what needs to be done. My fate is elsewhere."

Nimrod waited, but the General didn't move. Arguing with the man was pointless, Nimrod knew that.

"As you like," said Nimrod, but he said it quietly and he wasn't sure if the General heard.

Turning on his heel, head instinctively bowed against the slowing blades of the helicopter seven feet above him, Nimrod jogged across the helipad, gesturing to the three waiting agents to join him inside.

The view was spectacular. Manhattan glowed in the night, a thousand million jewels in the damp air. And beyond, New Jersey on one side, Long Island the other, and seven million people between. The wind had died down, even up here, nearly nine hundred feet from the street below.

Nobody had stopped him. The helicopter was hardly discrete, and there were few people on top of the building; those who were there knew who he was, or at least recognized his rank.

Nobody had stopped him as he walked to the edge of the

helipad and jumped the railing until he was standing on the edge of the setback, the lip of forever, arms outstretched, toes of his immaculate black shoes poking out over the edge. The stonework was clean, like new, too high for most birds to settle, although plenty would be flying overhead during the day. General Hall shuffled a little to his left, and raised his chin to the breeze.

Then he opened his eyes, and he could see forever. No, more than that, he could see beyond, to worlds unknown, to the Fissure, to the Empire State, to lands yet undiscovered.

And he could see her. He smiled and blinked, and watched as the glowing blue woman hovered in the air six feet out over the edge, nothing but endless air beneath her feet. So, she'd come, despite the fact that this was the Empire State Building, the place of her death and the place of her birth. It pained her to be here, he knew.

Their eyes met. He smiled; she didn't.

"You're too late," he said. His heart soared, and his head felt like it was filled with helium. He felt like he could do anything in the world. He felt like he could fly.

The Ghost of Gotham said nothing, but floated backwards, slowly, her blue glow fading, her expression flat. But her eyes... oh, there was such light there, light that was blue and spun like diamonds. She knew. She knew.

General Hall closed his eyes, and held his breath, and jumped.

The Director watched him fall, and then she was gone.

FORTY-TWO

The floor was cold and smooth. Rad could feel it against his cheek, against his hands. With his chest pressed to it, the cold had seeped into his skin like damp in an old house. When he opened his eyes, he saw that the floor was white, streaked with black veins. Marble. He closed his eyes again and wished he would die so the buzz-saw vibration in his head would leave him in peace. Even with his eyes closed, the darkness spun around him. Stretched out on the hard floor, he felt like he was tied to a gyroscope set on high, the ground rolling and bucking as it attempted to throw its unwanted occupant off.

Then the buzzing died a little, and Rad felt his chest tighten with adrenaline as he remembered what the feeling meant. He'd experienced it before, only that time he'd been wearing a mask to help alleviate the worst of the symptoms.

Rad opened his eyes, gritting his teeth against the nausea, and pulled his chin across the floor to look up.

They were in New York.

There were boots nearby, tall with black pants tucked into them. From somewhere above a voice came, annoyed, impatient.

"Hey, buddy, wake up!"

Rad blinked, but when his eyes reopened there were more of the black boots. He'd passed out, maybe only for a second, he couldn't tell. He tried a breath. It was OK, but it made his head spin. Crossing into the Origin without a mask... damn, it hurt. He wasn't going to be much use for anything for a while, that much he did know.

Carson. Dammit. Which also meant...

Rad turned his head, ignoring the way his cheek tugged on the cold floor. Next to him was another prone form, a long bundle of green winter coat topped with long brown hair. Special Agent Jennifer Jones, out for the count, her golden mask facing away. The men around them – the police – were in for quite a surprise if they hadn't seen her already.

Two hands under his armpits and Rad was on his knees. He sagged between the officers as the world spun, his breathing rasped, his eyeballs two red-hot coals. He felt the tears stream down his face. He blinked to clear his vision.

They were in Grand Central, back on the main concourse. It looked the same, although there were features not present in Carson's version – a big, long kiosk not quite in the center of the space, and signs with arrows. Grand Central in New York City was clearly in full use.

The middle of the space seemed to be sectioned off by police tape reaching right to the wide sweeping stairs that rose up on either side of the concourse. Beyond the tape more cops corralled people – lots of people, in hats and coats, holding newspapers and briefcases and umbrellas; people talking to each other, talking to cops who shook their heads, people craning to look and see what the commotion was; men and woman and children holding hands.

Then Rad closed his eyes and let himself hang between the cops, the sensory overload threatening to pummel him into unconsciousness again.

He could guess what had happened. He and Jennifer had popped into existence right in the middle of the concourse, right in the middle of all the people who were now crowding around the police line.

That would have been quite a surprise for the good people of Manhattan.

"Hey, hey," said a voice. Rad opened his eyes and found a scowling policeman clicking his fingers in his face. Rad flinched, each snap like being hit on the back of the head with a rubber mallet.

The officer backed away, and one of his colleagues leaned in for a pow-wow.

"Are they drunk?"

"Or worse."

"Call said they'd just appeared out of thin air."

"Call also said my mother is the Queen of England. Come on."

Rad opened his eyes. The police reapplied their grip, and he was on his feet.

"And her."

Rad struggled to stay alert. He watched as more cops tiptoed towards Jennifer, each of them with one hand on his gun. After shaking her gingerly, satisfied that she wasn't going to leap up and knife them, they holstered their weapons and rolled her over.

"Jesus H Christ!" said the first officer. The second just shook his head, and put his hands on his hips. Then he shook his head again and waved over the scowling cop.

"What the hell?"

The scowling cop reached for Jennifer, but then Jennifer moved. In one quick motion she was on her feet, and she spun around, the long split tail of her winter coat spiraling out around her like a fancy ball gown. She turned, and looked left and right and all around, her golden metal face bright in the lights of Grand Central, her gloved hands out on each side, fingers splayed, ready for a fight.

The cops were fast too, forming a circle, a dozen guns

pointed at her, a dozen voices commanding her to stand still, to give up, to lie down, to get down, to not move lady, to freeze right there. The circle moved, expanding outwards, the cops circling, not sure what they were dealing with.

Then Jennifer seemed to see Rad and she stopped turning and moved towards him, causing another round of shouting. The cops holding Rad up dragged him back a step, and then someone took the initiative and tackled Jennifer from behind. She fell with a cry, her metal face connecting with the hard floor with a surprisingly loud and bright sound, and then a cop put his knee in the small of her back and she was handcuffed and Rad passed out.

When Rad woke again he felt better, although his throat was as dry as sandpaper and his nostrils were filled with the scent of old urine and damp concrete. The surface below him was still hard but Rad could feel slats underneath the naked skin of his head. He was on a narrow wooden bench in a small room.

He swung himself over the edge, his head pounding but bearable, mostly. The buzzing behind his eyeballs flared with the sudden movement but quickly reduced to a constant pressure rather than a panic-inducing pain.

Rad looked around. He was in a cell, and he was on his own.

"Rad?"

Rad jerked around at the voice. There was a grill high in the wall behind him. He stood on the bench, which creaked beneath his weight, and looked through.

"Gah!" Rad pulled back and nearly fell off the bench, and then he gripped the edge of the window with his fingers and pulled himself back up. Jennifer's golden face was six inches from his behind four thick grey metal bars.

"You're OK," she said, and there was relief in her voice

even if her artificial face was unable to show emotion.

"We're in New York," said Rad.

"I noticed."

Jennifer's mask tilted a little, quizzical. "Are you feeling OK?"

"Apart from a sore head and a little difficulty breathing, just fine and dandy, thanks. But last I remember that damn fool Carson was shooting at me with the honking big ray gun of yours."

Jennifer chuckled. "'Ray gun.' I like it."

Rad waved his hand. "Whatever. You're holding something back on that thing. The only time I saw you use it was when you shot at that silver robot, the one that called itself Elektro. Blew half of it away, as I recall."

Jennifer shook her head. "Only because I missed. I borrowed the gun from the Empire State Building when everything went crazy."

"Borrowed?" said Rad.

"Borrowed."

"Go on," said Rad.

"It's the same kind of technology used by Nimrod's Department here in New York to send agents across the Fissure, but while out in the field. Only modified. Improved."

Rad frowned. "To be used as a weapon?"

"Kinda," said Jennifer. "It sends the target through the Fissure, but not necessarily to New York."

"Where else is there?"

"Oh, nowhere in particular. That's the point."

"Ah," said Rad as the penny dropped. "Neat. And I assume Carson made his own adjustment when he fixed it, to make sure it sent us here and not into the hereafter."

"Worked, didn't it?"

Rad rubbed the back of his neck. The effort of talking was bringing his headache back.

"Yeah, worked all right. Don't suppose you have an aspirin? How do you feel?"

Jennifer shrugged, and stepped back a little on her own bench. "Never better. I was out for the count, but I feel like I could take on an army right now."

Rad frowned. He wondered what the King of 125th Street – the real king, her own brother, masquerading as the King's robotic servant, the Corsair – had done to her that made her immune to the effects of being in an incompatible universe. He decided not to go there.

"Must be the mask," he said.

Jennifer nodded. "Must be." Then she turned quickly to face the door, and said in a low whisper: "Someone's coming."

Rad turned towards his own door.

"I don't hear–"

There was a heavy clank as his cell door was unlocked, and then it swung open on big hinges, oiled and silent. Two uniformed police stood in the corridor outside. They glanced at Rad standing on the bench, then up at the grill that connected the two cells. Then one of them scowled – it might have been the bad-tempered one from Grand Central, Rad couldn't be sure – and entered the cell.

"Time to talk, pal," he said, lifting his hand to reveal a set of cuffs.

Rad sighed. He hopped off the bed, holding out his wrists.

"Take me to your leader," he said, but the cop didn't get the joke.

"What kind of a name," asked the plainclothes cop, "is 'Rad', anyway?"

Rad sighed and drummed his fingers on the table. The interrogation was going nowhere and fast, for the both of them.

The cop took a drag on his cigarette and then squinted down at the paper on the table like he was changing a child's diaper. Periodically his eyes flicked up to Rad's, the expression unchanging. Another cop, also in a suit but without a cigarette, sat next to the first and didn't take his eyes off Rad.

"It's just a nickname," said Rad.

Another drag. "Short for something?"

Rad nodded. "Bradley."

A final suck of tobacco. "So let me get this straight," said the first cop, pausing to grin sideways at his companion. "You're telling me your name is Bradley Bradley?"

Rad sighed and stilled his restless fingers. "So now you see why I might chose to go by something a little shorter."

The first cop seemed to hold his breath. Then one eyebrow slowly went up and he nodded.

"That so?" he said, with the air of someone who didn't believe a word Rad was saying. Which, as far as Rad could tell, was the case.

Rad smiled sweetly. "Yes, that is so, officer."

The other cop adjusted his tie and took a deep breath. At this, his colleague sat back, pushing his wooden chair on the hard floor and making it squeak. He reached into his inside jacket pocket and pulled out the pack of cigarettes. Rad eyed them, enjoying the smell of the smoke but not knowing whether he really used to have a habit or whether he'd never smoked in his life. Being from the Empire State, it was a little hard to tell.

"Your name is Bradley Bradley," said the other cop, "and you're a private detective in a city called the Empire State, which exists inside a Pocket dimension connected to New York by a gateway–"

Rad nodded. "The Fissure."

The other cop smiled. "The Fissure, right. And this Empire

State is being overrun with robots, and you and your friend were sent here by another version of a man from New York who you think is in charge here, to figure out whether there's another army of robots being built to fight the first lot, because a friend of yours saw them in a dream, along with some broad with blue eyes."

Rad's eyebrow went up. He wasn't sure whether that deserved an answer, but he said "Correct" anyway.

The first cop lit another cigarette, and Rad's nostrils twitched at the curl of smoke as the cop waved the match out like his life depended on it.

"And then everyone will be ready for when the little green men arrive in their flying saucers?"

Rad sighed. "Look," he said, slowly, carefully. "I'm not crazy. I need to speak to Captain Nimrod."

"Oh, I don't think you're crazy," said the other cop. His smoking friend nodded behind his cloud. "Not crazy, no. A wino, though. How much have you had to drink today, buddy?"

Rad sighed in disbelief and sat back heavily in his chair. "Drinking?"

"You and your girlfriend were found in a heap in the middle of Grand Central Station, and before that, people said you was screaming. Caused a fuss. Someone said you was screaming about a gun; someone else thought you had a gun. We had to shut down the whole damn terminal because of you, and now you're telling me that the Martians are coming."

Rad closed his eyes and took a deep breath. "Nimrod. There's a government agent by the name of Nimrod. He knows me. He'll sort it out."

The first cop gasped in mock surprise. Then he nudged his colleague with his cigarette arm.

"Hey, Johnny, get this down, will ya?"

He leaned forward on his elbows across the table from Rad, and he took a drag on his cigarette. When he spoke his voice was a low, conspiratorial whisper.

"So, tell me, this Nimrod. He FBI? Or CIA? Or maybe – oh, he's not KGB, is he? That would be bad. But, no, you don't look like a Communist. Oh, I know!" the cop leaned back, triumphant. "He's P-I-T-A! Just like you are, buddy."

Rad shook his head and wondered whether he should ask for a cigarette.

Jennifer's cell was empty, and had been for a while. Rad sat on the bench, his fingers straying over his scalp. He missed his hat, presumably being held with his trench coat, scarf, and belt in a box somewhere nearby. His shoes were slip-on, so at least he'd been allowed to keep them. And it was warm in the cell, and the ground wasn't shaking.

Rad wondered how long it would take for the collapsing structure of the Pocket to start damaging the Origin. Maybe it would take a long time, given the difference in size between the two dimensions. Or perhaps it would happen all at once, catastrophically, both dimensions vanishing down an eternal plughole.

If the robot war didn't destroy both dimensions first, of course.

A series of footfalls sounded outside his cell, then kept going. Rad stood, and a moment later Jennifer was returned to the cell next door. Rad was on the bench, his face to the grill, almost immediately.

"What happened?"

Jennifer stood in her cell, stretching out what must have been a leg made stiff by sitting in the uncomfortable chair in the interrogation room. She glanced at Rad, and then continued to rub the top of her thigh.

"Nothing much. They asked a lot of questions, and I

answered all of them. They didn't seem that interested, just noted it all down."

"Huh," said Rad. "You were lucky. I got the wise guys. They didn't believe a word I said."

"Why are they holding us here, anyway?"

"Well," said Rad, and then he paused. Jennifer had a point. The questioning was a lot of bother for two people who were supposedly just drunks causing a scene.

"They haven't said anything about charges."

"No," said Rad. "They haven't. They're holding us for something, though."

"For what?"

Nimrod? Rad didn't dare hope. "They took down everything you said?"

Jennifer nodded.

"And you told them about being an agent in the Empire State, and about the robots and all that jazz?"

"And all that jazz, yes. The never-ending winter and the falling buildings and all."

"And they didn't say anything?"

"Only to ask more questions. Maybe they were distracted by this." Jennifer tapped a knuckle against a golden cheek.

Rad tugged at his bottom lip. "If only we could convince them to get hold of Nimrod. He'd get us out."

On cue, there was a sound at Rad's door. Rad heard Jennifer hopping up onto her bed to see into his cell as he stepped down from his bench and faced the door.

The cell was opened by a uniformed officer, not one Rad had seen before. He held the door open for a man in a brown suit and hat. The newcomer was built like a football quarterback with a thick, almost non-existent neck.

The man glanced at the policemen, then at Rad. "So, you coming or what?"

Rad smiled. "Agent Grieves, are you a sight for sore eyes."

Mr Grieves raised an eyebrow, a tiny smile flickering over his small mouth before vanishing without a trace.

"Yeah, swell to see you." He glanced at the cop again, then cleared his throat. He waved at Rad. "Now hurry up. We ain't got all day."

Detective Steven Sachs took the second-to-last cigarette from the pack, then stared at the solitary remaining smoke before squeezing the pack in his fist.

"Shit," he muttered, his fingers automatically fumbling for the box of matches in his jacket pocket. Box retrieved, he lit his cigarette and then waved the match out with his characteristic flourish.

Bryson pushed his chair out from his desk and turned it around to face his partner. He leaned back, placed his hands behind his head, and sniffed loudly. "One of those days, right?"

Sachs nodded, not looking up from the paperwork on his desk. "You got that right."

"Lot of paper for those two drunks?"

Sachs sucked his cigarette and shook his head. "They're being transferred. Look at this." He held up one of the sheets of paper. It was onionskin, a carbon copy, and when Bryson took it it nearly tore. Sachs watched as Bryson's eyes flicked over it before settling on the symbol at the top of the paper.

"Holy shit, this is from—"

"Yep," said Sachs, snatching the delicate document back again without much care.

"So that stuff about the government?"

"Yep," said Sachs. He pulled the typewriter on his desk towards him, adjusted the paper he'd carefully loaded just moments before, and selected a single key on the keyboard. There was a clack, and he leaned forward. "Ah, shit," he said, adjusting the paper again.

"Detective Sachs?"

"The one and only." Sachs didn't move, but when Bryson sat up straight in his chair with a clatter, he sighed, sucked on his cigarette, and turned around.

Three men were in the office, dressed in black suits and black ties. They were young, clean-shaved, and each wore a black hat. Sachs thought they looked like a trio of advertising copywriters from Madison Avenue. He looked them up and down and sighed.

"Can I help you?"

The first man in black smiled. "We're here to collect the fugitives."

Sachs sniffed. "Bradley Bradley and the girl with the party mask she refuses to take off? Be my guest, buddy."

The man's smile tightened a little. "Thank you."

"You're too well dressed to be FBI," said Sachs. "You CIA or NSA?"

"No," said the first man. "Now, if you would be so kind?"

Sachs and Bryson stood. The agents looked at Bryson, who smiled self-consciously and straightened his tie. Sachs coughed, long and hard, and pulled his jacket from the back of his chair.

"OK," he said. "Follow me."

Sachs slipped into his jacket as they walked. After a few steps he saw the desk sergeant walking towards them.

"Sergeant Ross," he said, the sergeant touching the brim of his hat and coming to a halt, expectant. Sachs indicated the three agents with him. "Those two in the cells, from Grand Central. We're handing them over to…" He frowned as he glanced at the first agent.

The first agent smiled and gave a small nod.

"…these guys," Sachs concluded.

"Sir?" The Sergeant switched the clipboard he was holding from one hand to another.

"We're handing them over to another authority. They ready to move?"

The sergeant looked at Sachs and pursed his lips. He glanced at the trio of agents, and peeled the top sheet on the clipboard back and folded it over.

"Something wrong, Sergeant?"

"They've already gone," said Ross, turning the clipboard around to show his superior. Sachs grabbed it and starting flipping through pages like he was a doctor surveying the chart of a dying man. "They were collected just fifteen minutes ago. An agent signed for them already."

The men in black crowded Sachs; he could feel their breath, smell their aftershave. He continued to scramble through the paperwork until the clipboard was snatched out of his hand by the first agent. The detective didn't protest, but in the silence that followed as the agent read the sheet he fixed Sergeant Ross with an angry glare.

"A Federal agent signed for it?" said the agent, turning the clipboard around, his finger next to the signature line on the release form.

Sergeant Ross peered closer, the color draining from his face as Sachs watched.

Sachs grabbed the clipboard back and read the line. "Agent..." he peered closer, deciphering the spider scrawl. "Shit. Agent 'Kissmyass'? What are you, a moron?"

He slapped the clipboard against the Sergeant's chest. Then he turned to Bryson, who was standing with his hands in his pockets, looking at the floor. "And don't think you can squeeze out of this either. They only left fifteen minutes ago, we gotta be able to–"

A hand was on his chest, the fingertips only brushing his shirt but somehow there was strength and purpose there. Sachs looked up and the first agent shook his head.

"We'll handle this," he said. He nodded to his colleagues,

already drawing guns from holsters beneath their jackets. The first agent looked at Sergeant Ross. "Take my agents to the cells. Follow their directions. Move. Now."

The sergeant turned on his heel, the two agents on his tail.

Sachs sighed.

"Who would have come in to take them?" asked Bryson.

"Enemy operatives," said the first agent. "Don't worry, detective, you will be fully exonerated. I need a phone."

Sachs led the way back to his own desk, then stood smartly to one side as the agent lifted the black phone off it. He tried to see what the agent was dialing, but he lost track of the turns. It didn't seem to be any kind of regular phone number.

"Enemy agents?" asked Sachs. He shook his head. "What, like... Communists? Spies?"

"Morrison," said the agent into the receiver. "Cloud Club."

Sachs raised an eyebrow. Wasn't that an old nightclub at the top of the Chrysler Building? Perhaps it was a code.

"Morrison," said the agent again, and then he nodded as he listened to something. "Nimrod is out?" A pause. "Understood." he said.

Sachs clicked his tongue. Nimrod? The name mentioned by the black guy. So, who were they, really? Spies? Communists? Secret agents from the government? This was exciting. And the agent – Morrison? – had already said that no blame would fall on Sachs.

Sachs puffed his chest out a little. Here he was, in the middle of a spy thriller like the kind he was so fond of reading.

"Confirmed," said Morrison. He replaced the receiver and lowered the phone back to the desk.

Sachs was on tenterhooks.

"The fugitives who escaped are the two most wanted criminals in the United States of America," said Morrison.

Sachs couldn't help but gulp.

"We need to put out an APB, and inform the FBI that there are felons loose in Manhattan. Armed and dangerous. They are spies who are acting against the government of the Western Hemisphere. Do you understand me, detective?"

Sachs nodded. He now understood that the statement Bradley had given him and Bryson – and the one taken by Mortimer and Zapf from the girl – were all part of a cover-up, a clever disinformation plan to confuse the police, to buy time to let someone else – an inside man – come and get them. Sachs's brow knitted as he tried to untangle it all inside his own mind. "They're really that dangerous?"

Morrison's expression was firm. "And as of right now," he said, "Rad Bradley and Jennifer Jones are both public enemy number one."

FORTY-THREE

They kept coming, and coming. Wave after wave, the King's hidden army now fully active, pouring from their hiding places around the city, following a single order: reclaim the Fissure, reclaim Kane.

Kane had another thing on his mind. It was likely that only Carson could solve the problem of the Empire State's impending demise, and it was up to Kane to protect him, buy him time.

He knew that now, as he hovered in front of the colonnades of Grand Central. He was powerful – he was the Fissure now – but the power had its limits. He'd felt it already, a small tug at the base of his spine – hardly anything at first but getting stronger the more he worked, and occasionally giving a real wrench, sending a cascade of blue-hot pain right down the center of his back. It did that when he opened up the tank, letting the Fissure's power leak out of the gaps he'd made in his suit at the wrists.

Keeping the robots at bay was hard work. They didn't carry weapons – they didn't need to. Their glowing eyes spat rays of energy, wide cones of heat and death crisscrossing in the air as they attempted to knock Kane out of the sky. It was hard work avoiding the rays, but at least it kept the robots occupied, the front ranks coming to a halt as they took aim at their target.

Kane had been lucky so far, but he knew his own energy

was running out – the more he flew, the more energy he directed back at the robots, the weaker he got. He wasn't even sure whether the King needed him alive or just his dead body to plug back into the machine in Harlem.

Kane dodged another series of blasts that came from three different directions, converging on where he had just been in a brilliant red haze of energy. He paused in the air, reorienting himself, and heard a thunder-like rumble from the distance ahead. He looked up, saw lightning flash on the horizon, and saw black shapes moving. The distance was huge, the shapes enormous: two office blocks collapsing like wet cake as the city began to crumble, unable to tolerate any longer the lack of energy from the Fissure.

The energy he was rapidly using up.

The robots gathered, regrouping. Park Avenue surrounded Grand Central on all sides, but around the periphery were the numbered avenues, moving out like spokes from a hub. The machines crowded every street.

Kane couldn't win. The sheer force of their numbers would overwhelm him and the robotic horde would breach Grand Central, taking him and Carson and the others back to Harlem. He hoped Carson's plan, whatever it was, was going to work. And fast.

The robots surged forward, and Kane swept down. He brought his hand back, opening the gap in the Skyguard's suit, and the Fissure flowed out of him like water. Tendrils of blue energy floated away from him like eddies in a stream, and then came the tugging sensation, strong now and surprising. Kane wobbled in the air as the pain clouded his senses, his vision splitting into a kaleidoscope view before it snapped back into tunnel vision, and blue fire spat from within him. The beam connected with the street, carving another great trench, causing the robots to back away. Kane moved the beam onwards, catching the front row of robots. The machines exploded almost instantly, silver arms and legs and heads flying through the air as the power of the Fissure cut through them.

Kane gritted his teeth against the pain, and touched down on the street in front of Grand Central. Time was almost up.

"Carson," he said to the air. Something in his ear clicked.

"A little longer, Mr Fortuna. We are not ready yet."

Kane shook his head. "I can't keep this up. The power is running out."

Carson clicked his tongue, the sound close and wet in Kane's ear. "I need a little more time."

"Can you get us away from here? The tremors are getting worse. The city is falling apart."

"Yes, we can hear it. How far away is the event horizon?"

"Six or seven miles uptown maybe. But the structure is getting a might thin here too. A block on the corner of 43rd fell as I flew past. I didn't even touch it."

"Very well," said Carson, and then there was a rustling noise. When he spoke next the tone was different, like he was facing away from the microphone. "Five minutes. Be ready to leave. Tunnel 17a. But wait for my signal."

"OK, but Carson–"

"Hold them off, Kane. Listen for my signal."

Kane nodded and clicked the radio off, forgetting Carson couldn't see him. But his mind was racing. He looked down at the street.

The robot army was stationary now, the rows and rows of glowing red eyes dimmer, like they were considering a new plan of attack.

Kane searched the army, but he couldn't see their leader, the real King of 125th Street. He hadn't seen the silver machine man at all.

The thunder rumbled again. This time Kane could feel the bass vibration shake the street, making him stumble.

The army tottered, a thousand silver soldiers banging into each other as the tremor increased in strength. Further down Park Lane, a huge building sagged at the waist and telescoped downwards, throwing up dust and debris that swept over the robots like fog.

Kane flew higher to see. How much of the city was left standing? But as he flew up, the unpleasant tug at his spine increased. He hissed in surprise and pain, and then he dropped.

It took four seconds for him to hit the street, and when he did he bounced twice, then rolled over, gasping for breath, struggling for purchase. The fall had hurt like hell, but the pain faded almost immediately. Kane moved, pushing himself up, and felt pins and needles all over and the tug at the base of his spine once more. He understood – the power of the Fissure had saved him from the fall and healed him, but that had just used more of its energy.

If the Fissure died within him, was that the end of the Empire State? Carson was going to put the Fissure back where it was, wasn't he? Back in Battery Park, where it would burn bright and blue, reconnecting the Pocket universe to the Origin and restoring the energy balance. And the Empire State would be saved, and all would be well.

He had to buy Carson time. On his hands and knees, Kane shook his head.

"Looks like it's just you and me, pal."

Kane looked up. James Jones, the real King of 125th Street, stepped forward in front of his army, his metal feet loud on the tarmac. Kane went to stand but James pushed him back with his foot. Kane fell backwards and immediately rolled to the side, but he couldn't stand. His body felt like it was made of lead. He craned his neck as James took a step forward and placed one foot on either side of Kane's body. He flexed his fingers, and Kane was sure the square metal jaw was grinning.

"Dead or alive," said James, "you're coming with me."

FORTY-FOUR

Carson tutted as he worked at the control console, his soldering iron moving with precise strokes, jeweler's eyepiece rammed into his good eye. He tutted again, then raised the board at arm's length and admired his handiwork.

"I fear for Mr Fortuna's safety, sir."

The Captain hrmmed. "And what of our safety, Byron? What of the safety of the Empire State itself?"

"I can sense a change in the world," said Byron's voice, filling the airship cabin from nowhere.

"So can I, my old friend, so can I."

"I can sense a change in Mr Fortuna."

Carson looked up. "The Fissure?"

"The energy signature is weak."

Carson frowned and returned to his work. A moment later he let the eyepiece drop into this lap.

"There," he said, slapping the control console closed. He flicked a switch, and sat back in the pilot's chair and stroked his beard.

"We are ready to leave?"

Carson nodded. "I've integrated the control systems of Ms Jones's gun into the ship, while the weapon core itself is mounted on the nose. All we need now is to give it a little kick and we should be able to transfer across and assist our friends." The Captain looked at the ceiling, head tilted, like he was listening to something. "It's quiet."

There was a click from somewhere close. The Captain turned in the pilot's seat, but the flight deck was empty. "Byron?"

A shadow moved across Carson's field of vision as Byron went to check.

"Anything?"

A pause, a beat. "Someone approaches," said Byron.

"Kane!"

Kane stumbled across the threshold, one arm across his middle. His suit was intact but scuffed and dirty, covered in dust and long scratches. He collapsed at the Captain's feet.

"Mr Fortuna, my dear chap?" Carson immediately lowered himself to the floor on the knee above his wooden leg.

Kane rolled onto his back and didn't move again.

Carson looked up to the ceiling. "We leave at once."

"Sir," said Byron, and then: "Have you a plan to start the transfer? Kane is too weak. It would exhaust the Fissure completely. The energy flux is unstable as it is."

Carson pushed himself to his feet. "I always have a plan, my friend." Unstable on his wooden leg, he overbalanced and fell back into the pilot's seat, then quickly spun it around and readied the controls. The sound of the engines filled the flight deck and he pulled back on the yoke. The Nimrod shook and the floor tilted as they took off, the tunnel flashing past the windows until they exited, and flew out into the night. Carson pulled back to gain altitude and turned the craft until the Empire State Building was ahead of them.

"All for one, and so on, and so forth!" Carson cried out over the roar of the engines as he pushed the Nimrod forward.

"No!"

Carson glanced over his shoulder as someone rushed towards him from the lip of the bulkhead door. Tall, silver and sleek, man-shaped but big. A robot – James Jones, the machine king.

Carson cried out. As he did, Kane's body jerked into life and stood, then rushed towards James, tackling the robot to the floor. The King of 125th Street screamed as the pair thrashed about.

"Sir, continue," said Byron, his voice coming from Kane's black mask. "Kane is safe, as is the Fissure. I have him."

Carson turned back to the windows. "Good show," he said. The engines thrummed as he accelerated towards the Empire State Building, but his attention was on the struggle behind him reflected in the airship's forward windows.

James had got behind Byron, thick silver arms wrapped around him. Byron grabbed hold of the metal forearms across his chest and struggled to stand, pushing backwards and lifting the attacker's feet from the floor. Advantage in his favor, Byron ripped one arm free from his neck and shot his elbow back, connecting with James's abdomen. James toppled backwards and hit the rear wall of the flight deck. Byron spun around and marched forwards, grabbing the robot by the shoulders, but James jerked into life, pushing Byron away. Byron staggered and James came at him again, throwing two punches, a left and a right, at Byron's face. Each blow connected silently, and Carson realized he was watching the fight in a kind of daze, the sounds of the scuffle hidden under the steady roar of the engines as they pushed the Nimrod towards its final destination.

Carson wanted to help, but he knew he couldn't. His only aim now was to keep them flying on target, trusting Byron, in possession of Kane's dying body, to hold the robot king off until transference was complete. Carson flicked a switch. The ship juddered and the nose rose in the air. In the reflection in the front window, Carson saw the tilting ship throw off James's center of gravity. The silver man staggered backwards, arms windmilling, as Carson corrected the ship's course with a sudden yank on the yoke. Byron, used to the motion of the craft, remained upright, braced with both hands against the wall behind him.

Carson allowed himself a grim smile, and increased the throttle. Impact in... ten...

"What are you doing?"

Carson refocused his gaze in the window, shifting from the blue and red lights of the Empire State Building to the ghostly reflected form of the real King of 125th Street behind him.

"What are you doing?" James screamed, his voice breaking in anger, his reflection leaping forwards towards Carson's back.

Seven...

Byron intercepted, throwing his body in the way. The two crashed into the back of Carson's chair, jolting the pilot. Carson hissed in pain as something blunt dug into the space between his shoulder blades.

Five...

Byron pushed James, and they stood, two brawlers, each wary of his opponent, each looking for an opening.

Four...

The Empire State Building was very close now. Carson flicked his eyes from the window to the control panel in front of him. He moved his hand over a row of buttons and paused, his thumb hovering over a single control. The ship bucked again and Carson gritted his teeth, feeling the ache in the hand that was still gripping the yoke as the machine, as though sensing what was about to happen, tried to free itself from his control.

Two...

James lunged again, not for Byron but for Carson, grabbing the top of the pilot's seat even as Byron tackled him around the waist. Byron pushed, but the robot king was stronger. Carson slid on the seat as it was rocked by the struggle behind him, the fight dragging his thumb away from the button. He hissed in annoyance as he strained to reach it, but the button was suddenly too far away as James pulled the pilot's chair around.

One...

The ship banked sharply. Through the windows, the horizontal lines of the Empire State Building's façade flipped until they were almost vertical and began to slide diagonally out of view with alarming speed.

Zero...

Carson let go of the yoke and threw himself at the console and the row of buttons. "Transference!" he cried, like shouting the word would make it so.

The hurricane sound of the Nimrod's engines swelled as they encountered the resistance of the building in front of them. The nose of the ship connected with the Empire State Building, hitting the stonework between two huge windows. The windows shattered and the stonework cracked, and Carson found himself pushed hard against the controls as inertia took over, trying its best to keep Carson moving while the airship came to a complete and sudden stop.

The metal framework around the Nimrod's front windows kinked suddenly. Carson was only dimly aware of this, watching events happening in slow motion, knowing that he had failed.

Then everything went blue and white, and Carson felt fire and wind and a terrible buzz-saw vibration in his skull.

FORTY-FIVE

Nobody was taking a second look at her, for which Rad was thankful. The atmosphere in the office filled Rad with a sort of nervous excitement.

He heaved a breath and glanced at Jennifer Jones. She seemed fine, unaffected by the transition from one universe to the next. It was the mask, had to be, or whatever else her brother had done to her. He noticed that she hadn't removed her heavy winter coat. She seemed more comfortable that way. Maybe she knew what was going on underneath, and that wasn't something everyone needed to be a party to.

Rad coughed, suddenly feeling light-headed. New York was making him dizzy. He'd felt better at the police station, but that was because he'd been sitting still in the cell. The little jaunt from the precinct house to the Empire State Building, which was hardly any distance at all on foot, had taken it out of him. Mr Grieves had been in a hell of a hurry, and when Rad had finally had to stop, leaning against a lamppost as his almost non-existent stomach contents threatened to make an appearance, Grieves had paced back and forth, eager to keep going.

But there was something in the air at the office, too. Rad thought there hadn't been much of a time dilation between the here and the there. Somebody had shifted some desks, and he didn't remember the two rubber plants, but Grieves didn't look much older. But then Rad suspected Grieves was one of those men who got to middle age and then seemed to freeze in place for thirty years. Lucky for some.

No, everyone was waiting for something. That was it. He and Jennifer were standing in the middle of the office. When they'd been led in, through a fancy lobby with couches and magazines, Grieves had paused, looked at the unoccupied furniture, and cursed before letting them through the main doors with a passcode spoken through a hatch. Rad had wondered what was so disturbing about an empty couch, but his vision was going grey at the edges and his legs were made of rubber, so the thought flitted away like music on the breeze.

"What are we waiting for?"

Rad looked up. It was Jennifer who spoke, her voice loud and clear, not a wheeze or cough. There were maybe twenty people waiting in a semicircle, most smoking, all of them looking uncomfortable. Nervous. Grieves was on the phone. Rad nodded to him. "Agent?"

Grieves held up a hand and muttered something into the mouthpiece. He hung up. "Confirmed. He's coming down."

Rad looked at Grieves. "Who?"

The main doors opened, splitting in the middle and swinging apart with sudden force. Everyone in the office turned at the sound, but the man paused at the threshold, wry smile on his pale features, was not looking at them. He was looking at Rad.

"Private Detective Rad Bradley," said Captain Nimrod.

Rad stood, taking a deep asthmatic breath. He felt that little thrill somewhere, of meeting someone who was the same as a man he'd left in another universe.

"Captain Nimrod. It's a pleasure. May I introduce Special Agent Jennifer Jones, former employee of the Empire State."

Nimrod flicked his smile to Jennifer, who inclined her head.

"Charmed, I'm sure," he said quietly, his eyes moving over her metallic features.

"I'm sure pleased to see you, Captain." Rad huffed another breath.

Nimrod clicked his fingers at Mr Grieves. "Agent, fetch a mask. Our friend here needs some help acclimatizing."

Rad waved his thanks and pushed his shoulders back, blowing his cheeks out as he fought for air.

"As pleased as I am to see you again, detective, I fear you come as a herald of catastrophe."

"Uh-huh," Rad managed.

"Any particular reason, Captain?" asked Jennifer, her hands back on her hips. "Or do you just have a flare for the dramatic like our version?"

Nimrod's mustache bristled. "Your version of what?"

"You."

"Ah, yes," said Nimrod. "The remarkable Captain Carson. No, my dear, I speak the truth. I assume if Carson found a way of sending you through to here, then it is either to ask for help or to offer it. As we have had no contact with the other side for some time, I assume it is the former. But as you have arrived at a particularly precipitous moment, your presence could not be more welcome."

Rad nodded, and looked around. Where the hell was Grieves with the mask? His eyes were about to pop and his vision spun like he'd had a belly full of moonshine. "There's an army in the Empire State. Robots, lots of them, built to defend against an invasion from here. I was hoping you were going to tell me that was a load of baloney."

Nimrod's eyes narrowed. "Robots?" he asked.

Rad nodded. "Robots," he said, and then he fell over.

Rad awoke to the smell of rubber and charcoal and he breathed deeply, savoring it. In and out, in and out, his breathing light and effortless, the crushing weight on his chest gone. He felt about ready to save the world.

Opening his eyes, he saw Jennifer's golden mask and Nimrod's lined pale face staring at him. Nimrod frowned, then nodded, and sat back behind his desk.

Rad wondered how long he'd been out. He turned to Jennifer. "You filled him in?"

She nodded. "Robots, the big freeze, Kane's dream. The works."

Rad turned back to Nimrod. "Make any kind of sense to you?"

Nimrod steepled his hands. "I'm afraid it does. And we haven't much time, detective. It seems Kane's vision of the future will come true. Since your last little visit, a new organization has arrived. Created on the orders of the president of this country, they call themselves Atoms for Peace. They are a peaceful, independent foundation, aimed at scientific endeavor and cooperation between power blocs that are otherwise hostile. A noble sentiment, I'm sure you'll agree. Atoms for Peace are headed by a miracle, a woman who has returned from the dead."

"Excuse me?" said Jennifer.

Nimrod smiled. "Evelyn McHale, their director, was killed several years ago in… an accident. It made the papers – Life magazine, even – so when she returned, there was quite a furor, I can assure you."

Rad and Jennifer looked at each other.

"Don't tell me," Rad said. "She has something to do with the Fissure?"

Nimrod nodded. "Top marks. She is linked to it, a part of it somehow."

Rad huffed through the respirator. "So the President of the United States of America hired a ghost to run some kind of a scientific institute?"

"Indeed he did. But Atoms for Peace are not what they seem. It is a front, a cover, for something dark and something terrible. The Director wants to control the Fissure, but to do that she must control my department. Atoms for Peace have built their own army, an army of machines. They are planning a war, one which I fear none shall survive. Mutually assured destruction."

Rad shook his head. "What the hell for? What kind of a war is one you can't win?"

"I would agree entirely," said Nimrod, "but the Director is doing this for another reason, a reason I have not yet been able to fathom."

There was a bang from somewhere outside the office, like a door slamming. Rad jumped at the sound, but Nimrod merely pursed his lips. Then the old man slid open the top drawer of his desk and took out a gun and placed it on the wooden surface in front of him.

Rad's eyes moved over the weapon – it was a revolver, and an old one, maybe the same vintage as its owner. But it was clean and the black of it shone under the desk lamp. There was a little loop at the end of the handle, and a fabric cord was attached to it. Rad liked that; it made sense, because presumably you'd attach that to the holster or belt and you'd never drop your gun.

Nimrod's hand rested on the desk near the gun, but he didn't touch it. Rad and Jennifer exchanged a look.

"Time is up," said Nimrod. He raised his head, the thin skin of his jowls pulled taut. This was the Nimrod Rad remembered.

No. Not Nimrod. Carson. Rad ran a finger around the rubber seal on the underside of his mask. His breathing was easy, and he wondered if he'd acclimatized yet.

"So if this Evelyn McHale is at the heart of it all, how do you stop a ghost?" asked Rad.

Another sound, louder now. Some people talking, men, raised voices. As Rad watched, Nimrod's hand slid over the handle of the gun.

"Every agent I was able to contact is here, in this office," said the Captain. "It's not all of them, not even a large fraction. But it's all I have. Atoms for Peace have been ordered to shut us down, and it seems they are now making their move."

Another bang, then another. Gunshots. Gunshots inside the office.

"I really don't like the sound of this," said Rad. He pulled the mask off, up and over his head. His eyes felt dry and hot, but he felt OK.

Jennifer jumped to her feet as another gunshot rang out. Rad wanted to, but took a deep, experimental breath. Nimrod was holding the gun, pointing it at the closed office door.

"Take as many agents as are left," he said. "I should be able to hold them off. They won't shoot me... well, not straight away, anyway. I imagine there are a few people who wish to speak to me before the sentence is carried out."

"Before the sentence is carried out?" asked Jennifer, her voice incredulous behind the frozen face.

Nimrod laughed, and this time it was loud, happy, the explosive bark Rad knew from the other version of Nimrod in the Empire State.

"Yes, my dear," said Nimrod, chuckling to himself. "I'm afraid I'm as much a fugitive as the two of you. This may well be my last stand." He held up a hand, stopping the objections of Rad and Jennifer. "I am not going to sacrifice myself just so you two can slip out the back. But I will be able to buy you enough time to get from here to the Cloud Club."

"The Cloud Club?"

The sounds outside the office reached a crescendo, and looking over his shoulder through the frosted glass, Rad could see shadows moving quickly. Any second now, and the place would be swarming with Atoms for Peace agents.

"It's at the top of the Chrysler Building. Here." Nimrod turned and tore a map off the noticeboard behind him. Rad recognized the outline of the Empire State – of Manhattan – but when he took it from Nimrod, a lot of the street and building names were different from what he knew.

Nimrod jabbed a finger at the map. "It's not far. Stay under cover if you can, but don't dawdle. Once this department falls, the Fissure is hers, and I doubt she'll waste any time enacting her plan."

"What do you suggest we do when we get to this Cloud Club?" asked Jennifer.

Nimrod tutted. "My dear young lady, you must stop the Director. Her army cannot be sent through. Stop her and stop them, at all costs."

"But how?" asked Jennifer.

"We'll think of something." Rad looked at Nimrod "We need agents and guns."

Nimrod nodded and strode around his desk. He yanked the door open and marched into the main office, heedless of the chaos around him.

The sound of gunfire stopped, and Rad could see several of Nimrod's agents turn from where they had hidden themselves behind overturned desks and cabinets.

Mr Grieves was nearest to them. Nimrod motioned to him, and Grieves waved the remaining agents to follow. Running at a crouch, despite Nimrod standing tall and bold in the center of the room, the agents filed past Rad and Jennifer. Rad counted five.

Five agents, with whatever ammunition they had left, to save the world. Rad didn't like the odds.

Grieves came up behind Rad's shoulder. "What's the

plan?"

"Cloud Club. Know the way?"

"Sure," Grieves whispered. "We can get out the service elevator."

Rad nodded. "Jennifer?"

"What's he doing?"

Rad peered out through the crack in the door. Nimrod was standing in the middle of the Department. In front of him, twenty black-suited, black-hatted agents from Atoms for Peace stalked towards him, each aiming their compact automatic pistol at his head.

"Captain Nimrod," said the agent in front. He had short blond hair under his hat, and an elegant face with strong cheekbones. "You are under arrest. New York City is now under the control of Atoms for Peace."

"I see," said Nimrod. "In which case, I believe the phrase 'take me to your leader' is most appropriate."

The agent's face broke into a smirk. "I don't think you're in any position to make demands."

"Oh," said Nimrod. "That wasn't a demand. No. Now, this, this is a demand."

In one swift movement Nimrod raised his antique firing piece, aiming it squarely at the blond agent's forehead. The agent was so close the barrel nearly touched his skin.

Rad saw the agent's face slacken, his eyes widen just a hair.

Nimrod pulled back the hammer of his revolver. In the dead silence of the office, the click the weapon made as the spring and catch engaged was surprisingly loud.

"I said, take me to your leader."

Rad felt a tug at his elbow. He turned to see Mr Grieves holding out guns.

"Come on," he said, and another agent hit a hidden switch on the bookcase at the back of the office. There was a click and the bookcase swung out to reveal a dimly lit corridor.

"Two agents front, two agents rear, our guests in the middle. Got it?"

The agents nodded, and Grieves pointed the way with his gun.

"Move."

FORTY-SIX

The Nimrod bucked like a rodeo bronco, bouncing Carson on the pilot's seat and throwing both their stowaway and Byron to the floor. The ship slid sideways through the air, out of control, the tilt too steep, the speed too fast. Through the smashed front windows the lights of the city were bright, brighter than anything Carson could remember. The view, and the buzz-saw vibration that wanted to pop his eyeballs, told him what had happened. He had done it. The device, fashioned from Jennifer Jones's gun, had worked; the impact with the Empire State Building had provided the energy needed to kick-start the transfer of so large an object as the airship.

They were in New York.

Carson pulled at the yoke and the ship responded. It seemed his theory about the overlapping geographies of Manhattan and the Empire State was correct: not everything was exactly aligned. It had been a risk, but a calculated one: if the Empire State Building had been in the same place in both cities, the Nimrod would have simply continued the collision that started in one universe in the other, and their journey would have ended very quickly indeed.

Carson grinned and ground his teeth as he pulled on the yoke with all his weight, trying to get the ship back level. They were flying down the middle of a great canyon formed by the skyscrapers lining an avenue in the heart of the city, but the Nimrod was drifting right. Carson leaned to the left as he willed the craft to turn, but a second later the armored side of the craft clipped an office building, dragging a trench along the structure. The ship juddered, then pitched violently to the left as it ran out of building and the controls suddenly responded.

Ahead towered another skyscraper. Carson hadn't seen it before, but it was impressive and elaborate, even more decorative than the city's tallest skyscraper. The top of the building was steel and glass, seven narrowing arches of stylized sun rays tapering to a spire; at the base of the remarkable cap were protrusions, also metal: lions, shining in the night, leaping from the building, frozen in sculpture.

And they were heading straight for it. Carson pulled back yet again, and the ship responded, sailing higher despite the protesting engines. The building was narrow, the decorative upper stories forming a neat cone even easier to pass safely, Carson thought. He took a breath at last and found it was painful and raspy. Incompatibility sickness.

Two arms wrapped around his chest and pulled. Carson gasped, the rhythm of his careful breathing interrupted as the robot King of 125th Street used the pilot's seat to pull himself up. Carson felt something heavy and cold on his left cheek. He recoiled and turned to see the silver sculpted face nearly pressed against his as James stared out of the crumpled nose of the Nimrod.

The mechanical man hissed and pushed Carson aside, reaching for the yoke. His new robot form was strong and Carson was thrown bodily from the pilot's seat. As he fell he saw the yoke spin of its own volition as James, once more mesmerized by the view ahead of them, froze at the controls.

Carson pushed against the decking with both hands, but his chest burned, every breath hot flame against his throat, and he collapsed back onto the floor. He was old, aged beyond his years as he travelled the universes in his ship, looking for Byron. He tried to rise again, but the ship lurched and a warning bell sounded as James, released from his reverie, grabbed the yoke and pulled with one hand while hammering the console with the other. Carson rolled on the floor, coming to rest against the wall of the flight deck.

Booted feet stomped the metal decking by Carson's face: Byron, controlling the Skyguard's suit with Kane's body still inside, raced forward on the sloping, bouncing floor and launched himself at the stowaway. James pushed him off, releasing his hold on the yoke and causing the ship to tilt again, sending Byron tumbling against the opposite wall.

Byron regained his footing and threw himself at James, grabbing him around the neck. The robot rammed back an elbow and it connected, but Byron hardly seemed to register the blow. With a roar, metallic and terrible that could be heard above the engines, James turned and threw a left hook at Byron, who ducked and planted a fist in the robot's abdomen. There was a solid, echoing clang, but James seemed almost unaware of the attack. Byron threw more gut punches, left and right, left and right, but all this did was give James more time to prepare, pushing Byron back, moving his hands up to the Skyguard's altered helmet in an attempt to rip it off.

The two men grappled. Another alarm went off, then a third. Carson reached for the console, now a bank of red lights flashing and dials spinning. The steel and glass crown of the remarkable building filled the flight deck's entire view, the triangles of the Art Deco sunrise sharp and angry. The ship dipped, and a lion, all steel majesty and power, tore through the nose's remaining glass as the Nimrod hit the building at an angle.

The control room was turned upside down. Carson saw Byron and the robot King of 125th Street go flying as the floor became the ceiling. The last thing he saw was the wheel of the main hatch approaching his face at high velocity.

The noise was colossal, impossible. It stopped cars; it stopped people. The major telephone exchanges feeding New York City froze as the system was overloaded with calls, and the police and fire departments went into high alert, cars and appliances racing out into the streets without a clue where they should be heading.

Reporters rushed to 405 Lexington Avenue, or as far as they could get before being stopped by the traffic or stuck in the mass of people who stood and stared and watched as a giant craft, something crossed between an old-fashioned zeppelin and a vast armored crab, crashed into the crown of the Chrysler Building. Some on the street fearfully recalled the Chicago airship crash of 1919. Others cried out that airships were full of hydrogen and the thing would blow, raining burning metal and debris from its skeleton like the Hindenburg had.

The Chrysler Building – the most famous building in New York, prettier than the Empire State Building although not as tall – shook, the vibration throwing people to the sidewalk and making cars jump on their suspensions. Those still standing gasped. From the street, the airship looked small, dwarfed by the Art Deco crown of the landmark, but the building was immense and the altitude great; everyone knew the horror that was unfolding before them.

The crown of the building buckled around the impact, throwing a huge cloud of smoke and flame, brilliant against the night sky. People screamed and the drone of car horns from the stationary traffic died as car doors were thrown open, the vehicles' occupants desperate to escape.

And then they ran, everyone, running for their lives as the crown of the Chrysler Building shattered, steel, stone, and glass exploding like fireworks. The sunrise spire bent and then toppled, taking out a huge chunk of the building as it fell nearly directly downwards.

The first pieces of rubble hit the street, bouncing cars like toys, and people screamed and ran from the great billowing cloud of dust and smoke that enveloped the street like a sandstorm claiming a desert city.

The remains of the Nimrod continued to travel through the upper floors of the building, sheering the crown completely from the skyscraper. The crown flopped and folded like wet paper and fell on the opposite side, and the ship, powered by gravity, plowed into Grand Central Terminal in a second mushroom cloud of flame and smoke.

FORTY-SEVEN

Nimrod opened his eyes to the light, and found himself standing in a familiar room, huge and empty save for a desk and a chair. On his left and right were two rows of columns like a Greek temple, and beyond, a wall painted with a vast mural of New York.

He was in the Cloud Club. The old faithful service revolver in his hand was pointed at Evelyn McHale.

The Ghost of Gotham floated in front of her desk; a desk spotless and dust-free. Nimrod could see it faintly through her. She smiled, and Nimrod felt slightly embarrassed, as though he'd caught her in her slip.

"I don't mind, if that is what you are worried about," she said.

Nimrod's mustache bristled. "I didn't used to be able to see through you. You used to be as substantial as the rest of us."

The Director glided forward, towards the barrel of the gun.

"Yes," she said, "I was. But it gets harder and harder. I'm being pulled down. It takes all my will and effort to stay tethered to this universe."

"So why stay? You want New York – you want the Fissure – but if you can leave, then leave! You are not needed nor wanted here, and I dare say you have never seemed particularly enamored of your situation. Let yourself go."

314

The Director shook her head, her eyes hidden slightly behind her spectral veil. "To leave is a fate worse than death."

"Forgive me, my dear," said Nimrod, "but I do believe that fate has already befallen you."

"I cannot leave," she said, her voice rising.

Nimrod adjusted his grip on the gun and raised an eyebrow. He wasn't entirely sure why he was pointing the gun at her – it was a habit, perhaps even an instinct, and as such it made him feel better, so he kept his gun arm raised, ignoring the growing ache in his arm.

"If I let go of this world," said the Director, "I will fall through the fabric of reality. There will be nothing to stop me, nothing to break that fall."

"And?"

"An eternity of nothing but falling, of never-ending existence trapped inside... nothing. Nothing at all. Do you understand?"

Nimrod sighed, and lowered his gun. "A fate worse than death."

"Indeed," said the Director, inclining her head. "My grip is slipping, and the energy it takes to keep moving just to stay in this space and time is too much and is growing more and more with each passing moment."

Nimrod glanced to the great windows of the Cloud Club. It was dark outside. Perhaps it was just the light from inside the room, and the blue glow of the Director herself blotting everything out, but he couldn't see the familiar red and white sparkle of the city.

"I don't understand. You don't want to leave, but you can't stay forever. What has this to do with usurping my authority? You want the Fissure, but why? Surely you, of all people, don't need it."

"Haven't you heard me? I can't leave. To move between

here and the Empire State, and the worlds beyond, I would first have to let go here, and if I do that then the tide will catch me, ripping me away from reality. I'm trapped here, for as long as my grip will hold."

Nimrod sighed, and looked around the Cloud Club. It was a magnificent room, even if the Director's acquisition of it as an office didn't make any sense.

"I used to come here," she said, following his gaze. She turned away from her prisoner and floated slowly around the room, tracing the mural with her fingers, leaving a sparkling blue trail of dust that hung in the air.

"It was a beautiful place, full of life, and music, and dancing. Oh, the dancing!" she breathed, and spun on her toes a foot from the floor, her face alight with a smile as she remembered her old life.

"That life is no longer yours," said Nimrod.

The Director's smile dropped. Nimrod blinked and she was in front of him again, blue fire in her eyes. Nimrod recognized the light well, the light of the space between the universes. He backed away quickly, and raised the gun again.

"That day," said Evelyn, spitting the words out like poison. "Do you know how I regret what happened that day? That day that trapped me, here, now, in a world I don't know and don't belong in."

Nimrod ground his teeth together and aimed for the Director's forehead. She drifted forward slowly, and Nimrod moved as well, keeping the distance even. Evelyn's eyes shone a terrible blue.

"I wanted him to save me, like he had saved so many. But no, the Skyguard was gone. He'd died a long, long time ago. They all had – the Skyguard, the Science Pirate. And before them the New Yorker, the Scienceers. All of them. They betrayed and abandoned all of us. They abandoned me!"

She stopped moving as Nimrod felt his back hit the plate-glass window. Evelyn's expression was a grimace of pain and sadness.

Nimrod gulped. "I can help you. Tell me what you need me to do, and I will help you."

She shook her head, her sadness lifting from her.

"You need do nothing except what you already are. Events will conspire. I can see the past, the present, the future. Time passes for me, I can see it, and measure it, but linear time has no meaning. What has happened has already been. Events will run their course. There is no alternative."

She pointed past Nimrod, to the window. Nimrod turned, her words casting a chill into his heart.

Nimrod looked down on New York, then blinked, trying to comprehend what he was seeing. The aerial view was just that – they were too high, the city too far away. Manhattan spread out below him, the Empire State Building small, toy-like. Nearby was a broken skyscraper, smoke pouring from its shattered crown.

"Impossible," he said, his breath fogging the glass in front of his face as he recognized the damaged structure. "The Cloud Club is *inside* the Chrysler Building."

"The Cloud Club is my domain," said Evelyn, shaking her head. "The Chrysler Building has been hit by your counterpart's airship. The original Cloud Club has been destroyed, and the building has been damaged down to its foundations."

Nimrod gasped. "Where are we?"

"The Cloud Club is my domain," she said. "It is wherever and whenever I need it to be."

Nimrod watched the city below, now understanding the dust and faded glamor of the room he had visited before he had been black-bagged and dragged to Washington.

Evelyn met Nimrod's eye in the reflection. "But our fate

lies elsewhere."

Nimrod swung around from the window, brandishing the gun. He braced himself, with no clue what would happen when he pulled the trigger.

Evelyn smiled, and Nimrod took aim, and everything went blue and bright.

FORTY-EIGHT

Mr Grieves led Rad, Jennifer, and the small group of agents through the police cordon on Lexington Avenue with barely a pause, only Jennifer sparking any interest from cops and onlookers alike.

"Doesn't look like there's a Cloud Club for us to visit anymore," said Grieves, pointing to the broken cap of the Chrysler Building.

The group came to a halt. It was carnage as they got closer, and Rad couldn't even tell whether they were standing on the street or the sidewalk. Rubble the size of cars formed a maze around them, the air thick with dust and smoke. There were fires, too; Rad could feel the heat on his face from smoking piles of stone and metal, some lit from within by glowing red and orange.

"Come on," said Rad. "Let's find out what happened."

They continued, the smoke and dust getting thicker the closer they got.

"Here!" Jennifer was ahead, apparently impervious to the acrid tang in the air. Rad squinted, and saw her golden face bobbing as she waved back at the group.

The rubble changed suddenly, and Rad realized they were on the other side of the building. Ahead, smoke rose from the shattered shell of Grand Central. Here there was stone and dull metal but glass and steel too, brilliant and electric, untarnished from its fall from the crown of the building –

and a twisted framework, black and burnt, of something else.

Rad swore and leapt over the nearest pile of rubble. His coat sliced open as the tail caught on an Art Deco sliver from the roof of the building.

"What is it?" Grieves called from close behind.

Rad reached Jennifer just as she pulled a hulking panel to the side, revealing a large box-like structure with a conical front, the nose crushed. Rad realized with a start it was the front of the Nimrod, flight deck and all, separated and thrown from the primary crash site.

Rad and Jennifer paused, looking at each other. Then Rad turned back to the wreckage. "Carson?"

They began digging into the debris, pulling, bending the remains of the downed airship aside as they fought to get into the detached flight deck. Finally an open hatchway was cleared. Jennifer didn't pause as she stepped in, Rad following her into the dark interior.

The flight deck was unrecognizable. It was merely a space, bent metal walls enclosing an obstacle course of twisted metal, wires, and shards of stone, steel and glass.

"Here!" Jennifer called from a few steps ahead, and she stepped back so the others could see. Rad swore again and rushed forward to help.

Under a cradle of riveted metal frames was a figure, kneeling on the floor, his body hunched over, protecting something. Jennifer yanked the heaviest pieces of debris away, and the figure rose up on its knees.

"Kane!" Rad pulled at his shoulder, and the figure uncurled. The Skyguard's suit was battered and scraped, but it was intact.

The figure turned its head and Rad paused, unsure. The figure shook its head, and when it spoke it was with a different voice.

"Kane is safe, Mr Bradley. I am looking after him."

Rad's eyes went wide. "Byron?" But his train of thought was interrupted by coughing from the floor, long and labored, followed by a wheezy intake of breath.

"My dear detective, I am so very glad you made it."

"Carson!" said Rad. He reached forward, then stopped, wondering whether he should touch him.

Captain Carson was on the floor, his great white beard matted with blood that looked too bright, too arterial. He smiled and the beard moved; then he coughed again and put a hand to his chest. His eye patch had been torn off, and set into the socket Rad saw what looked like a miniature camera lens.

The Captain closed his eyes and sighed, and in desperation Rad looked at Byron.

"What the hell happened?"

The Captain answered from the floor, his eye still closed, his voice quiet but strong enough. "I decided we should follow you. The Empire State was collapsing, and while I had utmost faith in your abilities, I felt it would be something of a waste if you were to encounter unforeseen circumstances only to have myself and Byron trapped, unable to provide any assistance."

Carson coughed, and Rad's eyes were drawn to the blood that covered his body. He turned back to Byron. "How badly is he hurt?"

"I fear I am unable to answer, sir." Rad winced as the voice that didn't belong to Kane came from somewhere inside the suit. "I believe I shielded him from the worst, but there was some violence to our collision with the building."

"You took the top right off it," said Jennifer. "It's a scene out there, that's for sure."

"What happened?" asked Rad.

"We were Shanghaied, my dear detective," said Carson

from the floor.

Jennifer shook her head. "What?"

Carson opened his eye and fixed it on Jennifer. Rad watched the camera lens in the other socket rotate, focusing.

"Bushwhacked. Ambushed. Hijacked! We had a stowaway..." Carson collapsed into a fit of coughing.

Rad frowned. Carson needed help. He looked over his shoulder at Grieves and the agents, but Grieves was already on his feet, turning to his men.

"Get this man out and to the ambulances by the police cordon. Move."

The agents moved in, and Rad gently pulled Byron to one side.

Jennifer looked at Rad, and Rad thought he could see her blink deep within the eyeholes of the golden mask. She turned to Byron. "A stowaway made you crash?"

Byron inclined his head.

Rad looked around. "He must be buried under this lot somewhere." The stowaway's chances didn't look good.

"It was the robot commander, the one who called himself the King of 125th Street," said Byron.

Jennifer jumped like she'd been given an electric shock. She whirled on Rad, the tails of her long coat flying.

"James," she said, breathlessly. "James is here. He came through."

Rad grabbed hold of Jennifer's arm. "I don't like to say it but I'm not sure he would have made it. Look at this. It's a miracle that the Captain and Byron got out like they did."

"Rad!"

The call came from outside the wreck. Rad and Jennifer looked at each other and raced to the exit, Byron close behind.

Mr Grieves was kneeling beside some torn debris that matched the metalwork of the crashed airship, his three agents carefully making their way towards the police cordon with Captain Carson carried between them.

Rad dropped to his knee, Jennifer by his side.

"What is it?" she asked.

Rad peered at the ground, then looked at her, his expression set. "Looks like... blood?"

"No," she said as she trailed her gloved fingers in the substance. "Machine oil. Lubricant. From a robot."

"There is more here," said Byron. The trio moved, and Rad quickly caught sight of the oily spatter that formed a trail through the rubble, towards the husk of the Chrysler Building.

Rad and Grieves exchanged a look.

"He's gone inside," said Rad.

"If you're going to say we need to follow the trail, I'm not sure the building meets city regulations right at the moment," said Grieves. Rad stared at the man for a moment, then turned around.

But Jennifer had already left, walking at pace towards the shattered entrance.

"Yeah," said Rad. "Good luck with that. Come on."

Rad turned and jogged after Jennifer. After a moment, he heard Grieves follow.

FORTY-NINE

The gun kicked in Nimrod's hand, the sound loud, reverberating off the thick plate glass behind him. He blinked the smoke away and his nostrils were filled with the smell of fireworks and dirt.

Evelyn McHale smiled, and Nimrod took a breath and fired again, and again, five more shots. Then he sighed, his arm dropping to his side. He stepped forward, until he was within touching distance of the Director's rippling blue aura. Through her he could see the marks on the New York mural where the bullets had struck.

"Well?" he said, his eyes dark and narrow. "What do you want from me? You have what you want. You have the Fissure. Your organization has control of the city." He waved at the cityscape below and behind them. "I must have a purpose. You said that everything does, that free will is an illusion and that you can see into the future, down our predetermined paths. So what is to become of me, hmm?"

The Director tilted her head, and when she spoke it was with infinite patience. Nimrod had to control the rage burning inside him. He could already feel the heat in his cheeks, the tremble in his jaw as his anger grew. And all the while, she was calm, quiet. A ghost out of time.

"Is that a question you really want the answer to, Captain?"

Nimrod raised his head and stared at the Director down

his nose.

"Do you want to know the future?" she asked "Do you die in bed, peacefully? Does cancer claim you, eating you from the inside out? Do you choke on a fishbone at a restaurant in Maine? Do you take a vacation to New Zealand and die in a car wreck? Does someone shoot you in Times Square, accidentally, perhaps the police chasing a dangerous felon as you are caught in the crossfire? Or do you die here now, with me, in my Cloud Club?"

Nimrod raised an eyebrow. "It hardly seems to matter, does it? You already know. You already know the outcome of this very conversation. How awful it must be for you, reading lines from a script as you do."

"I can tell you what happens. Don't you want to know?"

Nimrod laughed. "If that is supposed to be a threat, then it fails completely. It does not matter if I know. What will be, will be, and it appears I have little choice in the matter. If I am to meet my end here, then there is nothing I can do about it, because it is already written in the stars."

The Director smiled. Nimrod viewed her warily, rolling his fingers along the grip of his seven-shot revolver.

There was one bullet left.

"I need you, Captain Nimrod."

"Is that so?"

Nimrod raised the gun to his temple and pulled back the hammer. Perhaps he could cheat fate, disturb the universal harmony. Perhaps everything the Ghost of Gotham was saying was a lie, another of her games to pass the torment of eternity. He could understand that.

Nimrod pulled the trigger, and he heard the gun go off even as the floor dropped away from him. Surrounded by blue light, when he blinked he was somewhere else.

The Director of Atoms for Peace was still floating in front of him, but they had left the Cloud Club. They were standing on a circular platform with a grilled metal deck. Below them stretched the great factory floor buried deep underneath Manhattan, where a thousand silver robots stood in their ranks, active but awaiting orders. The glow from the floor was a brilliant red and orange and the light moved as the fusors inside each robot torso churned. The platform on which he was standing was directly above the main fusor reactor, the great torus suspended in the center of the factory. Mounted above the reactor's control panel, hanging underneath the platform above, was a large mechanical digital display, nothing but an empty black rectangle.

Nimrod was lifted into the air slowly, a foot at a time until he hung there, floating higher even than Evelyn. She pointed to him, gesturing with her hands, and he felt his arms being pulled outwards until he hung like a crucified man. The empty gun was still in his right hand.

"You cannot cheat fate," she said. "You do not die in the Cloud Club."

"I can see that, Madam," said Nimrod. The tingle of the Director's power surrounded him like a warm bath, but it was getting hotter, and more intense, quickly. He gritted his teeth against the burning pain.

"Now you know what it is like, being dragged through the universes against your will. Pain – infinite, eternal."

Nimrod said nothing, focusing instead on dragging air through his clenched teeth.

The Director lowered herself to the platform, and began to walk around its edge, trailing ghostly fingers on the railing and leaving a trail of sparkling blue dust in their wake. She surveyed the robot army below her.

"Elektro?"

A robot walked out from the beneath the platform and turned to look up at the Director. The machine saluted, cigarette smoke curling from its mouth. "At your service, boss."

"We are almost ready. Begin synchronization."

"You got it," said Elektro. The machine puffed on its cigarette and walked back underneath the platform. Nimrod dragged his head down as much as possible, and through the grilling saw Elektro operating the controls of the torus. The steady hum of the device increased in amplitude, the glow of the ring brighter until it was almost white.

The Director looked up at Nimrod, pinned like a butterfly to a board in midair. "My army of atomic robots. They are necessary, Nimrod. Do you understand? The atomic army is required. Now that I have control of the Fissure, I can move it here, to the factory. My army will be taken as one through to the Empire State, and there each fusor reactor will be detonated. Each will yield twenty-five megatons. Multiply that a thousand-fold and the energy released will be enough to cause the Pocket universe to collapse."

Nimrod hissed, and she resumed her walk around the circumference of the platform; with each step she rose a little higher in the air, until she was floating free again.

"Yes, Captain. The Pocket and the Origin cannot exist without each other, not anymore. They are tethered. The implosion will start a chain reaction, one that will continue, consuming the very fabric of this universe, accelerating exponentially until every universe, all the worlds beyond the fog, dissolve."

Nimrod growled and forced his mouth open. His tongue was dry and his teeth hurt as the tendrils of energy from Evelyn swirled, looking for the quickest way to the Earth through his body.

"You would destroy everything?" Every word was a struggle, every syllable spat out against a tidal wave of pain. "That isn't war, Evelyn. It's not even madness. You would destroy all of creation." He hissed a breath, and expelled one final question: "Why?"

The Director tilted her head at him and frowned. Perhaps it was madness, thought Nimrod. Perhaps that is what being brought back from the dead did to you.

"So I can be free," she said. "The universes will be no longer, and I shall be free."

"You would destroy everything, just to save yourself?"

"Enough!" The Director's eyes flashed blue, and she turned away from Nimrod in the air. She floated to the edge of the platform and raised her arms out towards the far wall of the factory. "I control the Fissure. It is mine."

Blue energy, smoke-like, ethereal, streamed out of Evelyn's arms, towards the factory wall. Nimrod watched as a small spot appeared, black against the flat grey concrete, then increasing in size, the edge ragged and glowing blue. Within seconds, the blackness had swallowed half of the wall and was still growing, the blue energy pouring off Evelyn.

Then he felt it, the vibration, the pins-and-needles sensation behind his eyeballs, the same feeling he got when he was standing next to the Fissure down in Battery Park. The blackness on the factory wall seemed to flash blue, the edges still spreading as the Director of Atoms for Peace dissolved the barrier between the Origin and the Pocket.

A cold wind blew in from the blackness. It flashed again, and then Nimrod saw it: a street, buildings shrouded in darkness. As the factory wall vanished, he realized he was looking at a street in the New York night, empty and cold, frozen in winter.

No, not New York. The Empire State. Evelyn had moved the Fissure into the factory, ready for the invasion to commence.

Nimrod wanted to cry out, to scream in anguish and rage,

but he was held firm in Evelyn's grip. He ground his teeth.

"Stop," he whispered. "You will destroy everything."

She ignored him. The portal to the other universe opened, she lowered her arms, blue energy curling off and spinning towards the gateway like smoke on the wind.

"Elektro," she said. "Activate."

From directly below him, the main reactor ring spun into life, deep bass notes increasing in volume and pitch until they were howling like a tornado. With an almighty crunch, the robot army turned to face the interdimensional portal, the dark glass windows in their chests now spinning with bright red light. As Nimrod watched, they began to march, their synchronized steps vibrating the platform above the reactor as they walked slowly towards the Empire State.

Nimrod wanted to die. This was the end of all things, and he couldn't guess why she was keeping him alive. She could see the future, and had spoken of it. Which meant it was going to happen. Her plan would work; the Empire State would die in a nuclear maelstrom, taking the rest of reality with it – not just one universe, one pocket dimension, but all of them.

The end of everything.

FIFTY

The inside of the Chrysler Building looked perfectly intact to Rad, though the lighting was low and yellowish, some kind of emergency back-up after the main power was knocked out by the airship crash. The interior was similar to that of the Empire State Building, but if anything even more ornate – all marble and glass, Art Deco motifs decorating the walls. Looking up, Rad stared at an image of the silver-crowned building itself that took up nearly the entire ceiling, and wondered why there was no equivalent structure in the Empire State. Not everything was reflected, it seemed.

"It's quiet," said Jennifer, wandering the lobby, looking up at the magnificently decorated ceiling.

Rad nodded. "Quiet as a grave."

He turned his eyes to the floor. The marble was lighter than the walls, the blocks streaked with darker veins and laid out to make geometric patterns. In the dim light it was difficult to see if any of the markings were robot blood or not.

Byron stepped forward slowly, turning his head from side to side.

"What you got? You hear something?" asked Rad.

"There is an energy signature," said Byron.

Jennifer stepped forward. "Energy?"

Byron gave a slow half-bow, reminding Rad of late-night conversations in an old house in another universe.

"The signature is unmistakable," said Byron. "Unique."
He paused, then took a step forward. "There. The trail
continues."

Byron walked to the corner of the lobby, which lay in
opaque shadow. "This way," he said, and he vanished into
the dark.

They'd been walking for what felt like hours. It was
the unfamiliarity of the surroundings, the total lack of
knowledge of where the corridors went, when they turned,
what lurked behind each door. In Rad's line of work it
wasn't an uncommon sensation.

Except now they were in the dark, traveling by the beam
of a flashlight Grieves had found in the security guard's
desk in the lobby, being led by the ghost of Byron piloting
Kane's body in the Skyguard's old suit.

It made Rad's head spin, so he tried not to think about
it. He also tried not to think about what they were going to
do to stop the agents from Atoms for Peace, down here in
the dark. They were just four people with a flashlight and a
couple of guns, walking into the lion's den.

"So," he said, like he was trying to break the ice at a
party. In front of him was Byron's back; behind him Grieves
and the others were so close he could feel Jennifer's coat
lapping at the backs of his legs. Underneath their feet the
trail was unmistakable, now that he could see it gleam in
the light. There was a surprising amount of oil. Too much.

Jennifer's voice echoed in the corridor as they walked.
"I'm fine," she said. "Keep walking."

"What are we going to do when we find him?"

"He needs help," said Jennifer.

Grieves stopped and turned around, spotlighting her face
with his light. The beam was split into a dozen more by the
contours of her mask, golden light thrown around the corridor.

"He needs to be arrested, is what," said Grieves. "From what you've said, he's involved with all this."

Jennifer stepped forward, bringing her golden face an inch from Mr Grieves.

"He's injured, agent. And he was protecting the Empire State from an attack from this place. If anyone needs to be arrested, it's your people."

"Oh yeah?" said Grieves, rolling his shoulders. "For what, exactly?"

"For doing nothing! For letting this Atoms for Peace walk all over you. For letting them plan a war right under your nose."

Rad sighed and pushed between the pair.

"Quit it," he said. "We don't know what we're going to find down here." He looked Grieves in the eye. "Carson sent me and Jennifer to New York to stop whatever it is that's going on from destroying the universe. Universes." He turned to Jennifer. "And that might just mean your brother does have something to do with it. He wasn't exactly altogether there in the Empire State, right?" Rad tapped his temple. "He was building his own army and keeping them doped up to keep them under control. That doesn't sound too savory."

Jennifer sighed behind her mask. "Let's just find him," she said quietly.

FIFTY-ONE

James Jones – formerly the Corsair, the real King of 125th Street – staggered down the corridor, reeling. He came to rest against the wall and leaned back, one hand pressed firmly to his side where it was soft and pliable. He grimaced, or at least he thought he did, the phantom memory of his flesh-and-blood face twisting in agony as he stopped for breath. It took him a moment to remember he didn't need to breathe, not anymore.

There was a large hole in his side. He reached in, not looking, and felt something thin and slippery move. Somewhere, buried in his mind, he felt nausea and pain and he felt dizzy. But it was distant, abstract. He wondered how much of him was left inside, how far the processing had gone before his blind servant had released him from the machine. Not every part of the process was automated; his complete conversion needed someone else to finish the job.

James pushed off the wall, leaving a rectangular smudge of black, thick fluid. He caught sight of it out of the corner of his optics and turned, surprised at how much of the substance he was leaking. He was leaving a trail easy enough for anyone to follow, he knew that, but it wouldn't matter, not now. He turned back around, the memory of a smile playing across his frozen metal face.

He recognized the place. He was home, in his underground

lair, the network of tunnels and basements built underneath Harlem, the subterranean train system that had lain dormant underneath the Empire State since the beginning of time.

His brothers, his family, were near. He knew it. He could feel it in his lubricant oil and in the coolant that bathed his rubber-sided heart. The army that he had built would be waiting for their creator, and he could lead them and they would march to victory against the evil ones who had been sent through the fog to wage terrible war against the Empire State. And their victory would be glorious.

Logic gates tripping madly, feeding the artificial part of James's mind false data, he fell over. The ground met his face with surprising speed, the collision at just the right angle to crack the remains of the nasal septum that existed behind the metal mask. He registered the sensation, the sliding of bone, but again the pain was somewhere else, academic. He reached down and tried to push himself upright, like a solider doing pushups, only after a thousand hours (or was it more? Or maybe it was less?) he found he was still on the floor, his hands sliding hopelessly on the polished cement in something that was thick and warm and red and black and smelled of old coins and gasoline.

"James!"

There were people here, in his domain: there was big man in a hat and a thin man in a hat and someone else who looked familiar and a woman with a green coat and a golden face. She was on the floor with him, her fingers trailing over his face and coming away sticky with oil. James smiled, or thought he did, as he strained and scraped along the floor, trying to get up.

The big man was standing over him now. His skin was dark, and when he took his hat off James could see he was bald. The thin man kept his hat on and he said something but James couldn't hear it over the music that filled the air, music he could see and touch, the air pulsing, shimmering to the beat. He knew this number. It was one of his favorites.

James found his voice, and new strength. He grabbed the woman's arm and pulled her close. The big man shouted and pulled on her shoulders but she shrugged him off.

"It's OK," she was saying. "It's fine, it's fine," and her long brown hair fell around her face and tickled James.

"We're home," said James, his voice the hiss of a punctured tire. "Where are my brothers, my family?"

"I'm here," said the woman with the golden face but that didn't make any sense at all. James shook his head, hitting it on the wall behind him.

The big man was rolling his hat between his hands and then James's vision went grey and fuzzy and tore at the edges.

"It's OK," said the woman again, and then she kept saying, "It's fine, it's fine, it's fine," like that meant something, but James could hardly hear it over the music.

"What's he saying?" asked the thin man who was standing away, arms folded, in the electric fog that seemed to fill the corridor.

The big man sighed. "Something about jazz."

"Sounds like he's bought the farm."

The woman with the golden mask pulled back, oil on the front of her green coat, black and thick and shining. "He can be fixed."

"Jennifer, look…" said the big man, but she was shaking her head.

"He's a machine, Rad. He can't die. He can be fixed."

The thin man tapped his foot. "There's going to be nothing to fix if we don't get moving."

The big man nodded and pulled at the woman's arm again. This time she didn't resist, and she stood.

"Then go. End this," she said. "And then we can fix my

brother. I'll wait with him." And she knelt on the floor again, her metal face looming large in James's crumbling vision.

The last thing James Jones heard was the big man's voice, nearly buried under the jazz. He was asking where Kane was, and the others didn't look like they had a clue, but then the corridor broke up into static and all James knew was the music and the darkness.

FIFTY-TWO

Black and white and blue and white and her eyes burning blue
they are blue her eyes are blue cold blue the light at the end of the

Kane shook his head and found himself standing by a door in a corridor of polished grey concrete. He was awake, although he had been dreaming again. Dreaming of the woman with the blue eyes, dreaming of his old friend Captain Carson, hunched over the controls of his mighty airship as it flew towards a tall building with a silver and steel cap, like the decoration on a fancy wedding cake. He remembered Byron, who had saved him... but Byron was gone now, just a thought, an echo ringing far away. And he remembered something else, something angry and silver and fast. Something strong.

Kane blinked. The corridor was gone. He was in a room, a vast space with a ceiling so high it was invisible. He was walking between two huge ranks of robots, silver, impassive, all facing the far wall of the room.

Kane stopped, but it took effort, like he wasn't in control of his body. He turned to the far wall and saw a street swathed in night, air as cold as a razor pouring out of it. He thought he recognized it, but perhaps he was dreaming. Soma Street was inside a room, a room full of robots, each of them facing the street, ready to...

"You."

Kane looked up. There was a platform ahead, suspended

over a huge red donut structure that pulsed with an internal light. Above the platform, a woman, floating in the air. She was blue and glowing, tethered to the image of Soma Street on the wall by tendrils of ethereal energy.

Blue and white and her eyes were blue they were blue they were blue

"I... I cannot see you," said the woman with the burning blue eyes. "I can't see your time."

Kane had no idea how he had got to where he was, or where his friends were. But he felt a pull towards this woman with the blue eyes, something magnetic, electric. It was comfortable; it felt right. He took a step forward, and the woman smiled.

"You're like me," she said.

Kane nodded. He knew it was true. He knew that she was the woman from his dreams, that here was her army, ready to march into the Empire State, ready to end it all.

She floated down from the platform until she was almost on the floor of the chamber. This close, Kane felt alive, aware, his body sharp and real and powerful. In response, her aura flickered, growing larger, brighter, so close he could reach out and touch it.

"Come to me," she said, holding out her arms. "Come to me and we will die together."

FIFTY-THREE

They found first a corridor and then a door, following a roaring in the air, low and rhythmic, like an animal breathing. Through the door was a platform. Rad moved to the railing, and looked down into the largest room he'd ever seen – like a half dozen of the huge hangars the Empire State Police Department kept their blimps in. The vast space was lit in spinning red by a huge glowing ring at the center and, there, standing between rows and rows of robots, two figures flashing blue. The machines were all facing the impossibility that formed the entire left side of the space.

The wall there was missing; instead, Rad looked out into a street in a city at night, windswept and icy, the sky above tinged orange. The Empire State, cold and decaying, connected directly to this underground space in New York City.

Rad heard Mr Grieves swear quietly beside him as he took in the view.

This was it. The robot army Kane had seen in his dream, the one James Jones was preparing to fight. It started here, in this room, a nuclear holocaust that would unravel the universe itself.

Mr Grieves called out and Rad snapped his head around, too late. Two of the robots were on the platform with them, between them and the door. The machines towered over the pair of them; Rad knew at once that resistance was a waste of time. In one fluid movement, Rad's upper arm was enveloped by a huge silver hand, and he was pulled down the stairs, Mr Grieves and escort right behind. The robots dragged the pair across the factory floor below, towards the two shining blue figures. They stopped and Rad pulled at his captor; to his surprise, the robots released him – but there was nowhere to go.

"That's bad," said Grieves next to him. Rad glanced at him and then squinted into the blue glow in front of them. Two people: a woman in a skirted suit wearing a hat; a man in a kind of black jumpsuit, the helmet missing, his hair waving in the energy aura like it was a summer's breeze.

Kane and Evelyn McHale. The woman from Kane's dream, the living echo of the Fissure that Nimrod had told them about. In his mind, Rad agreed with Grieves's summary of the situation. He thought perhaps Kane and Evelyn shouldn't get too close.

"Kane!" he called out, and Kane jumped like he'd had a fright. Evelyn turned with him to face the intruders.

Mr Grieves cleared his throat and raised his head. "Where's Captain Nimrod?"

The Director smiled and floated a foot into the air. Kane was still entangled in her blue halo but he moved backwards, away from her, his own blue glow diminishing with each step.

"Nimrod?" said Evelyn. "You can have him. He is unnecessary."

Nimrod's prone form appeared on the floor in front of Rad – there was no flash of light or slow fade-in; one second he wasn't there and then he was. He hit the deck and rolled, moaning in pain. Mr Grieves dropped to his side immediately, but Nimrod clambered to one elbow. He faced Evelyn and coughed.

"He's an anomaly, isn't he?" he asked, nodding at Kane.

"You didn't see this."

"Anomaly?" asked Rad.

Nimrod chuckled as Grieves helped him to his feet. He stood on his own with a slight stoop, one arm around his middle, but his voice was clear and strong as he addressed the Director of Atoms for Peace.

"An anomaly," he said, pointing at Kane. "He is as much part of the Fissure as she is, but from the other side, from the Empire State. Kane doesn't exist in the same space and time as the rest of us. Which is why she couldn't see him." Nimrod laughed. "Your plan has failed, Evelyn. The future is not as predetermined as you thought."

Wind and freezing mist blew in from Soma Street. Rad grabbed his hat before it flew off.

"Whether she's a fortuneteller or not," said Rad, his voice raised over the squall, "this robot army is still going to blow up my city."

Nimrod leaned into Mr Grieves, as Rad turned his back to the portal to shield the old man from the wintery blast.

At the room's center, Kane took another step back and doubled over in pain. Blue energy licked his body, and he fell to one knee. Evelyn's image flickered like a frame of film with a torn sprocket. When she stabilized Rad saw her face clouded with doubt.

Nimrod laughed again. Rad didn't like the mood the Captain was in, no matter what the Ghost of Gotham had done to him.

Evelyn held out an arm to Kane, but Kane didn't move. Rad saw Evelyn stretch, strain to reach him, but she seemed fixed in the air. She flickered again, pain crossing her face as she closed her eyes.

"What's happening?" he asked.

"No," said Evelyn, her eyes searching the room, like she couldn't see it. "I can't go. The world is moving away from me, faster, faster."

"She's losing her grip on the world," said Nimrod. "It's Kane. Together, they stabilized – both sides of the Fissure in the same place. But I'm afraid you interrupted them, unbalanced them. She's slipped, and without Kane's energy she will fall, forever."

"No!" Evelyn screamed. "I will not fall. I have the power, here and now. Elektro!"

From behind her, under the main reactor torus, Elektro strode out. He stopped beside the Director's floating form and regarded Kane with hands on hips.

"He don't look so good, boss. Looks like he could use a little juicing."

Evelyn ignored the machine as she flickered again. "Commence the countdown."

"Anything you say, boss."

There was a deafening bang, enough to shake the floor as the robot army turned on their heel to face the central reactor. Elektro gave a salute. "Wind 'em up, gentlemen."

On each of the robot's torsos, the spinning red disc of their fusor reactors flashed white as the machines entered their destruct sequences. The hum of the torus increased; above the reactor's control panel, the mechanical digital display flipped over with a clack.

The countdown began.

Rad blanched. Sixty seconds. Sixty seconds until the robot army detonated.

"She's going to destroy the world here?" Rad scanned the room. "I thought she needed to get her army into the Empire State."

Nimrod's face fell. He walked towards Evelyn, stepping over Kane's prone form. "No, this is different. She is falling and needs the energy just to stay in the world."

Forty seconds.

Nimrod turned back to his friends. Rad looked around at the robots, their spinning lights now flashing in time with the glow of the torus reactor, in time with the digits flipping down on the clock, marking time until the end of the world.

Thirty seconds.

"We need to get out of here," said Rad, knowing even as he said it that it was a naïve thought. Nimrod shook his head.

Twenty-five seconds.

"Each robot has a reactor inside it. There are enough here to destroy the East Coast of the United States. There is nowhere to run."

Fifteen seconds.

Rad looked at Mr Grieves, but all the agent did was take off his hat and shake his head, like he'd just lost a bet on his favorite baseball team.

Ten seconds.

Rad looked at Soma Street. It was dark and cold but it was home. Rad missed it.

Five seconds.

Evelyn screamed.

FIFTY-FOUR

Kane pushed himself up from the floor. As he moved, the lines of power connecting him to Evelyn snapped tight, sending white-hot pain flickering across his whole body. He gritted his teeth, focused on the pain, concentrated on the tugging sensation at the base of his spine.

The power of the Fissure, the power he had nearly exhausted defending his friends in the Empire State – it was here, now, in this room, in the portal to his home city open behind him and in the wraith floating in the air in front of him. And she was falling, slipping away from the world.

Kane reached out towards her. He understood the power, understood how to control it, to make it his, to wield the blue light of the gap between universes, shaping it, molding it for his own use. He had disturbed the balance, coming here; he was an unexpected guest, a future she could not see. Because they were alike, the two of them. No longer people, just parts of the Fissure, two sides of the same coin.

Kane summoned his strength, pulling energy from the window to Soma Street, pulling energy from Evelyn McHale's quantum event horizon. It was like flying in the air above Grand Central, as easy as pie.

But he needed more, a lot more. Evelyn did too, but she was going to kill millions of people to do it, just to stay in the world, a place she didn't even want to be.

There was another way.

Kane stood and Evelyn screamed. He saw fear on her face, desperate and cold and black; it was bottomless despair, the expression of the damned.

He turned, and saw Rad and Mr Grieves and Captain Nimrod, frozen in time.

No, not frozen. Time moved on, but Kane had sidestepped it, jumping off the track. Kane had all the time in the world, the countdown to destruction paused at four seconds forever.

Kane looked into the workings of the fusor reactors that powered the army. Despite his being outside of time there was still movement within, the quantum states of the subatomic particles flipping back and forth, back and forth, like they couldn't quite decide which state was best. It was the Fissure and the two universes, the Pocket and the Origin, slammed together in the underground chamber, Kane knew that. Each universe was incompatible with the other, not enough for anything cataclysmic, but enough to make things difficult.

Kane cancelled the countdown and stepped back into the time track. The fusor reactor in each robot flashed white and then the red spinning power within was slower, calmer, duller.

One.

The countdown clock clacked to zero, and stopped. There was no explosion, no atomic end of New York. The torus reactor hummed, and the robots stayed exactly where they were.

Evelyn flickered and she wasn't quite there, not anymore. Kane watched her face, watched the fear. Then the factory flared blue as he was pulled by her gravity back out of time, into the interstitial nothingness.

None of this was her fault. She hadn't wanted to come back. All she'd wanted to do was die, properly, the pain of existence too much. But now she had slipped and was scrambling to get hold once more, and she couldn't.

Kane was falling too, slipping away from time and space, dragged down by her. He'd used up what energy he could tap in the room. There was no more. And with the countdown stopped, there would be no more for Evelyn either. Together they would fall, forever.

Kane took a step forward. It was harder than he expected. His event horizon was locked to Evelyn's as they sank down through the foundations of space/time together into a dark place without end. Her eyes were on his, and she didn't move, couldn't move. She faded again, and Kane felt the pain in his spine.

She didn't deserve her fate, and Kane didn't want to join her, but he needed help. Perhaps there was some power left, some scrap to cling to, something he could use or direct.

A plan formed in his mind. A desperate one, one that he wasn't sure was even possible. But he had to try.

Kane reached out, his mind brushing another. A person he could trust, who would do his all, his level best, Kane knew. And Kane smiled.

"Rad?"

"Kane," said the detective behind him. "I... what's going on?"

Kane shook his head, keeping his eyes on Evelyn. "I need your help, old buddy. We don't have much time. I need power."

"I don't understand. Where are we? Everything's, ah, blue."

Kane kept his voice level, and he spoke slowly and clearly. The countdown to atomic annihilation might have stopped, but Kane and Evelyn were teetering on the edge of oblivion.

"We're in the factory. I've pulled you sideways out of

time. I need your help. I've given you a little of the Fissure's power, but I need more. Much more. Evelyn and I are locked together. I can't do it on my own."

"Where's Byron?"

A beat. "Byron is gone."

"Gone? Gone where?"

"Just gone," said Kane. "Rad, I need your help here."

Rad stepped forward slowly until he was level with Kane. Kane glanced sideways at him, and saw Rad with his hands in front of his face, looking them over as a moving blue aura crackled around them. Rad's eyes were wide as he looked at his friend. "OK. Tell me what to do."

Kane managed a weak smile. Then he slid to his knees. With some of the Fissure's power syphoned over to Rad, the pain running down his back was brutal, white-hot. The fall was imminent.

"Elektro," Kane said, and from behind Evelyn the metal man stepped out, red eyes rolling. A whining came from its voice unit, like a radio stuck between stations. "The robot, Rad. Take the fusor and give it to me."

Rad stared at the robot, then at his hands.

"Kane, I–"

"Trust me, Rad! Do it!" Kane collapsed onto the floor.

He watched as Rad rolled his shoulders and walked towards Elektro, hands outstretched. The robot backed away, but the movement was jerky, like it was pulling against something. Then Rad was standing in front of the machine, the top of his hat coming not quite to the robot's chin.

The fusor spun lazily in Elektro's chest, the red light mixing with the blue glow of the room outside of time. Rad reached forward, his hands almost touching the robot's chest.

Elektro was fast. Rad cried out as both wrists were

gripped by the robot's massive metal hands. Elektro leaned forward, forcing Rad to his knees. Rad cried out again, his face contorted in agony.

"You're gonna have to do better than that, friend," said Elektro. It pushed again, and Rad moaned as he was released. The detective toppled sideways to the floor as the robot straightened up and turned to Kane.

Kane shuddered, the pain too much, and the factory flickered into monochrome as he fell through the gap between now and now and returned to the world. The hum of the torus reactor seemed as loud as a hurricane and the footsteps of Elektro like collapsing mountains as it strode towards him.

A blurry shape flashed an inch past Kane's face, something dark green and flowing, a woman in a long coat, her tall black boots shining beneath the tails, her golden face reflecting the glow of Elektro's red eyes.

The robot stopped but Jennifer didn't pause. She powered towards the machine, pulling back her right arm like she was about to loose an arrow.

"I picked this up from a friend," she said. "Sometimes a punch can save the world."

Her fist connected with Elektro's jaw and kept going, tearing the steel apart and turning the robot's head into a twisted clump of scrap metal. Elektro whined from somewhere inside his torso, as loud as a jet engine, and fell backwards to the floor. Jennifer straddled the machine's frame as it twitched on the ground; reaching down, she yanked the chest plate off and pulled the fusor reactor out.

"Jennifer?"

As Kane watched, powerless even to rise from the floor, Rad got to his knees and then to his feet. Jennifer held the fusor reactor up and stared into its glowing heart. She looked mesmerized by the light, and if she saw Rad coming toward her, Kane couldn't tell.

Then she fell, telescoping straight down, the fusor leaving her hands as they dropped away.

Rad was fast and his face was a grimace of determination. He grabbed the fusor before it was halfway to the floor. Then, as he fell over Jennifer's body, he shouted something. What, Kane couldn't tell over the ocean of noise in his head, but craning his neck he saw Rad toss the fusor reactor like a football towards him.

This was it. One chance. With a cry, Kane concentrated and pushed at the world, willing the power to rise from somewhere inside him, where the Fissure was hidden. He forced himself to stand; as he did, Evelyn screamed and flickered.

Kane caught the fusor. The light within was red and orange and warm and even holding the device was enough to invigorate him. Then he looked up at Evelyn.

"I don't want to fall," said the Ghost of Gotham. She held out her hand to Kane, her blue glow almost extinguished, leaving her grey and cold, an afterimage burned into the universe on that May morning in 1947.

Kane smiled. "Neither do I." And then he tore off the glass cap of the fusor reactor. He summoned the last ember of his power and gave the ions within a little push, setting the reactor to destruct as the delicate balance within was disturbed. With one hand he pressed the cylinder to his chest as the device began to whine, the tone higher and higher, and he walked towards Evelyn. He took her hand, feeling pins and needles as their skin touched. He drew her into an embrace. And then she understood. She relaxed in his arms, resting her head on his shoulder, her feet touching the ground.

"I remember that day," she said softly. "I thought I could fly."

Kane smiled. "So did I, once." He pulled her close and they walked to the portal, to Soma Street, passing through the assembled robots like they were smoke. Time slowed. Kane could feel the heartbeat in his chest and he thought he could feel the heartbeat in hers too, but he wasn't sure.

They stood over the threshold, one foot in New York, one foot in the Empire State, standing in neither.

Kane held Evelyn and Evelyn screamed, screamed as she fell from the top of the tallest building in New York, her clothes caught in the wind, the wind that wrenched the shoes from her feet, that tore her stockings but that couldn't take her hand from the pearls around her neck, the pearls she held onto until the very end.

Kane held Evelyn and Elektro's heart detonated.

FIFTY-FIVE

Rad cried out. He rolled on his side and remembered the woman with blue eyes falling from a tall building. Then he looked up. The ground was cold, freezing, and the sign that shone in the icy air said Soma Street.

He jerked up, his head pounding. Someone said "Easy, tiger," and a hand pressed down on his chest. He blinked, clearing his vision, and saw Mr Grieves looking down at him, standing in a sea of silver men.

Rad cried out again, and spun around on the floor. Soma Street was to his left, close enough to touch. The army of robots was on his right, impossibly tall from his position on the floor. Lying next to him was Jennifer, face down and very still. Of Kane and the woman with blue eyes there was no sign, but when he blinked he saw their outlines moving, right on the border between the two universes. It looked like they were dancing, dancing until the end of the world, but Rad blinked again and they were gone and maybe it had been his imagination anyway.

Rad winced. He hurt all over. His head felt like it was going to explode. He turned his attention to Jennifer, his hands on her shoulders. She didn't respond, but Rad felt her body gently move. She was breathing, at least.

"What in the hell?" he asked of no one in particular, but Grieves moved away as a familiar laugh barked out.

"Welcome back, Mr Bradley," said Nimrod. He was

standing by the torus reactor, now dark, silent. He looked tired, his face slick with sweat and his safari jacket a little crooked, but he was alive and standing with his hands clasped behind his back.

"Son of a bitch," said Rad, pulling himself to his feet with a little help from Mr Grieves. "What happened? Where's Kane and the blue lady? And why aren't we dead?"

He turned to look into the Empire State. The portal that formed the wall of the factory was as large as ever but different somehow; the edge of it, where one universe cut into another, was not torn and flickering as it had been before, but a solid blue outline, curved and bold. It was still cold, standing so close to the winter city, but the wind was gone. Soma Street was still, quiet, like the robots surrounding Rad.

"The portal is quite stable. We have Mr Fortuna to thank for that, and Evelyn, of course. But I think you and Jennifer saved us all."

Rad looked at Mr Grieves, but the agent just shrugged, rubbing the back of his neck like he'd just gone two rounds with someone a little bigger than he was.

"I remember," said Rad, turning on his heel to survey the factory. "The robots were counting down to the end of the world. Kane stopped them but it was too much for him. Said he was locked to McHale and couldn't do a thing."

"You spoke to him?" asked Nimrod. "Fascinating."

Rad nodded. "Said he needed my help. He gave me a little touch of the power he carried, but… I guess it was too much. He asked me to take out Elektro, but I couldn't. The robot was too strong."

Nimrod walked forward, and Rad jumped back as the two robots immediately behind him stepped with him in time. Nimrod clapped his hands, rubbing them together like he was starting a fire between his palms.

"Fret not, detective. While you two were out for the count I had a look at the master control circuit." Nimrod gestured to the control panel underneath the torus reactor. "This army is now mine."

"Uh-huh," said Rad. He eyed the robots. There was something about the way Nimrod seemed so pleased to be in command that he didn't like, not this time. There was a hardness in the old man's eyes when he said it.

Jennifer moaned. Rad dropped to his knee and helped her sit up.

"Kane was the key," Nimrod said, watching the pair. "Evelyn couldn't see his timeline because, like her, he existed outside of the world. They were two sides of the same space-time event."

Grieves loosened his tie. "The Fissure?"

"Precisely," said Nimrod. "Polar opposites, perfectly balanced. They fed off each other."

"But the Fissure was inside Kane," said Rad. He pointed to the portal to Soma Street. "How could both sides be here, in New York?"

"They couldn't," said Nimrod. "He pushed Evelyn off her axis, and she began to fall, dragging him down. He realized this, from what you say, which is why he needed your help to tap into another power source. The injection of energy from the fusor reactor was enough to pull them both back up so the convergence could be complete. Two became one, the opposite sides of the Fissure balancing once more. Et, voilà."

Nimrod spread his arms open like a showman as he stood in front of the giant portal to the Empire State. Rad moved forward, expecting to feel the buzz-saw vibration, but there was nothing. Nimrod glanced sideways at him and chuckled.

"It's quite stable. The Pocket and the Origin are not

merely tethered, they are tightly bound together."

Jennifer sighed and rubbed the back of her head.

"That was quite a punch you threw," said Rad.

"I followed your lead on that one," she said with a small laugh.

"Are you OK? You tore up Elektro but then collapsed."

Jennifer nodded and rolled her neck. "I think so. I heard you from outside. Sounded like you needed help, so… I just ran." She flexed the fingers of her right hand. "I guess I'm stronger than I look. But that was all I had in me and it was lights out." She looked around. "I take it it worked."

Rad nodded. "We wouldn't be here without you, so thanks. With your brother out there…"

"Stop," Jennifer waved Rad off. "Didn't seem much point wishing I could get James fixed if the world ended, right?"

"True enough," said Rad. Then he saw his hat on the floor. He scooped it up and put it on. The band was cold against his skin. "And Kane?" He turned to Nimrod. "He's dead, I take it?"

Nimrod's mustache rolled under his nose as he surveyed the blue boundary of the portal. "I don't think he was ever alive, not really."

"Never alive?"

"Well," said Nimrod, waving his hands. "Alive, in a sense, the same as the Fissure is alive. But like Evelyn, it wasn't him. He was an echo, an afterimage."

Rad nodded. "A ghost. Like her?"

"Indeed. Evelyn McHale died in 1947 at the bottom of the Empire State Building. The Director of Atoms for Peace was not the same woman, not really."

Rad pondered this, but it all seemed too big, too dreamlike. He wasn't really sure Nimrod knew as much as he claimed, and while there was an empty sadness at the thought that Kane had never come back to the Empire State, not really, there was a calmness too, melancholic and cool but one that filled Rad with a kind of nervous hope.

He turned to Soma Street, to the Empire State. To his home.

"Sir!"

Rad turned as two of Nimrod's agents rushed in, the same men Grieves had left to help up top. Nimrod frowned.

"Yes?"

"It's Carson, sir," said the agent in front.

Rad froze. "What about him?"

"He's in a bad way. He said to get Captain Nimrod."

Rad turned to Nimrod. Nimrod brushed his mustache with the back of a thick finger.

"The incompatibility. It must be exacerbating his condition. He needs to get across the portal, quickly."

FIFTY-SIX

They stood in front of the portal: Rad and Jennifer and two of Evelyn's robots and two of Nimrod's agents. The two robots carried the metal body of James Jones between them, while Nimrod's agents held a stretcher, on which lay Captain Carson. The old man breathed deeply but too slowly for Rad's liking, and when he exhaled there was an asthmatic rattle.

"He'll be better when you get across, trust me," said Nimrod, his eyes on his other self. "The incompatibility sickness is making his condition worsen. Are you ready?"

Rad pulled his collar up and his hat down, and he looked at Jennifer. She nodded.

"And the sooner we get back, the sooner we can work on getting James help," she said, looking down at her brother's lifeless machine body.

Rad frowned. Inside he hoped she was right, but he also knew that getting James fixed, if that was even possible, depended largely on whether Carson would pull through. Carson and his New York counterpart were their best hope, but Rad wasn't too sure about relying so much on Nimrod's co-operation.

"OK," he said, turning to Nimrod. "We're ready."

"Very good," said Nimrod. "These robots will obey your every command. With luck, they will be able to overcome the programming of the robots on the other side, and those will in turn begin reprogramming their brethren – and so on, and so forth. The process will be exponential. When you are ready, simply give them the command, and they will go about their work."

Rad shook his head. "There's an awful lot of assuming going on there. You should come with us. We'll need your expertise, not just with the robots but with James here too."

"I have much to do here," said Nimrod, "but I shall try to be quick. With the portal open, we can come and go as we please."

Jennifer tapped Rad's arm. "We need to go."

Rad nodded. He shook Mr Grieves's hand and reached out for Nimrod's, but the Captain merely took a step backwards and bowed.

"Quickly, detective."

Rad frowned. He turned to the robots and the two agents.

"Follow me," he said, then he hunched his shoulders and walked into the Empire State, the others right behind.

They watched Rad and Jennifer for a moment, and then Mr Grieves coughed. Nimrod turned to him.

"Excuse me, sir," said Mr Grieves. "We're still federal fugitives, aren't we? Even with Evelyn gone…"

"Yes," said Nimrod, fire in his eyes. "There is something we need to do." He turned to the two robots behind him. "Come with me."

In Soma Street the hour was early, but there was something different. Rad paused, letting the others go ahead, as he looked at the sky. Morning would come soon, and it was still cold, colder than the coldest winter in the Empire State, but the deadly bite was missing, the chill that made Rad fear for his life. The Pocket and the Origin were reconnected, and now perhaps the Pocket was healing.

Rad turned around. The middle of Soma Street no longer existed. Instead, there stood a huge arch of shimmering blue, three or four stories tall and just as wide. Evelyn's New York factory was right there, the silver army frozen in place just beyond the threshold. Rad guessed the portal would be permanent, which meant access to Soma Street would have to be restricted. Something to worry about another time.

Nimrod and Mr Grieves were nowhere to be seen. Rad sighed, stuffing his hands in his pockets. He liked Captain Carson, but there was something about his New York counterpart that made Rad nervous.

"Rad!"

The detective turned. Jennifer waved at him from farther down the street, the agents and robots trudging forward, carrying their charges.

"Coming," said Rad. And then he pulled down his hat and jogged to catch up. Beneath his hat he smiled.

Home sweet home.

EPILOGUE
REGIME CHANGE

The men, near to thirty of them, sat around the circular table so large it occupied the entire room, a great ring of polished wood that circled two desks in a central arena. At these desks – themselves large, expensive, and tax-payer funded – sat two clerks, both female; one was checking through a vast stack of paper while the other prepped her stenotype for the second half of the meeting, due to commence in just a few minutes. Around the room, portraits of the great and good looked down upon the senate subcommittee: Abraham Lincoln, George Washington, and a dozen other presidents – some famous, effective; some less so.

The recess was nearly at its end, the committee members slowly returning to their seats, sipping from their fresh coffee and laughing about their poor games of golf that weekend, the episode of I Love Lucy from TV the previous night, and the chances of the New York Giants against the Cleveland Indians in the forthcoming World Series. The Giants were going to get their asses handed to them was the general consensus.

The double doors of the committee room opened and a man walked in, leading three others; behind them, two walking machines, hulking silver men nearly seven feet tall, their features a rough parody of human faces, their chests lit with spinning discs the same glowing red as their eyes.

The man in front wore a brown suit that was most definitely bottom rack, while the three behind wore matching black suits of a quality cut with black hats to match. All four were holding guns, and they strode into the room quietly and at speed, stepping through the gap in the circular table that allowed entry into the central space. In just a few seconds the three black-suited men spaced themselves out around the table, each covering enough of the committee members to ensure nobody did anything they might regret later. The two robots stood by the doors, still except for their eyes, which scanned the room back and forth, back and forth.

The clerks seated at the desk made to stand, but the man in the brown suit shook his head and motioned with his pistol for them to sit tight.

The committee members began to mutter, quietly at first but with gathering volume. Most seemed canny enough to keep still. All except the committee chair, a tall man wrapped in immaculate blue pinstripe, his hair snow white and perfectly parted. The Secretary of Defense.

"Who are you?" asked the Secretary. "What do you want?"

The man in the brown suit raised an eyebrow.

"You can call me Mr Grieves," he said, before turning back to the clerks. He clicked his fingers at one of them. After a moment the young woman realized what he wanted and picked up the phone, offering it to him. Mr Grieves nodded at her. "Dial for me."

The clerk put the receiver to her ear. "Um... what number?" she said, almost adding "sir" to the end of the question.

Mr Grieves smiled.

"The Oval Office. Get me the President."

The phone rang twice. The man sitting in the chair behind the big desk ignored it, his attention instead on the gun pointed at him, unmoving.

The phone rang four more times. Nimrod glanced at the black-suited agent and the robot standing by the door, and then picked it up.

"Oval Office," said Nimrod, a happy lilt in his voice. Behind the desk, Dwight D Eisenhower scowled at his former special aide, but he didn't speak, his lips tight, his left eyelid twitching. Nimrod kept his eyes on him and kept the gun perfectly level.

"Ah, Mr Grieves," he said into the phone. "I take it everything is in order? Yes? Good. What? Ah, the Secretary of Defense wishes to speak to the President? I'm afraid he will have to speak to me."

Nimrod smiled at Eisenhower as he waited on the phone. There was a movement in his ear, muffled, as the phone was passed over.

Nimrod raised the gun, stretching his arm out straight, pointing the barrel directly at the center of Eisenhower's expansive forehead.

"Ah, Mr Secretary? How charming to speak to you again."

Nimrod pulled his thumb back, cocking the revolver.

"Now, listen very carefully. These are my terms."

EPILOGUE
THE CLOUD CLUB

She took a glass of champagne from a passing waiter and sipped it, enjoying the tickle of bubbles against her nose. Glass half-drained, she kept it high, and peered over the rim at the man on the other side of the room. The man raised an eyebrow, his mouth twitching into a smirk. Then he turned away.

The band struck up again, and soon people were back on the dance floor.

"You've been looking at him all night."

She lowered the glass and turned her back on the room and her attention to the vast window that formed nearly the whole of the wall. She took a step forward and pressed one gloved hand to the glass. Manhattan stretched out before her, the lights of the city kissing the invisible horizon in every direction. If she squinted, just a little, the lights fuzzed and spun, turning into the whirly stars of the Milky Way, bathing her in their magical blue light, the light of...

"Seriously," said her friend, sipping from her own champagne. "You can't keep this up all night."

She smiled. "I can keep this up forever."

"If you don't do something soon, I'll do it for you."

She blinked, and the city returned. She turned away

from the window and watched the patrons of the Cloud Club drink and talk and dance.

"He looks nice."

"Yes, he does," she said. Then she frowned.

"What's wrong?"

She shrugged. "I've seen him somewhere before, that's all." She searched the room. "Where is he?"

Her friend smiled and slid sideways, back towards the window.

"Excuse me."

She turned. He was there, smiling at her, his eyes big and brown. His hair was dark, slicked back, one escaped lick flicking across his forehead. She decided she liked that.

The man bowed and glanced at her friend, who smiled before burying her face in her glass. "May I have this dance?"

She laughed, glancing at her friend, who nodded furiously. She turned back to the man and held out her arm.

"I'm charmed, Mr..."

"Fortuna. Kane Fortuna."

"Evelyn McHale." She took his arm.

"Ms McHale," he said, "the night is ours."

The pair weaved their way to the middle of the room, joining the mass of dancing couples.

Outside, New York sparkled, the lights of the city like jewels on velvet, like the stars in the sky, their light the light of the gap between the universes, the light of the end of the world.

And in the Cloud Club, the music played on and the couples danced, and danced, and danced.

ACKNOWLEDGMENTS

First and foremost, I have to thank my literary agent, Stacia JN Decker, for work above and beyond the call of duty on this manuscript. The Age Atomic wouldn't exist if it wasn't for her, and for that I am forever grateful and forever in her debt (thankfully she accepts payment in wine and chocolate, so we're sweet).

For support, advice (both moral and editorial), and late nights on Twitter, my thanks to Lauren Beukes, Joelle Charbonneau, Kim Curran, Will Hill, Laura Lam, Lou Morgan, Emma Newman, James Smythe, Steve Weddle, Chuck Wendig and Jennifer Williams.

Special thanks to Mur Lafferty, whose ear I was able to bend, and bend frequently, during the course of writing and editing this book. The gin is (still) on me.

Thanks once more to the Angry Robot team, in particular my editor Lee Harris, as well as Marc Gascoigne and Darren Turpin. And thanks to Will Staehle for yet another glorious cover.

As a writer, inspiration sometimes comes from the strangest – and saddest – of places. Evelyn McHale jumped from the 86th floor observation deck of the Empire State Building on May 1st, 1947, and landed on the roof of a United Nations limousine. A few minutes later, Robert Wise took a photograph of her body, which ran as a full page in Life magazine a couple of weeks later. This photo, which became known as "The Most Beautiful Suicide", was later used by Andy Warhol for a print entitled "Suicide (Fallen Body)". For more information about Evelyn, and the photograph, visit *http://www.codex99.com/photography/43.html*

Finally, to Sandra, my wife, forever supportive, even on those too-frequent days when I had to shut myself away from the world to get the work done. Here's another one, just for you.

ABOUT THE AUTHOR

Adam Christopher was born in Auckland, New Zealand, and grew up watching Pertwee-era *Doctor Who* and listening to The Beatles, which isn't a bad start for a child of the Eighties. In 2006, Adam moved to the North West of England, where he can be found drinking tea and obsessing over superhero comics and The Cure.

adamchristopher.co.uk
twitter.com/ghostfinder

THE AGE ATOMIC PLAYLIST

Music is important to me during the writing and editing of any book, and *The Age Atomic* was no exception. Here's a list of ten tracks I had on high-rotate for the last nine months. Each captures a moment or a mood of the story, from the epic melancholy of *Plainsong* that seems to describe Evelyn's sadness, to the classic Harlem jazz of Duke Ellington that might have floated around the King of 125th Street's theater workshop.

1. *The Cure – Plainsong*
From the album *Disintegration* (Fiction Records, 1989)

2. *Duke Ellington and Louis Armstrong – Drop Me Off In Harlem*
From the album *The Great Summit – The Master Takes* (Roulette Records, 1961)

3. *Black Rebel Motorcycle Club – Generation*
From the album *Take Them On, On Your Own* (Virgin Records, 2003)

4. *The Bird and the Bee – Preparedness*
From the album *The Bird and the Bee* (Blue Note Records, 2007)

5. *The Velvet Underground – Ocean (outtake)*
From the album *Loaded: The Fully Loaded Edition* (Rhino Records 1997)

6. *Duke Ellington – Take The A Train (live)*
From the album *Ellington at Newport* (Columbia Records, 1956)

7. *Wild Flag – Boom*
From the album *Wild Flag* (Merge Records, 2011)

8. *Dubstar – Everyday I Die*
From the album *Random, Volume 1: A Gary Numan Tribute* (Blanco Y Negro, 1997)

9. *Arcade Fire – Black Mirror*
From the album *Neon Bible* (Merge Records, 2007)

10. *Count Basie – Midnite Blue*
From the album *The Atomic Mr. Basie* (Roulette Records, 1957)